THE SCROLL

DONALD NASSR

ICAM
Publishing Company
Rouses Point, New York   Montreal, Canada

THE SCROLL
A Novel by Donald Nassr

ICAM PUBLISHING COMPANY
This is a work of fiction. Plot, characters and dialogue are products of the author's imagination. Any resemblance to living persons is entirely coincidental.

Copyright 1997 by Donald Nassr
All rights reserved including the right of reproduction in whole or in part or in any form.

Published in United States and Canada
by ICAM PUBLISHING COMPANY

Library of Congress Cataloging-in-Publication Data
The Scroll / by Donald Nassr
1. title
Library of Congress Catalogue Number 97-93380
ISBN 0-9642463-2-5

Design and calligraphy by Dufour & Fille Design Inc.
Printed in Canada

I dedicate this book to my wife Kathryn and my brother John,
and to the readers of my first novel,
In The Shadows Of The Cross
who enthusiastically asked for this, a sequel.
Enjoy.

PROLOGUE

IN the years after the birth of Christ, Imperialist Rome had consolidated its conquest of Europe and the Middle East while it persecuted Christ's followers, crucifying them for their faith, sending them into the arenas, making them slaves. However, after Constantine the Great, the roles of the meek Christians and Romans had reversed. The persecuted had become the persecutors. Christian knights had replaced Roman centurions, and people continued to die for their beliefs.

The first crusade, inspired by Pope Urban II, who had declared it "just and holy", was to rid the Holy Land of Muslims and free the ancient city of Jerusalem for Christians. In 1099 A.D., 150,000 knights and foot soldiers, mostly Norman, surrounded the city. Although they wore the white tunic and red cross of Christianity, they were descendants of the barbarian Goths who centuries earlier had sacked Christian Rome and who, when they were christianized, fought for their new master with the same genetic ferocity.

Once the great walls of Jerusalem had been breached, the knights showed their savage Norman colors, killing indiscriminately – men, women, and children, Muslims and Jews, all in the name of Christ – screaming Urban's battle cry, *Dues vult*, God wills it. The streets ran red with blood as knights and soldiers pillaged, murdered, and raped, leaving a scar on Islam that would never be forgotten. The rampaging knights desecrated that most holy shrine of Islam, the Dome of the Rock, occupied the Al-Aksa Mosque, and destroyed Jewish synagogues. Thus the Christian knights reprised the utter destruction of the city by Titus and the Roman legions centuries earlier.

In the Al-Aksa Mosque, Ibrahim Rasha Zangi, son of the great Arab conqueror, huddled in fear with his wives and children. On the floor of the mosque were three chests filled with gold with which Ibrahim believed he would buy safe passage for his family out of Jerusalem. He approached his youngest son Nur, as horsemen in chain armor cut a bloody swathe to the temple doors.

"Quickly, my son. Help me with this stone piece," Ibrahim had said, straining to pry loose a section of flooring in the temple. "Take this scroll and place it in the cave at Qumran, that I have showed you, until you have need of it and its secrets. Then find a safe hiding place from these Norman animals. More than all the armies of Islam, this scroll, which our family has safeguarded for a thousand years, can destroy the Christians and topple the House of David." He handed his son a rolled sheet of copper. "Below you will find your way out of Jerusalem as David found his way in. It is dark, and you will have immeasurable fear. But follow the sound of the water." The boy, barely nine years old, his dark eyes moist with tears, embraced his father and disappeared into the dark void as Ibrahim replaced the heavy stone and returned to his family and the bloodied Norman now prying open the chests with his broadsword.

"As I agreed to with your leader, Godfroi," Ibrahim said, pointing to the chests, "for our freedom."

"For your freedom, heathen," the Christian knight said, laughing, raising his sword in a two-handed overhead slashing hold. The screams of the victims rang through the ages.

The boy, Nur, found his way through the tunnels, across the Judaean wilderness, to the caves at Qumran and hid the copper scroll: a scroll which would not be found for nine hundred years, and one that had been scribed by a Greek student of Dionysius at the time of Christ's death. Nur climbed the cliffs and fell on the sand, crying, frightened, and hungry, too weak to run from the two knights who thundered up on enormous horses.

"This great Arab has escaped our blades," one said, laughing and prodding the boy with his lance as he climbed down from his horse. His tunic and metal armor were covered with blood.

"He's mine," the other said, drawing his broadsword.

"He's small, but we can divide him fairly," the first said, laughing even louder, raising his sword.

Within fifty years the hatred of Christians by Muslims for the Jerusalem massacre bred bloody wars across the Levant and into Egypt, with the armies of Saladin eventually defeating the crusaders, at times with horrible retaliation. The jihad continued.

A little more than a hundred years later, Pope Innocent III, a man made pope before he was an ordained priest, ordered a crusade against French Christians of southern France. These were the Cathars, and to Rome, they were heretics. Thirty thousand knights and foot soldiers swept into the Languedoc region of the Pyrenees, decimating the population in an attempt to eradicate the heresy.

At the mountain castle of Montegur resistance had failed after a long bloody siege. A young man, trained for one purpose, opened a secret door and descended a stairway deep into the mountain to a cavern. Behind him a massive stone hid the entrance. He knew what the knights were after and he would die protecting his charge. He stopped before a thick wooden door and withdrew his sword, placing the haft firmly in a carefully chiseled crack in the floor. Then he climbed to the natural opening of the cave, which gave him light and air, and looked out onto the valley far below him.

Farms and fields burned. Even if they did not find him, even if he could climb down, what was there to live for? Everyone would be dead, put to the sword in the name of Christ and by the will of the Pope. He wept for his family and did not understand why they had to die. He had not known he was a heretic who believed differently than the French knights and their pope. He went back to his sword at the door and read the words *Rex Mundi* carved into the wood. He knew what they wanted behind the door, even though he didn't know the meaning of the words. He reached up and tied a thick rope around his left arm, gripping it with his hand. Then he leaned over the sword, placing the sharp point in the soft tissue between his chest and abdomen and waited. If they came, he would fall on his sword and pull the rope as he died. If they did not find him, his people would teach their secrets to their children, and they to theirs.

This crusade, the Albigensian, the only one directed against Christians, wiped out the population of Languedoc, and as the few who survived the first crusade in Jerusalem had done, the survivors continued keeping their faith and their secret behind the door.

Seven hundred years after the massacre at Languedoc, twelve men met in a conference room of the world's largest building. They met six times a year, arriving by private jet from leading nations. The polished wood on their round table glistened in the subdued overhead lighting. A rainbow of color reflected on the dark slate walls from the hand-cut facets of crystal water glasses placed before each man. Their offices occupied an entire floor of the World Trade Center and had been extensively modified for security purposes. Large windows gave a panoramic view of the city, except when meetings were held and the heavy drapes were closed. Adjoining areas contained offices, conference rooms, and carefully screened clerical staff. One large room held computer-driven electronic communication and security equipment that could connect the members to any place in the world with absolute confidence against outside surveillance.

The men seated around the table were extraordinarily wealthy and powerful: international bankers, industrialists, and those whose wealth extended back for generations. Like the popes who had ordered the crusades, these men held a global ideology, one that had been developed over the ages. This council, or as they called it, "the Ring," represented the driving force of a secret organization that had existed under different names for hundreds of years. Most of the members were on the Supreme Council of the Thirty-Third and Last Degree of Freemasonry. Some were also Rosicrucians, and one held high office in the Catholic organization known as *Opus Dei*. All were executives of the Federation of the New World Order.

Much like the fabled knights of Camelot, these men had a vision of a utopian world united under one government, one monetary system, one language, and one religion. They had the power to impose, and the patience to wait. In the world's arenas, members were rarely seen; their enormous wealth, like their personal lives, was carefully shielded from public view.

The chairman of the Ring, an old man who would be replaced at his death by another council member, was also the director of the Federal Reserve Bank. He held a high office in the Rockefeller Foundation and was a personal friend of David Rockefeller and George Bush, a man who would be President of the United States years after this chairman's death. The chairman was a soft-spoken, immaculately dressed man, slender and frail, but ageless in mind.

"Gentlemen, the Jerusalem scroll has emerged from its dark sojourn through the shadows of history." He sipped water and remained seated as he spoke. "Smuggled out of Israel, it is in the hands of five men, archeologists, who are struggling to translate it." He looked around the table at each member. All dwelt on the meaning of this announcement, which they and their antecedents had sought for centuries. "Our time approaches. In due course, I, or my successor, one of you," he nodded respectfully, "will notify the French, and then the world." He addressed a younger man who had raised his hand to speak. "Please, let me finish; then discussion."

"We will need ten years. Their work must be finished or an alternative solution found. We must be fully prepared in Jerusalem and Iran. You must expand and then consolidate your positions in preparation for our final operation. We must keep in our hearts the one truth that motivates us. Failure! Throughout the course of recorded history, mankind has failed to establish universal peace and harmony. Politics, economics, nationalism, personal psychology, and, above all, religion, have failed. We will not, we must not fail."

Chapter 1

"The Blessed Virgin Mary was voted into office," the professor said with shammed nonchalance as he peered through his magnifying glass at the piece of copper scroll laid out on the oak library table in front of him. The woman, less than half his age, casually dressed, strikingly beautiful, looked up from the manuscript she had been reading. By now she knew his tricks and said nothing, letting smoke from her French cigarette drift into the musty air. A smile showed at the corners of her mouth.

"And so was 'papal infallibility,' Juda," he added, "and by a narrow margin at that." He looked over the top of his glasses perched half-way down his nose at his companion, as he dusted an area on the copper sheet with a camel's hair brush. Juda had waited patiently, enjoying his testy questions that always ended their late hours.

"Is that what your Aramaic reads, Professor, or what you read into it?" She responded to the bait – part of their game. Her English was flawless, showing no hint of a French accent, her tone warm and friendly. Repartee had replaced life and death interrogations for Juda Bonaparte, recent graduate, former assassin.

"You know it's Hebrew, not Aramaic, and damned near impossible." He wiped a part of the scroll with a soft cloth, shaking his head. "Even if I had the whole thing rather than this piece…"

"No wonder your scroll is so valuable, Doctor, it's magic. It anticipates the Council of Chalcedon, or was it Ephesus? and the First Vatican Council fourteen hundred years later. Truly a marvelous document."

The professor put down his magnifying glass and covered the scroll with an oil-dampened cloth. "I thought your doctorate was in oriental studies, Juda, not the cloudy history of the Catholic church."

Remembering the Vatican, Juda thought, not "cloudy," Professor, "dark."

"I'm tired," he continued. "Let's quit and go have some coffee. My brain is as weak as your history; it was the Council of Chalcedon, and in 451 at that," he said with a self-satisfied smile. "I cannot make any progress as long as you keep up that chatter about your church."

He shook his head, and she noticed that, for a moment, the playful sparkle in his eyes changed. Worried and tired, he looked down at the covered scroll.

"Too much is missing, too damn much. We shouldn't have cut it."

"You've been doing all the talking about the Church and not sounding like the good Catholic you are, Doctor. This scroll, as I've said, is brainwashing you into an agnostic or skeptic like your late friend Allegro." She smiled, adding, "You'll be excommunicated." She remembered her last meeting with the Pope: hallucinations, tears, and the death of an old monk, the man she killed, the life she left.

"Where are the other pieces of the scroll, Professor Baxter?"

He looked at her seriously, replying, "With friends, Juda."

This was the answer he always gave. She knew there were five sections cut from one. "My idea to cut it," he had admitted, shaking his head, when he had first told her about the scroll, "and a crazy one." Not all the Dead Sea Scrolls had made it to the Rockefeller museum. Many had been sold privately to collectors and museums after being smuggled out of Jerusalem, as this piece had been. Some were still secreted in the Middle East. "Others," he had told her, "no doubt are yet to be found in the caves at Qumran. Some are probably still with the Bedouin."

"Yours is different, copper, not parchment or leather," she had observed.

"It's like the first copper scroll, which was discovered in 1952, five years after the Dead Sea Scrolls," the professor had answered. "The one that obsessed John Allegro. That scroll was thought to be an inventory of the treasure of Solomon. Allegro had it sent to Manchester for cutting and opening. Unlike the other scrolls in every way, it ended up in Jordan in the Archeological Museum at Amman, and not in the Rockefeller Museum or the Shrine of the Book.

"My piece," he had continued, "with the other four, is different from all Dead Sea Scrolls." He had looked past her into the clutter of his laboratory, into the past. "Ours have never been public. They will fit together like a puzzle and reveal... What? Someday, Juda. Who knows?"

Now, ready to rest for the night, Professor Baxter shook his head again, closing his notebook. "The scrolls may not be deciphered in my time, but my work is in here." He patted his notebook and chuckled. "...if they can understand it."

"And when they're deciphered, what then? From the worried look on your face you'd think your scroll is the one..."

Baxter laughed and said, "They all thought that, Juda. The fear..."

"What the scrolls would reveal?"

They had never quite gotten past this point in their discussions. Now she waited in silence, a hard-earned lesson from her years in analysis, smiling inside at what she had learned. The professor did not answer. She knew that the matter of his copper scroll was closed, but he surprised her with: "It may, Juda. It may cause quite a rumble."

Since coming to England to study, and after defending her thesis, Juda had stayed at the university working as an assistant to Professor Baxter, who, though he was many years older than she, she had learned to love. She helped him, almost every night, on his special project, the copper scroll – a scroll that seemed as indecipherable as her own past.

"Which is it, Dr. Bonaparte?" the professor challenged her. She liked the sound of the title and he knew it. "Agnostic or skeptic, you think I'll become?" Together they checked the simple security of the room: barred windows and dead-bolt locks on the door that opened onto the polished wood hallway of the old university building. They went into his adjoining office. Juda locked the door.

Professor Baxter's office was filled with stacks of books, journals, manuscripts, and specimens from a lifetime of archeological digs. They covered the walls, the floor, and most of the desk top. A cave of curios, it smelled of coffee, strong Irish pipe tobacco, mustiness, and another scent Juda knew so well, the desert. She had spent hours in here reading and examining charts of the Judaean desert, memories of which, worse than death, still haunted her dreams.

"Now where were we, Professor?" she said, as she poured coffee from a stained electric percolator, grimacing at the smell of the stale dark brew, which was a far cry from the rich Arabic she preferred. Though she had changed her life, tastes cultivated over a lifetime remained. "Somewhere between Nestorius and infallibility, or was it Jesus Christ and your Qumran documents?" Her eyes sparkled as she sat beside him in a small corner they had carved out from the clutter and reserved for their long discussions on archeology, religion, philosophy, and rarely, their lives.

"You know where we are, with Qumran. I mean, nowhere! After fifty years of study, skullduggery by scoundrels, elusive bits here and there, cover-ups by everybody involved, lost scrolls, interferences by the Church and state, political changes, scholars rushing to publish, godforsaken theories, and now these, our impossible pieces of copper," he paused and added, "from hell. It wasn't anything like this at Nag. Just plain outright Arab butchery, but at least it all came out in Robinson's work." He became silent and his eyes misted over. "No Catholic cloak and dagger stuff like what's going on at the Rockefeller. The Egyptians just cut 'em up… "

"Nag Hammadi?" Juda felt a quickening in her chest. "You were there too? You never told me, Harold." Her voice softened. She felt his distress.

The professor smiled. "I'm old, and have a lifetime of stories, Juda, but not tonight. You invite me for one of your French dinners and I'll tell you the story of Nag Hammadi. It's a funny thing, Juda, that three ancient documents, nearly two thousand years old, which could have a profound bearing on the way we view Christianity and Judaism, were all found in the Middle East and Egypt, within the first fifty years of this century." He shook his head, adding, "Too coincidental to suit me."

"Nag Hammadi, the Dead Sea Scrolls, and… ?"

"The Damascus Document. Found in a Cairo synagogue just before the turn of the century. Barely fifty years between all three discoveries. Funny thing. Now, what about that dinner?"

"Sunday at three," Juda offered with a warm smile, still thinking about the three scroll discoveries and looking forward to another Sunday with Dr. Baxter.

"And let's talk about you and the assistant professorship you could have with just a nod. But, no, you chose to stay and work with me for next to nothing."

Juda gagged on the bitter coffee and smiled at this raggedy old man, with his uncombed bristly hair, weathered, leathery body, and a religious dedication to his science, and silently refused to analyze the relationship further. For Juda, analysis had died in the Syrian desert after she had been assaulted and her beloved doctor had given up his life for her. That part of her life was buried in the Vatican. She took the professor's arm as they left the ivy-covered building with its tile roof, and ornate cupola, and laughed with him when they both turned to check, as they had often done, that they had turned the lights out in the lab and office.

"Professor, how would you like to join me for a pint of bitters and a pastry at Barnie's? That coffee..." Her mouth turned downward into a simulated scowl: a beautiful mouth, upper lip thinner than the lower, free of lipstick.

"You mean 'pasties,' little English meat pies, not pastries."

She started to laugh. "In France 'pasties' are not exactly what we would ordinarily call 'meat pies.'"

"Well, Juda," he joined in her laughter, "pasties or pastries, beer or bitters, I can't go with you tonight, I have something I must do."

Juda embraced him, enjoying the feel of him in her arms, a warmth like the heat of the desert against her skin. It didn't last. Tonight the cold English air chilled her as she walked home, reminding her of Paris and lonely walks by the Seine. She flipped up the collar of her Burberry. France and the dark confessional for sins which were to be, were behind her forever, like those she had loved, dead – murdered.

In his second floor flat, which was in as much disarray as his office, Professor Baxter made tea and placed it on his desk beside a plateful of cookies and a hard scone and next to his notebook. He glanced at the small crucifix hanging behind his desk and a picture of a young woman, his wife, the pyramids of Giza in the background. For a moment he remembered her fiery death. For the rest of his life, he would blame himself and the scroll he had been after. Now he looked at his desk, pausing as if he were not sure where to start. Absent mindedly, he thumbed through the stack of mail he had carried from his office. Still thinking of his night's work on the copper scroll, he looked at the last page of notes he had made. The notebook contained, in his secret cipher, all of his work on the mysterious sheet of copper that dated back to Christ. He snapped on his computer and smiled as he typed his password; then he entered his notes.

For almost forty years he had worked on scrolls, first from Egypt, and then Qumran, but this last piece, the copper scroll that his friend at the Palestine Archeological Museum had taken out of Israel at great danger was different, ominously different. It was an obsession that possessed him, a formless ameba devouring him, an evil temptress, promising – never yielding, maddening, exciting, with an impossible code, impossible language – dangerous. He felt it whenever he touched the copper scroll, knowing now they had been wrong when they agreed to keep it and divide it into five pieces. It forebode evil and promised eternity. Not at all what they had expected.

Picking up his mail he had tossed next to his computer, Professor Baxter opened a card from Juda thanking him for escorting her to London for the scientific meeting on AIDS and the play the weekend before. He smiled, noting she had not mentioned the drinking and dancing. He remembered her kiss. What did it mean? Then he opened a brown envelope post-marked in Jerusalem. It was not the usual letter from Jean Legault, but was from Jerome Legault, Jean's younger brother. Baxter let out a painful gasp as he read that Jean was dead – murdered. They had been friends since boyhood.

Father Jean Legault had been assigned to the French École Biblique et Archéologique in Jerusalem, and he alone of their group had become a member of the original 'International Team' set up to study the Dead Sea Scrolls. The letter described Jean's grisly murder and ended with a warning: Baxter, you and your friends' lives are in danger; Jean's piece of the scroll is missing. I think someone wants your scroll.

Baxter put his head on his desk and cried. His fear over the scroll, over what they had done and what they had learned, was realized now in Jean's murder, which, in the dark shadows of his mind, forebode the death of Christianity.

Chapter 2

After her workout and shower, Juda prepared her supper of fresh eggs scrambled in heavy cream, the way Franke, her mother's servant, had shown her when she was a child. The eggs, an indulgence to tastes she had all but abandoned since coming to England, were still warm, as she had wanted, when she retrieved them from a milk pass-through. Now she watched them glistening in the low heat of the burner, a deep country yellow, warm, soft, and smooth, enriched with Jersey cream. At the end of her carefully timed production, she gently tossed them with butter, the *pièce de résistance*. To hell with cholesterol. She downed the golden buttery nuggets, wiped her plate with toast, then blotted her lips. English food was so otherwise boring. Smiling at her rationalization, she poured a cup of dark French roast coffee, lit a cigarette and looked for Professor Baxter's manuscript, which, after a quick search, she realized she had forgotten at the laboratory. She finished her coffee and went to her bedroom.

Juda threw off her robe and glanced at herself in the mirror. Her body was flawless in every way. Powerful muscles, discretely hidden beneath a thin mantle of fat, showed only when she called on them – now during workouts and not combat. Her back, which was straight and slightly broad across the shoulders, bore smooth thick columns of muscle on each side of her spine from hips to neck. Her small waist, thickly muscled, swept in smooth curves to full hips and long legs. She opened her dresser drawer full of neatly stacked underclothes: small lace bikini panties and matching bras, and sturdy cotton ones and support tops for exercise. A cylinder rolled from under some scented fluffy silk. Made of brushed stainless steel and four inches long, it bore a threaded nipple at one end. Juda picked it up, rolled it around in her fingers, examining, smelling the perfume rather than cleaning solvent and smiling at the incongruity. Then she wiped the silencer with a silk scarf and replaced it next to the matching weapon, a Walther PPK 9mm short with specially fitted grips. She tucked them beneath the layers of her underclothes. *Why? Why did I bring them? I'm finished with that.*

She pulled on blue jeans and a faded chambray shirt and tied a cashmere sweater over her shoulders. At thirty-one, Juda was even more beautiful than when she had trained in Israel, first as a commando, then, because of her extraordinary skills, as an assassin. But it was another Friday night and she had nothing to do, her social life limited by her past and her fears of the future. Her choices she knew. *C'est la vie*, she shrugged, looking to the place where she had buried her weapon. She would go back for Baxter's document and read it tonight as she had planned. Thinking of the eggs, four of them, and eyeing her waist with a tilt of her head and a smirk that went more to one side than the other, she knew the walk to the lab would be just what she needed. At the door she paused and took off the sweater, deciding the eggs demanded a run rather than a walk. Food and exercise, she knew, substituted for yearnings that would be forever unsatiated. She had learned that in her psychoanalysis, and had found it forcibly realized in her failed relationships. She smiled thinking of her weekend in London with Professor Baxter.

Juda had had to bribe Baxter with a play and the best dinner in London to get him to take her to the meeting of London's Royal Society of Medicine, of which he was an honorary member. It was held at the Society's exclusive Belgrave street quarters. The presentation by Professor Peter Barnes, a Nobel laureate for his work with Dr. Medwar on immunological cloning, had been to an elite group of London's most eminent physicians and scientists. The paper had been entitled "Towards a New Theory of HIV Disease." Baxter had not questioned Juda's curious interest in AIDS – part of her nightmares – he had balked at the formal attire and stuffy manners demanded at the meetings. But he had finally given in to Juda's persuasive charm, and had beamed when he and Juda entered the meeting room and all eyes turned to him and the beautiful woman on his arm.

Professor Baxter, dressed in the required tuxedo, shaved, his gray hair combed, had looked quite handsome, Juda had thought, not so old, as they crossed the meeting room to chairs at the front. The only woman in the room, Juda had worn a simple black silk dress by Givenchy, slit on the side to just above the knee, that hinted at, but could not hide the curves and muscular grace of her body. A black wide-brimmed hat framed her smooth oval face, wide-set eyes, and shoulder length hair that glistened with a silken sheen the color of desert sand. As eyebrows rose and eyes shifted from the sixty-five-year-old professor to the beautiful woman, Baxter gently nudged his young associate. Hesitatingly, he whispered that she looked quite beautiful, as they took their seats. After the presentation, as waiters served sherry in Lennox crystal etched with the society's seal from small silver trays, Juda had met Dr. Peter Barnes and Dr. George Gamash.

As she recalled the meeting, her jogging to the lab picked up speed. Juda thrilled to the exertion of her body, sailing into the wind, leaving her phantoms.

"Baxter," Barnes had said, "a little far afield, what? Nice to see you. You know Dr. Gamash." Turning to Juda, he said, "Dr. Gamash is London's leading cardiovascular surgeon, almost as much a stranger to my presentation as England's authority on the Dead Sea Scrolls. And who is your lovely friend?"

Juda offered her hand first to Barnes then Gamash, noting the intensity in Gamash's dark eyes, and something familiar. Where had she seen him before? He wore a full mustache and had thick black hair amply laced with gray. Fiftyish, of medium height and build, muscular, immaculately tailored, Gamash took her hand, flashing perfect white teeth through moist sensuous lips. "What is a young graduate doing at a meeting of stuffy old scientists?" Dr. Gamash had asked, paying little attention to Baxter as he continued holding Juda's hand. "If you are working with Dr. Baxter, immunology is not your interest, rather the riddle of the Dead Sea Scrolls."

"Nor yours," Baxter replied, irritated, as Juda withdrew her hand. Privately enjoying Baxter's annoyance, she pressed a little closer to him, demurely inquiring:

"'Gamash,' Arabic is it not? Lebanese?"

"Beirut, Dr. Bonaparte. Have you been there?"

"I've traveled in the Middle East, and my degree is in oriental studies." Turning to Barnes, Juda said, "From my understanding of your presentation, Dr. Barnes, you're saying the AIDS virus may not follow pathways of transmission as presently understood, especially by the Americans. You believe the victim to be already immunologically compromised to be susceptible." Not likely after a single assault, Juda thought, remembering her half brother Shamir, his ordered assault and attempt to infect her, and the carnage in the desert – the bloodbath that followed.

"Very astute, Dr. Bonaparte. That's exactly what my work leads me to. Preexisting disease, repeated assaults on the body's immune system by infection, malnutrition, and drug abuse, are the real culprits. But, I say, you are very well informed."

"A relative, perhaps, has been a victim?" Gamash said, quite taken with Juda's beauty.

"Then how do you explain the transmission through single accidental needle pricks, Dr. Barnes, to nurses and doctors apparently not so compromised?" Juda asked, feeling Gamash's eyes on her, disregarding his question.

"We're doing case by case studies, but I have no answer to that as yet, Dr. Bonaparte. And, of course, it doesn't apparently fit my theory. George, what do you say to that?"

"I am a surgeon at heart," Gamash said, smiling at his pun. "Immunology is a special interest – a hobby, that's why I am here."

"A relative perhaps?" Juda quipped with a smile.

"*Touché*, Doctor... may I call you, Juda? Unusual name." Gamash smiled again. "Perhaps the three of us could discuss our common interests in Peter's work over lunch tomorrow."

"Harold and I are staying at the *Au Quatre Coins du Monde*. Why don't you join us there for dinner," Juda suggested coquettishly. "We're seeing *The Phantom* afterwards."

"A marvelous production. How beauty and evil can exist in one person touches something in us all."

"Like the surgeon with his knife," Juda said.

Gamash took Juda's hand once more and said he would not join them for dinner. His rakish eyes held hers.

"Juda, somehow I know we have met before. Perhaps in the gaming rooms at Monaco or Venice? Have you been to Las Vegas? I'm sure we will meet again."

"Las Vegas is my favorite," Juda answered still trying to place Gamash.

Later that night in the hotel restaurant, Juda and Baxter had been greeted by Cordon Bleu chef, Pierre LaCourt, who came to the table and embraced Juda. Kissing her on the cheek, he exclaimed, "Juda, Paris was not the same without you, so I followed you to England. God knows they needed me."

Juda thought: They needed me in Paris to kill people in Rome, South America, the Middle East, wherever God or country thought it right that someone should die. Oh, they were right. They needed to die, but now it won't die in me, they killed my soul. Juda returned his embrace with a kiss and a warm smile.

LaCourt snapped his fingers and a waiter brought a pâté decorated with a single fanned black olive. "Something special for you, Juda, it would be lost on the tastes of the English. Your American friend in the wheelchair said you were living in England. How could you, Juda? Paris is your heart."

"You've met T.J. Troubble, Pierre?" Troubble was an American security agent, crippled in a gun fight with terrorists.

Spreading some of the pâté on a thin triangle of toast, Juda looked at her old friend and thought of another Pierre who had loved Paris, Dr. LaCroix, dead because of her. Remembering, she smiled at LaCourt, raised her fingers in a circle of perfection and said it was an exceptional paté, just the right amount of Henessey; but she could not mask the sadness in her eyes. She introduced Harold Baxter as her friend and said Paris had indeed been her heart. Juda looked down, saddened. She remembered the men she had killed in Paris while saving Michael and Susan who were to become her dearest friends.

Sensing her discomfort the chef urged her to enjoy her meal and to join him in the kitchen some afternoon for some cooking lessons. "Like in Paris, Juda," he added, embracing her again before leaving their table.

Baxter frowned, noticing her sadness. "Paris brings painful memories, Juda?" he asked. "Do you want to talk about them?"

"Like your Nag Hammadi story. I, too, have lots of stories, Harold, but not tonight. I want to eat and drink, and have fun.

If you will indulge me?" She sliced into the rare chateaubriand, dipped it into the bernaise sauce, and offered the first bite to Baxter. "The first is yours, Harold, the way of the Arab." She downed her Pernod, tilting her glass towards him.

"French liqueur, Arab ways, English scholar. Juda you are a delightful enigma as puzzling as my scroll, with an appetite like a Welsh coal miner, I should add."

"I exercise a lot." I had to, to be the best at what I did, and to drive away my demons, she thought. The drinks warming her, Juda smiled between bites and sips, beginning to enjoy the pleasant sensations of food and drink and the exchanges with Baxter and earlier with Chef LaCourt. She knew that her mystique was heightened by the fact that she had a Jewish general for a father and an Austrian countess for a mother. "I could add to your enigma," she said to Baxter, "with a past that would knock your Bayfords off, but let's save that. I want to dance."

Taking her hand Baxter said he was old enough to be her grandfather and hadn't held a woman in his arms since his wife died, but if Juda wanted to risk having to resuscitate him and getting her feet crushed, he'd love to dance. And dance they did. Slow, quiet, safe, Juda enjoying the comfortable feel of the man in her arms the way she enjoyed food, and fast and hot like Pernod, when the music changed and the alcohol played in her head. The professor carefully paced himself as Juda twisted and whirled, shimmied and kicked around him, expending unabated energy that had consumed her, until she was breathless and the professor exhausted. The band picked up her tempo as she moved into a belly dance before she quit, embarrassed and unsatisfied. Afterward, at the door of her room, warmed by the Pernod and dancing, hair tousled, silk clinging to sweat-wet skin, Juda had kissed Baxter passionately, testing his lips with the tip of her tongue, before pulling herself away and closing the door. Tears in her eyes, she had thrown herself on the bed.

As Juda fell asleep with nightmares of the AIDS virus intertwining in a dance of death with her own DNA, Dr. George Gamash was making a call from the Iraqi embassy not far from where she slept. By international agreement all embassy calls are free of surveillance and all materials sent in the official diplomatic pouches free of inspection. Gamash withdrew a cigarette from a gold case as the call was forwarded to the headquarters of a Palestinian training camp a hundred miles from Baghdad.

"Abu Keeftan, *keefect*, how are you? Does Hussein treat you well in your new home?"

"We live like dogs, my cousin. What of London?"

Gamash, London's consummate cardiac surgeon, Arab terrorist, and mass murderer, who with Keeftan would soon orchestrate another airline bombing while cleverly shifting the blame to Libyans, smiled and said, "My friend, is Mohammed ready with the radio I ordered? One that will play a different tune over Scotland?" His dark eyes followed smoke rings he blew into the empty room provided for him at the embassy. "There is something else you need to know, Rama. Juda Bonaparte is in Birmingham and sleeps in Harold Baxter's bed. The Israelis must know. Be careful with this operation you do for Nadir. He cannot be trusted."

In Iraq, Abu Keeftan clenched his hand knuckle-white around the phone. "I have already sent my people. Allah curses me with Nadir, and now Juda Bonaparte. *Khayak*, cousin, I am sickened with the Palestinians, the Jews, and Pan American Airlines. Your radio and the other favors will be in the diplomatic pouch on Monday, and I will be there myself for our visit to the University."

Halfway to the archeology building, Juda picked up her pace into a long soaring run. The jog barely winded her. Exhilarated by wind and rain, she felt weightless when she arrived at the building. Unlocking the door, drenched and dripping, she ran the three flights to Professor Baxter's office. A block away a man in the back seat of a sedan watched her through night-vision binoculars. He picked up a small two-way transmitter. "A woman has entered the building, kill her if she goes to the laboratory."

Juda pressed the old push-button light switch and looked around the office for the manuscript. It must still be in the lab beside the scroll, she thought. About to unlock the door, she paused, distracted by a burnt coffee aroma. She had forgotten to turn off the percolator. Stopped, alerted, remembering, she looked back at the coffeepot, then at the dead-bolt on the door to the laboratory, which was now unlocked. Before entering the darkened room, she stood absolutely still, breath suppressed, every sense awakened, listening.

The lab was dark – silent. Her heartbeat? A movement? A scent? Breathing sounds? Fine blond hairs on her arms sprung to attention. Action replaced thinking as she dropped and rolled into the room. The long knife, which would have removed her head, whistled through the air and embedded itself deep in the door jamb. Juda kicked high into a shadow standing beside the worktable. A curse and scream followed the crack of a breaking bone as a gun went clattering across the room. She spun back to the doorway, and using the speed of her turning momentum, drove the heel of her hand into the face of the silhouette trying to remove his knife from the heavy oak trim. He uttered *"sharmu..."* the word unfinished – and died – as the sharp bones of his nose split, and ripped into the base of his brain under the force of her perfect blow.

Powerful arms held her, crushing her chest, cutting off her air – a giant of a man gripped her from behind. Thrusting her hands overhead, Juda twisted, slipping out of her wet sweater, at the same time bending, grasping flesh and heaving, using her body as a fulcrum. A gunshot exploded, splintering the door, as the man flew over her shoulders, screaming in pain from the hold she had on his genitals. She slipped her hands to his head and jerked his chin sideways as a second shot muffled the sound of his vertebrae cracking. He died before he crashed to the floor at her feet. Hit with a powerful blow, Juda collapsed as a blinding white light burst inside her head, and she fell into a sea of blood and broken pottery.

Fighting for consciousness, blood pouring from her head, Juda dragged herself across the floor and found the weapon. In the darkness engulfing her, she raised the Uzi and emptied the clip, firing three long bursts through the window as the injured and frightened assailant escaped.

On the street below, the sedan moved quickly to the man running from the building. He held a bleeding, broken arm against his chest. Gasping and trembling he spoke to the occupant in the rear seat, Rama Abu Keeftan. "There was a fight," he said breathlessly, "I think Kahlil is dead and the other injured, maybe dead. I was lucky to escape with my life. My arm is broken – a, a woman."

"Where is the scroll?" Abu Keeftan demanded. He spoke in a near whisper, controlling his rage while raising a weapon from the darkness of the back seat. Police sirens screamed in the background.

"Nowhere. There was no scro…" His body flew backwards onto the pavement as two silenced 9mm bullets drilled a path into his chest.

"Drive," Ram Abu Keeftan said to the frightened young man behind the wheel.

Chapter 3

FRANCE

It was a place of miracles. The Blessed Virgin Mary had appeared here in 1846 warning that "priests and religious orders will be hunted down and made to die a cruel death." But now the hunted had become the hunters and the man kneeling on the oak priedieu before a framed cloth painting that looked like Christ's head was the order's best. Sworn to poverty and chastity, his life had been orchestrated from childhood for one purpose, the protection of the Church. He lived in a mountain monastery near the shrine of La Salette, high in the French Alps. He ate fruits, vegetables, grains, milk, and cheese, never the flesh of any animal. He had never known play or recreation or the touch of a woman – except in his dreams. Prayer, meditation, study, exercise, and practice with weapons had been his daily activities for as long as he could remember. Once he had completed his formal and supervised education, his interactions with others were limited to solitary instruction by tutors and trainers. When called upon to do so by his superiors, he would kill, as he had been programmed to do.

Out of habits imprinted in childhood, and with the adult indifference to rote learning, René Gervais thanked God, but did not make the sign of the cross, for this was not a requirement. He stood up from his prayer stand and took off his exercise suit. Powerful muscles glistened with the sweat of his workout and five mile mountain run that ended his day – every day. Naked, he walked to the window of his tower apartment and stared at the mountains on the horizon, the snowcapped Alps dark against the blue sky, and then at the mist settling on the lake below the village. His hair, shiny black and thick, fell loosely to below his ears. He looked young, his face smooth and boyish. His eyes were as blue as the sky over the alpine lake, and even more striking because of his dark complexion. Like the waters, they were icy cold.

In the village square below he watched large-breasted girls carry unsold goods home from the market and noted his reaction as a sin for his next confession as he felt a rush of passion encompassing his whole being like a whirlpool with its vortex in his groin. Footsteps in the hall meant much-needed food, nothing else. He turned to the door even before the knock and shamelessly opened it. A small man, old and bent, wearing the coarse wool habit of a monk, carried in a large tray of vegetables, steamed grains, and a loaf of warm bread, which he placed on a low table. The man seated himself cross-legged on a mat in front of his food, silently turning his broad back to the monk, and lowered his head in prayer before his meal. The monk told him the director would see him in two hours.

Always alone, Gervais ate slowly of the massive quantities of food, unadorned by salt or sauce. He had almost forgotten the beans and sausage and the smell of frying fish in his mother's kitchen. Afterward, he showered, dried himself with a rough towel, and rested on his bed, a solid wood slab suspended from the wall at each end by chains, on which a thin straw-filled mattress was laid.

He was a Knight Templar, a holy brother sworn to the service of Christ for the protection of Christians. The bells of the church marked this, his time of meditation. He closed his eyes and asked the Holy Spirit for strength, but he was answered with thoughts that tormented him. The Templars were a renegade and secret society whose simple mandate was death to those who would threaten or endanger the Church.

The Templars, or the Poor Knights of Christ and of the Temple of Solomon, developed as the brainchild of a French knight in 1120 for the protection of pilgrims to the Holy Land. The Templars competed with other orders for knightly services, and they alone survived. They became the most enduring and powerful Christian order in the world, and also the richest. The order endured secretly in southern France and the Pyrenees even after it had been disbanded by Pope Clement V in the fourteenth century, its vast properties confiscated and its leaders roasted over coals. Its treasure had never been found. Throughout its history mystery shrouded the Templars.

Through the ages the Templars continued an underground existence administered in secret from Marseilles. Gradually distancing themselves from Rome and the Vatican, they aligned themselves instead with other secret societies and religious movements. Sanctioned by their self-righteous convictions of purity and might, they replaced broadswords, shining armor, and mighty steeds with powerful handguns, Kevlar vests, and fast cars. Like his predecessors of the past nine hundred years, the handsome young man in the tower apartment of La Salette, his stomach full but his needs unsatiated, longed for the excitement of joustings and the kill for which his life had been programmed from childhood.

The monk's immediate director was Raymond Lagare, Benedictine priest and head of the monastery at La Salette. He stared in silence at René Gervais, who had just entered his sparsely furnished office and was seated before him. Lagare knew that the time he dreaded had finally come. Earlier that day he had received instructions from Fra Jean-Baptiste Sancta Croce, director of the secret Templar society centered near the city of Marseilles. Sancta Croce was the religious head of the basilica and monastery of Ste-Marie-Magdeleine at St-

Maximin-la Ste-Baume. Nowhere in the world was devotion to Mary Magdalene more evident than in southern France, the home of the Templars.

"René," Father Lagare said, "our people in Jerusalem and Spain were able to gather the information in the file you have. When we have finished our talk, and before you leave us forever, you must memorize every detail and then we will talk again." He got up from behind his small oak desk and placed his arm over the young man's shoulders. "Now come walk with me through the village, to the paths where you run every day. I have much to say before you leave us on a much different path.

"You have been extensively educated in the Catholic Christian tradition, René, an education that has been very costly to our society and one that would make a Jesuit's pale by comparison. Between your formal education here in France, at the Vatican, and in the United States, you have been constantly and privately tutored and supervised. You have never questioned your somewhat unusual lessons in the use of weapons or in the martial arts. Yes, you have learned well and it has not been in vain. You knew that we would call on you one day for unhesitating obedience in applying what you know, while at the same time living the vows you have made. But first, I will talk about the Church."

They walked in silence through the damp halls and stone stairways of the near empty monastery, which in 1125 had been a staging post for the Knights Templar. When they entered the town square, it was dusk.

"We are Roman Catholics in name only," Lagare said. A small man, bent and shrunken with years, he walked in striking contrast to Gervais, young, tall, straight, and muscular. "From the time of Christ there has been a systematic effort made to Romanize Christ's teachings. Your file contains my own dissertation on this; study it well. It is old like I. Jews were blamed for Christ's crucifixion, although, in fact, it was a classic Roman penalty for political enemies of the state. Then Constantine made Christianity officially Roman in the fourth century, converting himself just before his death. Even when the king of France tortured our grandmaster, Jacques Molay, and confiscated our lands in 1307, the Vatican remained silent as our brothers were murdered, our property seized. Be that as it may, the Catholic Church is very much Roman and has been so throughout history. And, as you already know, Rome made the cross its symbol. But was this Christ's intent? Or St. Paul's?"

René Gervais listened, but remained silent. He didn't care. The old man continued.

"The Templars' mission, as ordained by Hugh de Payens, our founder, was, in the beginning, to protect Christian pilgrims to Jerusalem, protect them from robberies, murder, and an Arab society known as the Assassins. The Assassins, or Nizaris as they were known in the Arab world, had been formed a few years before as a secret Islamic order by Hasan ibn al-Sabbah. They had as their mandate, protect Islam, kill Christians, and destroy the Templars. Sworn to kill each other, the Templars and Assassins, in a fateful twist of history, embraced each other after most of the Assassins were destroyed by Hulagu Kahn in North Syria. Soon afterward, the Templars met a similar fate on the orders of the French king, and Pope Philip IV, and then Pope Clement V. Bedfellows now, the Templars and Assassins who remained continued in secrecy into modern time, distancing themselves from their Christian and Islamic beginnings and sworn in blood to destroy the Roman, Islamic, and Judaic religions because of their parochial, ethnic, and racial biases. They would replace these with a world religion, incorporating universal principals.

"Over the years," Lagare continued, wheezing from exertion, "the Church has violently suppressed radicals and heretics up to the Inquisition and past, well into modern times – a concept encouraged by no less than the great Augustine himself, who spoke of a holy and just war to suppress heresies. Even when the papacy moved to Avignon in 1309 and seven popes ruled in France until 1377, the Catholic Church was still Roman. The cry 'where the Pope is, there is Rome,' spread throughout the world until the French papacy failed." The old priest again found a resting place, his breathing difficult in the rarefied mountain air. René Gervais, bored with this old man and his history lesson and wondering where all this would lead, assisted the priest, patiently and silently as he had been trained to do, wanting to choke him – another sin. Would he go on forever with his fabrications?

"Wearing the cloak of Catholicism, the Roman Empire still lives, René. Even when it fell, it absorbed the conquerors. Next to the Egyptian dynasties it became the longest lasting empire in the history of the world – only now it is under the guise of the Holy Roman Church and more than one billion Catholics listen when the Pope speaks. It is based on one finite historical truth, that Christ was the Son of God."

As they walked in silence for a while, past stone, vine covered houses, narrow paths, and the walls of the ancient church, the old man took the young man's hand as he had done since René was a child. "What I am about to tell you will change the way you think forever, René, and it will move you, and it could move the world.

"A house has been arranged for you in Marseilles. There you will have all the resources you need: money, intelligence, men, and weapons. You will no longer receive orders from me but from Fra Jean-Baptiste Sancta Croce, and you will go to Spain for training. I am only one in a chain that connects the world and reaches into the highest offices of all nations, and now my work is finished, my son."

"What must I do, Father?" The young monk with the innocent blue eyes put his arm around the waist of the priest to help him as they continued their walk. He could feel the fragile bones beneath his fingers. "We have walked far enough," he said, "Ahead, it is very difficult; you are tired and the light poor. Let us turn back."

Comforted by the strong arm supporting him, the old priest said, "The file contains everything we know about a scroll stolen from the caves of the Dead Sea – a copper scroll scribed in a secret code by the student of Dionysius at the time of Christ's death. We Templars have kept the legend in our hearts even after our documents were seized and sealed in St. Peter's Vault. Now that the scroll has been found, we must have it in its entirety, all five pieces; then all those who have viewed it must be silenced. And you must be prepared for others who are after the scroll – violent men driven by avarice."

"What will this scroll reveal, Father?" the young man asked, releasing his arm as the path eased. "Why must men die for it?" The old man stopped. His head trembled as if what he was about to say was utterly inconceivable, collapsing a lifetime of belief.

"You are forbidden to ask questions, René, but I will answer this one time. As I said, Christianity is based on one truth. That Christ died on the cross and raised himself from death – the Resurrection. The scroll," he anguished, "the scroll will reveal what has been held by secret tradition for two thousand years."

Gervais stopped, looked the priest in the eye. "What will it reveal?"

"Where the body of Jesus Christ was buried, René, and," his voice faltered, tears welled up in his eyes, "and remains to this day, my son, buried in a secret vault here in France."

LONDON

"It was Juda Bonaparte, Gamash," Rama Keeftan said, his eyes fierce with rage. "Three men dead and no scroll. The Israelis sent her, I know it."

"Why do you involve yourself with Nadir and this scroll? He is garbage, a Syrian pimp without principles."

"Money! If he is a pimp, Iraq has made me the prostitute. My men must be paid."

"How much, my cousin?"

"Two million American dollars for all five pieces of the scroll. Five hundred thousand for each. One half more for operational expenses."

"Then the scroll must be worth twenty times that to Nadir. Why?"

"What do I know of scrolls? They are for Jews and Christians, and Dominicans. They fight over shit. Nadir is worse than a Jew."

"Where is Baxter's piece of scroll, *khayak*, cousin."

"Gone. There was no scroll." Abu Keeftan cursed in Arabic.

"Then the woman… " Gamash said.

"If she had it, then it is in Tel Aviv."

"Or, perhaps, still here, *akhuk*, brother," Dr. George Gamash said calmly. "We will find it, if it is. And if the Israelis have it, will you go after it?"

"As we speak, my people are in training with Sabri for a raid into Tel Aviv where the streets will run red again. But I cannot trust any of them except Sabri. Iraq is not their home and Hussein not their leader. And Sabri is not George Gamash or Rama Keeftan." Keeftan smiled, putting his arm over his cousin's shoulders. "Will you stay here forever, Doctor? I need you. I leave for Baghdad in the morning. Come with me." Keeftan walked to Gamash's fifteenth floor penthouse suite balcony and looked down at the city of London. "You must prefer English women, *Gideus*," he said in Arabic, though his English was flawless, turning his dark eyes to Gamash. "Surely not their food or climate. Perhaps the casinos?"

"And if this scroll is nothing, like the others? Something that moves academics to write books and embarrass the Vatican? What then?"

Keeftan shrugged. "A few men, and a little effort. We have wasted much for less. A night at roulette. If the scroll is what Nadir said, then we will – "

" – Topple Rome? Is that what you want, Abu Keeftan?"

"Believe Nadir only, and we will have more wealth than many small countries. Imagine the excitement of holding the Vatican as hostage, or the Israelis."

"What of that Syrian fool?"

Keeftan tapped an unfiltered cigarette on the railing then lit it, turning to Gamash with a cold, determined look. "Nadir is a pimp and a dead man. He sells himself to rich Americans to find the scroll, now he will use me to steal the scroll and sell it back to them."

Gamash laughed and said, "An Arab business man." He poured two drinks, tall glasses of Glenfidich on ice.

"I let his youngest son live to bring him the news that a woman killed his eldest. What greater pain for failure than that? And the Israeli-Christian woman, Juda Bonaparte, will be mine. She will die naked in my arms, screaming in ecstasy."

"You forget, Rama, I saw her first. Her old professor we will kill, but Juda Bonaparte is much too beautiful to die. I will make her mine."

Abu Keeftan laughed. "You have always said the *hammami* is mightier than the sword, my cousin." They both laughed and drank more Scotch whiskey.

Chapter 4

Juda blinked her eyes open to the dazzling light of her hospital room. Professor Baxter was standing over her. "You've been hurt," she heard him say through the fog and thunder inside her bandaged head. "You've had a concussion, Juda, but there were no internal injuries. You'll be all right, up and about soon." His beard had grown, he looked tired and frazzled. She felt something about his being there, like being a child again.

"You went to my lab." He sounded far away. "A fight – two men are dead, another on the street. They hit you with something. They might have killed you, Juda." His voice faltered, sounding old, broken. "Thieves," he said, "took the scroll piece."

She closed her eyes, remembering. The run in the rain, the unlocked door. Two men dead? She couldn't remember, but in her heart she knew and it sickened her. Death followed her like a shadow. Dead men – her life. He took her hand, soft, young and wrapped it in his. Comforted, she slept, and when she awoke he was sitting beside her. She had known he would be, but he was not alone.

A smiling man in a white coat said, "Miss Bonaparte, I'm Dr. Jones, Clayton-Cowell Jones." A young man, he spoke with an air of inflated authority. "You've been hurt, a head injury.

Aside from a headache, you'll have no permanent injuries except the scar, but with your hair, it won't show. We'll have to watch you for a few days. The outer table, uh, surface of your skull was fractured. Your memory will be a little spotty for the time around your injury, but there were no cerebral injuries. We did a CT scan and blood work when they brought you in. Now, if you can bear with it, an inspector from Scotland yard wants to talk to you." Juda nodded. "I've allowed him five minutes." He walked to the door and said, "Come in, Inspector Gillis."

Gillis was short, fiftyish, and thick waisted. He had leather elbow patches on his ill-fitting Norfolk jacket and wore baggy corduroy slacks. He smelled of tobacco and his thumb nail alone was dirty – a pipe smoker.

"Miss Bonaparte, Edmund Gillis, Scotland Yard." He automatically extended a chubby hand and then withdrew it. "I'd like to talk to you in private. If you'll excuse me, Dr. Jones, Dr. Baxter."

"You don't have to speak with him now, Juda. The police have a full report," Baxter said.

"I'm all right, Harold," Juda said, the pain in her head easing with the medication a nurse had given her. She managed a smile against this new violation to her life and offered the policeman a seat. "How can I help you, Inspector? Scotland Yard? CID, no doubt. You're out of your jurisdiction in Birmingham, are you not, Inspector Gillis?"

"Miss Bonaparte, or rather, Dr. Bonaparte, you're rather well informed about Scotland Yard. You also know we work closely with MI 5 and MI 6 in matters of national security. Three men are dead – Arabs we think, foreign nationals. One from a brain laceration, his nasal bones were hammered into his brain by a powerful blow. The other shot, but he was dead before he was shot, his neck broken. The third, poor sod, had a broken arm and two bullet holes in his chest, killed on the street. Very professional, I must say. Professor Baxter's laboratory's a bleeding mess, and a scroll, or a piece of scroll, has been stolen. You were there, miss, uh, Dr. Bonaparte. They found you unconscious, wet, injured, naked to the waist, and bleeding profusely from your head. What happened?"

"I don't know." Juda forced her mind to remember. Naked? Wet? "I went there for a manuscript. It had been raining. The door to the lab… " She paused, straining, her head aching again, trying to remember. "Unlocked? I remembered locking it." Her thoughts blurred: shadows, sounds, no images. Amnesia. She remembered awaking in the desert stronghold of Raol Shamir, naked, tied to a table and the horror that followed. Shaking her head, she said she couldn't remember. She felt outraged at the violence that had been forced on her again.

"Let me help you," the inspector said. "There were, we think, three men in the lab and a fourth driving the car. Gunshots were heard, an automatic weapon. We think you fired it out the window before you went unconscious. A large curved knife of laminated steel, made in Damascus, was stuck in the doorjamb. They tried to kill you. You fought and killed two of them, injuring the third before he hit you with an urn or pot and escaped with the scroll. He was killed on the street by the driver."

Juda remained silent. Inspector Gillis paused, holding his unlit pipe, looking at this woman, beautiful, even with her head bandaged, who had apparently walked in on a robbery and killed two armed assailants with her bare hands. Hard to believe, but not unexpected from what he had read in her file from MI 6. He stood up and gave her a card.

"Call me, Dr. Bonaparte, when your memories return. We can't have this kind of thing in England, you know." On the steps of the hospital he lit his pipe, tamping the ash with a callused thumb before getting into the waiting Jaguar sedan. Once back at the regional police bureau and his temporary office, he picked up a file on his desk, made some notes, then placed a call to London to report to the station director, Major Alistair Fitzsimmons.

"The report from MI 6 confirms that Juda Bonaparte is a private citizen of France and a legal alien in England not connected to the Mossad or, in fact, any agency. Three years ago Mossad honorably dismissed her and notified every secret service in the world that she was no longer involved in any work for the state of Israel and was returning to private life."

"Anything since coming to England?" Fitzsimmons asked. He was a big man, with a balding, large round head, a full, neatly trimmed mustache, and thin hair carefully parted and combed over the crown, giving him an endless face that looked like a full moon. He wore a dark suit with a gray waistcoat drawn tight over a heavy midsection and stood with an erect military posture.

"No, sir. Just her doctorate, and her work for Professor Baxter."

"She's a killer, Gillis. There's more, there has to be. Any contacts here?"

"She has few friends, no relatives. Occasionally dates professional types: professors, a doctor from London. No one regular, sir. She maintains an apartment building in Paris, ten units and her own. She has a large estate in Austria, inherited from her mother, and is rightfully a countess. A man named Troubble stays at her place in Paris, collects rent, and keeps it up. He's an invalid in a wheelchair, an American veteran, Special Forces. She maintains a small staff in Austria and rarely visits there."

"Jesus, anything else, Gillis? We don't have a thing. What about the scroll? That's all they took, wasn't it?"

"It's all what Professor Baxter reported, sir; the place was a shambles. As far as we can tell, just the scroll. Part of the Dead Sea Scrolls. He's a world expert, as you know, sir."

Fitzsimmons bristled red. "What about the scroll? Do we know anything? Christ, how do we know they were Arab?"

"They looked it, sir. Dark skin and black hair, Arabic features, and the knife… "

"You idiot. That could fit any Mediterranean, Spanish, Italian, Egyptian, Algerian. Christ knows."

"Sorry, sir."

"They came to England to steal a scroll, a bloody fucking scroll, and kill over it. An Israeli spy, now a Ph.D. A world expert on the Dead Sea Scrolls. Is she sleeping with him? Goddammit, Gillis, there are more scrolls in England than in the entire Middle East. This might be the beginning of an Arab rampage. That woman must know more, and the professor. Check with the royal society."

"Royal society, sir?"

"Gillis, this is England, we have royal fucking societies for everything. Half of them are Freemasons as well. Find out. And what about the dead men?"

"Nothing, sir. No ID, no prints to match. MI 5 and MI 6 came up with nothing on them."

"Bugger! What about their weapons?"

"An Uzi, short barrel type, a 9mm Glock, the knife, and one had a Mauser in a leg holster."

"Did they just carry them through our bloody customs? Have Captain Biggers put someone on her when she leaves the hospital, and the professor. And Gillis, get back to London. Report directly to me when you arrive. We have another Arab problem." He hung up the phone, walked to the window that overlooked the walled court of the New Scotland Yard. Indians, Pakistanis, Iranians, Africans, and now Arabs. "Christ, I won't be able to recognize a Londoner," he shook his head, talking to himself. Then he went back to his desk and opened a file entitled "Solomon Rashid." Beside the file was a small book entitled *The Last Prophet*.

Recovering from her head injury, Juda had time to think about the theft. She found herself troubled because it seemed to have peeled off a layer in her feelings about Harold Baxter. She now felt he was more than a gentle, eccentric scientist; she felt he was holding something back. Had she been blinded by her interest in his work and in him? Three unidentifiable, heavily armed professionals meant more than a simple theft.

"Tell me about your scroll, Harold," she said from her hospital bed when he returned. "Who would want it and why? I know you didn't tell the police everything." Juda watched his eyes, expressions, body movements, breathing, resenting herself as she did. "You had to know something and you couldn't trust me. Why?"

"They think… Juda, I don't know." He shook his head and appeared despondent. He covered his face to hide tears. "I don't know. They murdered my friend, Jean Legault. I only knew about it that night. I should have warned you."

"I'm so sorry, Harold. You think it was the same people who took your scroll?"

"No, it was different. They were religious fanatics. They… we were like brothers, since boyhood, Legault and I. But… his brother, I mean, they… whoever they were, wanted our scroll." Baxter shook his head, "I don't know, Juda, I don't know."

Juda, taking his hand, said softly, "When did it happen?"

He told her about the letter from Legault's brother and the warning, his voice cracking. He looked older, in pain. "Jerome's letter said that someone wanted the scrolls and that my life and my friends' lives were in danger. He didn't say that Jean was killed over his scroll, but that it was missing. It preyed on my mind." Baxter shielded his eyes with his hands and continued.

"Even after he entered the Dominicans, Jean and I worked together. He was the best there was on Semitic and North Syrian alphabets. Second only to the late Father de Vaux at the museum, and the only one of us to become part of the

International Team with Strugnell, Cross, and, until he too died, John Allegro, and the others. I should have called you. It's my fault, you might have been killed. I didn't want you involved."

"Legault had a brother? Both priests?"

"Dominicans who had worked under Father Roland de Vaux at the Rockefeller – all world experts on the Dead Sea Scrolls.

"The Rockefeller Foundation out of New York funds the Israeli Department of Antiquities," he continued. "It controls, through its resources, all work on the Dead Sea Scrolls done at the Palestine Archeological Museum – which we now call the Rockefeller Museum – at least all officially sanctioned work, and most of the scholars come from the French École Biblique. They're all priests; mostly Dominicans, one a Jesuit, all Catholics except, you know, Allegro who alienated himself over his copper scroll. One is a convert to Catholicism, Professor Strugnell, who is now the director since de Vaux died. Everyone on the team knew there were other scrolls; some yet to be discovered at Qumran, others that were sold in the black market by antiquity dealers like Kondo and his cousin. Some are still with the Bedouin.

"But no one under de Vaux ever saw our scroll, only the Legaults and our friends. Although Father Scantland knows about it."

"Who's he?"

"The Jesuit on the International Team, Jerome's friend. I would have let him in but the others didn't trust him. They were wrong. He's never let out a word all these years."

"Are you sure, Harold?"

Baxter looked away and said, "I guess not."

"What did you do with the scroll? You cut it into pieces…"

"We had it cut into five pieces after we smuggled it out of Jerusalem in 1973. And now Legault's dead."

"Why smuggled?"

"Jewish law, Jordanian law, Vatican law, and above all, Roland de Vaux's law. He controlled everything to do with the Dead Sea Scrolls with the apostolic seal of approval. In 1903 Pope Leo XIII created the Pontifical Biblical Commission which claimed authority over all religious artifacts found in the Middle East, or anywhere for that matter. It, not the Israelis or the foundation, controls the work on the scrolls through the exclusive International Team which, until recently, was under Father Roland de Vaux's control. He answered to Rome alone."

"What about the Bedouins?"

"They found the scrolls in 1946 and began selling them privately before representatives from the papal commission organized the International Team, and they probably still have some, though all scrolls have now been declared property of the state of Israel in direct conflict with Rome."

Juda, who had lived with a Bedouin tribe for a year as part of her training, knew that Bedouins would not show deference to the laws of Jews, Catholics, or any state, especially Israel. They were the law, older than all laws, and if they had scrolls and chose to keep them, they would, regardless of the value, country, or religion.

"What about your scroll?" Juda said. "Who has the other pieces?"

"Jean Legault, Helmut Van Dorn, Harrington Wolfe, and Angel McLaughlin, all professors of archeology and all close friends."

"Angel?" Juda smiled, finding it hard to picture an old archeologist with a name like Angel.

"Really Archibald, but we called him that since we were kids. He's six foot two now."

"Do you have any idea who would steal yours or Legault's piece?"

"I don't know, Juda." He looked down at the floor, shaking his head as his voice faded. "They're not what we thought in the beginning."

"You and Father Legault found the scroll?"

"No, the five of us. In a cave at Qumran. Because it was copper like the first copper scroll, we thought it would help us decipher the first one, which, as you may know, is totally different from all the other scrolls."

"How?"

"It's a thin sheet of copper, which may have come from ancient copper mines in the Sinai, and does not deal with the Essenes, Sadducees, Pharisees, nor the Qumran community at all; it seems to be an inventory of the lost treasure of Solomon. The first copper scroll I mean. That's what impelled John Allegro and caused him to split from the team. There have been a lot of useless diggings for Solomon's treasure all over the Middle East, especially in Jordan, since Allegro translated that scroll. Our scroll may not have been placed in the cave at the same time as the other scrolls and the first copper scroll, and it's not any kind of key to the first, and has nothing to do with the treasure or the ark."

"The Ark of the Covenant?" Juda remembered that after Jerusalem was conquered by the Assyrians under Sennacherib in 760 B.C. and the first temple destroyed by the Babylonians in 586, the Ark disappeared, along with the fabled treasure and the ten lost tribes of Israel, never to be seen again. Some suspected that it was in the Holy of Holies in Herod's second temple or, perhaps, beneath the Temple Mount.

"Our script was different, Juda, and from what progress I've made, written at disparate times. The copper scrolls shared two features only: both are made of copper, and both were found in caves along the Dead Sea."

"What about the work you've done?"

"Nothing. Religious material predating the Essene people, I think. That seems to be in the time from 100 years B.C. to sometime before the Romans sacked Jerusalem and destroyed Jewish resistance in 70 A.D., at Masada. It's impossible. Even if it were all together." He shook his head, as she had seen him do many times, struggling over his scroll. "A prophecy, perhaps something to do with the fall of the Teacher of Righteousness, who may have been Jesus, but there are doubts about that. And other bits I can't connect. It's become an obsession, Juda, one that only might be satisfied when all the pieces are translated. No one has made progress." He muttered on about the unusual script, the ciphers, and the cuneiform marks. Then he left her, promising to be back tomorrow.

Alone in her hospital room, Juda's compassion for Baxter at the loss of his friend, Father Legault, mixed with other feelings less comfortable. Harold Baxter, a man she loved, had lied, and was holding back something. And Baxter, alone in his flat sat at his desk and buried his face in his hands, wondering where the copper scroll would lead them. How many would be hurt. He picked up his telephone and called his friends, warning them. He hadn't acted when he should have on Jerome Legault's warning, but now he would. He couldn't make up for Juda's injuries, but he could see that no one else was harmed.

More than once he had wondered about Juda. Young enough to be a granddaughter, she had brought excitement back into his life and feelings he thought had died years ago in the Egyptian desert, at Nag Hammadi, when his wife was killed – murdered over another scroll. He would end this curse once and for all.

The next day Juda had more questions.

"Juda," Baxter answered, "there were the five of us who knew the scroll existed. All friends, trustworthy, close from high school years, two before that, and all experts in our fields. Then Wolfe got us involved with the American computer millionaire, Bill Hickman, who began to finance our work. We were all financially secure, I think. Old men, none of us interested in the wealth we thought the scroll promised. We wanted to publish. Every team member wanted that, and the competition was fierce. That's why we excluded Scantland. He would have rushed to publication. He's already a world expert with several books published. The only Jesuit on the team, brilliant but radical. He's written some troubling theology that got him close to being excommunicated, like de Chardin and Hans Küng, but a genius in the scrollery in the museum.

"Our group had been excluded from the International Team, except Legault, but we had our scroll and wanted to upstage their precious inner circle with a full translation. It wasn't money, Juda, it was our secret game, our egos and arrogance. Wolfe was already wealthy from an inheritance. Angel McLaughlin was semiretired, and Helmut an old widower like myself. And Legault a priest..."

"How much did Hickman pay you?"

"Fifty thousand dollars each year. He wasn't interested in money. He's one of the richest men in America. We were all on some kind of an ego trip by then, even Hickman and his wife. She wanted to present the lost treasure of Solomon to the world, a treasure that we all thought would make the Tutankhamun treasure pale in comparison. My friends and I wanted to present a full and clear translation of one complete scroll – something all those working under Father Roland hadn't done after forty years of jealous bickering and infighting, while excluding all Jewish and non-Catholic scholars from the International Team." Baxter slumped in the chair beside Juda's hospital bed, looking old and defeated.

"What is it Harold? What are you thinking?"

"Don't you see, Juda?" She waited, listening, watching. "We were all on the same side, no one else knew about our scroll. If one of the others wanted mine, I'd have given it for the asking.

We needed each other and accepted that without argument as friends. Who would steal it? We were all on the same side, no one else knew."

JERUSALEM

Nadir al-Nadir picked up a glittering silver-mounted knife and speared a ripe fig. He carefully sliced it, impaled a piece on the tip of the blade, and walked to his balcony that sparkled from inlaid tiles of gold, green, and blue. Before him was the skyline of Jerusalem marked by the glistening Dome of the Rock. The cool evening breeze picked up the scents of ripe fruits, pistachio nuts, coffee, and rosewater flavored Arabic pastries arranged in front of him on a lacquered table inlaid with exotic woods, ivory, and mother of pearl. Below him, at the entrance to his residence, a locked gate closed off a walled courtyard. Two armed guards, their automatic weapons cocked and ready, waited for any attempts at encroachment. Jerusalem was not a safe place for a Syrian merchant dealing in silks, spices, exotic foods, imports from all parts of the world, and, his most lucrative commodity, contraband weapons. In this city, sacred to Christians, Jews, and Islamics, there always had been intense racial conflict and hatred, good for business, but dangerous. His guards were well trained, and his protection money well placed. Security for Nadir al-Nadir, the gun dealer, came at a small price.

Nadir had lavishly adorned the interior of the house with art objects, oriental furniture and carpets, security devices, and weapons for protection against the violence he nurtured for profit. He had found Jerusalem a better market than Damascus, his home, for transacting his secret sales of weapons. He sold Egyptian made AK 47s, German H&K automatics, American M 16 rifles, the Israeli Uzi, and the popular 44 magnum Desert Eagle to Palestinian groups dedicated to freeing their country of the hated Jews by any means, including the wanton slaughter of Jewish children in the settlements, schools, farms, and on buses. He also sold weapons, without pause, to outlawed bands of Israeli vigilantes who carried out no less fierce atrocities on Palestinian settlements.

A former supplier to the "Fat Man" of Damascus and the retired master terrorist "Carlos," Nadir al-Nadir had expanded his market to Jerusalem after the loss of Raol Shamir, the Syrian Druze, the half brother of Juda Bonaparte. With connections to arms manufacturers and dealers in Russia, the United States, Germany, Czechoslovakia, and even Israel, Nadir found Jerusalem, more than Damascus, hungry for his goods.

He waited impatiently for the return of his sons from England, and the copper scroll they had taken from Professor Baxter's. His heart lightened when a dark Mercedes sedan pulled up to the gate. Passing security, the car stopped in the courtyard and discharged its single passenger, Nadir's youngest son. Nadir rushed to meet his son at the door, dreading what he already knew.

"*Biyak*, father, Kahlil is dead, and the Bear." The young man, tall and dark, embraced his father, patting his shoulders, tears in his eyes. "Keeftan killed Micha, whose arm was broken. The bone was sticking through the flesh." His voice was hesitant, breathless. "While Kahlil, Micha, and the Bear went in after Baxter's scroll as you ordered, I had to wait in the car with Abu Keeftan. We saw a woman run into the building. In a few minutes, I heard the shots, then a whole clip from the Uzi. Micha came running out, sobbing that his arm was broken and the woman had killed them, killed Kahlil and the Bear and broke Micha's arm. When Keeftan heard there was no scroll he shot Micha, just like that, twice in the heart."

"A woman killed my son?" A look of utter despair and desolation contorted his face. "A woman?" He fell back on an overstuffed chair, tears in his eyes. Nadir, who believed that his one devotion in life was his children, looked at his son, his youngest. "Leave me and wait. I will call for you." He fanned the air with his hand, waving his son out of the room. "After I weep, I must hear of this woman who could kill the Bear and my son."

Finished with his solitary mourning, Nadir called for his son. "There was no scroll, *biyak*, but these clippings from several papers say that a scroll was taken from Baxter's laboratory. Micha had nothing, not even his gun." Nadir scanned the papers, then howled with rage.

"Juda Bonaparte. Dr. Juda Bonaparte, with Baxter? By Allah, how could this happen? She killed my son. *Sharmuta*, whore!" His head rolled in anguish and he sighed heavily. "Oh, Kahlil, Kahlil, you let a woman kill you, a *sharmuta*, a *shaitan*, whore, devil, kill you."

"It is natural, *biyak*, I had many hours to think," the younger man said. "I have reasoned that Juda would choose to study under Baxter. He is a world authority on the Middle East. When she left her work for Israel, if that is true, she went to England to resume her schooling after she and her Jew-bastard father killed Shamir, our best customer. For three years silence, not a word of Juda Bonaparte. Now she emerges from the darkness like a *shaitan*, a devil. I do not know how she is involved with Baxter and the scroll or if she is still working for Israel, but I think so." Nadir's face twisted into a dark hateful scowl as his son completed his analysis.

"Mossad must know about the scroll. The Jews have always claimed the scrolls were theirs. Juda is still their agent. They have it and have tricked us. Juda, Baxter, Mossad. Allah, I am cursed." Nadir speared a ripe fig and carefully fitted the whole fruit into his mouth, past his thick mustache and thin cruel lips. "And Legault is murdered. Crucified with ropes."

"Crucified? What of his scroll, *biyak*? Do we have it? Who did this?"

"Islamic fanatics. Who knows? There are many wild seeds in this land. This is the birthplace of religion, and there are many sects: Christian, Jew, and Islamic. But I think Islamic fundamentalists would do that to mock the Christians. No, we do not have his scroll or any scroll, and we are poorer by a half million dollars and one son."

"You would still pay Keeftan after he failed?"

"We agreed." Nadir stood up. He was thick, short, and muscular, fat around the waist. His hooded lids seemed to lower even more over his expressionless eyes as he adjusted his fez and gazed out over Jerusalem, his ring-bedecked hand grasping the steel rail of the balcony, knuckles stretched white through the folds of dark, hairy skin. "Juda Bonaparte," he said through clenched teeth. "Kalid, we are betrayed. For five years I have played the scroll game, listening to those fools bicker, waiting for them to finish. Now, my impatience has cost me a son and a woman has made me the fool." He clenched his fist, tapping his large nose with his thumb. "We must have Baxter's scroll. His holds the key. The others have said that too often. Unlimited power, my son, beyond your wildest dreams, power that comes only from wealth, will be ours – yours, your children's children, your brother's children, when we have all the scrolls. But now, more than anything else, I must have Juda Bonaparte's throat in my hands as I slowly squeeze the life from her. This is blood, my son."

"What would you have me do, *biyak*?"

"First, we must have the scroll of the priest, Legault. Then the others. It began here in Palestine, and it will end here. We will use Rama Keeftan and his men again. Next to that bitch Juda Bonaparte and her Bedouin friends, no one knows more of the Middle East. Get him. Go to Baghdad. Pay him for his failure and offer him more dollars."

"Keeftan? He is an animal. He did not have to shoot Micha."

"We failed, Micha failed," Nadir shrugged. "This has now become a killing business, thanks to Juda Bonaparte. Keeftan is the best. It isn't the only time in history that the Dead Sea Scrolls are stained with blood. Now, I swear by the blood of my son, it will not be the last. If your path and Juda Bonaparte's cross, cut her throat. Do not fail, Kalid." The man who believed he loved his children, this son, more than life itself added, oblivious to the incongruity of his beliefs, "… or I will kill you." Then, embracing his son, he said, "Before you leave, tell the woman Annamar to go to my room. The food tonight was fit for dogs. I need other comforts, I am sickened with grief."

Alone, angry, and in utter despair, his stomach burning with its old pain, Nadir picked up a telephone and dialed a number in New York City. A woman with a musical voice answered "the Rockefeller Foundation" and connected Nadir to an electronic menu which, after he pressed the appropriate numbers, got him to the director of archeological fundings, Harrington Wolfe, Baxter's friend and confidant in their copper scroll conspiracy.

Nadir announced that he would be attending the conference at Lake Como in northern Italy, and answered that he was aware that Baxter's scroll had been stolen. "You and the others must complete your work before all is lost to our senility." After he hung up, he balled his stubby hand into a fist. "By Allah, I will find the scroll."

MADRID

Brother René Gervais, Knight Templar, boarded a DC 10 that would take him to London. Traveling First Class, he wore a conservative blue business suit of relaxed fit. His long, black hair had been trimmed and styled into a fashionable cut – part of his new image. Charming the stewardess with a smile, he ordered a Pernod and water, remembering the file he had studied on the copper scroll, the archeologists, and Juda Bonaparte – a most detailed file complete with photographs, biography, and her likes. Later he ordered a filet done rare, the first of his lifetime, and another drink, this time a single malt scotch. He toyed with the steak, cutting into it, watching the red juices spread on his plate and felt a wave of nausea. Afterward, he lit a cigarette, a Gauloise, and inhaled for the first time. He smiled at the pleasant burning in his throat, then wretched with bile. His head swam. He sipped water. Later he put on headphones and relaxed to the good life.

After leaving the monastery at La Salette, he had spent a week of study, exercise, and training in the use of drugs and weapons at the secret headquarters of the organization known as Euzkadi Ta Azkatasuna (ETA) hidden in the Pyrenees mountains – Basque country – in northwest Spain. The ETA, made up of Basque terrorists seeking autonomy from Spain, had welcomed ties to other terrorist groups, including the many in Israel, Jordan, and Iraq, as well as the IRA, the Italian Red Brigade, and the remnants of the Baader-Meinhof group. In their hidden camp, they provided training in assassinations, murder, weaponry, bomb making, and intimidation. René Gervais had no taste for causes, and he found the Basques strange with their ancient language and customs that seemed more Middle Eastern than Spanish or French. As ordered by the Knights Templar he completed the intensive courses, then drove to Madrid where he purchased a new wardrobe before boarding this flight to England and his first assignment in Birmingham to find Baxter and get his scroll.

But the blue-eyed monk, smoking another cigarette and sipping on his third drink as his plane droned to England, was slowly developing his own ideas about the scroll, and especially Juda Bonaparte. Above all, he thought the wheezing, shriveled old priest at La Salette a fool and liar.

Chapter 5

JUDA was feeling surprisingly good in the warm afternoon sun, in spite of her recent ordeal. Out of the hospital and aware that she was being followed by a not-so-unobtrusive policeman, she shopped for the meal she would prepare on Sunday for Harold Baxter when he would tell her the rest of his story about the scrolls and finish the one he had started about Nag Hammadi where he had lost his wife. Eyeing the detective, who was about to lose her in the crowded store, Juda walked up beside him, her purchases in her arms, her eyes sparkling, and whispered, "The game's afoot." Then she left the store and hailed a box-like black Austin taxicab.

Of course, the police knew about her from their computer files in SID, and they would also know that for three years she had lived peacefully in England, unattached to any secret service. Her father had seen to that, it had been his parting gift: a clean slate. The theft of Baxter's precious and mysterious scroll, and the death of three men, had prompted the police tail, which kept a discrete distance behind her. But the police didn't know Harold had kept something back. He hadn't told them the scroll was copper. Why not? The death of Baxter's friend must be connected with the theft. If there was no lost treasure of Solomon, and the theft was by professionals, then why? Her headache came back like a gunshot. She was in no mood for analytical thinking. I'm getting soft, she thought, as memories of her work for the Israeli secret service painfully came back, as did her analysis with Dr. LaCroix – interrupted by his cruel death.

In spite of the jackhammer working inside her head, she wondered about Baxter. *Would he tell me everything, or just what he wanted me to know? Trust him, you're not involved.* (She scanned for the right word – love, friendship, respect. "Oedipal," Dr. LaCroix would have added, to define her relationship with Harold Baxter.) Only he and his friends knew about their scroll. *Even if Harold didn't know everything consciously, there were ways with drugs.* Before she went to bed she looked through her drapes to see the black Hillman parked in the shadows up the street and smiled at the thoroughness of British police work.

Three days later, her simple dinner ready for final assemblage, which she planned to do with a flair deserving of her skill in the kitchen and marketplace when Baxter arrived, Juda relaxed with a tall drink. She had slipped a cassette into her tape deck, dimmed the room lights, and kicked off her shoes to listen to the sensuous music and the rich tenor of Michael Crawford, and to recall London and *The Phantom*. She remembered the drinks and dancing, and the Peter Barnes lecture, and the dashing surgeon, George Gamash, who seemed as out of place at the lecture on AIDS as she was. There was something familiar about Gamash, but she still couldn't place him. Her eyelids dropped, she became sleepy. Warmed by the fire and the golden liquid she twirled in her glass, she stirred with different memories.

Her life had changed so much since leaving Mossad, she mused in her near-dream state. She felt herself drifting, yielding to her body, remembering another Michael, running her fingers over her lips, remembering Venice. The scroll, the copper scroll. *Focus! What questions will I put to Harold tonight?*

Why? What am I afraid of? The music moved her and she could feel her skin, sensitive, turgid, touching the silk of her blouse. *What had Harold found in his scroll, after all those years?* Unruly blood rushed to her skin and parts forbidden by priests and childhood sisters – memories. Distracting. *Why now, why ever?* She remembered her husband; he and she had been babies playing at love. She felt his sweating body convulsing onto hers, his orgasm sweeping over him as he fought it, struggling to be her lover, failing, crying in her hair. How she had tried to reassure him it wasn't his fault, and how, in the springtime of her desires, she had secretly accepted his beliefs and fought the idea that it was. Warned by a tightness in her chest she turned back to Baxter. *What was he hiding?* Let it go, she thought, unable to focus. Intrusive thoughts, memories, and feelings swept into her consciousness.

Dedicated, persistent, gentle. They were like that, the men she loved. She remembered her young husband, a fledgling biologist, his smooth, pink body covered with blood. What could a sixteen-year-old girl know about lovemaking? *The nightmares, why didn't I listen to them?* The animals had come after her husband's death, not just in her dreams. Real men smelling of sweat and tobacco, and alcohol; unwashed tattooed men who hated her less than she hated them. Vomiting blood and bile. Drugs, nose bleeding – gagging on stomach acids. Then came those who died from her bullets or her knife, the men in her crosshairs, clean smelling psychopaths, easy to kill in the name of the Father or fatherland, and sweet relief. Juda could not escape the smile that forced itself on her, as arousal once more froze in bas-relief in her psyche, leaving a hideous caricature – a killer. Then there were the doctors. Her doctors. Men she loved. She wiped her face, bit her lips which had changed from moist to parched, and drove her fingers through her hair. Sweat stained her blouse. "Oh Christ," she cried.

Juda got up, turned off the music and inhaled deeply on a cigarette, then dropped it into her drink. Angry feelings coursed through her. Muscles throbbed, mean steel bundles. She looked at her watch, two hours until Harold would save her from herself, her dreams.

They were alike, the doctors, her husband. Baxter blamed himself for his wife's death. Michael tormented himself over his guilt and wanted vengeance. Baxter had given his life to scientific curiosity, research, and a search for meaning or vengeance in the Dead Sea Scrolls. He was afraid, young and inexperienced, but had gone blindly into the Hamaras at Nag Hammadi, where they killed his wife. *I would have been afraid too, but for things my father taught me in Israel and Bekaa, and what Hashim did in the desert.* Restlessly, Juda walked into her kitchen and opened her refrigerator. Full of waiting food, it offered nothing and rattled defiance when she slammed the door. *I would have taken the gun and the knife and killed the Hamaras, and I would have killed more with my hands and feet – and teeth. I would have killed them with my body, my sex, like my dad. Dad? You were afraid and unskilled, Harold, as you charged with those boys, and you scared them away. Yet you suffered guilt for the death of your wife? You've lived your life angry at God for what men did.* Angry tensions screamed in her pelvis, her powerful thighs. She poured another drink, as if to quench the fires inside her. Then it all stopped, and like a child, she curled up on the couch and fell asleep.

She dreamed she was with Sheik Ali Hashim in the Negev, where she had spent a year after her training in Israel and where she had learned about the desert and the Bedouin and, surprisingly, how to enjoy being a woman. She awoke in the dark, recalling with a laugh the words of the sheik from her dream: "So many daughters, Juda, Allah has cursed me for my sins." As her head cleared, she relished the dream and the memories of the sheik, the idea of children that came from ghosts. But then her heart started its warning tempo inside her chest as she realized it was still Sunday, quite late, and Harold Baxter, always early, had not shown up.

As Juda dreamed about Sheik Ali Hashim, Harold Baxter sat quietly at his desk writing her a letter, the warning letter of Father Jerome Legault beside him. "Baxter, you and your friends' lives are in danger; Jean's scroll is missing. I think someone wants your scrolls." Prophetically correct, the underlined words haunted him. He had warned the others, his friends, but he still had to find out if Jean's death was related to their work, and he had to find Jean's scroll. For now, more than ever, he was convinced that the scroll spawned evil and must be destroyed or sealed in St. Peter's tomb. Two hours after the courier had picked up his letter and a carefully wrapped package, he heard another knock on the door.

It was a voice he didn't recognize. "Dr. Baxter, I'm Father René Gervais. I must talk to you about your scroll." Hesitatingly, Baxter opened the door and saw a young man dressed in a black suit, wearing a Roman collar; he was soft-spoken, with trusting blue eyes.

"What business could you have with me, Father. My scroll is gone, thieves. You must know. Every paper in England carried the story." Baxter held fast to his doorway.

"I'm from the Pontifical Biblical Commission, Dr. Baxter. We're charged to investigate all scrolls removed from Jerusalem and the Dead Sea, including your copper scroll," the young man said in English, his French accent evident.

Baxter bristled. "How do you know it was copp..." Suspicions aroused, his voice rose. "I have nothing to say, and no time. I am leaving for a..." Frightened and angry at the dark automatic weapon Gervais raised from the shadows and pointed at his chest, Baxter backed into his room.

"I still have questions, Dr. Baxter," Gervais said with his new smile.

Though it was late, Juda called Baxter's apartment and then the lab. Impatiently she listened to the ceaseless ringing, realizing how little she knew about him. She recalled his friends. The only one even close was Peter Barnes in London, and George Gamash, but Baxter hadn't mentioned either since their trip. She went to his flat. The only answer to her knocking was her heart's warning beat. Juda let herself in with a steel pick she took from her purse. Alerted by the darkness, she waited and listened. Hearing faint breathing sounds, remembering the lab, she entered cautiously and snapped on the light. Harold was slumped on his easy chair, half on the floor, unconscious. His mouth sagged open, his respirations were shallow.

Juda quickly checked for wounds and injuries, felt the pulses at the carotid arteries, examined his pupils, swept her finger in his throat. A stroke she thought, as she dialed for an ambulance then carefully eased him to the floor. His breathing stopped. Tears in her eyes, her own heart pounding, she held her ear against his chest, listening to his heart; she heard soft sounds like a humming bird, then silence. She pressed her mouth to his, whispering, "please Christ," as she held his nose and breathed into him. Then she ripped open his shirt and crossed her hands over his sternum, depressing it against crackling sounds of cartilages and joints stiff and old yielding to her strength. Without losing her rhythmic efforts at lungs and heart, she shouted, "Breathe, Harold," ordering him to live, feeling him dying beneath her lips. Balling her fist she hit him on the sternum as she heard the ambulance siren on the street and her heart echoing its cry.

At the hospital, an emergency room registrar, who looked too young, approached Juda after a resuscitative team had taken over. "It could be a stroke, or a hemorrhage, Dr. Bonaparte. We have him on a respirator. There are unusual features. Fixed pupils and no reflexes. No Babinski, that's a, uh, reflex. He's in a deep coma, fully unresponsive to stimuli. He'll need a complete work up. Any empty bottles around when you found him? Pill bottles, I mean. I've seen patients like this from an overdose. Has he been depressed?"

"No, I saw nothing. Did you smell his breath? Some kind of floral odor. I didn't recognize it. Please do a toxicology screen. I think he's been poisoned." Juda had followed the ambulance to the hospital, but first she had thoroughly examined Harold's room, noting the packed luggage on the floor, the absence of signs of a struggle. His desk had not been touched, it was still its usual mess. She had gathered up some badly labeled disks from beside his computer and dropped them into her purse.

Baxter was still unconscious three days later when Juda met with Dr. Hastings, chief of neurology, and the senior registrar. "We've detected no organic lesions, Dr. Bonaparte. His electroencephalogram does not support a concussion or coma. There's normal sleep architecture, including alpha rhythm and REM sleep. An NMR tomogram of his brain was entirely normal."

"His heart had stopped," Juda said weakly.

"I know, Dr. Bonaparte. If you hadn't… Well, he had a normal electrocardiogram. You got there just in time. Blood chemistry and gases were normal with one exception. On urine chromatography, we've found an abnormal spot that could be a toxin of an unrecognizable sort. Clinically, he is sleeping, even dreaming, and cannot wake up or be awakened. This means damage or toxicity in the brain stem, the reticular activating system." The registrar seemed nervous as he spoke. "We think it's poison as you thought, an unidentified one so far, and we have reported it to the police as such."

Containing her anguish and rage that violence had once more scratched the thin varnish of her staid life, hurting someone she loved, Juda asked what was to be done now. "Wait, Dr.

Bonaparte, keep him alive," Dr. Hastings, who had silently listened to the report by the registrar, said. "We are maintaining nutrition by tube feeding and we're doing further tests. There's no immediate threat to Dr. Baxter's life. The body is a wonderful healing instrument, Dr. Bonaparte. It may do what we cannot and detoxify the poison."

"What about dialysis?" Juda asked.

"You are well informed, Dr. Bonaparte, though your degree is not in medicine. And yes, we will dialyze if there is no improvement in two more days. But I must tell you, don't hold out much hope for that procedure. The substance appears to be confined to the central nervous system." They walked into the corridor together. "We'll do everything in our power to help your friend, Dr. Bonaparte."

"Not just your power, please Doctor. Call in any consultant, the best, here or anywhere in the world. Money is not in question. I'm very wealthy," Juda emphasized, knowing that physicians were moved by Juno as well as Asclepius. Back in the waiting room she lit a cigarette and over the flame of her lighter said to the single occupant, "Hello, Inspector Gillis, I thought you would be here."

"Violence seems to follow you, Dr. Bonaparte."

"*C'est-la vie*, I'm afraid, but true no less. How can I help you?" Her voice was soft and sounded sad. She offered him a cigarette and a forced smile.

"What happened?" he asked. "Do you mind talking?"

"I don't know." She made no attempt to hide her tears.

The next morning she received a letter from Harold.

I lied about the scroll, Juda. I thought I would be safer if they believed it was taken. I blame myself for what happened to you. When you read this I'll be in Jerusalem. I must find out about Jean. I have sent my scroll to your Paris address. Please have it put in a bank vault and tell no one you have it. I have warned the others of the danger. If anything happens to me, give the scroll to Father

Emile Peush. My friend, Professor Van Dorn, will give you his portion.

I'm convinced that our scroll portions need to be sealed and stored in St. Peter's Vault and never be translated.

Juda, thank you for your friendship.

Juda reread the letter and its closing, *Love, Harold,* several times, tears in her eyes.

TEL-AVIV

Benjamin Kerns had led Israel through four wars after carving the state of Israel out of Arab territories in 1948. Before becoming director of Mossad, he had been the highest ranking military officer in the country. A man of great strength and intense passions, he personally joined his men in commando raids against terrorist groups hidden in the Bekaa Valley, Golan Heights, or, his last, deep into Syria, where, with his daughter, Juda Bonaparte, he had destroyed the desert stronghold of the assassin Raol Shamir, killing Shamir and all his men.

It was this unauthorized attack into Syria, when overtures of peace with Assad were being made and Arafat was indicating a possible rapprochement with Israel, that right wing members of the Knesset used to force Kerns' retirement, which Kerns thought he would welcome, for the blood on his hands from the raid in Syria was his son's, Raol Shamir's, and now, like his daughter, death sickened him.

Provided with a secure home in southern Tel-Aviv, guards, a housekeeper, and an adequate pension, and ordered by his friend Shimon Peres to write his memoirs, Kerns was a virtual prisoner in the country he had helped found. He knew what Peres had in mind with the goddamned biography he demanded as he pecked and hunted in front of the computer so generously provided by the state; keep the old man busy and out of trouble. The last time he had turned on his computer he had become enraged at the smiling little face on the screen and had shouted "fuck you" with a smack that sent the fiendish monster to a repair shop.

Then they had given him help, a secretary who soon left after claiming he had made indecent advances. Kerns roared with laughter at the hearing, saying he did nothing except out of the boredom the state had imposed on him, and that he didn't want a secretary anyway, particularly that old witch. If he wanted a woman he'd pick one thirty years younger. He'd write what needed to be said himself. A year later, staring at the screen on which he had typed two words, "Chapter One," and had deleted many, he thought of Juda's mother.

Looking out into his walled courtyard and through the iron gate he could see the blue Mediterranean where, in the mornings, he would roll up his pants and walk barefoot in the sand and water. He enjoyed the feel of the wet sand between his toes and the cool water on his painful feet: feet that had walked thousands of blistering miles, through five wars, for a thankless Israeli state. Two Mossad agents, their long coats hiding automatic weapons strapped over their shoulders, would keep pace behind him. At the beach, with the four-thousand-year-old Egyptian pier in the background, stretching and curling his toes in the water, he would think of the countess and her love for the sea, and Juda. Where was Juda? A daughter he had barely gotten to know: powerful and deadly, beautiful and lonely, he thought, like he was. For this honorable solitude, he had given up a daughter and a wife, killed a son. For Israel, this dried up piece of camel dung surrounded by a people who would bury us in the sand, and rightly so, they believed. He watched a Lancia sedan pull into his driveway, raising one of the security guards who was half asleep at the gate.

Kerns recognized Samuel Scharkes, head of the Mossad, in the back seat: the man who had replaced him; a man he didn't like. What did Scharkes want of him? that Jewish-American prick. Anything would be better than this, he thought, as he went to the door; maybe a war.

Unshaven, dressed in wrinkled military fatigues, his opened sweat-stained shirt revealing curly gray chest hairs, Kerns dwarfed the meticulously dressed, compact Scharkes as he extended his giant's paw and encompassed the director's hand in his. He forced a smile and welcomed Scharkes into his study.

"What does my Ivy League successor want with this old retired general?" Kerns asked, as he offered Scharkes dark Turkish coffee. Scharkes declined with a hand gesture as he removed a brown file from a thin leather briefcase. Scharkes, lean, smooth shaven, fortyish, with brown kinky hair streaked with gray, threw the folder on the coffee table in front of Kerns. He lowered his dark eyes and said:

"There's trouble, I need you."

"We've had nothing but trouble ever since we took this god-forsaken desert from the Arabs. Now there's this *intifada*. Trouble goes with your job, Samuel; they want our asses out of here; it'll never change." He opened the folder and whistled through his teeth, "Jesus Christ," as he examined the color photograph of a crucified naked man. Kern's tanned, furrowed brow collapsed into a frown. White wrinkles spread out like spider webs from the corners of his eyes against his leathery tanned complexion as he turned the glossy picture over in his hands, looking at the processing marks on the back. "Where did you get this picture, Scharkes? It's recent." He seemed puzzled. He had seen a similar picture thirty-two years earlier in Jerusalem during the 1956 war when he first took the ancient city.

Responding to an urgent radio message, Kerns, then commander of the occupation force, had driven his Jeep into the Kotel plaza square as the early morning sun glistened on the Dome of the Rock and cast long shadows that textured the ancient stone of the Western Wall. Here a few Hasidic Jews in their dark suits and hats, braving the war, had come to pray to God, tucking their petitions into the cracks of the venerated wall. That morning they had backed away in fear, murmuring to themselves, when, in the shadow and light, they saw a man, his arms outstretched as if crucified, hanging from the wall, their most sacred wall. His head hung lifeless on his chest; he was naked. Closer inspection showed that coarse ropes, not nails, ran through bloody holes in his wrists to the top of the wall, where they were secured by large iron nails driven tightly into the old mortar. Blood caked around a wound in his right side.

Israeli soldiers, who had occupied the ancient city, cut the body down and Kerns identified him as Rabbi Svika Herzl, whose father Theodor had been the founder of Zionism. Above the head of the victim a scroll had been suspended by string between the ropes. Written in Aramaic was one word, the name *Abraham*. The war overshadowed the crime which remained unsolved but was, nevertheless, attributed to Palestinians; now this color photograph, the same scene thirty years later.

"The picture was taken yesterday, Kerns, tomorrow you'll see it in every newspaper in the Middle East. That's Father Jean Legault strung out like Jesus Christ, naked and crucified."

"Not 'Jesus,' Scharkes, 'Herzl.' Who's Legault?" Kerns rubbed his chin as he studied the photograph, grimacing, shaking his head slightly, drawing his mouth up on the left.

"A priest. French. He was to replace Father Roland de Vaux as director of the International Team at the Palestine Archeological Museum, but Professor Strugnell was chosen instead. Between de Vaux, Legault, and Strugnell, they controlled the release of all the materials on the Dead Sea Scrolls, a near Catholic monopoly, probably directed from Rome."

Another Israeli mistake, Kerns thought. That's all we've done with the scrolls. But he said, "Not Rome, Scharkes, the Vatican, sticking its finger where it don't belong. Hell, we're not even a state according to them, they're worse than the PLO. The scrolls are Jewish – Hebrew documents, found in the state of Israel. We should have taken them in '57, goddammit."

In 1957 Kerns and Ariel Sharon had devised a plan to capture the scrolls. After all, they were documents of the early Hebrew Church, they thought. Jerusalem, a city four thousand years old, built and rebuilt many times, had been taken by David about 1000 B.C., but it was Solomon who had built the Great Temple and established Jerusalem as a city of wealth and beauty – until the Babylonians destroyed it.

Jerusalem, one of the world's oldest cities and once the most strongly fortified, was originally occupied by the Egyptians, and later by the Phoenicians. Built on rocky hills, it was laced by a natural karst system of sinks, caverns, and tunnels, carved by groundwater leaching through the limestone and dolomite rock. In this underworld of caves there were remains of structures more than five thousand years old.

The tunnels had almost killed Kerns when he and Ariel Sharon had tried a raid on the Rockefeller Institute to capture the scrolls. Water, rats, and sewage dripping from the city above them, and most of all, an indescribable fear, forced them to turn back, Sharon cursing all the way. Secretly Kerns, who David Ben-Gurion was to say had balls bigger than his brain, tried again alone.

Crawling on his belly in a tunnel that David might have used when he took the city nearly three thousand years earlier, carrying a pack of oiled cloths to protect the scrolls when he got them, cursing God, the Jews, the Christians, Rockefeller, and above all himself for wanting to show up Sharon, dirty, drenched, and angry beyond words, he was stopped cold in the maze of tunnels he had followed by iron bars he could not budge. He pressed his face into the bars, as his flashlight found a black void beyond, a room or cavern as black as hell. Then there was a thundering sound rushing behind him, the *wadi* roaring like a train, water crushing him into the bars, taking his flashlight and pack into the space, stealing his already fetid, sparse air. Barely alive, he crawled back promising God he'd leave the scrolls to the Dominicans and the tunnels of Jerusalem to the water rats.

Kerns looked at Scharkes with his fine mohair suit and saw him in the sewers. "What's written on the scroll over his head? The first had one word, 'Abraham.'"

"Here, look." Scharkes handed Kerns more photographs, enlarged to show details. The scroll over the priest's head, again written in Aramaic, translated read "Abraham," and beneath it, "Jesus." Another photograph showed the detail of the wounds through the wrists and the single triangular wound into the liver. Like in the first murder over thirty years earlier, the letter Z was deeply burned into the forehead.

"Fuckin' 'Zoro' again. Like the first," Kerns said, excited now, feeling his pockets for cigarettes. "Goddamn," he muttered, remembering he had quit smoking as ordered by his doctor. That went along with the glass eye and the surgery to insert it.

"The Church of the Holy Sepulcher," Scharkes said, "that's where he was pastor or deacon, or something, not just the Rockefeller."

"What do you make of it? Thirty years doesn't exactly fit for a serial killer, or a copycat. Someone's trying to tell us something. The Z, what do your CIA friends make of it?"

"A cult, they think."

"No shit! Is that all your combined brains could come up with? A cult?" He wanted to say something to satisfy this little fart. "Abraham," "Jesus," "Z," crucifixion with ropes? "I'll tell you one thing, Scharkes, get that picture suppressed. No newspapers. Whoever did this wants everyone to know. What do you want me to do? I'm retired."

Scharkes stood up. "I want you back, you know more about the crazies in Palestine than anyone."

"I'll do it, because I know it's not over, Samuel." He didn't understand why he said it, but, above all, he knew it was the truth. The scrolls, the accursed scrolls overshadowed his thoughts and those goddamned tunnels. He thought of Juda. "I'll need help, Scharkes."

BAGHDAD

Five hundred miles east of Jerusalem in a terrorist training camp north of Baghdad, Abu Keeftan, back from London and still seething with anger over his failure, ranted about his new enemy, Juda Bonaparte. A tall man with closely cropped black hair and a full mustache, Keeftan had carried out raids against Israeli settlements south of the Golan heights and had fought against Israeli commandos of which Juda Bonaparte had once been a part. Driven out of Lebanon and given silent shelter near Baghdad by Saddam Hussein, who supported other Palestinian factions in Iraq, Abu Keeftan had continued his friendship with Dr. George Gamash, his cousin, and with Baghdad bomb maker Ibrahim Mohammed. Using Mohammed's undetectable plastique explosives sewn into the seams and linings of garment bags and triggered by barometric switches, Keeftan, Gamash, and Sabri Youssef, coerced by the Iraqis, had carried out Mohammed's personal vendetta against Pan American Airlines, each time effectively shifting responsibility for the bombings to other terrorist groups. Their last would be the carefully planned destruction of Pan Am 103 over Lockerbie, Scotland, eventually bringing the airline giant to its knees and bankruptcy and uniting the free world against terrorism, particularly Moammar Kudafi. This unity would lead to what Keeftan had fought against for most of his life, a rapprochement between the Arabs and Jews, led by turncoat and once friend, Yassser Arafat.

"You are restless, Abu Keeftan. Your rage will kill you. Come and eat," the dark haired woman dressed in dusty military fatigues said.

"You know what happened in England," Keeftan scowled, "and you offer me food, while that bitch Juda Bonaparte lives and laughs at me."

The woman withdrew a large knife from a sheath fastened to an American-made webbing belt and sliced pita bread into small wedges; she dipped one piece into a bowl of *hummus* and offered it to him. "If we had her, I would serve her to you in little pieces, like this pita. Maybe then you would sleep at night, and make love again."

"Did you make this?" he derided her, reaching for another piece. "It is for goats."

"It's from Baghdad. Who could make anything in this place from hell? I may go back to Bonn, or Paris."

"And marry some fat industrialist like your sister?"

"You will come with me. I think you're sick of this business of killing Jews. They'll never go away. It would take another annihilation – a Diaspora – not the thousand men you and the others train here."

"No, Gamash and I will do it with airplanes lighting the skies, and I will find a way to use these crucifixions in Jerusalem and…"

"You've settled with Sabri? It will be Lockerbie? What about Tel Aviv? You and Gamash have formed a dangerous liaison with Ahmed; one that will bring down Pan Am, not Israel. Sabri Youssef is old for this work, and Ahmed is crazy."

"Sabri is my most trusted man. Saddam Hussein with his Scuds and gas may bring our cause to Israel if we fail. With the scroll we will have something greater than guns and bombs to use against the Jews. I will have Solomon's gold and the Ark of the Covenant, if Nadir is right."

Looking out the window at a dust trail left by a black Mercedes as it followed the narrow road through the valley below of orchards, olive groves, and pistachio bushes, he said, "There's Nadir's son."

"How do you know?" The woman approached him, putting her arms around his neck.

"He's alive. My guards would not have passed him through."

"What does Nadir want of you now, my love?" Shapely and young, she pressed her body close to him, kissing him on the ear and neck.

"What do you want?" He smiled and crushed her against him as she slid her hand between them, feeling him respond. Then she broke away and pulled her knife.

"I want you in there, now." She flipped the knife in the air, caught the sharp blade in the flat of her hand and, flashing a smile through clenched teeth, in one continuous movement sent the weapon spinning through the air. It made a perfect one hundred and eighty degree turn and embedded itself deep in the center of a door across the room. She pranced to the door and withdrew her weapon. Turning to Keeftan, eyes drooping, mouth sensuously wet, she slowly stripped off her clothing, leaving only the webbing belt with gun and knife around her waist, and small bikini panties. "Do not be long with the son of Nadir al-Nadir, Rama. I am bored of this place." The telephone interrupted Keeftan, two long and two short rings.

"It's Gamash, wait in the room until I call for you, Shalima."

"*Keefect uhmo*," Abu Keeftan exclaimed, as Gamash reported that Baxter had lied to the police about the scroll being stolen.

"An insurance fraud, my friend, is that what the good professor is doing? There was no scroll? Baxter's the thief."

"He's in the hospital, poisoned. I have good reason to believe he gave the scroll to Juda Bonaparte first."

"Poisoned? Juda Bonaparte?" Keeftan's face contorted in rage.

"In a coma."

"Another trick? Mossad?"

"No trick, Rama. Doctors will speak with each other. Baxter will not survive." Keeftan paused, watching the black Mercedes drive into his compound.

"Nadir," he said, narrowing his eyes as Kalid Nadir emerged from the car. "We have cast our lots with thieves, liars, and scoundrels, Gideus. My people will take Juda Bonaparte within twenty four hours. We must get the scroll before she delivers it to the Israelis, and you, my cousin, must change your plans about making love to this Frenchwoman, unless you prefer a corpse over your English women. Not much difference I am told." Still laughing, Keeftan hung up and opened the door to Kalid Nadir and his two guards, surrounded by Sabri Youssef and a squad of Keeftan's men led by Tunnous Manni. "Come in, son of Nadir al-Nadir. You have my money?"

Abu Keeftan opened the briefcase presented to him by Kalid Nadir. Tunnous Manni, Keeftan's lieutenant, remained at the door, his hand on his weapon. Keeftan quickly counted the stacks of American dollars then became enraged, his eyes narrowing on the young man. "This is half what your father and I agreed on, Kalid. Where is the rest?" He stepped back from the table. Nadir's two guards, dressed in tan cotton fatigues, their heads covered by short *kaffiyehs*, cocked their automatic weapons, Russian AK 47s, aiming them at Abu Keeftan. "One shot and Tunnous will have a hundred men who would cut you down in a moment."

"And you would be dead," young Nadir said.

"Lower your weapons. We will talk." He signaled Tunnous to replace the automatic now in his hand.

Kalid remained standing, his men at alert. "You failed in England and have not delivered the scroll. My brother is dead, killed by the woman. You killed Micha, my friend."

"Kalid, Micha was badly injured." Keeftan's voice softened. "Would you prefer a hospital and a British prison?" Keeftan shrugged. "He is comfortable now, with Allah."

"When you have all the scrolls, we will pay the two million, as agreed."

"My men are on their way to find this Bonaparte woman. If she has the scroll, they will get it, and trust me Kalid, she will die."

"We live in shame over our failure, Rama Abu Keeftan. My father will double what you have there when you bring him proof that Juda Bonaparte is dead. Bring her to us alive and he will double it again. Debts will be paid, but with the woman it is a matter of honor and blood."

"Agreed," shouted Keeftan, slamming both his hands on the table. "My woman will bear witness," he said loudly. The bedroom door opened. The guards died instantly from the forty-five caliber bullets that blew them across the room, their heads shattered, blood spattering the walls. Keeftan smiled and raised his hand as Shalima pressed her gun barrel against Kalid Nadir's forehead. "You have not lost your skills, my lovely," he said, examining the dead bodies.

"Manni, put these back in their car and drive them to Jerusalem with Kalid." He signaled Shalima to put down her weapon. "Kalid, you come to my house with guards and weapons. Your father cheats me. I could kill you now and send your body back to him with them, but I will not. You tell your father I will accept his offer for one million dollars for Juda Bonaparte delivered to him alive or dead and two million for all the scrolls on delivery, in cash, United States dollars. One half regardless, or I will go into Jerusalem and destroy the Bhite al-Nadir, the house of Nadir."

His face frozen, Nadir agreed to the terms.

"Abu Keeftan," Manni said, his head bowed, "it is over one thousand kilometers to Jerusalem and very hot. They are very dead. I will die a thousand deaths from the stench." Keeftan laughed. He turned to Shalima after they left. "Now for your promises of the bed, my deadly friend."

"Now you must wait," Shalima said, throwing her head back. "Why did you signal me to kill them, Abu Keeftan, and spare Kalid?

"You are a woman and Nadir sickens me. Two of his men killed by still another woman will make him crazy. In the end, I must destroy Nadir and all his family. Kalid will be dangerous to me for as long as I live, or he lives. It is the way of the Arab. Nadir will be maddened with anger – irrational with his thirst for blood, first Juda Bonaparte's, then mine. He will make mistakes. The scrolls, the money, and the Bonaparte woman will be mine, but first I must have his money for my men."

"You will be with Bonaparte on Nadir's death list. And now, I will be there."

"A *ménage à trois,* my dear." Keeftan smiled and wrapped his arms around her. "That may still your boredom. Pack some things, we're going to our camp in Palestine."

Chapter 6

Juda read Harold Baxter's letter several times, noting the names and addresses that followed his closing: Juda, I'm sorry. Love, Harold. She thought of him dying, of things they had done together, of that part of his life that he had shared with her. When the tears stopped she called Paris, confirming that T.J. Troubble had received the package. She asked him to take it to her bank as Harold had wanted.

"I need a report on everyone connected with research on the Dead Sea Scrolls at the Palestine Archeological Museum, the Albright Institute, the Rockefeller Foundation, the French École Biblique, and the Vatican. And I need a list of world authorities on poisons. I'll be there as soon as I can. I'm sending you a stack of floppies I found on his desk, see what you can get from them with that array of equipment you've been charging to my accounts." She talked about Baxter, his permanent sleep and her feelings about him. "T.J., I need to know about him. I have to help him. I…"

The next day Troubble called her, giving her four names – men connected to the British Palestine Exploration Society. "There's a Professor Pribble, lives in Manchester. One's a priest who's been murdered in Jerusalem."

"Pribble? I know about the priest. He was one of Harold's friends. He told me about him, Father Legault, and about a

Van something, McLaughlin, and an American. Who's Pribble?"

"A past president of the British Palestine Exploration Society and a big name in scrolls. He's the guy who developed the method of cutting them open, or something like that. Worked with Baxter years ago in Jerusalem. Another is retired and lives in Jersey, Channel Islands, a Professor Helmut Van Dorn. Funny name for an Englishman. One guy, name of McLaughlin, was with the Palestinian group until 1965. I can't get a lead on him after that. His last address was in London. The other is in the good ol' U.S. of A., New York City, but lives in Long Island, a guy by the name of Harrington Wolfe. I'll give you his address when you get here. He heads up a department at the Rockefeller Foundation that provides grants for archeological digs in Palestine, I mean Israel. Wolfe was in Palestine with Baxter and the others." T.J. hesitated, his voice lowered. "Juda, are you OK? How's your head? Outside and inside."

"I'll be all right T.J." Juda said, feeling it was a lie.

"I'll fax you a list of toxicologists."

"I want you to call Baxter's three friends, Van Dorn, McLaughlin, if you can find him, and Wolfe. Wolfe or Van Dorn might be able to help you locate McLaughlin. Tell them that Harold's been poisoned and that his scroll was stolen. There's good reason to believe they too are in danger. They should contact their local police and get private security. Tell them to expect a visit from me."

That same day Juda flew to Manchester to see Professor John Pribble. Pribble had been on the board of the Palestine Archeological Museum as the British member from 1952 until 1975; he was the man who had developed the method of cutting the first copper scroll.

Pribble's office at the Manchester College of Technology, unlike Professor Baxter's, was neatly decorated with walls of books, a large, world globe on a cherry wood stand, and framed photographs of the rocky cliffs and caves of the northwest area of the Dead Sea known as Qumran. The professor, a short man, neatly groomed like his office, stepped from behind a large desk on which there were several brass curios and ceramic pieces all carefully arranged on the polished wood, and which was otherwise free of clutter. He greeted Juda, offering her a seat in a Queen Anne chair beside his desk.

Juda, conservatively dressed in a pleated Black Watch skirt and a v-necked cashmere sweater, removed her trench coat and sat down. Observing every detail of the man and his surroundings, Juda explained that Harold Baxter was her mentor and friend, and that he was sick, in the hospital, and in a coma. She watched his face carefully as she spoke.

Dr. Pribble showed genuine concern. Juda told him that he might have been poisoned and that a scroll had been taken from his laboratory. She told him that just before the scroll was taken, Baxter had called her, very excited, saying he had found the key to deciphering the scroll.

"My dear, Dr. Bonaparte, a fascinating name, if I do say. I'm so sorry Harold is ill, sounds like a stroke. Eh, what? Poison, I doubt it. Who would poison him? Sounds dramatic. And what scroll are you talking about? I've known that curious scoundrel, a delightful man, all his life, and in the most god-awful circumstances at times, let me tell you. Does he still maintain there's another set of scrolls from Nag Hammadi that have never been found? Poppycock, I say to that one. Always have. He got obsessed with that after losing his wife. They killed her, you know, in a tribal blood feud."

During one of their Sundays together, Harold Baxter had told Juda the story of Nag Hammadi and the lost scrolls, when his young wife had been murdered by the Hammara tribe. Juda recalled his tears as he relived the story and remembered his embrace and kiss on the cheek when he said goodnight and thanked her for listening to a babbling old man.

Juda looked at Professor Pribble, a little younger than Harold, white thinning hair, portly, pompous, and said Professor Baxter had told her the story. She asked him if he could say anything about the stolen scroll.

"Do you mean to say, Dr. Bonaparte, that Baxter really had the lost scroll of Nag Hammadi? Or was it another? Perhaps from the Dead Sea. God knows, he spent enough time there with those Dominicans."

"No, it was another, I think. A conundrum he called it. Small, incomplete."

"Well, my dear, I can't help you." He moved to the large globe beside his desk, spun it, then slapped his hand over the Middle East. "If someone poisoned Harold to get his scroll then he's back here, no doubt. Probably, Jerusalem, Baytal-Mugaddas as the Arabs prefer, rather rightfully, I dare say. This is speculation, you know, with the scrolls and the Middle East, but poison is a favorite of the Arabs – before guns that is. Goes back a long way. That's the way it's always been, and why I'm out of it. Trouble, always conflict and trouble over the Dead Sea Scrolls. Like they're afraid."

"Afraid?"

"I dare say, Jews, Christians, especially Catholics. It's been like that from the start. Catholics claimed a monopoly on the early history of Christianity. Then these scrolls show up, written right around the time of Christ and in caves maybe thirty miles from where He died. And they're the only documents we have of that period. The gospels were written later, much later, and we have no originals. Even the authorship of the books is a matter of dispute." He stood up, his thumbs hooked into the pockets of his waistcoat.

"So, right off, the scrolls were considered a threat to Christian history as they saw it. Then the Vatican stepped in with all the Dominicans in that exclusive club of Catholics they called the International Team. No place for an Anglican there, so I got out. Maybe that's why old Baxter fit in so well. I mean with the Dominicans. He's Catholic, you know, and he had a close friend who was a Dominican." The professor returned to his desk, took hold of his lapels and protruded his lower lip.

"Anything else, Professor Pribble?" Juda said, annoyed by his haughtiness.

"You've come to Manchester unnecessarily, my dear, Miss, Dr. Bonaparte. As you've seen, I mean heard, I haven't been able to help you. Don't worry about Harold, he'll get through this. He's as tough as… as leather. Good stock, you know. He'll be back working with another absconded copper scroll. Oh, by the way, he had another close friend, still in Palestine I think, Professor Delbert Markham. Retired now. For the life of me, really, I could never understand one taking one's retirement in Jerusalem, or anywhere in the Middle East for that matter."

Two miles away – the effective distance for the perimeter transmitter Juda had placed under the overhang of the professor's desk – she stopped her rented Jaguar and tuned in a silent FM band on the car radio. Had copper been mentioned in any of the press releases about the stolen scroll? To the police? If not, then Pribble had to know more than he let on. If he did, why? The radio remained silent. Juda waited. What if he did know something? He was Harold's friend and probably privy to knowledge of the copper scroll. But, if so, why lie? She was about to drive off when she heard a knock in the professor's office, and his voice saying, "Come in, Agnes, you're right on with my tea. Thank you." Juda looked at her watch, four o'clock. Predictable Englishman, she thought, and listened, uncomfortable at her passivity. There were other ways to get the truth, drugs, or a gun in the mouth – the brain-splitting sound the hammer makes as it's cocked against shaking teeth, sending fearful messages through bone and into that part of the brain that screams for self-preservation. "Agnes, have there been any calls from Harold Baxter, when I was away last week? He's sick, in the hospital you know, poor bloke."

"Oh dear, I'm sorry about the professor," she heard Agnes reply, "I do hope he'll be better soon. Sir, all your messages are in your daybook, and if you had looked, you would see there were none from Professor Baxter. That doctor from London called three times – rude man." Juda heard pages being turned and a muffled laugh.

"Ah," he said as he apparently found the name of the man she was referring to, "McLaughlin," and he chuckled again. "Thank you, Agnes. I wonder… " Juda heard the door close and then she counted the digits as Pribble dialed a long distance number. "I've just had a visit from a Dr. Juda Bonaparte. Yes, a friend of Baxter's. No, not that, too young, although, I daresay, it would be a delightful idea." Juda smiled, listened, and waited. "Harold Baxter's in the hospital. The Bonaparte woman says he's been poisoned and his scroll's been stolen. This might affect your work."

At the Rockefeller Museum in Jerusalem, Father Howard Scantland, Jesuit priest and scroll expert, hung up the telephone. He looked at his watch and calculated the time he would contact the senator. Violence was not a part of their arrangement.

When she returned to Birmingham, Juda checked the newspapers and the police report. There had been no mention that the scroll was copper. Yet Pribble knew. He had made an international call. Who was Howard? Why had Baxter lied? She called the hospital for a report on Harold and asked that Dr. Hastings return her call. Juda looked out her window: a dark rainy night. No police car. Her eyes narrowed, scanning the shadows. Baxter had lied, and Pribble knew more than he should. She would pay him another visit.

Tired from her day, she fell asleep on the couch, waiting for Dr. Hasting's call.

She awoke from a nightmare, face flushed, body wet, and looked at her watch. Nice dream, she thought, rubbing her eyes, hearing the rain beating outside on her patio as she stripped off her silk shirt, damp with moisture. By the time she entered her exercise room, slacks crumpled on the floor, naked except for the panties clinging to her, she had given up her dream, yielding to the tensions in her body. Mindlessly she pressed against a heavy barbell; it felt hard and cold like a man. She touched the steel with her fingertips, but turned instead to her exercise rings. The hangman's nooses she called them – new to her program. Juda checked the floor flanges and guy cables then started swinging, the aching in her muscles easing with the stretching. Effortlessly she soared, inserting her hands through the rings, grasping the straps the way her instructor had taught. Dr. LaCroix flashed through her mind, his naked body hanging cruciform in Shamir's prison, arms pulling from their sockets, dying for her. She let her head fall to her chest imagining for a moment what he had felt, hanging and dying. How long could one last? Christ, she thought more as a prayer than a profanity, hadn't lasted long on His cross. Then holding with one hand, she grasped her ankle with the other – the figure four – and swung, stretching thigh muscles painfully – exquisite pain.

Body arched, she twisted and rolled, one arm then the other. Legs overhead, toes pointed, head high, muscles straining to escape from the confines of skin and flesh, and heat. Exhausted, she hung head down, arms outstretched, an impossible hold except for the strongest. Finally, her shoulders aching, she dropped to the mat below and, pulling a robe over herself, fell asleep once again, a deep dreamless sleep.

When she awoke the rain had stopped. Sunlight beamed through the windows. Juda rubbed her eyes and blinked at a shadow sitting by the door – a man. Letting out a screech she clutched her robe to her chest. "What the hell are you doing here?" Her *coup d'œil* picked up every detail: the glass eye, older, fatter, thinning hair, desert tan, leathery skin, spider wrinkles at the corners of his eyes. "How long have you… ?"

"Long enough, Juda." Benjamin Kerns flashed a broad smile, and his one eye sparkled. "You're even more beautiful than your mother."

Chapter 7

A GASTROSTOMY had been done on Baxter, making an opening from his stomach through his abdominal wall for feeding purposes. "How long?" Juda demanded of Dr. Hastings. "When will he come out of this?" Benjamin Kerns, feeling his daughter's irritation, gently squeezed her arm and led her to the lounge where she cried. Afterward, angrily resigned, Juda arranged for around-the-clock nursing care at a private facility the doctor had recommended. He had reassured Juda that they had not given up and would continue investigations and treatments. He said he had not been able to secure a toxicologist, but had sent specimens to several, mentioning a world authority at the University of Chicago, a Dr. Richard Grodzinski. Composed again, Juda took Benjamin to the office and laboratory where she had worked with Baxter, showing him where the fight had taken place and, childlike, showing him her healing head injury. "It's all over for him now, Ben. I know he'll never wake up."

Kerns looked over the laboratory and office, still in a shambles. "You killed two of them? Becoming a doctor hasn't slowed you down," Ben said, trying to change the subject of Baxter's imminent death.

"A Ph.D.," Juda answered, enjoying his interest. She wondered whether it was the doctorate or her other, father-given abilities that stirred his pride and her feelings of gratification. It didn't matter. She liked it and felt weak that she did. She wished, more than ever, that she was still in analysis with Dr. LaCroix; killings did that to her, and now she had other feelings: for a father she was getting to know and like, and a friend dying, a man she loved.

Patting her father's thick waist, she said, "And I do keep up my training or I'd be your size, and just as slowed down. I noticed how you were breathing when we climbed the stairs to the lab." Catching herself she added, "I'm not proud of what I've done, Ben, killing people I mean. I came here to start something new. Death follows me like my shadow, not just in my nightmares. I hated you for a long time, blaming you for what I was. But not now. I know it was me. Something repugnant in my soul released the beast I became, one that found political and pontifical justification. I became a Darth Vader. It was easier the other way, blaming you, I mean."

Putting his arm over her shoulders, Kerns said, "Come on, Juda, let's go home, and on the way, tell me who's Darth Vader?"

"And you tell me why you're here."

Two weeks before Benjamin Kerns arrived at Juda's, another body, that of an Islamic holy man, had been found crucified and hanging from the tower of the Dormition Abbey. The abbey, built on the site where the Virgin Mary had fallen asleep at the end of her life, was a venerated Catholic landmark and tourist attraction, was now desecrated by murder. It was within gunshot of the Islamic Dome of the Rock and the Israeli Western Wall, where Father Legault's body had been found. The inscription over the victim's head read, "Mohammed, Abraham, and Jesus," in Aramaic. The people of Jerusalem were outraged, filled with even more contempt and fear of each other.

Fueled by the newspapers and a shocking photograph of the naked man strung out on ropes through his wrists like the others, fighting broke out in Jerusalem for the first time over religion. This was something the official Israeli policy had tried to avoid from the beginning of the last occupation in 1968, continuing an unwritten tradition of religious toleration that had been in place over two thousand years, except during the first Crusade. Racial hatred between Arabs and Jews, driven by the Israeli takeover of Arab territories in 1968 and military-backed Israeli settlers on Arab lands, had been enough to provoke the endless round of hostilities; father the Palestine Liberation Organization and more than a dozen splinter terrorist groups led by violent leaders such as Carlos the Teacher, Raol Shamir, Abu Nidal, Yasser Arafat, Charles Haddad, Abu Keeftan and others; and divide the world's allegiances. The Americans, backing the Jews and Arabs, sold like arms to both, while the Vatican, alone among non-Arabs, had not acknowledged that the Jewish state even existed.

Two days after the third murder, a young Jew had exhorted the crowd gathered on the Kotel plaza in Jerusalem that it was time the Jewish people reclaimed the site where Solomon had built the first temple, a temple on whose ruins "heathen" Muslims in 688, sixteen hundred years after Solomon's glory, had defiantly built the Dome of the Rock. Here, a thousand years after Solomon, Herod's magnificent second temple had been destroyed by the Romans. Fanatical Jews wanted their sacred area back.

David Hashan, a dark-haired, wiry young man, was a member of a Jewish cult centered in an abandoned Arab village in the Lifta Valley near Jerusalem. Deeply tanned because of the cultic ritual of always facing the sun, he, like other Semitic people, could easily be taken for an Arab. Inflamed by the crucifixion of Rabbi Svika Herzl, Hashan and his followers believed that a third Jewish temple should be built where the

Muslim shrines of the Dome of the Rock and the Al-Aksa Mosque were situated on the Temple Mount, a site claimed by Jews, Christians, and Muslims alike as holy.

"We have reclaimed our land," he shouted to the crowd gathered on the plaza. "It was here that Abraham offered his son to God. Now let us build the temple of the one God, Elohim, the temple of his chosen people." The crowd – mostly old men, Hasidic Jews dressed in black, coarse serge with broad brimmed-black hats and curls of hair hanging down their temples, and a few women and children – murmured as they advanced up to the Temple Mount. Facing them at the top stood the small contingent of Israeli soldiers who had been assigned to protect the mosque ever since a fanatical Australian had bombed it. David Hashan tore his shirt during his oratory, showing the crowd scars from beatings he had received as a small child after Palestinians guerrillas forced him to watch them kill his father.

Fed by fear and hatred, the crowd moved forward to the Dome, but stopped at the sound of automatic weapons fired over their heads. David screamed, "They won't kill us; they're Jewish soldiers and we're Jews. The temple is ours." He called on God for courage. The Israeli lieutenant, uneasy over his orders to protect the Islamic temple, leveled his Uzi at David and shouted that he would shoot anyone forcing entry.

"They're our people," a soldier said, lowering his gun, his face contorted in fear as the crowd pushed closer to the temple.

"My orders are clear," the officer shouted, sweating profusely and holding his weapon tremulously. "Disperse! Disperse!" he again yelled in Hebrew and stepped backward into the doorway as the crowd of Jews egged on by the now bare breasted, screaming David, pushed past the soldiers into the sacred Islamic temple.

Frightened, the officer lowered his weapon as the frenetic David danced like his historic namesake into the shrine, waving the crowd on. He climbed over the wall protecting the black granite rock, the *Even Shetiyah*, called the *Sakhrah* by the Muslims. He screamed that the temple was once again back with the Jews.

The lieutenant, sweat streaming down his face, fired a short burst. David collapsed on his knees as blood erupted from three holes in his chest, and in one final supplication, he called on God as the soldiers, hysterical with fear, let loose a wild undisciplined staccato of 9mm rounds into the advancing crowd.

It was over in seconds; a dozen unarmed Jews, including three children, lay dead and bleeding on the steps and within the mosque. The officer, his face white as the temple mosaics, parched mouth open, dropped his weapon and climbed to the dead boy who had led the outbreak. Crying, he cradled the young David, as his men ran from the temple. A few stragglers began throwing chips of temple stones gouged out by the bullets at the officer, but stopped as the man, robot-like, but with tears in his eyes, withdrew a small German Mauser pistol from a black leather holster and in one smooth unfaltering move, put the muzzle into his mouth and fired.

At Mossad headquarters in Tel Aviv, Director Samuel Scharkes had gritted his teeth and slammed his telephone down when he had heard of the slaughter of Jews in the Dome of the Rock. He closed his eyes, called on Christ, and then told his secretary to get Benjamin Kerns on the phone. He waited, strumming his fingers on his desk.

"Benjamin? Scharkes."

"I know – Jerusalem…"

"How the hell? Benjamin, I need you. Intelligence that's all. We're about to have a civil war."

Kerns had said nothing, listening to Scharkes' heavy breathing.

Juda, who had been listening to Ben's story as she prepared their dinner after they had returned from the hospital, slammed the heavy French chef's knife into the chopping block, sending bits of onion and celery flying like missiles around her kitchen. Kerns ducked. "Jews killing Jews in the Dome of the Rock! Ben, you've got a war coming. That's one of the most sacred places in all of Islam."

"And three religious men, Juda, crucified – a Catholic, a Jew, and an Islamic."

"Who was the Catholic?" Juda asked, knowing he'd say Father Jean Legault, Baxter's friend. *Why didn't Harold tell me?* Religious fanatics, Baxter had said. Juda poured dark coffee from a French-press coffee maker and lit a cigarette, quieting the anxiety she felt beginning in her chest.

"That's why you came. You want me to go back with you. Well, you just listen da… Damn! I can't even say it." She heard herself sounding like a child. "From now on you're Ben. This is a first for me, having my father visit and for dinner, and with the wildest imaginable story." She went back to her food preparation. "Ben, I'm hungry and can't think now. I've eaten hospital food all week." She wrinkled her nose disdainfully. "This will be good, the best homemade dinner you'll have had in a long time. So pour a drink and a Pernod for me, have a cigarette. Let me think. After dinner, I'll tell you my answer. Be prepared, my life is different now. Then you can go back to your mistress Israel."

"Someone's stirring a new kind of pot, Juda," Kerns went on, "setting religions against each other. Jews, Muslims, Christians are all on edge. Churches have guards posted. Israeli soldiers guard churches, mosques, and synagogues, and they're locked at seven o'clock. In two months the Pope is supposed to visit and walk the Via Dolorosa, but our people have warned Vatican security it must be canceled. Who knows? John Paul's one stubborn man."

"You don't think there'll be another assassination attempt, do you? You can find someone else, I'll never get over the last."

She remembered the old man with his rifle over a half mile away from the pope's balcony, then the vision in her scope had turned into a collage of red as her bullet found its mark.

"I want you to come back with me, Juda. This forced retirement is killing me."

"And cook for you?" She smiled. "Keep you company in your retirement? Listen to your stories about your troubled people and the equally troubled Palestinians, and do a little intelligence work on the side? Find out who's killing these holy men and setting innocent people against each other? How about some assassinations for the honorable state of Israel? Or would you rent me to the Vatican again? Get me papal sanctification and earn a place in heaven with the lost tribes of Israel?"

"You're upset about your friend Baxter. I'm sorry, Juda. My timing could have been better. Do you still think he was poisoned?"

Juda collapsed into a chair near Benjamin, making no effort to hide her tears. "Yes, and so do the doctors and the police, but they haven't identified the substance, nor do they have any leads. At first it seemed more of a coincidence, the theft and the murder of his friend, but not now." Juda took a deep breath and asked, "Were the other victims connected with scroll research in any way?"

"No, nothing so far. Just Legault. The murders may be what you say, unrelated to scrolls. Crazy religious fanatics seem to thrive in the Middle East." Kerns slurped his coffee, commenting that it was excellent, as Juda went back to her kitchen.

"Al Mocha, Arabic, do you like it?" Juda said, proudly displaying her abilities with knife and food processor as she chopped and sliced a dozen different foods, peered into the oven, and fanned a second container of coffee, carefully testing the aroma for the right strength, then deftly pressing the plunger on the French coffeemaker. "I think they're connected, the scrolls and his attempted murder, but I don't want to talk about it now."

After a long, leisurely meal, Benjamin Kerns leaned back on his chair at Juda's table, smoking one of her Gauloises, drinking more coffee, sipping a liqueur. Satisfied, he patted his abdomen. "Juda, that was the best meal I've had since I was a kid in my mother's east side New York apartment. French, Arabic, and, I think, Greek. Those little spinach pies you made! You handle that Sabatier like a professional. What's that machine you used to make the *kibee?*"

Juda smiled proudly, wiping the big French chef's knife on her apron. "Yes. I'm good with a cook's knife too." *But with my stiletto I can pierce a franc at three meters, or a throat.* "This is a Moulinex," she said wiping the processor. "I thought Arabic food would please you. Wasn't your first woman Palestinian?"

"Druze. Shamir's mother. A fine woman, Juda, but still Arabic." His tone was almost apologetic. Juda hid a smile.

"You may not know," he said, changing the subject, "that the Roman Curia is about to recognize our state. After forty years! Rome will acknowledge that we are a political entity. Your church moves slowly. It took them nearly two thousand years to lift the blame from us for killing Christ. Maybe they'll shift it subtly back to the Romans where it belonged in the first place. That was the first big cover-up. Israel owes you for this, Juda, thanks to your 'in' with Karol.

"The problem now is Jerusalem," Kerns went on, kicking off his shoes. "With a cutthroat political climate going on for forty years, religious conflicts we don't need. We have respected religious freedom since the occupation; actually learned that from the Muslims. But we've got to know what these murders are about, Juda. The people are scared. Jews killing Jews, and in an Islamic shrine no less! Christ, there could be a holy war, and I'm sure someone is behind it all, manipulating the people, playing on their fears, pulling their strings. What do they want?"

"Your generals could handle a war. Give them a chance to try out all that American hardware they're buying. Just do another pre-emptive strike on the Islamics, six hundred million of them." Juda knew there were radicals in the Knesset who would love to do just that, wipe out every threatening Arab nation – particularly Iraq and Syria, with Iran thrown in to boot. "Maybe you just want me to take out Khomeni, and Hussein, and Assad. Are you so proud and confident in the skills you gave me?"

"Yes. You're the best of the best, but I didn't do it. You drove yourself. You worked harder and learned more, became stronger and faster than any agent we had. I think you were driven by demons. But it's true, a religious plague is being stirred up in Jerusalem, not a political one. We don't need a war with God after what He did to Sodom."

"And Gomorrah. More biblical myths." In spite of extensive excavations, funded by the Rockefeller Foundation, the sites of the ancient Biblical cities destroyed by Yahweh remained a mystery. "Do you still believe in the Old Testament, Father?" Juda's look became serious. "Well, do you believe in your Jewish faith? The Torah? Obviously," she smiled mischievously, "not in their eating customs. I need to know."

Kerns scratched his chin and laughed. "Circumcision and beanies, hell no. And when I die I'm going to heaven with all the Christians and Muslims. I'm not waiting for the Messiah, and I'm not coming back. I've seen enough hell right here. The Mosaic laws? The Commandments? Yes. I think they fit everybody. Now, why are you testing me, Juda? What do you believe in?"

"What your people taught me, what you taught them, and things I've been trying to teach myself, about being a woman, I mean, and liking it, and forgiveness. I let myself fall in with you, the politicians, and the cardinals. It's men who have been the movers and shakers of bloody history. Wars, murders, assassinations, greed, power, anarchy, atomic bombs, death camps. You name it. Did you ever hear of Mrs. Genghis Khan? And the closest Eva Braun ever got to a gas oven was the one in her kitchen." Juda poured another Pernod and lit a cigarette. "Now finish your story. Would you like another liqueur? B & B? Chartreuse? Mine's Pernod." Juda paused. "There's more. What is it?"

"Yes, one more thing. It ties in all right. The victims were first poisoned, Juda, an unidentified drug."

"Like Baxter? Why did you hold that back?" Juda asked, reminded of her anguish over Harold Baxter. "What was the letter or symbol on the heads of the victims?"

"A 'Z,' Juda; we think, for Zoroastrians?"

"An ancient Persian religion that influenced Judaism, and whether we like it or not, Christianity."

"Iran backs many of the Islamic fundamentalists. Maybe this."

Chapter 8

WHEN they had finished eating and having coffee, Juda said she would go back to Israel to help Ben, unofficially, and on her terms. "You give me what I need: passports, new identifications, equipment when I ask for it, and a carte blanche to do what I want and I'll see what I can find out about this cult, if there is one. I may need intelligence from Mossad, KGB, CIA, and others. I'll listen to you, but I'm not going to take orders, or do any dirty work for Israel. First I'm going to find someone to help with Harold Baxter."

"What does this Dr. Baxter mean to you, Juda? Are you in love with him? You didn't answer me before."

"I know. He's my friend, and didn't ask me questions. He helped me get started after my depression, let me work with him. In love? I don't know. I was in love with my husband when I was fifteen and it's not like that. I've never felt that again, even though I've loved since. I loved Dr. LaCroix and Michael, and Susan. And now Harold Baxter. And if you believe it, you," she gave him a warm smile adding, "a little."

"Susan?"

"She was great, Dad," Juda teased, gesturing with a slight wriggle of her shoulders causing her breasts to ripple.

"A woman kind of 'Susan'?"

Juda got up and sat beside her father, a smile on her face. She placed her hand on his. "She was a friend, and in love with Michael." *As I was*, she thought. "The only female friend I ever had. She saved my life in Rome. But not a lover." Her eyes sparkled mischievously. "And what if she was a lover? How would you handle that one?"

"Juda, I'm too old, and have too few surviving gray hairs to be surprised by much. Even a little teasing by you. I knew you were playing with me. Now tell me what you've learned about your archeology professor."

Over the past weeks, Juda had investigated all connections in England, and, working with T.J. Troubble by telephone at her place in Paris, became convinced that Baxter's poisoning and the theft of his scroll were tied together, but the meaning eluded her. She mentioned it was never made public that the scroll was copper, yet Dr. Pribble knew it was, and had let on he knew nothing, and that after her visit, he had talked to someone named Howard. There was little else to suggest what Juda deeply felt. "These murders in Jerusalem and the poisoned victims seem to bring it together. Five were working on the scroll: Legault had been murdered; he and Baxter had both been poisoned." Other than names, she said she knew little about the other three scroll experts.

"Everything connected to the Dead Sea Scrolls is shrouded in mystery," Ben said. He told her about his effort to steal them in 1957 and almost being killed in the tunnel.

"You were trying to show up Sharon and it backfired." Juda laughed, a husky belly laugh.

Kerns laughed, too, admitting that that was why he had gone back into the tunnels. "I thought I was going to die down there, alone with the *wadi* driving me into the bars."

Before going to bed Juda stiffly embraced her father. "After this is over and we find your assassins, Ben, and whoever did that to Harold."... *I'll kill them*, erupted into her consciousness like a volcano. "I'm not going to move in with you – but you'll come live with me in Paris. I have a whole building of rooms and toys, where you can busy yourself. I'll show you when we get there." Thinking of her sleek BMW Motorcycle, Juda saw her father navigating the traffic of Paris on the powerful bike and muffled another laugh. "And when you're bored with Paris, you can go to my estate in Austria and get it fixed up, and whenever you want, we can go back to Israel for a visit."

"When this is over, Juda, I'll give you my answer about that one. Paris? Austria? I've been to your estate; you wouldn't know." The old man smiled, remembering her mother. "We'll see, Juda, we'll see."

LAGO DI COMO, ITALIAN ALPS

Sheltered on a treed bluff overlooking beautiful Lake Como in the Italian Alps, the mansion, built by Emilio Lugi, the Italian automotive industrialist, had once been owned by the Rockefeller Foundation and used as an academic retreat. Ten years ago, Bill Hickman, the American computer billionaire had bought it and fully modernized the estate, adding high security fences, steel gates, and an airstrip suitable for small twin engine jets. It was now used by the Hickmans as their European residence for parties and meetings. There were separate quarters for the staff of cooks, servants, and armed guards.

Hickman had made his money in computers, producing IBM clones in his South Korea plant that sold for one third the price of the originals. He sometimes had new models ready for the market ahead of Big Blue, thanks to inside help. He simply copied new specifications from files his father would bring home. William Hickman Senior had been the CEO until the stock plummeted from near two hundred dollars to the low fifties. By then, his father welcomed retirement, basking in his son's success. Hickman Junior's personal fortune, at current estimates, was three billion. Much of it had been made from selling short the large stock holdings inherited from his mother. Now in company with the wealthiest men in America, such as Ross Perot and Bill Gates, Hickman, spurred by his wife B'Ann, had set his mettle on new sights – the Dead Sea Scrolls, and the treasure of Solomon, one of B'Ann's avid pursuits. The other, her religion, Baha'i, he wouldn't touch.

Dressing for dinner, the Hickmans looked forward to the current report from the archeologists on the scroll. Bill smiled, watching B'Ann's reflection in the bathroom mirror as she dusted herself after her bath and slid naked into a silk dress of some Italian designer currently the rage among the young and wealthy. After eight years her beauty still stirred him. Cold, almost aloof, a young genius in his business, Hickman saw B'Ann in counterpoint to himself, giving him balance with her warmth and passion.

Wanting nothing material, the Hickmans seemed a perfect couple, beautiful people to the societies of New York, Rome, Paris, and Palm Beach, their favorite places. It was not the wealth of Solomon they sought, but the prestige of presenting to the world an invaluable treasure that would make Tutankhamun's pale by comparison.

"I'm ready, darling," his wife called, emerging from the dressing room to parade her dress and figure. "How do I look?"

"More beautiful today than yesterday," he mumbled in French, bringing a laugh to her face.

"Not exact, or original," she smiled. "You need more work with tapes and tutor, but I love it." He slid his arms around her waist, feeling her nakedness beneath the soft crepe, and kissed her on the cheek. "Who's here?" she asked, enjoying his tumescence through the thin silk.

Hickman laughed. "You mean here or downstairs?" B'Ann chided that this was not the time for his antics. Hickman backed away, pretending to be hurt and said, admiring her revealing dress, that she did not look much like a nun.

"Bill, you know there are no nuns in our order." They both laughed at her pun. The conventional idea of nuns might be especially outlandish in Baha'i, since it was a religion that believed in the essential worth of all religions, the unity of all races, and the equality of the sexes. B'Ann's religion, like her fetish for the scrolls, was not a contest between them. He indulged both. "Now who's here, Bill?"

"Wolfe, Van Dorn, McLaughlin, and al-Nadir."

"Any word of Harold Baxter and his scroll?"

"He might as well be dead. He's in a nursing home, with a stroke or something. His scroll was stolen."

"Baxter gone, Legault dead. We're in trouble. Two scrolls missing. All that time wasted." A petulant pout, disarming and attractive, belied her fierce, angry eyes. "And what about the warnings they received from Baxter, and also from this Juda Bonaparte?"

Hickman frowned. "I know. Van Dorn's scared. McLauglin's a mess."

Their guests, wearing tuxedos and waiting in the library stood to greet B'Ann and Bill Hickman. Nadir, impeccably dressed, wearing a sheik's plain white *kaffiyeh*, took Mrs. Hickman's hand, bowed low and kissed it. "It is a great pleasure to meet you, Mrs. Hickman." His dark eyes penetrated hers. "What I have heard from your husband is now confirmed in the flesh." His tongue darted across his lower lip. "You are indeed very beautiful and as fair as a gardenia." She smiled, unembarrassed, and extended her hand to the other men.

"Professor Van Dorn, good to see you again. Are you feeling better? And Professor McLaughlin, and you, Dr. Wolfe. Bill, have drinks sent in. Gentleman, let's sit over here while our waiters serve appetizers that I personally prepared for you."

It was a little over ten years since Wolfe, who was now with the Rockefeller Foundation in New York, had told Hickman about the scroll, their secret copper scroll. Angry at first over Wolfe's breaking their secret, the archeologists had agreed to a meeting at the Hickman's Long Island estate, where they had accepted the first of an annual gift of fifty thousand dollars each. With this allotment, Baxter, Wolfe, Van Dorn, McLaughlin, and Legault agreed to give the rights to the treasure, if it was found, to the Hickmans, who would present it to the world and ultimately bequeath it to the Smithsonian. Bill Hickman, agreeing to Baxter's demand, arranged that the scroll be cut by a new laser technique rather than the faulty method used by Pribble with the first copper scroll – thus preventing the oxidative deterioration of the cut edges and allowing perfect reunion of the parts later. Each year afterward, they would meet at *Lago di Como* for a review of their progress, study, sharing of ideas, and an examination each other's scrolls. Here, Hickman would give them another gift of money.

Before dinner Mrs. Hickman met privately with Harrington Wolfe. "Are you sure, Harrington, that you'll be able to translate the entire scroll? Everything we do from now on depends on that."

"Yes, don't worry, between Father Scantland and myself we'll do it, but Baxter's section is the key. We must find it. B'Ann, don't expect the treasure. Scantland's research points in other directions."

"I know what Baxter believes, but let's get it done."

At dinner Hickman introduced al-Nadir. "Gentlemen, no one has more resources available for actually locating and recovering the treasure in Jerusalem than my friend Nadir, who works under our retainer." Nadir looked at each man, tipping his head, flashing a brilliant smile and bowing slightly. He told them he could do nothing until they were finished with the translations and analysis of their work.

"We'll need more than a dealer in arms to find the treasure of Solomon," McLaughlin said. "I'm afraid, Mr. Hickman – if I am correct, and I'm not sure – the scroll will have more to do with Paul of Tarsus than the treasure of Solomon. I'll show you in the workshop. But how can we finish with Baxter's and Legault's scroll gone and our lives in danger?"

Hickman interrupted. "Gentlemen, for those of you from Europe who may not be abreast of the American political scene, I've recently won a seat in the U.S. Senate. From now on, my work with you will be deferred to my wife, B'Ann. She will have the full authority of our resources in the matter of the copper scroll. She also assumes directorship of our companies, freeing me for the challenges of the political world ahead."

Uninterested in politics, Helmut Van Dorn said to Archibald McLaughlin, "No, Angel, it's John the Baptist not Paul, and I think whoever made this scroll was a man playing tricks with history, an educated and conceited fool, like us. The languages and symbols, do not – "

" – Helmut, I've been asking you to stop with the 'Angel' for years, dammit. Now please, no more!"

"No, Archibald, let me finish. It's been bothering me a long time. All the scrolls, I mean the eight hundred or more already found, not just the copper scrolls, were written, we think, at the most significant time in history, the birth of Christ, the beginnings of Christianity. Yet they contain not one word of Christ. His name is not mentioned. I know. I've read every publication those fools in Jerusalem have produced and I've examined scrolls, bits and pieces, for thirty, no forty years." Van Dorn's voice rose and he trembled. "The Dead Sea Scrolls," he said, "are the biggest hoax in history and we are history's biggest old fools."

"Gentlemen, gentlemen, it makes no difference. It's the location of the treasure of Solomon, or perhaps the Ark of the Covenant, you must find," Nadir said. Laughing, he added that it was only on Abraham, Solomon and Allah that Muslims,

Jews, and Christians even barely agreed. Then Nadir's eyes became harsh and he looked at each one in the room. "Yes, I am a gun dealer, and when we find the treasure you may need my guns. Removing it from the state of Israel will not be without danger, but perhaps by then," he proffered a weak smile, "there will be no Israel and no Nadir."

After dinner they went to a large room in the lower level of the Hickman mansion. Hickman pressed a button on a small remote control unit taken from his pocket and motorized drapes drew back over large plate glass windows, giving a magnificent view of the lake and the dock where his ship, an eighty foot cruiser was anchored. Another button turned on an array of discretely placed outdoor lights, illuminating the grounds and the dock.

"Gentlemen," B'Ann said, "our home is large and very secure. If any of you choose, you can live here where you will be safe until your work is finished." She smiled graciously and turned to examine the scrolls.

Arranged on a large table under a sheet of glass were three scroll sections. McLaughlin had said that their studies were worthless without the pieces belonging to Baxter and Legault. Measuring forty-two inches wide, the scroll had been cut into five pieces with a middle section, Baxter's, irregular in shape, containing parts from the other four.

"Without Harold Baxter's and Father Legault's sections what we have is worthless, ten years for nothing, and now intrigue, murder, and danger." McLaughlin sounded angry.

"Not for nothing, Dr. McLaughlin. We've already paid you, each of you, large sums of money. Bill and I are as concerned as you. I assure you we will take nothing lightly. Here at Lake Como we're perfectly secure. If you return to your homes to work, Mr. Nadir will arrange special security for each of you, as you wish. We'll find the scrolls of Baxter and Legault." B'Ann Hickman, a beautiful woman with a disarming smile, took

Professor McLauglin's arm, asking that he come with her to the billiard table. "Gentleman, please, Bill and I have something to show you." She pressed a switch that turned off the recessed lights over the table. Somewhere above them a motor began turning wheels and the entire ceiling over the pool table slowly descended revealing a model of the city of Jerusalem.

"Marvelous," Angel McLaughlin said. "The detail is amazing."

"The scrolls, gentlemen," B'Ann Hickman said, "are not the only way we have of finding the treasure of Solomon. Give us every detail and perhaps Mr. al-Nadir can find it here in Jerusalem."

"Impossible," said Wolfe. "There are no details, no directions in what I have. We should never have cut it in the first place. Damn Baxter for that. And where the hell is his piece? Without the center piece, Chris…"

"Easy, Harrington. McLaughlin has some different thoughts," Van Dorn said, muffling a cough and grimacing in pain. "You get too excited. Always have. The real issue now is the danger. Baxter's gone, probably dying. Legault's dead. Who's next? I'm not sitting around waiting for some *uneheliches Kind* to shoot me over some worthless scrap. I'm too old and too sick."

That night after their guests had retired, B'Ann approached her husband wearing a scanty negligee, carefully chosen to be discreetly revealing. "Bill, I so appreciate your enthusiasm in this project," she said. "I know your heart isn't in it." She leaned over him and kissed him gently. Her movements were liquid, sensual, and calculated, as he pulled her to him. Their love making was perfect – practiced. As the tempo of his passion increased, B'Ann arched her head and closed her eyes. She had learned it helped to control her nausea and hide her disgust.

As Juda slept, three of Keeftan's men entered her house through a patio door from her garden. Awakened by instinct or the sound of silence, Juda listened, then slid her hand under her pillow, reaching for the gun that was no longer there. Now she heard them, two, maybe three. Suddenly the room light went on and a dark-skinned man holding a Browning automatic entered, behind him two others. He warned her not to move even as she, naked to the waist, sat up in bed screaming in shammed fear, trying to cover herself. The African slapped her hard across the mouth. "Shut up, bitch, no one's here to help you," he snarled, leveling his weapon at her face. Cowering and sobbing, Juda covered her face, which was quickly reddening from the slap. "Tie her in the chair," the African said to the others.

"Watch her, she kills easily."

"Not today, my little friend," the black said. He was large and muscular and spoke with a French accent. "Give me Professor Baxter's scroll and notebook and we will leave you unharmed. Refuse, and in a little while you will beg to tell me, and then you will die. And bitch, you will not die quickly. I promise you that. I heard about you."

"Let me have her," the smaller man said, showing a lewd smile at Juda's nakedness. "I'll coax her with my little friend." He passed a short-bladed lock-back knife from hand to hand in front of her, smiling lasciviously.

Her head down, sobbing, Juda said, "Cover me and I'll give you the book, but I don't have the scroll, it was stolen." Her voice cracked; the man laughed and slapped her again. Then Juda looked into his dark eyes, and for a second could not keep up her charade. "I promise you that."

The dark man laughed again, showing crooked white teeth, but this time nervously, fear in his eyes. "Will you? So easy to give in. The great Juda Bonaparte. I think not. Kamel, search the house." The black man was the most formidable, Juda thought, strong and fast. He would die first.

"I live alone," Juda said, with controlled apprehension in her voice as Kamel left the room. "I lied, there is no book – not here."

"Make it easy, Miss Bonaparte. Death can come in many ways." He motioned to the second man, short, slender, unshaven, with deep-set eyes, tattooed arms, who held a Mauser and played it close to her face. "Search the house; leave her to me."

The man called Kamel searched the kitchen and living room, examining rows of books, sweeping shelves, opening drawers and dumping their contents. In the workout room he tested the weight of a heavy barbell, grunting in surprise. As he snapped on the light in the second bedroom, a giant hand clamped over his mouth and nose and another squeezed the back of his head. Before he could get his gun around, Kamel knew, and in the split second before he died, his bladder emptied. His last living memory was a warm wetness on his leg then nothingness, as Kerns jerked, shearing Kamel's spinal cord against a vertebra. Silently easing the body to the floor, Kerns took his gun. He checked the clip and pulled back the slide enough to see a bullet in the chamber. Barefoot, in boxer shorts, Kerns went silently to Juda's room. Before he fired his weapon he saw an amazing sight.

Juda had turned the steel-framed dressing room chair into a lethal weapon. Sliding and twisting, her hands still behind her back tied to the chair, she had spun the chair into the black man. Gun still in hand, he was doubled over, a horizontal streak of red showing on his white shirt were the leg of the chair had caught him, ripping his abdomen. The other man was on the floor, his left arm broken above the elbow. The black man screamed an obscenity, trying to level his weapon at Juda. Kerns fired twice, the man exhaled once, convulsed and died. Then he turned his gun to the other. Juda shouted, "Don't kill him!"

Kerns hit him on the side of the head instead, then untied his daughter, a big smile on his face. "I'm not as slow as you thought. It's like old times, Juda. Are you all right?" Juda smiled, slipping into a shirt. Bending over the unconscious man she tied the belt of her robe around his neck. Then, with her foot in the small of his back, she pulled tightly on the belt, tying his ankles together, bending his legs at the knees, arching his body like an English longbow. She squeezed his cheeks together and stuffed a silk scarf into his mouth. Then she felt his arm for the fracture and tied his wrists together in front, gently prodding the broken arm. The man groaned into consciousness.

"In a little while your legs will tire and cramp and try to extend themselves. Though you'll fight it, you'll slowly strangle yourself. Your arm will turn black first. You'll fight to breathe and will try to loosen the tension at your neck, but your legs will fail. Before you die, before your muscles kill you, blood will pound in your brain and your eyes will burst from your head," she whispered close to his ear. Turning to her father she said, "Let's go, this will sicken me. This one will soon join his dead friends." The man on the floor did not see the smile and wink as Juda took her father's arm and, stepping over the body of the dead black man, left the room.

At Lake Como, Nadir al-Nadir, alone with the Hickmans and Harrington Wolfe, said, "It will take men and money to find Baxter's scroll and to take it away from the thieves, and to find Father Legault's in Jerusalem, if it's there. Money for bribes, for information, and for other things you don't need to hear about."

"How much Mr. Nadir?"

B'Ann looked at her husband momentarily then at Nadir. "Bill will have five million transferred to your account, Mr.

Nadir, but you will be accountable to us. We will have the scrolls."

Nadir bowed. "You are most generous, Mrs. Hickman, Mr. Hickman. Trust me."

"What of the others?" Wolfe said. "Van Dorn and McLaughlin are quitting."

"We have you, Harrington, and other resources," B'Ann Hickman said, "and other scroll experts."

Chapter 9

"Rama Keeftan!" Kerns howled when the assailant Juda had tied and nearly garroted finally confessed. "That murdering bastard."

The last of Keeftan's men, his head veins bulging as he gasped for breath, groaning in pain and fear, had confessed that he had been ordered by Keeftan to get Dr. Baxter's scroll and notebook from Juda and to kill her afterwards. He uttered that now Keeftan would find him and kill him. He prayed that his death would be swift, not at all like what he had just been through with his legs and neck tied together. He sobbed in Arabic that Juda was a worse bastard than Keeftan for causing pain, not realizing that Juda could speak and understand Arabic. Nor did he see the carefully hidden smirk on her face when he added that she was a *sharmuta* only worth one fuck before she died. Now, lashed to a chair, waiting for the police, he said a British prison would be heaven compared to what Juda had done to him. Kerns raised his hand as if to strike him and told him to shut up.

"Tell me more about this Keeftan, Benjamin," Juda said, inhaling deeply on her cigarette, her efforts at quitting forgotten.

"As bad as they come, Juda. I should have killed him when I had him in prison or pushed him from the copter like I wanted."

"An animal who will kill all of us, very slowly," their prisoner screamed, risking Kern's threats of backhanding him.

"A freelance assassin, a hired gun, who took up the cause of the Palestinians. We took him out of Bekaa. I had him in my hands over Gaza, but I had orders from the P.M. Keep him alive, no drugs or torture, they said. I think that murdering bastard had a cousin in the Knesset. Anyway, we traded him for twenty of our boys. Now the bastard is trying to kill you and me. I should send him a box of parts from these schmucks."

"What does he look like? How old?"

"Mid-forties now, tall, thick shoulders, slender waist, very powerful. Big arms. Fast. At least he was. An expert shot and as good a street fighter as I've seen. Good-looking. He always wore his hair cut short, right against the scalp, and a heavy mustache, like Hussein and the rest of the Arabs. Oh yes, Christ, how could I forget? He has a tattoo on the back of his hand, a tiger."

"Tiger men, I've run into them before."

"In Venice, I know. They're gone now, all dead except for a few living stragglers who got away. We did a raid on their camp like we did on Shamir's. But Keeftan got away. Now he has a training camp in Iraq near Baghdad and we can't touch him. They're all under Hussein's protective umbrella. The Americans politely refuse to deal with that one. They want Iraq on their side. No one listens to me. Iraq is far more dangerous to the Middle East than Iran or even the Palestinians. There's only one way with these killers. Kill them first. Get them in prison and they get out, sooner than…"

"What would this Keeftan want with the scrolls? Or Baxter's notebook? It's hard to believe that book's worth anything without the professor. I watched him make notes and they were in an unreadable scrawl, all abbreviated and in his own shorthand; coded I think." The computer disks she had taken from Baxter's desk, Juda thought, remembering their illegible labels in smudged pencil. Troubble would find out if he could read Baxter's notes. Now, Juda had another kind of trouble to deal with, the police knocking at her front door and two dead men to contend with.

By the end of the four-day workshop at *Lago di Como*, the frustrations over working on the partial scroll had erupted into a bitter argument among the three scientists. Despite the reassurances by the Hickmans, especially B'Ann, Van Dorn said he was through, and was soon joined by Archibald McLaughlin. Their impatience, furthered by the loss of Harold Baxter from the group and the theft of his scroll, was reflected in the complete lack of progress in deciphering the three fifths of the divided scroll they had to work with. Van Dorn, the oldest, had been working in front of McLauglin's scroll and notes. He threw down his pencil, then got up and walked to the vast expanse of glass that overlooked the lake.

"It's madness," he said, turning back to his friends. "It is now, and was then. Baxter said it, I say it. Whoever made that scroll was insane, as crazy as we are trying to read it. How do we know it wasn't some psychotic? We have them now, and I'm sure the Jews had their share. What kind of language did he use? Certainly not Aramaic. We not only have missing parts, we have someone who used an unintelligible cipher, some *Got verboten* code." Van Dorn began to flush through his sallow, ashen-gray complexion. "If he was here I think I could kill him."

"Easy, Helmut, you'll burst a cerebral vessel," Angel said, getting up and walking to his friend. The lanky Archibald McLaughlin put his arm over Van Dorn's shoulders and said he agreed the scroll was written in a code and he too was sick of it. He looked at the Hickmans and Harrington Wolfe, the youngest of the friends, and said, "I'm leaving tomorrow and I'm sure Van Dorn is with me. I'll wind up my work over the next few weeks and send it to you, Bill. I'm finished with it, and I don't want any more money. I just want to live out my life in peace and finish the book I've been writing for the past ten years." He raised his hands in front of him and said, "Don't say anything. It's final. I'll finish what I can and send you the scroll and all my notes in a week or two."

The next morning Van Dorn and McLaughlin flew to London where Van Dorn took a connecting flight to Jersey, his home, and Archibald McLaughlin rented a car and drove to Birmingham. He sat with Harold Baxter in the nursing home, Harold's emaciation furthering his resolve to end his involvement with the copper scroll. McLaughlin touched his friend's forehead and took his hand. "It's Angel, Harold. You were right, Harold," he whispered close to his ear. "The scroll was cursed, and we were wrong. Come stay with us when you're well." At the doorway, he turned and looked at his friend, tears in his eyes. "Get well, old friend," he whispered into the silence.

The next day he boarded a train that would take him from Victoria station to his summer home at Brighton. As he ate the traditional Welsh rarebit and sipped hot tea and milk, he could almost smell the salt water and feel the breezes coming from the Atlantic. There near the ocean he would compile his notes and finish his work on his part of the scroll, though he knew it would never reveal its secrets. Baxter's probably going to die, and Van Dorn's next, he thought nervously. The scrolls will kill us all. Anticipating being with Mona, his wife of forty-two years, he paid little attention to the few passengers in his car – especially the occupant ahead of him, reading the *Times*. It was fall, Brighton a resort town, the young man was probably on his way to visit retired parents.

As the train rumbled on, René Gervais looked up from his paper to watch the green, rolling hills of the English countryside, enjoying his freedom from the cold stone walls of La Salette.

Chapter 10

After the police investigation, leaving England was easy once Benjamin Kerns had spoken with Prime Minister Thatcher. On the Hovercraft taking them to Jersey, the home of Professor Helmut Van Dorn, Kerns told Juda he had known and admired Mrs. Thatcher for many years. "If she were single and younger, I might have initiated a... a liaison," he said to his daughter, his eyes sparkling mischievously, much like Juda's. They were on the upper deck, the ship's engines roaring, keeping it just a little above the churning waters.

"You mean, if you were younger, Benjamin." Juda laughed, the Channel winds blowing her hair, her skin fresh and radiant in the brisk weather. She was enjoying the company of her father much more than she had anticipated. Do you find safety in years, Juda? Dr. LaCroix had asked in her analysis; her answer had been angry and regretful. But with Benjamin Kerns, her father, "older man" was something different. Different than Baxter, and the doctor, and the old priest at Notre Dame Cathedral, the dedicated Jesuit who had given her orders from the confessional to kill, and how he had died as she had held him in her blood-stained hands, his chest sucking air from a fatal gun shot. The memory brought sadness.

"Ben," Juda said, banishing her thoughts, turning her blue eyes and smile on her father, "If you'll let me, I'm going to take you shopping when we get to Paris and show you the city." She put her hand over his on the ship's railing. "After that, Israel and her wars will seem tame."

General Benjamin Kerns, a man who had fought five bloody wars, recognizing that it would be useless to argue against such female weaponry, said yes, knowing that few men could say otherwise to Juda's charm. He shook his head and said he suddenly understood why the Arabs covered their women head-to-toe, leaving only their eyes to be seen, and why the Bedouin used to cast their baby girls into the desert to die, while proclaiming their pride at having sons, many sons. Fear, he said, men were afraid of women.

"Why, Ben?" Juda waited, knowing the answer. Every woman did. He remained silent, an unbeliever. A smile broke on her face.

"It's because we don't have to have pissing contests," she exclaimed. Kerns roared with laughter, putting his arm around his daughter.

"I guess you're right, Juda. Now tell me why we're going to Jersey. What about this Van Horn? I should be back home killing bad guys."

"That's what I mean about men's war games. Not me, I need to know what I'm doing, and why. This 'Van Dorn,' not 'Horn' was Baxter's friend, one of five with a piece of the scroll. I said I'd go back with you and help, and I will. You're retired anyway and Israel's problems will still be there under the not-so-able hands of Samuel Scharkes, didn't you say?"

"Why they picked him to follow me, Christ, I'll never…"

"I know him," Juda said, remembering, pulling up the collar of her Burberry against the cold salt spray. "A bad choice." She looked out at the water and Jersey's craggy coast ahead. "Are you getting hungry? I know a great restaurant on Jersey."

"You've been here before? And you remember every good restaurant? What about the bad ones?"

"Gone forever," she said, snapping her fingers. "Just like that. It's like a mistake… " Juda paused, then said, "or a sin. Once you see it, you have to let it go, call it for what it is. I do, then I don't go back. Jersey's a popular place for both French and English: nearby, good shopping, no duties or VAT, and great beaches. No income tax either. It's close enough to Paris for a nice weekend. And fish so fresh it dances on your plate when they serve it. You'll see. I've asked Professor Van Dorn to join us for dinner. He didn't sound well — frightened, I think, but sick too. We'll have time for a quick tour of the island first."

Just past customs, Juda rented a Saab turbo convertible and they drove the south shore road past St. Aubin's Bay through St. Helier to Gorey Harbor, stopping at the Moorings Hotel. Their adjoining rooms faced the harbor with Mt. Orgueil Castle high above it — a spectacular view. In two hours they had completed a quick drive around the island, Juda obviously enjoying the sports car and her role as tour guide for her father. Deftly handling the shifter on a tight curve at St. Queens Bay, showing off a little, she said with an exuberance that invigorated Ben, "Look, there's a German bunker." Stopping quickly and setting the hand brake she said, "Let's look," and was out running up a narrow path on the grass-covered cliff to the strategically placed concrete structure high above the rocky north shoreline, its guns long removed. "The Germans were here during the war. They built bunkers and practiced with manned torpedoes on Alderney. Then they left, leaving these concrete scars. Look, Ben, over there, across the bay, Grosnez Castle. It's haunted. Let's go!"

"No! Juda, you wear me out. Let's get back. I want to freshen up for dinner. I do have clothes, other than these fatigues. Maybe you won't have to take me shopping. That's something

I hate even more than climbing a cliff to see a beat-up old castle."

"I knew you'd worry that one to death, the shopping I mean," her smiles came easily now. "I won't make it too painful. Wait till we get to Paris."

That night they sat around the piano bar in the restaurant, enjoying the panoramic view of the harbor and castle. Juda, beautiful in a simple dark suit that fit perfectly, sprinkled Tabasco, lemon, and pepper on the large tray of oysters between them, sipping Pernod as she ate and talked. Tilting the liquor from a shell into her mouth and gently slurping it, she commented that next they would have ormer stew, an island specialty.

"I'm going to try it, Juda. But the oysters are all yours." About to finish the last, a waiter interrupted her with a message from Dr. Van Dorn.

"He's not feeling well and asks that we come to his house after dinner. I do want to eat first." At dinner they were served another house specialty, *Fruits de Mer*, an array of seafood arranged on an elevated platter like a pizza tray: filets of plaice, crab, poached salmon, coquilles Saint-Jacques Mornay on the side, and the chewy ormer stew, the abalone exclusive to the Channel Islands. Eating with her usual gusto, swirling a scallop in the rich cream sauce, Juda suddenly felt someone staring at her. She removed a gun-metal makeup case from her purse. He was young, dark, very good looking, with cold, penetrating blue eyes, and he was clearly watching her. She said nothing and continued her meal, finishing with a large bowl of ripe strawberries and Jersey cream. Warmed by her food and drink, Juda raised her frappe of Chartreuse to her father. "Now let's see what's worrying the professor." She used her make-up mirror again. The young man was gone.

Dr. Van Dorn's home, an English Tudor, was just outside St. Helier. A buxom housekeeper, young, with a friendly smile, showed Juda and Benjamin to the book-lined study. The professor raised his small frame to greet them. He was neatly dressed, though his clothing was oversized and baggy; his white shirt hung lose from his thin neck; he had an ashen, sickly look. The room air was dense with cigarette smoke. Juda extended her hand. "Dr. Van Dorn, I'm Juda Bonaparte, a friend of Harold Baxter, and this is my father, Benjamin Kerns."

Kern's bristled. "I'm going to kill you, you Nazi bastard. Juda, meet Major Carl Conrad Nagel of Buchenwald."

Van Dorn raised his hand. "Before you do, General Kerns, let me give you this. I'm already a dead man." He opened a leather document case, and there, between two sheets of plastic, was his portion of the copper scroll. He offered them drinks and bid them have chairs.

"I was a soldier, following orders, like you have done, General Kerns. When we left Jersey they sent me there – to Buchenwald and the horror."

"A war criminal, murderer." Benjamin's eyes narrowed and his mouth pulled up to his left, in an expression of disgust and rage. Juda placed her hand on her father's arm as the professor bent his head, trembling.

"Please, there are no charges against me. Even Wesenthal cleared me. An officer, yes, but I was never arrested. I followed orders. The shame of the Reich has haunted my life. I came back to Jersey years later, changed my name, married. And now, I'm dying. I'm alone. My wife is dead. I have my work and my few friends. Harold said you would find me, and now he too is dying."

"Baxter? When did you last speak with him?" Juda looked at the professor, her eyes soft, her tone genuine, then at her father, noting that his rage at the sickly professor had subsided.

"The night he had the stroke. Oh yes, I found out."

"What did he say?"

"He told me of the stolen scroll, and about you, and the men you killed there in his laboratory, and that you had become friends. And that you were young and very beautiful. He was going to Istanbul to see Professor Zacher and then to Jerusalem where he would stay with Markham."

"Who's Zacher?"

"A religious authority, ancient religions, mostly Middle Eastern and Persian. He's been a colleague and friend for many years."

"Why would Baxter go to him?" Juda asked.

"The scroll. It's religious, at least as far as we've gotten with it. McLaughlin thinks so too. Nothing so far to suggest the whereabouts of Solomon's treasure."

"What about the others working with you? An American, what was his name?"

"You mean Harrington, Harrington Wolfe. He's with the Rockefeller. There were five of us, Wolfe, Baxter, Legault, McLaughlin, and myself. Legault's dead – murdered. Baxter's scroll is gone and he… he's about dead. Now I'm finished with it. And I'll soon join Legault. It's all yours, Dr. Bonaparte. We're finished. Old men on an adventure that's over, one we could never finish. You have in there my scroll piece and the results of my work on it. Over ten years of it. And let me tell you it means nothing. It's not all Aramaic, or even Hebrew or any Semitic language. It's Sanskrit or a variation of it or some lost language, or a mix. If you ever get them all together, Baxter's the best man to make sense out of it, and maybe Professor Zacher or Markham."

"Markham's in Jerusalem. Where did you say was Zacher?" Juda asked.

"Turkey. You keep my scroll, but you must assume the obligation I have to Bill Hickman and his wife. They paid me a lot of money and I've failed. They'll get what's left when…" The professor began to cough, covering his mouth with his fist. Reaching for a cigarette, he said, "Too late now to stop these."

Juda made a mental note to renew her efforts at quitting, then remembering the virus, as yet undetected, that could be living in her immune system's cells, she understood the old man's hopeless despair over his health.

"I'll accept your scroll, Professor, if that will free you from fear, and I'll see to it that Hickman gets it, if he's rightfully entitled, but I won't say when." She touched the professor's hand, dusky red with pale clubbed fingers. "Can you tell us anything else about the scroll or Professor Baxter? Please, and we'll leave you."

"When he called he was afraid. His voice trembled like mine. Strange. He's younger and stronger. I've never known him to be afraid. Even in the caves, when we were in danger."

"What caves?"

"At Qumran, when we found the scroll." He repeated the story of their finding the copper scroll in the undiscovered cave and their decision to hide it and later laser it into five parts. "We all thought it would be like the first copper scroll, but it wasn't. Not as far as anyone got with it."

"Who knew about it? Was there anyone else?"

"No, no one. Not by me, or the others as far as I know. No, that's not right. The Hickmans know, and that Arab they hired. Nadir al-Nadir, that's his name."

"Jesus Christ, you hired 'The Big One.' You might have hired the devil," Kerns broke loose.

"The Hickmans hired him, not us, not me. I..."

"Why?" Kerns demanded, visibly annoyed.

"To find the treasure once we translated the scroll and get it out of Israel." Van Dorn's voice faltered, he grimaced once in pain after another coughing episode.

"I'm tired," he said. "The medicine the doctor gives me is worse than the disease."

Kerns was about to say something more about Nadir, but Juda froze him with a cold look over Van Dorn's head, then told the professor where they were staying and that they would leave for Paris in two days. She gave him a card that simply read "Juda" with a phone number on it. "Call me if you think of anything, anything at all about the scrolls or about Dr. Baxter, please. I believe Harold Baxter was poisoned and didn't have a stroke. His doctors are of the same opinion. He seems to be in a permanent sleep. I'm trying to help…"

"Poisoned?" His body seemed to fold into itself as he fell back into the oversized chair. He waved his hand. "Please leave me."

Juda's skillful handling of the professor had not passed Kern's perception. "Why did you shut me up back there, Juda, with your Medusa glare. This Nadir is one major bastard of a gun dealer, unprincipled, worse than Keeftan. I've tried to get him many times, but he's a slimy snake with connections and high-priced protection. These guys are all crooks. The scrolls have been declared property of the state. And they wanted to smuggle the treasure out of Israel."

"Which state? Long before Israel asserted its rights over the Palestinians, the Vatican laid claim to all religious artifacts found in the Middle East," Juda said, softening Ben with a smile. She said she hadn't wanted to frighten the old man any more by talk of Nadir, of whom she also knew and who should have been one of her sanctions when she worked for Israel.

Kerns laughed and said he had saved him for last. "That phone number you gave him, it wasn't Paris. Where do you think we're going now?"

"Paris. It will be relayed to my flat," Juda said. "A holdover from my fast life in God's service." Calls to that number went to a telecommunications center inside the Vatican; untraceable, they were then relayed to her Paris apartment.

"Juda," Kerns said, "when do we go home? World war three could be erupting in Israel. I have to get back. They may have strung up…"

"In a few days. Promise. First, we're going to Paris."

They left by chartered helicopter two days later. "I wish we had time to take the Hydrofoil to St. Malo," Juda said, straining to see the impregnable castle and the narrow land bridge joining it to the old town. "There's a marvelous little restaurant there that makes a bouillabaisse as good as you could find in all of Marseilles." She missed her father's quizzical look at his slender daughter who had finished a large meal at the Moorings not an hour earlier.

Loosening his belt, Kerns said, "Perhaps we can find a snack for you in Paris, Juda," and choked a laugh.

Three days after Juda's visit, Professor Van Dorn had another visitor, a priest asking questions about the scroll.

"Father," Van Dorn said, looking at the man in the black worsted suit sitting across from him, "what does the Vatican want with this old professor?" He seemed too young to be a priest and an emissary from Rome.

"Dr. Van Dorn," René Gervais said, "I'm from the Pontifical Biblical Commission, and I'm investigating the copper scroll that you have. I would like to know what you've found, and I would like to see the scroll."

"Found? What do you mean by that? I didn't find anything." The professor's face reddened as his voice rose in excitement. "We worked, Father, over ten years on it. How many hours? More hours than you've lived." He coughed, started to stand and fell back, shaking his head. "How do you know about my scroll? No one knows. No one."

"You don't mean 'my' scroll, Professor, but 'ours.' We know about the others."

"How do you know so much of our secret? Who are you?" Van Dorn's voice trailed off, his body slumped back in his chair.

"We have full authority over all scrolls of the biblical period whether from Qumran, or Jerusalem, or Egypt, including the Damascus Document, Dr. Van Dorn. We have known of your copper scroll find for many years. May I see your scroll, please?" With its French accent, Gervais' voice was soft and flat, but authoritarian, his eyes frightening.

Van Dorn stood up, flushed and angry. "No you cannot see my scroll. Leave my house, Father. Leave now. Not you, nor the Church, nor Jesus Christ has authority over me in my house. The scrolls will embarrass your church, Father. Is that what you're afraid of?" He laughed, and coughed again. "From the beginning, that's what worried all of them. Well, I'll tell you now, the Vatican has nothing to worry about. Whoever wrote them was as mad as writers we have today. Now, go! Marie! Marie, show Father... Father. . ? You never told me your... What are you doing?" Gervais had walked behind Van Dorn and clamped a folded handkerchief over the professor's mouth. Van Dorn kicked and flailed his thin arms, his eyes wild with fear, but was helpless in the powerful grip. His head started to swim as he was sucked into a slippery, wet whirlpool. Even as his consciousness faded from him, he recognized the gas with its sweet odor and frantically fought to avoid the spinning vortex, but nevertheless fell into a chloroformed sleep. René Gervais loosened his grip.

Gervais removed a long latex catheter and deftly passed it through Van Dorn's nostril, guiding it down the back of his throat into his stomach. He attached a syringe and tested the contents with litmus. Satisfied it was gastric juice, he filled the syringe with a milky fluid from another vial and emptied the fluid into the professor's stomach. Lighting one of Van Dorn's cigarettes, he sat back and waited for the chloroform to wear off and the haoma to begin its work. "Soon you will tell me everything, old man, and then you must die."

The professor awoke in hell. Fires blazed, devils danced. He cowered in fear. Jews lined up before gas furnaces and he was with them, old, withered, and naked. He screamed a silent hallucinated scream even as he heard the priest's first question about the scrolls and his last answers about Juda Bonaparte and her father.

When he was finished, Gervais dragged the body of the housekeeper he had killed into the library next to the professor. Then he took off his priest's attire and dressed in a simple casual outfit he had taken from his rented car along with a container of petrol. Bending over the dead girl he parted her blouse, revealing her ample breasts and the small hole where his bullet had entered. He touched the tissue, testing its consistency, feeling the heat of his fingers against the cooling flesh, remembering the beauty of the woman, Juda Bonaparte, he had watched in the restaurant and the girls of La Salette. He placed the barrel of his handgun behind the professor's ear and fired one silenced shot, ending his nightmares. Then he poured the gasoline around the room and over their bodies. At the doorway he threw a match. The room erupted into an inferno. René Gervais smiled as the flames lit up his face and played in his cold, blue eyes.

And all who have viewed the scroll must be destroyed.

Chapter 11

Paris was home for Juda, not England, where she had lived the past three years, nor the Middle East, which she loved more. In Paris she had lived a short time with her husband before his tragic death: a death that had driven her into such depths of despair that suicide had seemed her only option, but which, instead, had set her on diverging pathways. One led to infamy as an assassin for the Israeli secret service, and the other to the most meaningful experience of her life, her psychoanalysis with Dr. Pierre LaCroix, initiated by her sexual problem. An analysis interrupted by his murder in the course of her work for the Catholic Church and the State of Israel, strange bedfellows though they were. Afterward she had borne the burden of guilt, the continued sexual frustrations – for she was intensely passionate – and a new fear – AIDS.

Juda had found some relief in her studies and work with Professor Baxter and in reassuring AIDS tests every six months and consultations with such authorities as Dr. Peter Barnes. But, in the dark recesses of her mind, the fear and guilt lingered. Guilt, she had reasoned, for the dead still clinging to her.

Now she was back in Paris and the day was perfect, warm and sunny. The shops and restaurants and sights of young lovers, who, for Juda, were everywhere in Paris, would momentarily refresh her from the memories of England and Professor

Baxter, dying emaciated in a nursing home. Juda shrugged off her painful thoughts as she dressed for a day of shopping and dining later with Ben and T.J. Troubble.

During the day Juda enjoyed refurbishing Ben, despite his protests. As T.J. had scanned computer screens and waited for modems to download from giant data banks he had managed to tap into with secret access codes, Juda had shopped for her father and had returned loaded with packages. Luggage shops, tailors, shirtmakers all answered to her call with personalized services at her apartment. Benjamin squawked loudly but acquiesced.

"You'll be up there with Kissinger and Prince Charles as one of the world's best-dressed men when that suit is finished, Ben," Juda said, hiding a smile as her father, standing straight and tall, tried to tighten his stomach muscles and shrink his waist. "Just relax, it'll fit better, you're fine the way you are. A man your age is supposed to have a portly shape." She told the tailor to have the suits and shirts ready by six o' clock. "Tonight, Ben, you, T.J., and I are dining out and seeing some of the Paris night life. Then I'm off to Chicago."

"You're not coming back with me, Juda?" Ben's posture sagged to the tailor's objections. "Why Chicago?"

"To speak with Dr. Grodzinski. He's the poison authority Harold's physician sent blood samples for analysis." The thought of Grodzinski's failure to characterize the toxin sent a wave of despair through Juda which she resisted. "Ben, is there anything special you want to do before we go out? More shooting?"

They had spent the day before going through Juda's building, T.J. Troubble, in an electric wheelchair, proudly demonstrating the changes he had made. He had been equally proud to meet the famous Israeli general. "I took some ideas from your description of Shamir's place in Damascus, Juda: security devices, fire protection, video cameras, and a private elevator to the workroom. That was mostly for me," T.J. said, tilting back and balancing on the rear wheels of his motorized chair. "And the computer room, it's state of the art. My toy. You'd be amazed what tricks I can do with the codes I've been able to snitch from buddies of mine in the States: FBI, State Department, and CIA, no less. You'll see some in the report I gave you. Soon I'll be able to get into the Duxième through Langley, and next, the KGB."

Interrupting, Ben had said he would like to do a little shooting with Juda, in the range.

"I haven't fired a pistol in a few years, but I might be able to show you a few tricks, Juda."

"You're on, Ben," Juda said, loving the challenge.

At the soundproofed range, Juda opened a steel cabinet in which were stored several of the world's best handguns: a Colt .45, a 9mm H and K, a .357 Smith and Wesson, a .44 Ruger Blackhawk, a massive Desert Eagle .44 magnum, and several Walthers, including two of Juda's customized PPKs, one with a silencer. Pointing to several hunting rifles and custom Italian shotguns, Juda said they had been gifts and that she didn't hunt. They put on hearing protectors and shooting glasses. Juda placed boxes of cartridges on the counter as Ben hefted the forty-five. She had known he'd select the satin-finished Colt.

"This is a beauty, Juda, reworked by an expert, I see." He pulled back the silken-smooth slide checking for play and examined the customized sights and grips. Then he loaded two clips with wad-cutter ammunition.

"I'll show you something, Ben," Juda said, picking a 9mm Walther P 88. "This one's right from the factory. Decocks from left and right sides, and no safety, like a revolver." The heavy weapon seemed large for her hands, but she held it steady, aiming down the range.

"Ladies first, go ahead, Juda." Juda stood with her legs apart, arms out straight from the shoulders, forming a perfect triangle, body erect; the gun jerked and barked fifteen times, as she quickly emptied the clip, putting every round into the one-and-a-half-inch circle.

"The Walther's the best there is, Ben, but you go ahead with your forty-five."

Ben, awed by Juda's shooting, fired his seven rounds, shooting from just above the hip; all struck within a few inches of Juda's, the wounds not so closely spaced, but every shot fatal to the flapping target.

"Do you always shoot like that, Ben?

"No. Two hands like you, when I was younger and could focus on the front sight. My arms aren't long enough now, and my shoulder feels like its full of sand."

"I prefer my PPK, or at least I used to… Watch!" Juda snapped in the clip and turned her back to the paper target. "Move the paper, Ben, anyplace along the track." He waited, as Juda held her gun up against her chest. "Anytime; call it, Ben."

"Now!" Juda whirled and fired two shots without aiming. Both went into the one inch bull's eye at the three meter mark.

"Christ," Kerns whistled. "With a little gun like that you've got to be accurate, or they'll shoot back. And you, daughter, are very, very accurate, and fast. With a forty-five they go down wherever they're shot."

Smiling at her father, Juda said she would clean the guns and that she would like him to accept the Colt as a gift. He looked at her a little dumfounded, then embraced her awkwardly. "Let me try that little gun, Juda," he said, burying it in his large hand. They both laughed when he said it was so small he'd shoot off his finger first, and Juda commented, with a laugh, something about men preferring big weapons anyway.

After they finished, Juda broke down the guns for cleaning, then they looked at the rest of her workplace: reloading equipment, workbench, the exercising area, her cars, the BMW motorcycle, and the new addition, T.J.'s specially fitted Ford Van.

"That was some pretty sharp shootin', you two. Next time, I'm in. I didn't want to interfere with this father-daughter bonding thing." They all laughed and took the elevator to Juda's apartment. At the bar, Juda poured a short Pernod on ice for herself and a scotch for Ben. T.J. opened a can of American beer. Juda picked up Troubble's reports from a desk.

"I've broken the poisons down into several categories, Juda, some straight out of the CIA files and many you'll be familiar with. Like medications such as Inderal, digoxin, insulin, potassium chloride, and all the sedative drugs. Inderal was a favorite with the cloak and dagger boys for a while." T.J. parked himself by a table piled high with reference books and drank from his can of Bud. "The list of poisons from toxic plants goes on and on. In the right column I've listed what they do, symptoms, and how fatal. Trouble is, none fits the picture of Professor Baxter – permanent sleep, I mean. And that reminds me about something…" The telephone interrupted him. Juda answered.

Juda looked at her father, a mixture of sorrow and anger in her eyes. "That was Inspector Gillis of Scotland Yard. He's flying here tomorrow to talk with us. Van Dorn's been killed. Shot, burned, and he thinks poisoned. The day before, Dr. McLaughlin and his wife were killed, each shot in the head. McLaughlin was another of Dr. Baxter's friends with a scroll piece."

"Keeftan again," muttered Kerns. "I'd like to have my hands on him right now."

That night when they went out to dinner, at T.J.'s insistence they rode in his van with its lift and hand controls and other custom features, including a computer, two-way radio, fax machine, and hidden compartments. "The computer," T.J. said, "can access the big one in the apartment by way of a wireless modem, Juda." He pressed a hidden button on a panel that slid back revealing an empty compartment fitted with hooks and slings. "That's to hide things like Mac Tens, shotguns, and Uzis," he said smiling, "just in case Juda doesn't need me anymore, and I have to go back into the security business like I was in the States until those guys turned me into an armchair detective and computer hack."

Juda smiled and nudged Ben. "Just as long as you didn't prepare this tank for me, T.J. It looks like it's set up for an assault on Tehran. You didn't mention the bullet-proof glass or sidepanels. Is the floor reinforced against land mines too? I noticed the blowout-proof tires." T.J. pressed a remote from his chair; the door rolled back and the lift lowered. They climbed into the van with T.J. seating himself behind the wheel.

"What's a guy to do, Juda, you've been gone for three years. Hell, you gave me *carte blanche* with your account and I got bored. And yes, the floor is reinforced. Now where to?"

"La Cassolette, T.J. A twenty minute drive. I've made reservations. Easy parking for your limousine," Juda said, crawling into the rear seat, recalling the first time she and her husband had gone to the restaurant. She gave T. J. instructions on getting there. They traveled up the Champs Élysées, which was crowded with early evening traffic, to Place Charles de Gaulle and onto Avenue de la Grande Armée, as T.J. kept up a steady stream of complaints and expletives about Paris drivers and little French cars.

He turned onto Allée Longchamps, following Juda's directions, and drove through the Bois de Buologne with its dark wooded areas. In the park he asked if the restaurant was in France, saying he could eat a wolf he was so hungry.

"How about rabbit, T.J.? I don't think wolf is on the menu tonight. You should have told me earlier." Juda smiled, adding that it wasn't far to the restaurant. In the rearview mirror she spotted the black Citröen sedan two car lengths back.

"This must be someplace special for you, Juda," Ben said.

"Turn right here, T.J. Now!" Juda said abruptly, then "Yes, Ben, it is."

"Christ, this ain't no Ferrari, Juda," T.J. said making the hard turn against screaming tires as the van tilted smartly.

"It's about a mile or so ahead, on the left. Sorry about the turn. I was distracted." She relaxed her vigilance, seeing that the Citröen had not made the turn with them.

In the restaurant they were seated in a cozy bar by owner Henri Rogère, who had embraced Juda saying it had been a long time. He said he had something special on the menu tonight, one of her favorites, cassoulet. "Try a small bowl for starters, please, I only make it twice a week now."

"You're well known here, too, Juda," Ben said, remembering the restaurants in Jersey and England.

"We would come here when… Charles and I, when… " A tear welled up, she looked away. "That's a long time ago, Ben. The restaurant was small then, cassoulet a house specialty. You might say it was built on beans," Juda said, her smile back, putting away memories.

"I wish… Oh hell, never mind, Juda." She knew that Ben was going to say something about not meeting her young husband before his violent death. It had been this tragedy that had led Juda to join Mossad and become their preeminent agent and assassin.

T.J. looked around the large candlelit restaurant, gulping down his second beer, and laughed. "Beans caused their business to explode, no doubt," he quipped, as they were shown to their dinner table.

As a starter Juda had a small bowl of the bean dish prepared with duck, sausage, pork, and lamb, then another large bowl for her entree. After dinner, they had more drinks, and conversation which by tacit understanding avoided such topics as the Dead Sea Scrolls, Israeli conflicts in Jerusalem, and Professor

Baxter. When Juda finished a crème caramel dessert, she suggested they go to a jazz bar before going home. She saw that Ben was enjoying himself and seemed ready for more. She directed T.J. to La Villa, a nightclub just off Boulevard St. Germain in the sixth.

On their way to La Villa, Juda, leaning from the back seat between the two men, her arms on their shoulders, joined in a singsong. T.J. led off with a repertoire of American cowboy and country songs of which Ben knew a few and filled in with humming and mumbling when he couldn't remember the words.

"You got a good voice, there, General," T.J. said, driving the van competently despite several glasses of beer.

The nightclub was crowded and noisy, seats hard to find. The place vibrated with the tempo of the loud jazz group and the undulations of hundreds of dancers dressed in everything from formal attire to miniskirts, jeans, and tee shirts. Ben was amazed at the scantily dressed women and girls and by the hairdos and earrings on the men. He refused to dance at first, but joined in after Juda pushed T.J. and wheelchair onto the floor, his beer in hand.

Later they were singing their way back to the van when three men approached them brandishing weapons. The black Citröen was parked beside the van.

Juda quickly evaluated their situation: thugs, gunmen – tough looking and determined men with very professional weapons – two automatics, a Tokarev and Beretta, and an Italian revolver. One was French, short and muscular with coarse features. He stood too close, a dangerous mistake. Another time she might have taken them, but she was unarmed, and she knew her timing would be slowed by the alcohol.

"What the hell do you want?" Kerns bellowed, advancing towards them.

"One more step and you're dead, General Kerns, bang, just like that," the Frenchman said, aiming his weapon up into Ben's face.

"You little bastard, what do you want?"

Juda weighed her chances. No matter what she did, there would be shooting; Benjamin or T.J. would be hit by large caliber bullets fired at close range. She nudged Benjamin.

"You want something from me," Juda said with an icy calm, buying time, formulating a plan. "Money? I'm very wealthy and I'll pay."

"Shut up, bitch," the Frenchman said. He pressed his automatic against Kerns' forehead. "Open the van and get in." He motioned with his gun to T.J. and the general. Trouble looked helplessly angry, bristling for a fight, wanting a weapon.

"What the hell do you want with us, you ba – " One of the men struck T.J. on the side of the head with his gun, telling him to shut up. You'll be the first to die, Juda thought, memorizing his appearance and the license number of the car. Then, in a psychedelic collage of color, the gunman's head exploded, spattering blood, bone, and brain on Ben.

The Frenchman, wide-eyed, frightened, looked at Juda. An instant later he choked as a bullet struck him in the throat. The third man fell to his knees and died, his hands on his chest as if to stop the bloody gush from the third shot. Juda looked in the direction of the silenced shots to see a black Saab, its tires screaming, drive away.

Hours later, after they were cleared by the police and had returned home, Ben wondered aloud to Juda and T.J., "What the hell was that all about? Who were those bastards, and who the hell shot them?"

Holding an ice pack to his head, T.J. said whoever it was, he was one hell of a shot, three men dead in less than three seconds. "He could'a killed us just as easy. Nice friend to have as a backup."

"I don't have backups, T.J.," Juda said angrily on her way to her room. That night, for the first time in three years, she placed her PPK beneath her pillow, a bullet chambered and the hammer down, safety off. It may have been the gun sleeping close to its partner again or the horror in the parking lot that caused her to drift quickly into a fitful sleep and dream she was a young girl at home in Austria.

In her dream the countess and her husband were quarreling, screaming over his allegations of her infidelity; he was threatening to kill her. Juda ran from the chateau and went to the stable where she sat on a stack of hay watching Raol Shamir brush down a horse. "Your parents frighten you, Juda," he said, "they cannot be your friends. I am your friend, Juda." She shivered and started to cry, collapsing on the hay. He sat beside her, stroking her hair. "I am your friend, Juda. I am your friend."

Trembling with rage, Juda awoke, sitting up in bed, beads of sweat on her forehead and chest, her gun in her hand. She silently screamed, *No, you dead bastard half brother. No! I have no friends.* The private telephone by her bed was ringing its subdued chime. Only two people had the number, Father Oudi Yong, the Pope's private secretary, and Professor Helmut Van Dorn, Baxter's friend, dead in Jersey.

"I'm René Gervais." He sounded young, his voice soft-spoken. He told her in French accented English. "I killed the men in the parking lot for you. Now I must talk with you."

"Who are you?"

"A man of God."

In Jerusalem, Nadir al-Nadir echoed Juda's nightmarish rage when his son, Kalid, reported that the second team Keeftan had sent against Juda had been killed outside a Paris nightclub. "*Yalan denak*, damn your religion, *sharmuta*! Goddamned bitch, Israeli whore, she is blessed by Allah and I am cursed in everything I do for these scrolls. Do we send men against a *shiatan*, a devil, Allah himself?"

"Keeftan is here with Sabri Youssef," the young man said with forced serenity, knowing how dangerous his father could be when thwarted, especially by a woman. Nadir walked across the tile floor of his study to the doorway opening onto his garden. He inhaled deeply, swelling his chest, pressing his hands into his loins, arching his back.

"Have Amman and two men go around and sit in the garden with their weapons ready. Then tell the women to bring in food and coffee, and send in the Arabs."

Looking more the businessman than the terrorist, wearing a loose-fitting dark Armani suit and open silk shirt, Keeftan bowed and greeted Nadir with the Arab blessing. Nadir smiled, returned the greeting, his cold hooded eyes taking in every detail of Rama Keeftan and Sabri. "Welcome to my simple table, Rama Abu Keeftan, Sabri Youssef. Why do you come armed to Bhite al-Nadir? We are friends. Eat, then we will talk. Have coffee."

"Our weapons are simple automatics, Nadir, for Jerusalem, not you. Rabble run the streets, Israelis, Palestinians, hunting each other, killing a few Christian tourists as they do. We, too are disgraced by Paris, but it was not the woman Bonaparte, who killed my men. Someone else is playing with us. Perhaps there are issues of these scrolls and the woman you have not shared with me. Eight of my best men are dead, and one is in an English prison."

"The report I have from Baghdad says that they were shot in a parking lot from a distance, someone with a rifle, someone who was a very good shot," Sabri said, filling a small plate from the *maza* spread out before him.

"A bodyguard?" Nadir said, controlling his anger. "Who?"

"No guard, not for Juda Bonaparte. She was unharmed; so was her father and the cripple. They were followed. They had to be, but by who? There are other players in this game, Nadir." Nadir remained silent, puffing on an ornate *narghile*, the cool smoke from the dark tobacco rising through the glass bowl.

"You've failed twice to get the woman, Keeftan. Give up, she's too good for your men, for you. And the scroll is cursed for me, I will also give it up."

Keeftan laughed, "Give up? Tell me what is in this scroll that you offer so much money, and for so much blood? Your son's life, and the woman, I can understand. These scrolls are worthless except to scholars and the Church. The treasure of Solomon, is that what you want?" Keeftan smiled. "It's a Jewish myth, like their ark."

"I have a buyer, who's of no interest to you. I will make money. Did you doubt that? Do you think me a fool?"

"No, Nadir, I do not doubt you. You're a Syrian with the soul of a Jew and the money of the Rothschilds. It's Elohim, not Allah who curses you and me for this business. I'll get you this woman and your scrolls if it takes all my men. Now I will send my best. Sabri will go to France; he's no fool and will take this Mossad woman."

After leaving Nadir's guarded fortress, Keeftan and Sabri Youssef walked to a small bar near the King David Hotel. Their car followed. "Sabri, my friend, we've been together for a long time. You're like a father to me. Don't underestimate this woman. Take her and kill her. You may not be able to bring her here alive, but bring proof she's dead. And *biyak*, we must first have the scroll that's in her possession."

"And the other scrolls, Rama, what of them?"

"Nadir must know, Juda Bonaparte must know. Make her talk, my friend, before you cut her throat. Nadir is mine."

Three guards patrolled inside the closed Rockefeller Museum. Located in the Arab section of Jerusalem not far from the Damascus Gate where itinerant workers congregated waiting for transportation to their outlying villages and towns, the museum was in a hot spot of turmoil, even worse now since the murders of the religious leaders. Father Howard Scantland, a member of the International Team worked in his office by the Scrollery, waiting for a visitor. A Jesuit, he did not wear the traditional black cassock but dressed in light cotton slacks and shirt open at the collar. He peered through a magnifying glass at a photograph of Baxter's copper scroll, a curved Peterson pipe dangling loosely between his teeth. Scantland was in his sixties, had a few gray hairs on his round head and a ruddy complexion punctuated by small freckle-like plaques from a lifetime of exposure to the Judaean sun. "Who's there?" His voice was raspy, words clipped.

"It's the man from the States you were expecting, Father."

Scantland opened a drawer and pulled out a bottle of Johnny Walker and two glasses. "You still good for a couple, Senator?"

"It's one long, uncomfortable airplane ride from Kennedy to this god-forgotten Holy Land," Senator Graves said, taking the drink.

"I'm afraid he has forgotten it, Senator. You know about Father Legault? Sickening barbarism." Graves said nothing for a few moments.

"We want you to clean up your work and come back to the States, Howard. You're too valuable and Jerusalem's about to explode."

"I've not finished my work, and unless I get the originals, I never will. This photograph is impossible to work from. There are techniques using very high resolution photography available now. It's my fault it isn't sharper, dammit. I took it right under Baxter's nose; how many years ago?"

"We've arranged a sabbatical for you at Harvard Divinity. Write your book. Stay there. We'll provide everything you need. I'll bring the scroll sections to you when I have them. Are you sure you can translate it?"

"The Jerusalem scroll is the most significant find to come out of the Dead Sea. I've been studying the legend and working on this print for years. Yes, I can do it. Can you imagine the uproar?"

Graves lied. "I never thought of that, Howard. Your book should be a sensation. We will, of course, publish and promote it. Our people are working on that right now. How do you feel about it?"

"I'm not afraid."

"You'll be censured, probably excommunicated, like others who have gone against the establishment, or worse."

"Truth is greater than the fiction… " Scantland stood up. "I'll rewrite history." He looked around his office. "Yes, I'll leave. Take me a week to wind up. When are you going back?"

"Three days. I have other business in Jerusalem."

Chapter 12

BENJAMIN KERNS, wearing a new blue suit, his luggage packed for Israel, stiffly embraced Juda. "I wish you were coming with me. I…"

Juda returned his hug, enjoying the feel of his arms around her and being pleased with herself that she could. "When I return from Chicago, I'll fly to Israel and help you. But first I must meet this nonchalant killer, this man of God."

"Don't trust him, Juda, even if he speaks the truth. Truth can kill. I know you're armed, but be careful. Remember what that English policeman said."

Gillis had arrived in Paris the morning after the parking lot shooting. "What's going on, Dr. Bonaparte?" he had challenged. "I've got two dead women and two dead professors, and one, I'm afraid, almost dead, and they're all connected. We think Van Dorn was poisoned with the same substance that was given to Professor Baxter. McLaughlin and his wife, like Van Dorn, were killed with the same weapon, a twenty-two. Each with a single shot to the brain, behind the right ear." He asked if Juda had known McLaughlin.

"Poisoned, then shot?" Juda asked. "Were the McLauglins poisoned?"

"No signs. Wasn't taking chances like he did with Baxter. What did you and General Kerns talk to him about?"

Kerns was about to answer, but Juda interrupted.

"We asked him about the Dead Sea Scrolls. Baxter's was stolen; they were both scroll experts and friends."

"So who's killing them, and why?" Gillis asked. "And what has this to do with you, Dr. Bonaparte?" He looked at Juda, managed a smile, and said, "I don't think you're involved in these crimes, Dr. Bonaparte, but somehow you are a focal point. Bodies are lining up like Stonehenge around you."

Before he left, Gillis told them he had been taken off every case except this one and would be in Paris for two days. They could reach him through French security or the police. Gillis asked that they call him if they learned anything, and almost as an afterthought, he warned her to be careful.

Ready to leave for Israel, Ben stood back and looked at Juda, shaking his head, holding his arms on her shoulders. "Very beautiful, and very dangerous. Gillis shouldn't be telling you to be careful. Better he warn the Frenchman, Gervais." Juda embraced her father.

"Ben, getting to know you these past weeks has, well, I… "

Ben smiled and said, "You're as bad as me with good-byes. I know what you want to say. You be careful. We have a lot of time to make up – a lifetime, and a lot more Scrabble games to play and museums to see." Juda hugged and kissed him.

Dressing for her meeting with Gervais, Juda remembered the wounds of the dead men – massive tissue destruction made by fragmenting high-velocity, small-caliber ammunition like the thin copper-clad jackets of the American AR15 whose bullets were designed to circumvent the 1920 Geneva Convention agreement on nonexpanding or mushrooming ammunition. She chambered a Winchester hollow point Silvertip bullet (also an expanding bullet, but with no copper-clad deception) in her PPK and slid it into the secret compartment of the gray

Gucci purse she had had made especially for her. The purse complemented perfectly her gray wool suit by Victor Victoria from Bergdorf Goodman and gray accessories. She touched her ears, neck, and wrists with Joy and went to the taxi waiting outside to take her to Antoine's Cafe. She had chosen a sidewalk cafe just off the Champs Élysées for her meeting with René Gervais.

Antoine's had been there for a hundred years, a place for artists, lovers, and spies. The outdoor area contained small bistro tables widely separated for tête-à-tête rendezvous. Covered with starched cotton tablecloths held in place by circular sheets of glass, each table held a bud vase containing one red rose. The interior was dark, the decor seductive. Juda ordered a Beaujolais, lit a Gauloise, and waited, adjusting her gray purse on the tabletop.

The Frenchman looked younger than she had guessed, perhaps in his mid-twenties. He had a dark complexion, smooth, child-like cheeks without the signs of age and character seen in older men, black straight hair, and striking blue eyes. His full lips were slightly parted at rest, showing a thin edge of white teeth. Like his eyes, his boyish smile seemed to reveal only innocence. Danger warnings sounded in Juda's nervous system, along with something else she couldn't place.

"Sit down, Mr. Gervais." Juda smiled, offering him a glass of wine. "I could say thank you for your intervention in the parking lot, but I don't appreciate it. Tell me how you happened to be there so conveniently and with a 308 NATO rifle, undoubtedly scoped from my estimation of the distance."

He smiled, responding to Juda's test, saying it was an American Colt rifle, not a 308.

"You followed me. Why? No one follows me." Her face and eyes turned cold and angry.

"I'm a brother of the Benedictine order."

"The Benedictines have a venerable and at times checkered history in France." Juda met his troublesome, infectious smile with one of her own. "Perhaps you will explain. Being saved by your Order in this way is not exactly traditional, or what might come to mind."

"But it is traditional, Dr. Bonaparte, a secret tradition." He sipped the wine and asked to have one of her cigarettes lying next to her purse. "I don't drink or smoke, except when I am away from the monastery." He puffed but did not inhale and tilted his head upward, as he slowly let the acrid smoke drift from his nose and mouth.

"What tradition?"

"I'm a Templar, a knight sworn to protect the Church."

"An organization disbanded in 1307." She wondered how old he was and asked him. With this, Juda again found herself smiling, and feeling uncomfortable that she did, being drawn into his naiveté. She moved her purse and lit a cigarette. *KILL HIM NOW*, invaded her consciousness.

Gervais smiled and said, "I am older than you guessed. I'm twenty-seven, I think. Not young. My lifestyle and diet may affect my appearance." He shrugged indifferently, shifting in his chair. She felt his foot just barely touch hers. "I've taken all the vows of the Benedictines and Templars, but I'm dispensed now, except for chastity."

"Tell me about this modern-day Templar society," Juda said, moving her foot away.

René Gervais told Juda how his order had continued in secret, maintaining their vow to protect the Church, training men over the years to be capable knights. "Like soldiers," he said, "we follow orders and are skilled in the modes of defense of the day." He said he had been raised from an orphaned childhood by Benedictine monks, becoming a brother sworn to obedience, chastity, and educated broadly in religion, the arts, and in physical defense, both in Europe and the United States.

"Why did you follow me? Where did you obtain my phone number?"

"I was given a dossier on you and ordered to obtain all the pieces of the copper scroll. I have funds available to purchase the scrolls, but Professor Baxter is in a coma, and Professor Van Dorn is dead. Killed, I assume, by the same group that attacked you in England and who might have killed you here in Paris, except for my skill as a marksman. I believe you have Dr. Baxter's scroll and I am prepared to pay substantially for it."

"Do you have Van Dorn's?" Juda asked, watching his eyes, knowing the scroll was safely with Baxter's in her bank vault.

"His home was destroyed in the fire and he was murdered. I don't have it. It may have been consumed in the flames, or the murderer took it."

If he was lying, he did it well, Juda thought. Then she remembered the dinner at the Moorings, the man in her make-up mirror watching her.

"You were there, in Jersey. You killed Van Dorn." She slid her hand into her purse.

"Yes, I followed you from England, but I didn't kill the professor. I came to Paris after you."

"How did you obtain such a file on me and the scroll? Why do you want them?" Juda's angry suspicions were aroused, but she relaxed her grip on her gun and believed him.

"I only know that the scroll is thought to be necessary to fulfill our mandate of protection." He shrugged, innocently adding, "I'm a worker sworn to obedience, what do I know? We do have many sources of information, and I don't question my authorities, as I have been trained."

"Protecting the Church? What in an old copper scroll could threaten or harm an institution that has withstood the challenges of history for two thousand years?" Juda had no trouble accepting the idea that lust for the treasure of Solomon or even the Ark of the Covenant might move some to murder, but something vague, like protecting the Church bothered her. She remembered Baxter saying that the scroll might bring down the house of God. What had he meant by that, if he had not said it in jest?

"Brother Gervais, if you couldn't buy the scrolls, would you take them anyway? Would you kill for them?"

"Killing is against the laws of Moses, Dr. Bonaparte," Gervais said as a matter of fact, "and I live my life by the law. Would I follow orders that were against my conscience? Would you?"

"And what if Moses was just fable, René, and Abraham? If you've heard Professor Eckstein lecture on the Dead Sea Scrolls, then Jesus himself…" Juda stopped herself, seeing she was taunting him. Why?

"And you, Dr. Bonaparte? You've studied, read their books, worked with a world expert, and heard lectures. Do you believe?"

Juda paused, watching this young man of such striking appearance. "I watch and listen and you didn't answer me. Would you kill to get the copper scrolls?"

"I didn't answer, did I?" He smiled disarmingly again. "I said I would not do anything that was against what is in my heart, my conscience. Would you?"

"No." Juda replied, thinking, No, not now, but I have you, insolent child. But you're a killer, not a child. *Kill him now.* The shot would be muffled and she could walk away. "We have nothing more to talk about, Monsieur Gervais. Don't follow me. I don't need anyone in the shadows with a rifle ready to kill for me. His life would be in danger." Juda stood up, leaving money on the table for the bill. René offered her his hand. "You didn't tell me how you happened to be there in the parking lot."

"Yes, I know." Gervais stood up. "It's been my pleasure, Dr. Bonaparte."

What was that all about, Juda thought, as she entered a taxi, feeling that René Gervais was dangerous. What was it? Something incongruous about him. His dress? Simple, relaxed, as she might expect for a brother away from his monastery. His entire appearance, soft, youthful, innocent, bespoke honesty. Her own discomfort troubled her; she couldn't characterize her feelings – feelings that aroused her anxieties.

That night René Gervais screamed an agonizing animal cry then collapsed into the arms of a prostitute and began to sob. The woman stroking his head against her breast said, "That was the first time for you. I understand."

"But I'm a brother. I've broken my vows."

"We all break promises, *monsieur*," she laughed, still holding him. "One of my men is even a bishop. Don't be afraid. Your secret is safe with me. Like going to confession." He arched his body and touched her face with his hands. "Your hands are soft and gentle, like you. Such eyes, I have never seen." She smiled showing stained, carious teeth as he fondled her breasts. Then her eyes widened in fear as his hands moving upward found her throat.

Juda awoke to the smell of bacon and eggs. She sat up in bed thinking of the strange and erotic dream that had left her, as always, unsatiated. *My guardian never sleeps. Even in my dreams I'm sheltered. No, not sheltered. I protect myself? From what, Dr. LaCroix? Why am I forbidden to have what the young boys have in the moonlight of their passion when they sleep? C'est la vie.* She shrugged and jumped out of bed, naked and beautiful, calling to T.J., "It smells great, I'll be a few minutes." Then she laughed at herself as she stepped into the shower, laughing because the smell of food had displaced her erotic curiosity. *One day you'll be fifty, fat, frigid, and very much alone, and still hungry.* Her thoughts strayed to the young Benedictine monk. She might at least have dreamt of him. She banished the fantasy that was developing and thought instead of her trip to Chicago and the sad memories it conjured up. Toweling herself pink, she said *karma*, then threw on a heavy robe.

"So the guy who popped the men in the parking lot was a priest?" T.J. asked over their breakfast. "Strange. Are you going to give him the scroll?"

"A monk. No! I'll do what Harold asked, but not till I find out more about it and the killers. I don't care about the scrolls T.J., but some people do – religious fanatics and killers – and those who rightfully owned them, the archeologists who found them and whoever owned them before."

"Only Baxter and the American, Wolfe, are alive."

"I want this killer, T.J., but I've got to help Harold first." Juda lit a cigarette, sipped her *café au lait* and stared out the window. "I've got to get going, T.J., breakfast was great," she said without enthusiasm. "Very American."

"I set out your luggage, but didn't give you any weapons, because of the airline securities, except this." He handed her a small fiberglass-reinforced plastic stiletto. "Stick it in your purse. It can't be detected. It was made for the CIA and it works." Juda hefted the weapon and tested its edge, remembering when she had first used a knife such as this murderous piece of plastic. It sent repugnant chills through her, hateful feelings, a paranoia against governments, manipulators, and her own past.

Placing the stiletto in her purse, Juda smiled and said, "Thanks, T.J., I'll keep it. Who knows, it might be useful… for opening letters." Had T.J. watched her eyes he would have seen sadness rather than her smile.

"If I wanted weapons, I could buy anything in the U.S. right on the street, especially in Chicago, but I won't be needing any." She tossed her head back slightly. "You seem to forget I'm a Ph.D., not a secret agent anymore."

"Juda, I'm sure there are people out there who haven't forgotten your past, or who haven't followed your career since then."

"I want you to set up a meeting for me with Harrington Wolfe and the Hickmans before I leave the U.S. These people must also be in great danger over the scroll. Whoever went after Baxter's, Van Dorn's, and McLauglin's pieces is still out there. After I talk with them, I'm off to Israel to join Ben. I'll help him if I can, and I'll learn more about the Dead Sea Scrolls."

"How long will you stay in Israel?"

"Just long enough to help Ben and to get him to come back here to live with us, T.J., and a little time for me to go to the desert. I have an old friend I want to see again."

NEW YORK CITY

Erhardt Boeckerman, chairman and chief executive officer of the world's largest pharmaceutical conglomerate, and now director of the organization known as the Federation of the New World Order, sat in his office at the World Trade Center listening to a telephone report from United States Senator Henry Malcom Graves III. Graves did not know to whom he spoke or to where his call had been routed. A voice scrambler and security devices at both ends prevented any possible detection.

"The Templar has executed two of his tasks, and the first will not survive his illness," Graves said from his study in his Washington home. "He has recovered only one part."

Boeckerman inquired, "Does the woman have them?"

"He's not sure." The senator wiped his brow with a napkin. These calls always made him nervous. "There's something else. Others are after the... the objectives."

"Advise the Frenchman, through his control in Marseilles, to find them and remove them. What about Jerusalem?"

"Proceeding as planned. The city is in chaos."

"Is the engineering in place?"

"Yes, and waiting for your orders. And there's one more thing."

"What is it, Senator?"

"The knight may be a rogue."

"Watch him and replace if necessary."

"And the Jesuit? Will he be able to do the translation."

"He assures me he will, once he has the full scroll."

"We've initiated much that depends on you."

Throughout the following day, Boeckerman personally reported to the eleven members of the ring, placing calls to France, Germany, England, Switzerland, the Soviet Union, Tokyo, Beijing, and Seoul. Three of the calls were in the United States; one went to the White House.

Chapter 13

On the flight to New York, Juda could not sleep. She ordered a drink and opened her purse for a cigarette. In the cluttered recesses she felt the plastic CIA weapon T.J. had given her, the knife so cleverly designed to kill yet be invisible to airline security metal detectors. It reminded her of past horrors: assignments in the Golan Heights with Israeli Special Forces, her first assassination as a Mossad agent when her friend Saul Wiseman died, and her last and most secret, orders to kill that came from the Vatican through a confessional in Notre Dame Cathedral.

She opened her book about the Knights Templar, but the powerful turbines of the Concorde droning hypnotically caused her to lose her focus. The little French volume fell to her lap as her eyes closed. She fell into a phantasmagoric dream, a maelstrom, randomly displaying memories of dead men on a computer screen. She tried to banish them and failed. Then she was a little girl at a private school in Vienna, shy and frightened. Her teacher, a black nun, called her to her desk. Juda knocked over a statue of the Madonna standing on a snake. She saw it twist and slowly tumble to the floor, breaking into many pieces. The snake's head looked up at her. Juda screamed, opened her eyes and looked around, embarrassed that someone might have seen her. She ordered another drink from the stewardess and sat back in the soft gray leather seat. The plane would land at Kennedy in an hour. She thought of René Gervais, the Benedictine killer, but the handsome Arabic face of Shawi Haddad came back from her dream, and the death of Saul Wiseman.

Thinking of the dead terrorist Haddad, a man she had killed but not before his bullets had found Wiseman, Juda realized she had had that same physical awareness in his presence – an erotic magnetism – that she had felt when she met René Gervais; a feeling uncomfortable and very physical.

As the turbines slowed and the flaps went down for descent, she was jolted from her fantasies and thought about her meeting in a few hours with Dr. Richard Grodzinski, the renowned toxicologist. She prayed he would help her save Harold Baxter.

UNIVERSITY OF CHICAGO

Refreshed after the flight from New York, Juda went directly from her room at the Ritz Carlton to Professor Richard Grodzinski's office at the University of Chicago. The appointment had been set up by T.J. Troubble who had briefed the doctor on Harold Baxter's illness and Juda's effort to find an antidote for the unknown poison. The professor was old, with receding gray frizzy hair, a warm smile, and bright keen eyes.

"He's sleeping, Professor Grodzinski," Juda said, enjoying the coffee he offered. "He can't be awakened. A continuously monitored electroencephalogram shows regular REM stages of sleep occurring every ninety minutes, each stage lasting eighteen to twenty-two minutes. Normal sleep architecture, I was told. But he can't wake up, can't feed himself, and requires a catheter." She lowered her eyes. "He's dying." Juda tried to restrain her anxiety as she repeated the history of Harold

Baxter's illness to the toxicologist, but as she spoke she became visibly distressed and cried.

"My tests on the samples Doctor Hastings sent came up with no matches." He shook his head saying he was sorry. "You say they've tried stimulants. Methamphetamine? Ritalin? What about shock treatments and subconvulsive electrical stimulation of the brain?"

"No. Dr. Hastings didn't suggest that. Would it work?"

"It might work if he were in a psychogenic catatonia, but the description strongly suggests brain injury. But where? Not the brain stem as I thought, because of the dream activity. It's very unusual, Dr. Bonaparte. Let me think." He got up from behind his desk and walked to a wall of books, journals, and papers, looking aimlessly, running his fingers through his wiry hair. "You say you smelled something floral from his throat. What was it?"

"I couldn't recognize it."

"That may be the key. I've not been idle; it has vexed my aging brain cells. A poison given orally, possibly intravenously, or through the skin. Our skin is a very special organ, Dr. Bonaparte, it's impervious to most molecules. Dimethyl sulfoxide, however, is absorbed rapidly through it and can be smelled in the breath in a few seconds. A garlic smell, not floral, but it can carry in other substances – even toxins. There are hundreds of poisonous plants and flowers: hyacinth, iris, hydrangea, lily of the valley, mushrooms, the leaf of the rhubarb. Can you imagine a rhubarb pie and an ice cold tonic made from the leaves? A very deadly drink. And Socrates' drink – hemlock. But, I ask, why a vegetable concoction when there are so many deadly toxins that can be injected? Let me think."

What was it about these professors? His office was a mess like Baxter's. He looked as if all he ever did was think. "Think, Doctor, I'm prepared to pay very well for a solution, for your wisdom – for help."

"Solving a puzzle is it's own reward, Dr. Bonaparte, and if it can help someone, all the better. Let me – "

" – Then I'll grant a sum of money to your department, if personal wealth is unimportant to you, but I must have an answer."

"Yes, you can do that," he said offhandedly. "Tell me once more everything about the professor, maybe there's a clue. Don't leave out anything." Juda told him everything she knew about Baxter, the scrolls, and the others. Even about Van Dorn's and McLauglin's death and René Gervais.

"My God, so many dead. We must find the answer, Dr. Bonaparte, before others are killed. Give me your hotel number. I'll call you and we can meet again. First, I must have time to think."

After leaving the professor, Juda went to the library and copied a list of poisonous plants from Casarett and Doull's *Toxicology*. Next she took a taxi to the Field Museum of Natural History and began smelling plants and flowers, trying to remember the scent on Baxter's breath: a complete waste of time. Returning disconsolately to her hotel, Juda took off her clothes and fell into a dreamless sleep. Two hours later she was awakened by the telephone, the professor calling to say he wanted to meet her. He sounded excited; he believed he knew what the poison was. Elated, Juda arranged to meet him for dinner.

At dinner, Grodzinski was barely able to contain himself until he ordered his meal. "I was on to something, Juda," he said, when the waiter left. "I used my computer, wonderful toy, but I could have done it on paper. I made boxes and put in everything we knew: Baxter's condition and symptoms, the scrolls, the murders in Jerusalem, every detail I could remember. Pretty soon I had about a dozen boxes all filled with facts. Then it just about jumped out at me."

"What?" Juda felt his enthusiasm, felt hope.

"Zoroaster, Juda, his religion, and the scrolls. I called a friend, an expert in world religions. Zoroastrians used haoma in their religious rituals and still do, both in Iran and India. And it comes into the Dead Sea Scrolls."

"Haoma?"

"Not haoma, but Zoroaster, in the Manual of Discipline scroll, the Z you mentioned. Smyth, he's the world religion professor I called, said that the teachings and writings of Zoroaster had had profound influences on Judaism and Christianity, though not credited by church fathers. Clearly, the teachings of Zoroaster spread throughout the Middle East from around 500 B.C. There are sects still in Iran, India, and even here in the U.S. That brought me back to the killings in Jerusalem and some weird, religious fanatical group who might want the scroll and be using Zoroaster's cocktails on their victims. It ties in by some loose thread."

"What about the haoma? Is there an antidote?"

The professor shook his head. "I don't know, Juda. It's a hallucinogenic drug derived from a milkweed plant. What Huxley called soma. I thought I had it. It fit Baxter's symptoms. In a large dose it might have killed him, but you saved him. He could have just died in his sleep. Then Smyth burst my bubble. He called me back and said it could be soma."

"But you said they were the same, soma and haoma."

"That's what Huxley and others thought, but they were wrong. Soma is another hallucinogenic drug derived from mushrooms, the amanita muscaria. Same as the Mexicans used. It yields psylocibin, or psylocin when fractionated. It's used even today in Vedic ceremonies. Like haoma, it's part of Hindu religious ritual. Helps worshippers get in touch with their gods through a psychedelic experience. And it's not all that unusual in other religions, primitive ones we would say, to use drugs for mystical or metaphysical purposes. The trouble is both haoma and soma could produce a similar clinical state in overdose, I think."

Juda frowned, understanding that everything the professor said seemed to fit together somehow, but wondering how it could help Baxter. Grodzinski shook his head. He didn't know, but he wasn't finished. He said that the active compound of soma had only recently been found to be psylocin, and that no one knew what the toxic stuff in haoma was. "If I could get some I might... "

"I'll get it," Juda said. "Where will I find it?"

"I don't know. India or Iran, I'd bet. Maybe they used the drug as a truth serum. Scopolamine was used as a truth serum by the Germans in World War II. After that it had a little vogue in obstetrical anesthesia as twilight sleep. And its chemical cousin, belladonna, can be a deadly poison. It was a favorite of the Italians. It dispatched more than one pope over the centuries. Comes from a plant called Deadly Night Shade. Appropriate name." He gave her a wrinkled smile.

Unresponsive, Juda glanced into the past. *I know about scopolamine, Doctor, she thought. Mix it with lorazepam, it works even better. It would surprise you what I've learned about men who kill and how to kill them.*

The old man smiled at this determined woman. "You send me some haoma, I'll find out what's in it, if it's the last thing I do, Juda."

Juda touched his hand, thanking him and warning him to be careful. "People who have known me, Professor, as you now know, have not been good insurance risks."

Three hours later Juda was about to board a plane at O'Hare International Airport when she heard the professor call her name. She had just handed her boarding pass to the attendant.

"Professor, what is it, what's wrong?"

"I tried to catch you at your hotel," he shouted as the attendant asked Juda to board. She glared and said she would be a moment.

"Tell them to give him Rauwolfia," Professor Grodzinski yelled over the crowd. "It reverses the effects of soma, and won't hurt him. If he doesn't wake up, you can bet it's the other."

Crossing the Atlantic Juda tried several times to call Dr. Hastings. Rauwolfia? What was it? From India, a drug made from a tree . . ? She couldn't remember more, but it would work, she knew it. No answer at her apartment. Her heart pounded. Where was T.J.? Dr. Hastings? She called the nursing home in Birmingham again and spoke with a senior registrar who refused to do what Juda wanted.

"Bastard," Juda screamed loudly, startling the other passengers, "I'll do it myself."

Chapter 14

Immediately after landing at Charles de Gaulle Airport, Juda hurried home to change and pack a small bag for her flight to Birmingham. She greeted T.J. and told him she was leaving for England. She wanted him to get into his computer and find material on Rauwolfia. Excited to go to Harold with this drug, she failed to pick up T.J.'s consternation.

He wheeled behind her to the door of her room. "T.J., what's wrong? Oh God… Oh Jesus. When did it happen?" Juda collapsed on the bed in tears.

After Baxter's small funeral, Juda returned to Paris. Three days of listless melancholy was all she could take. "I'm going to my place in Austria," she told T.J., "to collect my thoughts. I have some things I want you to do while I'm there. Then I'm going to Tel Aviv. Get in touch with Benjamin, tell him to expect me in a week and have these ready for me."

T.J. pushed himself away from the computer and faced Juda. "I've got something coming in on the Zoroastrians, Juda. They still maintain a sect in Iran, on Lake Urmia near the Caspian Sea, but the main body is in India. I'll put everything together and you can have a look. You want me to go with you? I can be quiet and out of the way to give you time alone, and be company if you want, have a beer with you." Juda walked over to him and touched his hand.

"Thank you, my friend, but I want to be alone." Juda wouldn't be entirely alone though when she got to Austria. She had retained a couple that had worked at the Bonaparte estate since her childhood. The woman of the couple had been like a mother to her. She said, "I'll enjoy the drive," and smiled warmly at T.J. "I love your van, or should I say armored truck, but the Ferrari is better for my mood."

"I bet you'll tear up the Autobahn. How much will it do?"

"Faster than I drive," Juda lied.

"How fast, Juda?"

"Two hundred and three. That's miles per hour. Here's my list for Ben and one for you, if you have time."

"I ain't goin' no place, and I got all the time in the world for anything you want. Gimme your list." He looked over the list, puckered his lips, and said it should be no trouble. "Who's this Georgi Kirnski?"

"A friend. He's a retired KGB operative, lives on the Caspian. We worked together in Istanbul. You'll find his last phone number in my book. If it's not current, try the CIA with your modem and those access codes you lifted. If you can't find him let me know." Remembering Vatican security, Juda said, "I have another source." She packed as she talked, taking leisure and workout clothing, books, and a small leather case containing her Walther PPK, the silencer, four clips, two boxes of Silvertips, a box of her hand loads, and two stilettos.

"Have a little target practice in mind, Juda?" T.J. asked, examining the case. Removing one of the custom knives, he tested its edge on a finger nail, and whistled. "Christ, who sharpens these?"

Juda smiled, putting the knife back. "I do, on a buffing wheel with jeweler's rouge. I'll show you sometime, but its dangerous." Smiling, she said, "Do you want a shave?"

"This Kirnski, he's in Russia? That sea borders on Iran, don't it? You ain't going there, are you? The Ayatollah will have you for dinner, and a nicer shish kabob I couldn't imagine." T.J. smiled from ear to ear, disregarding Juda's disapproving glance followed by her warm smile.

"I told Professor Grodzinski I would get some haoma. It won't help Harold, T.J., but we may learn something. Reach Kirnski and ask him to call me in Austria, or at Benjamin's. You have the numbers."

"You be careful, Juda, and if you need me…"

Juda kissed him on the cheek. "You be careful, T.J. Remember you have the scrolls, Baxter's notebook, and his computer disks. These people are dangerous."

"After the last time, I'm prepared." He reached into a bag suspended from the right arm of his wheelchair and removed a government-issue Colt .45. "Like your dad's, Juda." He moved back to the computer workstation. "I've worked Baxter's disks backward and forward until I had the computer jitters. A sixteen-digit code is about impossible to break, and I think it's alpha numeric, making it even harder. I'll keep trying, but don't expect much."

Juda took the elevator to the garage and the freshly tuned Ferrari. Her last trip and the killings at Portofino flashed through her mind as she shifted gears through Paris, heading to the Autoroute A4 and the three hundred miles west to Strasbourg. She wondered how her friend Phillippi was after being shot, and for a moment, as her car became a red blur on the highway, she thought she was being followed. Remembering the past, she laughed at her paranoia and tossed her hair back into the wind as she pressed the accelerator to the floor. For a few kilometers, as driver and machine became one, she forgot the pain in her heart at Dr. Baxter's death, unmindful of the forces pulling her to her destiny.

Thrilling to the speed, running from shadows, but in no hurry to arrive, Juda stayed at a small chalet near Munich and enjoyed a sauerbraten supper for which the inn was famous, along with two glasses of German beer. The next day, and at a more leisurely pace through the Austrian Alps, she drove the last leg to Villa Bonaparte, forty miles from Vienna and overlooking the Neusiedler See.

Juda's home, a two-hundred-year-old chateau built in the once fashionable Italian Renaissance style, was a slant-roofed, three-story structure of heavy stone blocks, red tiles and arched windows and doorways. She drove past iron gates emblazoned with the Napoleonic crest onto a long drive, bordered by tall, old oak trees, which curved through well kept grounds. Juda stopped her car and gazed at her home. *Why did I come back, why now?*

The mansion had stood unscathed through two wars which had devastated much of Europe, due as much to the lavish parties thrown for German and Austrian officers and high-ranking Nazis as to its isolation from areas of bombing and combat. She looked past the house to the stable, the garage, and the woods beyond – the dark forest of her childhood fears. Across the lake were the snow-capped, imposing Alps. She remembered the riding trails and Shamir and Tora, and fear. *Oh, Christ, it will never go away.*

For a week Juda exercised daily: swimming, weight training, running, and riding. A strong rider trained in dressage, she preferred the saddle of the Bedouin on the one Arabian still stabled. Though Franke, her excellent cook protested, Juda insisted on simple foods: salads, light soups, grains, freshly made breads, fresh fish with no rich sauces, green tea, all served in the kitchen. Juda ate, as she had done so many times before, with Franke and his wife, Katrina, rather than alone at the long, formal table in the dining room.

She spent hours lying by the pool, neither reading nor sleeping, simply thinking of Harold. At other times, wandering through the pages of her life, despairing over the world, she read from Kahlil Gibran, the Koran, the Tao-te-ching, and the

Bible, finding comfort but not the answers she sought. As a child she had been afraid of walking in the woods, but she could ride Tora there, racing against the taunts of Shamir, afraid of showing fear. Then with the surges of bravery that come when you are nine, she had started to go alone to her secret dreaming place by the lake.

On one ride, while revisiting those childhood places, she reigned up, listening, alert to the sounds of the forest – or lack of them, feeling something different – someone there. Another time, while resting and sunbathing after a long run and an exhausting swim, she saw the glint of a lens (binoculars, camera, or rifle scope) in the woods.

Doubting herself, she snapped her bathing suit top in place. *I'm a Juda, not a child*. She slung a canvas beach bag over her shoulder. The bag held cigarettes, lighter, sunglasses, lotion, and her automatic, the small TPH. Juda walked into the woods. The adult brain looked and listened, the child felt the shadows that hid the wolf and made her afraid. A careful and skilled woman, capable and deadly, examined twigs and leaves, listened for the sounds, and looked. She found nothing, but she felt her child's heart beating beneath her adult breast – a warning. That night after a simple supper in the kitchen with Franke and Katrina, she dreamed of her mother and dreamed she was telling her dream to Dr. LaCroix.

Mother's doctor stood at the doorway and said it was over, Mother was dead. I pushed past him and took her hand. "Mother, it's Juda, I want you to know I'm all right, I'm safe, and I want to say thank you for everything." She came back, opened her eyes and smiled. Again, the doctor said she was gone, and again I called her back. She opened her eyes. It happened three times, Dr. LaCroix. In the dream, the child Juda sat up in the dark of her bedroom, tears in her eyes, but she was not afraid. It was not a bad dream, about mother. It had given me a warm happy feeling, Dr. LaCroix. As she fell into a deep sleep, Juda was still thinking of her analyst, wanting him to listen to her tomorrow.

Every morning Juda took the Volvo wagon to the nearby village for fresh produce, cheese, and meats. Today she changed her ritual. Two kilometers from her driveway she turned onto a small tree-covered lane that led to a fishing dock and the lake. Dressed in dark clothing, wearing her soft leather jacket that covered a suede shoulder holster and her PPK strapped tightly under her left arm, Juda began a fast run back toward her estate, traveling familiar pathways along the rocky edge of the lake. In a sheltered area, she tucked her hair into a dark brown balaclava, smeared dirt on her face, jacked a Silvertip into the chamber of her gun, turned off the safety, eased down the hammer and went back into the woods, slowly and silently working her way back to her chateau. The night before, in the darkness of her room, she had viewed the area with an NVM, night vision monocular, she had taken from the trunk of her car.

She knew where he was hiding.

Silently, crawling through grass and underbrush, scanning the woods with small Zeiss binoculars, she came within a few meters of him. A scoped rifle stood against a tree, its stock, barrel, and scope carefully wrapped in dark muslin. He was sitting with his back to her, head resting on his knees, when Juda pressed the muzzle to his neck. "Don't move." He turned, looking innocently into the gun.

"Hello, Juda," he said with a disarming smile, seemingly unconcerned with the gun a few inches from his face. Trusting eyes looked into hers as if he knew he was safe.

Juda screamed, "Bastard. René Gervais sent you." She spoke through clenched teeth. He was young like Gervais. Spinning on her foot while the other flew around her with awesome speed, she struck him a punishing blow that sent him flying backwards into the bushes. She could easily have killed him, but she turned her foot, checking the impact.

Angrily she told him to get up. Rubbing the side of his head the man asked, "Why did you hurt me, Juda? I could easily have taken you as you crawled through the bushes. If I had wanted, I could have killed you three days ago, just like that. But no, I'm here to protect you, and you kick me into the earth. There are others who would kill you."

"Shut up, and hold your hands behind you." Controlling her fury, Juda tied his hands together with a strong nylon tie, then she picked up his rifle, noticing that he had only a ground sheet and one blanket. "How long have you been here? What did you eat?"

"Food from tins. I buried my waste," he said, making no attempt to struggle. "I have no other weapons, only a Red Cross knife, in my pocket." Juda took the knife, a Victorinox Swiss Army knife, a multipurpose tool, observing how he trembled as she touched him.

"What's wrong with you? I didn't hurt you as I might have."

He hesitated, and said softly, "A woman has never taken a Red Cross knife from my pocket before, never touched me." She nudged him with the gun. "I'm a brother," he explained.

"Take the path to my house, no tricks, or I'll shoot you in the leg. You tell me, as we walk, why you're here, why you shadow me."

"I was ordered to follow you and protect you, even with my life if necessary, and for good reason."

Juda kicked him in the buttocks and screamed, "I'm Juda. No one follows me or protects me. Not you, not René Gervais, not God. *Tu es une merde.*" Juda holstered her weapon as they reached the clearing and started across the lawn. "Over there, by the pool." Her arm flashed and a stiletto appeared. "I'll cut your tie, but run and I'll shoot you. Do you understand?" At the table Juda picked up a portable telephone. Using the intercom she called the kitchen and told Franke to bring sandwiches and wine for two.

"I'm hungry, and you can join me before I kill you. Now tell me why Gervais sent you." She removed her weapon and placed it on the table close to her right hand. The man nervously looked around at the stable, into the woods, and back at the villa.

"They're here. I know it."

"Who? There's no one…"

"I followed you, they followed me. But first it was them. I had much time to think there in the bush. I passed them on the Autobahn and they followed. I know it. A Mercedes, four men, Arabs, I think… " He stopped when Franke approached with a tray of food and a bottle of wine. Though Franke had been with the Bonapartes for almost fifty years and had served Juda since she was a child, he still offered a slight bow with his apology for the food.

"You were not able to do your marketing this morning, Mademoiselle Countess Bonaparte, and therefore," he said with a show of indignation, "there is no Westphalian ham as you prefer." He unfolded a white linen tablecloth, waiting and saying nothing until Juda removed her gun. "A simple Beaujolais Nouveau, I believe, will be appropriate, mademoiselle… "

"Franke, just Juda, please. The tray is perfect, thank you." She smiled warmly, remembering her childhood and the treats in the kitchen Franke and Katrina would prepare for her, and coloring for hours at the kitchen table while Katrina worked. Examining the cheese, Juda said, "That looks like a good Apsberg, Franke. One of my favor – " Juda gasped and screamed "down" as blood erupted from Franke's chest and his body pitched forward across the table. The young brother, Juda's prisoner, fell with chest and abdominal wounds as Juda rolled to the ground and fired at an assailant at the corner of the house shooting with an automatic rifle. She let loose a full clip as she ran a zigzag course to the kitchen. Bullets tore up the grass behind her in a cross-fire. Juda found Katrina sobbing and huddled on the floor.

"They killed my Franke," she sobbed. "I watched it happen from the window. Juda, they're in the house. They cut the telephone."

"Quick, Kati, in here. Lock the door on the inside. Open it for me, no one else. Lie on the floor." Juda pushed her into a scullery off the kitchen as she snapped another clip into her weapon. She was about to step into the hall when she heard a sound outside the door. The door opened, pushed by the barrel of an H and K automatic rifle. Juda hugged the wall as the man let loose a wild burst, spraying the room. From her crouched position, Juda sprang. Grabbing the weapon and tearing it from his hands, she sent him flying across the room, crashing into pots and kitchen utensils, atop the worktable. The man reached for a handgun in his belt – too late. Juda's left arm flashed. The assailant gasped as Juda's knife embedded itself deep in his throat. Carrying his rifle, she ran full speed into the hallway and crashed into a second man coming out of the library. Juda and the cursing Arab went sprawling on the smooth hardwood floors. The man fumbled for his weapon, but Juda, gasping for air, stopped him with a kick to the chin. Then her other foot crashed down on his throat, crushing cartilages, killing him.

Checking the clip in the H and K, Juda raced silently through the house to the front door, the image of Franke before her. A Mercedes sedan was parked in front; an armed driver was standing beside it, his weapon on the roof. Not more than two more, Juda thought. Where? She opened the door, screamed, and pretending to cry, held the rifle by two hands over her head. The man at the car raised a radio transmitter to his mouth, pointing his gun on her. He won't shoot, Juda reasoned. They want me alive. The other man came around the corner of the house shouting in Arabic, "Don't kill her, you fool."

Sabri Youssef! She recognized the ruthless assassin, terrorist, bomber instantly. Juda became a blur, firing at the windows of the car, twisting and rolling as bullets gouged out bits of grass and dirt around her. The man at the car died instantly in a hail of 308 NATO bullets. Her final rounds ripped through the gas tank and the car exploded.

Youssef screamed, "Drop your weapon, Juda, and you'll live. Raise your hands or I'll shoot your legs." He was at least seventy feet away and held a powerful rifle on her. Juda threw down her empty weapon, turned her back to Sabri, and began walking to her house.

"Shoot now, you murdering bastard who kills unarmed women. I am going to attend my wounded housekeeper." She held her automatic against her chest, waiting, listening.

Sabri fired into the ground at her feet and approached her. "Stop, bitch, your legs are next."

Juda stopped, her back to him. "Sabri Youssef, you are too old to shoot well. Why are you here? You prefer to kill unarmed servants and boys rather than innocent Pan Am passengers?" Juda listened, measuring the distance. "I know, Sabri Youssef, I know about you and this Keeftan. Monsters, you will all die, and you now."

Sabri laughed. "I know you have your little gun, Juda Bonaparte. One move and I will cut you in half. Drop it now. Otherwise die… as you prefer."

It was over in a second. In an awesome display of speed and skill, Juda flew through the air, twisting and turning, her gun in her hand, as Sabri shot at her shadow. Sabri Youssef fell to his knees. His weapon dropped from his hands, his right shoulder irreparably smashed as Juda's expanding bullet destroyed joint and muscle. Juda stood over him, her gun aimed at his face.

"Kill me, Juda Bonaparte. I am dishonored."

"No, Youssef, you will die in prison, without a woman, and you will eat garbage and will never kill again." Juda fired.

Surgeons would save his arm but it would be useless, the left elbow fused, the muscles atrophied. "Nor walk well," Juda hissed, wanting to kill him, as her third shot destroyed his right knee. "And they will not take innocent hostages to exchange for a cripple, Sabri Youssef." She turned to the last man at the far end of the chalet. She holstered her weapon as the frightened killer raised his rifle. Juda walked slowly toward him. The trembling man fired three wild shots that hit the ground well in front of Juda. Still shaking, he screamed *shaitan*, devil, and threw down his weapon and began running to the gate, Juda rapidly gaining ground behind him. Before she caught him, he collapsed on the grass sobbing. "Die or live, bastard!" Juda shouted, driving her knee into his back and pulling his head back at a terrible angle.

"Who sent you to kill? Answer or you die." She jerked hard on his head, twisting and stretching the muscles.

"Keeftan," the man cried.

"Where is he?"

"He will kill me. Please."

"Then or now?" Juda hissed through her teeth, pulling harder on his hair, thinking of Franke and wanting to kill him."

"Jerusalem." Juda hit him hard on the side of his head with the flat of her gun, knocking him out, then she ran through the house to Franke. On the way, she yelled to Katrina that it was safe to come out. The bleeding from Franke's chest had stopped with his last heartbeat. Tears of sorrow and rage filled Juda's eyes as she fell on the ground beside him, her head on his chest. Then she turned to the brother, Gervais' man, curled up and holding his abdomen in agonizing pain, his hands covered with blood. He could not live long, Juda knew. Her anger gone for the moment, she touched his hand.

"You're dying," she said, "talk to your God."

Juda sat up, staring into the forest, her eyes taking on a fierce and frightening look. She thought of the two still alive at the front of her estate, Katrina wounded, Franke dead, René Gervais' dead guard, the gun dealer Nadir al-Nadir and his hired killer, Rama Keeftan. Going back inside, she reloaded her weapon and retrieved her knife from the throat of the killer in her kitchen.

Chapter 15

Along with Susan Pepper and Michael George, married and living in Ontario, Father Oudi Yong was among Juda's dearest friends. She looked forward to seeing him again, sharing her sorrow with him after Franke's funeral in Vienna, as she entered Rome's Augustea Restaurant. With its marble floors and pillars and elegant table settings, the restaurant suggested the opulence of the empire. The food would be as Oudi liked, classic Roman. Although she had dined with him in the past on the robust, tomato-rich foods of southern Italy – particularly the pizzas in Naples – this was his favorite.

Juda was dressed conservatively in an off-white Dior ensemble purchased that afternoon in the hotel boutique; she had come to Rome from Austria with only casual clothes. Father Yong, a Korean priest, a hard-nosed realist, was the Pope's private secretary and also director of Vatican security. More than others, he knew the intricate workings of the Vatican, and he was the man who, in the past, Juda had allowed to be her final control when the Pope's life had depended on her skill as a marksman. Yong was a man for whom Juda felt deep respect and a bond of kinship.

"Juda," the priest said as he ate, "there are a number of issues which I've investigated since your call. One, the Templars, we've known about for hundreds of years. At the time they were hunted down, they were the most powerful organization in the world, their wealth coveted by the French king and their power by Rome. Much of their history has been written, sometimes by scholars who were less historians then they were antagonists of the Church."

"I know, I've read the books, or rather some. Popularized accounts, spotty and biased from the start," Juda said, relishing a delicate, fried artichoke flower, remembering *Holy Blood, Holy Grail.*

"Trial documents of the charges against the leaders and reports of their executions are available in the libraries of France and in the Vatican Library," Father Yong said. "Were they true or trumped up? There are documents in St. Peter's Vault which might answer that question, but as you know, they're only accessible by the Pope. He's much too busy to do scholarly research for another doctorate. So there they remain until one day a pope opens wide the door."

"The charges against the Templars were shocking: sexual aberrations, spitting on and otherwise defiling the crucifix, murder and usury. Others. Were they true?"

"No one really knows, Juda. They didn't venerate the cross, that's probably true, except in their knightly garb at the beginning, when their tunics did carry a red cross on a white background. Later they venerated an unusual image, thought to be Christ – possibly John the Baptist, but the image did not include the crucifix. Some thought it was the image on the folded Shroud of Turin."

"Why, didn't they venerate the cross, Oudi?"

"I think it was because the cross was a symbol of Roman imperialism – a Roman punishment, extremely cruel, for those convicted of crimes against the state. The Templars focused on Christ, and possibly His resurrection. They came to view the cross as a symbol of Roman evil."

"After their persecution, or before? It makes sense as coming after, when they might have displaced their anger onto Rome and its symbol of punishment."

"When their castles were raided and other Templars killed, icons of Christ or John the Baptist were found in their places of worship, and symbols suggesting pre-Christian influences, but no crucifixes." Father Yong reached for a cigarette then changed his mind. "You know Juda, the early Church had little tolerance for those who held different Christian beliefs. Sometimes their methods of dealing with those so called heretics were disgraceful and murderous. I was thinking the Gnostics and the Cathars might have hooked up with the Templars in France. Certainly France was fertile soil for heretics in the Middle Ages."

Finishing her meal, Juda asked about René Gervais and the current Templar Organization. Gervais, the self claimed Templar, seemed to her neither knight nor priest. "I thought he might be delusional paranoid, not a Templar knight." Juda did not mention her other feelings.

"Perhaps paranoid, Juda. We know there are those who claim that the Templars are still with us, submerged in other religious groups, living secretly in monasteries under different identities. Historical fiction or real? Did they align themselves with other religious groups, which we know are real and mostly insignificant and bizarre, like the Rosicrucians? I don't know, but Professor d'Angello of the Vatican Museum, a scholar I greatly respect, believes it. Anyway, real or not, this Gervais is after your scroll, and dangerous, you believe."

"He killed three men and said so, without any concern. I think he felt it put me in debt to him. He said he would buy the scroll pieces at any cost."

"Possibly," Oudi Yong said. "The wealth of the Templars was enormous, and it was never found. And that raises the question of the scroll itself. Why does this Gervais want it?

Why Keeftan and Nadir? What could be so valuable about it that it would motivate murder and attempts on your life?"

"The Arabs may be driven by vengeance now. I've insulted them, killed their killers. Me a woman!"

"And a very beautiful woman, if the man side of my priesthood can speak, Juda." Father Yong smiled, sipped his cognac, and lit a cigarette. "But yes, I'm sure from what you've told me, and from what I know of the Arab mind, that they want you. The Arab has great respect for women, but for women in their place, not killing their sons. In ancient Middle Eastern religions, women were often priestesses and goddesses – feared and venerated. So you are in danger. Knowing you, as I do, I'm sure they, too, may be in great danger."

Juda smiled. "As always, you flatter me with your confidence, Oudi."

"You saved the Pope."

Between dessert and coffee, Juda reviewed with Father Yong what was known or speculated about the Templars. If they existed at all, they were no longer sanctioned by the Vatican and might still be a renegade society hostile to Roman Catholicism. Still Christian, they might be after the scroll to use against the Church's organization, or might they want it for another reason? Protection of Christian belief, in some way? Protection of Christians had been, at the start, their mandate.

"Was Baxter convinced that his scroll was written around the time of Christ, Juda?"

Juda paused, thinking. "No, not exactly. I presumed it was, like the others. He never said. But it was written in an ancient language, Aramaic, with some unusual symbols, like Sanskrit." She sipped her cappuccino and lit a cigarette, offering one to Father Yong, who reached for his pack of Camels.

"Thanks, I prefer these when I can get them," he said, lighting the unfiltered cigarette. "Juda, what are you going to do now?"

"I'm going to Tel Aviv to see my father and get what I'll need. Then I'm going to Jerusalem."

"To investigate these murders, the crucifixions?"

"Yes, I promised him I'd help. And I'm going to find out what I can about Baxter's scroll. His friend, Father Legault, was one of the victims and held one part of their copper scroll."

"Wait two days, Juda, I'm going with you."

"Father!" Juda said calmly, but surprised, "I work best alone."

"I know, and I won't interfere. I'll have with me a letter from John Paul that will open doors even you may find hard to open. You will no doubt want to talk with the members of the International Team, and visit the Rockefeller Museum and the École Biblique. There are areas in Jerusalem permanently closed to visitors. I'll get us in. Tomorrow I must present all of this to His Holiness, then I will meet with Professor Carlo d'Angello."

"Why, Oudi?"

"We're involved, Juda. Templars? Secret scrolls? A priest murdered? René Gervais, alleged monk, killer, who knew so much about you, your private phone number, which I alone knew? Whatever the explanations, I suspect we have an enemy in the Vatican." Oudi Yong paused in thought, then he said, "This scroll's secrets, if there are any, may be a threat to the Church, although I doubt this."

"Who is d'Angello?"

"A great scholar, Juda, an archeologist who directs the Vatican Museum and has for fifty years. An advisor to the Pontifical Biblical Commission, at times he reports directly to the Pope with regards to material he suggests be archived in St. Peter's Vault. He, more than anyone, is knowledgeable about the workings of the commission, the International Team in Jerusalem, the scrolls from Qumran and other places. He is old and wizened by a lifetime of study and writings. By last count more than five hundred scholarly papers and dozens of books have come directly from his pen."

Juda, remembering the past and how she had worked alone with drugs, gun, and knife, said resigned, "I'll wait two days, but I would like to meet Professor d'Angello tomorrow. Please arrange it."

The Korean priest smiled. He had expected nothing less from his friend.

Before she went to bed that night, Juda wondered about Oudi Yong's confidence in the stability of his church. It was like an inverted pyramid, beginning as it did with a simple and holy man who said things about man's relationship to his fellow man and to God. She had studied the biblical scholars who had extracted the "Jesus' sayings" from the narrated comments of the four Gospels, tediously laying the writings side by side, line by line. Indeed, Christ's sayings were simple and in many ways like those of other, non-Christian prophets, particularly Buddha and Lao-tze.

And what about the Dead Sea Scrolls, written purportedly by the Essenes, of which sect Jesus may have been a member? They were the only documents in existence written when He lived: documents that the Essenes had considered so valuable that they had hidden them in the natural caves at Qumran, and in some instances, had dug out caves for them themselves. Why? Juda thought. To protect them from the Romans? Why did they not write about Jesus, one of theirs. As Juda closed her eyes she prayed that Father Yong was right in the confidence he had in the Church.

In New York, René Gervais made his final plans to acquire Harrington Wolfe's copper scroll. For three days Gervais or one of his men had observed the movements in Wolfe's heavily guarded Long Island estate. The high fence, security lights, and ground sensors around Wolfe's property would present no insurmountable problems, but the armed private security guards could. Since the deaths of Legault, Baxter, Van Dorn, and the McLaughlins, the Wolfes had added two men outside, armed with handguns and shotguns, and one inside. The guards changed shift every twelve hours, circled the house every fifteen minutes, and reported to the man inside. The long and boring periods of their watch would make the time to strike an hour before the tired men were relieved at midnight. The Wolfes retired regularly at ten, into separate but adjoining bedrooms.

Gervais put down the night vision binoculars with which he had been observing the estate and spoke to his two men, both young monks, both Templars. They had parked their car off the road in the dark shadows of a large oak tree a block away.

"Marcel, you'll take the front guard and Henri the rear." Gervais spoke in English, his voice low and authoritative. "You must be quiet, avoid the alarms and sensors, or we'll fail. I'll enter the rear and take the interior guard before he can activate the central alarm. It's a silent alarm, so you won't know. If you hear anything unexpected from inside or on the street leave immediately. We cannot fight a dozen American policemen."

The rear guard, who had just left his counterpart at the side of the house, stopped and lit a cigarette on the back patio. He stood the shotgun beside him as he rested against a patio table beside the pool. Henri leapt from the shadows, clamped his hand over the guard's nose and mouth and pulled him backwards as he thrust a sharp stiletto into his right kidney area. Before he died, the guard collapsed in shock, falling into the assassin's arms.

Meanwhile Gervais explored the locked patio doors, running a thin magnetic card around the door until he found the alarm sensor. Then he cut a circle of glass near the lock with a diamond cutter and taped the area with duct tape. A sharp blow was all it took, and Gervais was inside and working his way to the front foyer.

The third guard was seated just inside the main entrance, twenty feet from Gervais, his shotgun across his knees, his head nodding. The killer removed his short woolen jacket and wrapped it around the long-barreled twenty-two, silencer attached, that he had withdrawn from a shoulder holster. The guard died silently, a bullet in his head. Gervais went up the stairs into Mrs. Wolfe's room. Silently, on rubber-soled shoes, he walked to the sleeping woman, again wrapped his gun and squeezed the trigger, sending a single shot to her brain. Then he went through the adjoining bathroom into the professor's room.

"Not a sound, Professor Wolfe, just get me your scroll and you'll live."

"Bastard," Wolfe screamed and reached for a gun beneath his pillow as a shot tore into his shoulder. Wolfe howled in pain.

"The scroll, now, and I'll leave."

"My wife… you came from . . ," Wolfe gasped.

"She's unconscious. Get the scroll now and you'll both live."

"Downstairs… locked… " Wolfe began to sweat and tremble.

"Get it now!"

Wolfe groaned and got out of bed. At the bottom of the stairs he saw the dead guard and knew he too would not live.

"I'll give it to you," he stammered, "and money, all I have. I'm wealthy. Don't harm my wife, please, you can have it. You killed Van Dorn and McLaughlin and his wife over a worthless scroll. Why? Why?" In the study he unlocked a closet tripping an alarm. As Wolfe opened the door, Gervais saw the sensor in the door frame. Fifty miles away a warning light began to blink at the alarm service center. A message was sent to the police.

"Here it is, now leave." Gervais smiled as he opened the leather folder and saw the copper scroll. The phone rang.

"Answer it, Dr. Wolfe, give them the code." Wolfe picked up the receiver, but could not speak. "The code word, Dr. Wolfe."

"Hello... I... I... HELP ME!" he blurted hopelessly as a bullet shattered the phone.

"Dr. Wolfe," Gervais said, still smiling, "I lied; your wife is dead." Wolfe let out an agonized gasp. Gervais fired once more.

That night, alone in his room, René Gervais sat on the floor beside his bed, his head on his knees, and cried. He remembered his father, screaming his paranoid accusations again at his mother, waving the gun René had tried to hide from him. Frightened, he had huddled in the corner, a twelve-year-old crying helplessly. Then the deafening sounds of gunfire had filled their farmhouse. He had opened his eyes to see his father crying over his mother's body, and had watched as his father put the barrel into his wine-stinking mouth. Before he squeezed the trigger he had looked wild-eyed at René. The boy had stayed there until the priest had come and taken him to the monastery.

Now he cried because the killings thrilled him.

ST. MAXIMUM-LA STE-BAUME, FRANCE

Marseilles had been a shipping port hundreds of years before the birth of Christ. Through Vieux Port Bay, guarded by the forts of St-Nicholas and St-Jean, fishing boats passed daily, supplying fresh fish to the homes and restaurants of France. Here fishermen's wives invented bouillabaisse, the seafood stew, to use up the oversupply of shellfish, sea bass, conches, and eel, or whatever was left unsold from the day's catch.

From the beaches at St. Tropez, where she sometimes vacationed from Paris's summer heat, Juda would drive to

Marseilles for a night of dining and dancing, or to buy special and illegal supplies when she had needed them in the past. In Marseilles one could buy drugs, weapons, explosives, and contraband of any type in small or wholesale quantities. Organized crime, the French Mafia, and every type of criminal thrived in Marseilles, an exciting but dangerous city. Marseilles was the city depicted in the *French Connection*, though heroin shipments from Turkey had all but stopped since the drug users of the world had been cleverly turned to the white powder from Colombia.

After René Gervais returned from Long Island to his headquarters, a house on the rocky cliffs northeast of Marseilles, he traveled to the nearby town of St-Maximum-la Ste-Baume. Here, in the fourth century, a cathedral had been built to St. Mary Magdalene, Jesus' dearest companion, a woman not liked by the other apostles, especially Peter, as told in the Gnostic gospels. The last of these gospels had come from the scrolls found at Nag Hammadi on the banks of the Nile a year before the discovery at the Dead Sea. Nag Hammadi was where Baxter's young wife had died in a tribal feud while he hunted for a scroll. Blaming himself and God, Baxter became obsessed with the scrolls and their secrets.

The cathedral at St-Maximum had been rebuilt and enlarged many times since its cornerstone was set in the fourth century. It had become, over the years, a great monastery and place for pilgrimages, for in the thirteenth century the skull of Mary Magdalene had been found there and somehow identified. It remains in a bronze reliquary under the floor of the cathedral, a major attraction for pilgrims.

Monks had left the rambling and rickety structure; tourists came. Popes visited when their palaces were being built in nearby Avignon. A town hall and pilgrim's hostelry abutted the church's massive entrance. This adjoining building also held the secret administrative offices of the Knights Templar, its director Fra Jean-Baptiste Sancta Croce.

Across the street, where vendors sold coffee, sandwiches, postcards, film, religious supplies, and trinkets, René Gervais sat in an outdoor cafe. He watched the steady stream of visitors, some with their heads bowed in prayer, others descending happily from tour buses, their Japanese cameras swinging from their necks. From his austere life at La Salette, Gervais had come to realize that religion was very big business.

He finished his coffee and entered the basilica through the large wooden doors, walked past the crudely chipped stone facade and was met by Fra Jean-Baptiste Sancta Croce. "Follow me, Gervais," the old priest said. He led him through a small door to the Cloisters. This treed inner garden was surrounded by empty three-story structures, formerly Monks' cells, and fronted a renovated cultural center. Structurally unstable, the area was closed to visitors. In many places giant timbers had been set in place to support the arches, hallways, and floors above from collapsing.

Gervais followed Sancta Croce through the refectory. They proceeded to a door which the withered old priest unlocked, and began a descent through dark passages and more locked doors to a windowless room deep beneath the structure. Sancta Croce remained silent as he seated himself at a simple oak library table and offered the one remaining chair in the otherwise barren room to Gervais. No sounds could be heard in the room which carried a thick coat of masonry over its stone walls. All corners had been rounded. There was one light hanging from the ceiling. Sancta Croce, old and shrunken, had a narrow wrinkled face that continued into his bald head. He wore a black cassock with a red sash. "You have the scrolls, Gervais, as you were ordered?" His eyes seemed too large for his face, bug-like through thick glasses.

"I have two parts, McLaughlin's and..."

"I don't need to know their names."

"I've killed eleven men. The professors knew nothing. The drug is unpredictable. What was its purpose?"

Sancta Croce bristled. "How dare you ask questions, Gervais."

"You lied. Lagare lied. This is about wealth not the body of Christ. They all referred to a treasure. The Arabs, Nadir and his assassin, Keeftan, are after the scrolls. They believe it will lead to a hidden treasure in Jerusalem. But Lagare said it would show where the body of Christ was buried, somewhere in France? Do you think I believed that? I am not a fool."

Sancta Croce stood up, his face reddened, his eyes glared. "René Gervais, you have failed your training as a Templar. I order you to give me the scrolls you have. You are to return to La Salette immediately, and never leave. Father Lagare was wrong, you are no Templar Knight." Gervais smiled, removed his gun and shot the priest in the abdomen. Sancta Croce fell back on his chair, moaning in pain.

"It's a small bullet, Father, you won't die quickly." Gervais walked behind the priest and clamped his hand over his face, squeezing his cheeks in his powerful grip. "Drink this old man, maybe you will speak the truth before you die." Gervais forced Sancta Croce to swallow the milky contents of a bottle he had taken from his pocket. He looked at his watch and waited. Soon Sancta Croce relaxed as the pain subsided and he drifted into a twilight sleep, but his abdomen became distended, and blood oozed from the tiny hole below his navel.

"Who directs the Templars?" Gervais asked.

Sancta Croce mumbled, "the Senator, the Ring"... His eyes rolled. "The Priory..."

"Who are they?" Gervais screamed.

"Rome." He started to sweat. Vomitus drooled from his mouth. He slumped over in his chair. Gervais tore open his cassock and examined his abdomen. Hard, the wrinkled skin was now stretched taut. Gervais pressed his hand against the flesh to see a small geyser of bright blood expelled through the wound. He knew his questioning was over. His bullet had hit a major artery, probably the aorta. Angry, he held his weapon against the priest's head, said "Old fool," and fired again.

In the Cloister, Gervais examined the old buildings and the large timbers holding the arches. He smiled and picked up a workman's sledge hammer. With powerful strokes he dislodged the supports. The lintels crashed to the ground. As Gervais walked calmly away, he could hear the stones groan in their final struggle to stay together. Like the Holy Roman Church, he thought. As he passed the turnstile into the cultural center, there was a thunderous roar as the entire wing collapsed into the refectory, burying Fra Jean-Baptiste Sancta Croce, director of the Templars, under tons of decaying rubble that was part of the Cathedral of Mary Magdalene.

Chapter 16

When Rama Keeftan, now in his safe house in the Arab town of Hebron south of Jerusalem, heard of the capture of Sabri Youssef by Austrian police and the death of two more of his best men, he went into a rage. Crying and screaming, cursing and smashing, he slapped Shalima, causing her mouth to bleed, when she tried to comfort him. Then he locked himself in his room. On the third day he called for her. "Bring me food and coffee – and Arak. Stay with me." His eyes were dark shadows, fierce, angry, his beard unshaved. After he had eaten he pulled her to him and began screaming and tearing her clothes.

"Wait, Rama, I will remove them," she said, trying to respond. But he hit her again and savagely attacked her. Shalima fought back with fists and feet, ripping Keeftan's clothes and flesh. They fell from the bed to the floor, onto the remains of the food tray which had crashed. Finally, still cursing her, cursing her father, cursing all women, Keeftan, with one final animal cry, convulsed and collapsed against her back, still holding her wrists. Bleeding, dirtied with food, she tore herself from him and crawled for her knife.

"That was not lovemaking," she said, breathing heavily, unsheathing her knife, brandishing the blade in front of his face. "Now my *hammami* will taste your blood."

"Kill me, Shalima. I am a dog." Keeftan turned his head and began to cry, his whole body trembling. Shalima threw down her knife, embraced the child, Keeftan, and began to laugh. "You laugh! Bitch, you laugh at my pain. I fail in every quarter; Sabri is gone, my men dead, and…"

"You are not a dog, my love, but you make love like one. Let me help you find this Bonaparte woman and avenge yourself."

"Sabri was like a father to me. I knew he was too old; now he will die in prison, crippled."

"We all die," she shrugged, "but he will die happy, knowing we have found the woman that shamed him, and we have killed her. I am a woman; I will know her ways." Keeftan, the storm abated, embraced his woman.

"We must find her," Keeftan said, reaching for the telephone. "We lost her in Vienna." By nightfall he had men in Europe watching for her at airports in Paris, Vienna, Berlin, and Rome. Others watched her residence in Paris.

In Rome, the day before they were to leave for Israel, Juda and Oudi Yong met Professor d'Angello. His office in the Vatican was in the same building as the Pontifical Biblical Commission and across a courtyard from the Papal Palace where Oudi Yong lived. Professor d'Angello was near eighty, tall, thin, stooped, his office cluttered and filled with books, charts, and manuscripts. One wall was covered with framed pictures, the largest being an aerial photograph of one of his successful digs, the ancient city of Mehrgarh in the Indus valley. "As old as any in Mesopotamia or Egypt, Dr. Bonaparte. It dates to more than 7000 B.C. – at least as old as Jericho," the Professor said, as Juda examined the pictures. "Mehrgarh challenges the concept of civilization beginning in Mesopotamia. I can't do field work now, but I can still write and do research with the help of the staff the Holy Father provides."

"Are you still working on the proposed new edition of the *Catholic Encyclopedia,* Carlo?" Father Yong asked.

"A much-needed one." His head shook regretfully. "But I'm afraid by the time it's ready for printing it too will want for another. There are so many radicals in the Church today that must have their place. But you are here to ask about the Templars, and this much-coveted scroll. I've done my homework, Oudi. Come, sit over here where we can be comfortable. Excuse the mess of my office, Dr. Bonaparte." The professor removed a stack of books from an old velvet couch. "I'm old and my time too precious to be spent making order for others – except in my work. This is my life and nearly my home." He spoke English with an Italian accent.

"Are they real, Professor? These modern day knights?" Juda asked.

"Yes, I'm convinced they are. But how significant?" he said, shaking his head. "That they continued after the death of their leader and grand master, Jacques de Molay, in 1314, cannot be doubted. They became a cult, and they lost sight of their origins and purpose, coming to hate the Church's administrative hierarchy, the Vatican. They blamed the Vatican for the killing of their leaders, the loss of their wealth and vast holdings of real-estate, and the schism that divided the Christian church into East and West; and they blamed the Vatican for the Reformation, which further split Christians. They sided with heretics, the Cathars, and others."

Remembering the strange alliance between the Masonic order and the criminal organization known as P2, Juda asked if there was a connection between the Templars and these. The professor smiled, saying he knew of that evil marriage of the Italian criminals and some of the leaders of Freemasonry. He said it had been shattered, never to recover, with the death of their grandmaster, the U.S. Ambassador to Italy, after the death of Cardinal Borgese and his sister the Countess Borgese.

Obviously, Father Yong had never revealed the true story of the Borgeses and Juda's involvement.

Juda thought, who would have believed it? She remembered the race through the burning mansion, carrying the wounded Michael, fire and death everywhere.

Carlo d'Angello looked directly at Juda and said, "You're probably not aware of the story, Dr. Bonaparte. The murders and burning of the Borgese mansion did make local news. You're from England, I believe, Birmingham? And that brings me to the scroll which seems to be at the center of this mystery, and to an arena in which I'm most comfortable."

"What about the Masonic Order and the Templars, Professor? Did they connect? You didn't say," Juda pressed her question. The professor hesitated.

"The answer is very difficult, Dr. Bonaparte. Yes and no. At the highest level, the Thirty-Third degree of the Masonic Order in Germany, and possibly France, the answer is possibly yes. No in the United States, where their center is in Charleston, nor in Italy and Portugal. In Scotland, where some Templars may have escaped, an organization known as Templar Freemasonry developed, and in Germany, the Illuminati. At the apex of secret organizations and brotherhoods throughout the world, the closest ties may be between the Templars, the Freemasons, and the Rosicrucians. And there are others. And all this is speculation, of course."

"What motivates them?" Juda asked.

"Mysticism, occultism, religious fanaticism... hermeticism... hatred, paranoia... power. Some suspect devil worship. I don't know." Professor d'Angello smiled and said jokingly it would all be in his book, all thirty volumes of the forthcoming encyclopedia. "The scroll must be the key, Juda."

"What do you mean, Professor?"

"I'm an archeologist. When the International Team was organized under Father Roland de Vaux in Jerusalem, I was in

India dusting and digging. Since then, I'd say the early fifties, I have been director of the Vatican Museum and on the board of the Pontifical Biblical Commission and, in all humility, an advisor to four popes. What the team in Jerusalem did, I knew about it. I even have some representative scrolls here in my museum. And I know there were absconded scrolls, like the one the late Professor Baxter had and the others who were part of his little team. I frankly doubt it will help find the treasure of Solomon. Like the first copper scroll, it's probably the work of… of religious fanatics or worse. We had them in the time of Christ, like we do now. But there may be another explanation, or rather hypothesis, for the copper scroll and its apparent value, one that excites my imagination. Are you familiar with the works of Flavius Josephus?"

"The historian? He chronicled the history of the Jews and Romans while in the service of the Emperor Vespasian," Juda said, adding, her voice trailing off with uncertainty, "I think."

"In a way, Josephus was like Freud, often quoted by those who never read the original work, but I have. Unlike the Dead Sea Scrolls, Josephus does mention Jesus briefly. But more important, he refers to a historian and follower of Jesus, one who wrote down what Jesus said and did, a young Greek student. The document has been referred to as the Jerusalem scroll."

Juda said, "The source, the book of *Q*."

"You're well informed, Dr. Bonaparte. According to Josephus, and some letters that exist, this young scholar was a student of Dionysius, our first saint, a man converted by none other than Saint Paul himself. This student had been sent to Jerusalem to study the new religious and political movements such as the Essenes and Zealots, and may have known Jesus."

Juda frowned. "I thought this book of *Q* was an extrapolation from the books of the Bible, the words of Jesus taken from the narrated comments – not real."

"Biblical scholars have noted great consistencies in the writings of Matthew and Luke. As if they were copied from a common source, hence the book of *Q*, or *Quelle* – German for the source."

"Carlo," Oudi Yong, who had been listening in silence, said, "The book of *Q* has been talked about for two hundred years. It's an academic fantasy. What is this Jerusalem scroll?"

"Yes, a fantasy," Professor d'Angello said, "but imagine if this copper scroll… It's unfathomable. A gospel written by a scholar who followed Him, was there when they crucified Him, when He died on the cross and when He raised himself from the dead. Wrote down everything – a reporter, if you will. The others, Matthew, Mark, and Luke wrote long after the events of Christ's life, forty or more years later, and, as you know, there is uncertainty about John of the Gospels."

"Yes, I know," Oudi said. "It's doubtful that the apostle John and the evangelist John were one and the same."

"Yet… " The professor became excited, short of breath, overwhelmed, "we have no autographs, original documents, or source documents of the New Testament, not a word, not a letter. Oh, God, if this scroll were *Q*, the source, an eyewitness account recorded as the events unfolded, its value would make the treasure of Solomon seem paltry in comparison. Imagine, an actual account of Christ's life by a Greek scholar. Or if, perhaps, it was the source, or Jesus' sayings! As you know, Mark was not an apostle, and Luke and Paul never saw Jesus."

"Professor, could it account for the wanton murders? And wouldn't this presuppose someone knowing about the scroll and its contents before Harold and his friends had translated it?" Juda asked, not able to hide her skepticism. "At the time of his death and Van Dorn's, in their own words, they were not even close to a translation."

"Gervais knew, Juda," Father Yong said. "Have you forgotten? He offered to buy them for the Templars. And the Arabs knew."

Juda was silent, angry at herself. How could Gervais have slipped her mind? Why did he want the scroll?

"Baxter and his friends were wrong," Father Yong said. "Others knew."

When they left Professor d'Angello's, Juda arranged to meet Father Yong at the airport. Her head was reeling with uncertainty as she packed in her room. She called Ben and gave him her arrival time. "Did you get the package I sent and the things I'll need?"

"Clearing them through customs unopened was no easy task, even for Samuel Scharkes." Kerns paused and added, "I… I'm looking forward to seeing you, Juda." Later, she had a call from T.J. Trouble.

"You wouldn't have heard about it yet, Juda, but the last one's murdered. The guy in New York, Harrington Wolfe and his wife and three guards. Looks like the same guy. Same method, head shots with a twenty-two, but he had help. Two outside guards were stabbed to death and the one inside the front door shot with the twenty-two. You gotta be careful, Juda. This guy's got balls, taking on an operation like that with a popgun." Juda hung up the phone, knowing why the killer had chosen a small caliber weapon – for the greater effect of the silencer; but that meant a very skillful marksman. The extraordinary rifle skill of René Gervais in the parking lot came to her mind. He had lied again.

At the airport Juda had drinks with Father Yong before the flight. The priest gripped the arm rests tightly on takeoff, apologizing to Juda that in spite of many flights he was always nervous at first. "I guess it's because I'm not in control," he said with a smile, taking a rather large gulp of scotch as the General

Electric turbines screamed to cruising altitude. By that time, Juda's eyes were closing.

"It's a long flight, Father, I'm going to nap for a while. Call me if you need... " Father Yong covered her with an airline blanket and began to doze off himself. Suddenly, he was awakened, and the other first-class passengers startled, as Juda, jerked from her sleep by a dream, uttered loudly HERETIC. She looked about her, covered her face and laughed.

"You were dreaming, Juda."

"My house was on fire," Juda said, still embarrassed and laughing, as she analyzed her dream. "Do you still burn heretics, Father?"

The priest joined in her humor and said, "Not beautiful dreamers, Juda. Not anymore. Do you want to talk about your dream?"

"Not now, Father," Juda said. "I've had that dream before and worked through it with Dr. LaCroix, though we never finished." Juda closed her eyes, remembering what her analyst had said, *You were having sexual feelings, Juda, that day...*"

"It's that drink you prefer. Pernod, isn't it? Like absinthe?" Father Yong said, his words interrupting her thoughts. "It may be a psychedelic."

"It just tastes like it, Oudi, there's no wormwood. Perhaps I am a heretic."

"Like most Catholics today. Popes write encyclicals; nobody reads them; few believe."

"You mean about birth control and abortion."

"He won't listen to me or to the voices of millions. There's no way. For the Church it's the indelible truth, chiseled on the stone of theology."

"Religious abstractions, Father. The Church is full of them: original sin, the Trinity, the Virgin Birth, the Immaculate Conception, Heaven and Hell, Purgatory. What about Limbo? I haven't heard about it since I was a child... " She stopped and apologized, saying she was speaking like a college student, pressing for an argument.

"What do you believe, Juda?"

She smiled. "I'm not sure what I believe anymore. You might say I'm a recovering Catholic, Father, but I know I'm going to find these killers. I don't care about the scroll or what's on it. I cared about Harold Baxter and, Father, I care about the others, the murdered scientists. So much so, it hurts me inside."

When they landed at Ben-Gurion International Airport, Benjamin Kerns met them with a Mossad car and driver. Juda embraced her father, smiled and said, "I told you I'd come, Ben. Meet Father Yong."

Kerns took the priest's hand in his. "The Pope's personal secretary. Why are you here, Father?" Before Oudi could answer, Kerns turned to Juda. "Are you all right?" He said it eagerly, knowing the full story of the attack at her estate in Austria and the capture of the wounded assassin, Youssef. "We've wanted Sabri for a long time, Juda. I'm sorry they killed Franke. How's Katrina?"

As they cleared immigration, they were observed by a tour guide in the airport, holding a card with a name on it over his head. The young man lowered his card and unobtrusively walked to a telephone.

JERUSALEM

Rama Keeftan listened silently to the phone call from the airport. "She's here, Shalima, as you said, and with her father and a priest. Now we have her."

"Juda has come to find you, Rama, but we have found her."

"No, there are other reasons that bring the spy home."

B'Ann Hickman picked up the telephone in her New York suite. "Have you heard about Wolfe and his wife?" Bill Hickman asked.

"Yes, it's in the papers. I'm so sorry for them and the others. Who would do these horrible things?"

"It's over, B'Ann. We need to take our losses and get out of this brainchild of yours. It's too dangerous."

"I know, Bill, they're all dead. The scrolls are gone and they're dead."

"I'd like you to call Nadir off and get our money back, minus expenses as we agreed. This whole thing sickens me. And you, are you staying in New York? Make sure Gerry is near you at all times and authorize him to get more security for you."

"Bill, you stop worrying. We were just peripheral to this scroll business. Whoever killed the others will have no interest in us. But I'll talk with Gerry. I'm leaving for Palm Beach in the morning. What about you? I miss you."

"It's been only three days. I'll meet you in Florida as soon as I get the boat out."

"Where will you dock it?"

"At Gidos, on the Costa del Sol. I'm going to take it out for a few days, then I'll be home with you. I miss you B."

B'Ann looked at her watch, added eight hours, and called Nadir al-Nadir in Jerusalem.

"Have you found this Bonaparte woman? My husband wants out, Mr. Nadir. It has become much too dangerous."

"We lost her in Austria, but I have my people looking."

"Bill wants the account settled, our money returned minus your expenses, as we agreed, but I must have the scrolls…"

Nadir fought to control his rage. "I'll need one week. Call me."

"Senator," B'Ann said to her mentor, Senator Henry Graves, seated across from her in the Hickman's New York apartment, "that was one very angry man."

"Pressure, B'Ann, properly applied can produce miracles. He'll work all the harder to capture the scrolls." He got up and put his arm around her. "Everything I've prepared you for depends on this."

"Henry, it's something more than the treasure. Tell me."

"Have I ever been other than truthful with you, B? You'll know when you need to know. Now tell me about Bill."

"He'll be taking his boat to a dockyard on the Costa del Sol, at a place called Gidos. Then he'll join me in West Palm Beach."

When the Senator stood to leave, he embraced B'Ann. "Ahead there will be difficulties and pain, my daughter, enough to test the mettle of a first lady. Be strong."

Chapter 17

TEL AVIV

"How long has it been, Juda," Ben asked, "since you've seen our little New York?" Indeed, Tel Aviv was like that: a coastal city crammed with tall gaudy buildings and crowded streets filled with shoppers and cars from every nation. A young and brash city less than a hundred years old on the Mediterranean. Much different than Jerusalem, the five-thousand-year-old capital fifty miles southeast. Juda asked if they were going to the not-so-secret Mossad headquarters near Netanya. Ben laughed. The sheltered, unmarked building nestled deep in the hills where Juda had trained years ago was well known to citizens as well as terrorists.

"We know where the terrorists are, Juda, in towns such as Bethlehem, Jericho, and Hebron; and," Ben gestured with a shrug, "they know where we are. Secrecy is a game we play. Some hide in the caves and cliffs along the Dead Sea and others in Jordan, right under King Hussein's nose. But he's too busy with his young and very beautiful American wife to give attention to murderers of children who hide in his land, and these are the hardest for us to catch. The cave people easily hide from our planes and patrols." As they turned on Ben Yehuda Street and drove through the old city of Jaffa, Ben said he was taking them to his house for the night.

The ancient city of Jaffa, with its marina and great Egyptian pier, was an island, a preserved tourist attraction, surrounded by Tel Aviv. Weaving through the narrow shop-lined streets, Juda removed her makeup mirror from her purse. This gunmetal instrument had been made to her specifications by Borman's of Paris. The optical lens gave her a perfect view of the road behind them, and the car following them. Juda read the license plate appearing in the reflected image and jotted it down.

"There's a young Arab in a Volvo following us, Ben."

"Like Mossad headquarters, where I live is no secret, Juda. Could you see the plate?" As they headed south to Bat Yam the car turned off. A few blocks ahead, the terrorist stopped the Volvo in front of a public telephone and called a number in Hebron. He told Rama Keeftan that Juda was in Tel Aviv, heading toward the house of Benjamin Kerns.

Keeftan's dark eyes flashed with excitement. "She's staying with her *bayak*, General Kerns. The spy has come home and now I will have her. Get the Syffer. I must make plans."

Tunnous Manni, the man known as the Syffer by all terrorist groups, came in, bowed his head slightly and said, "Salaam, Abu Keeftan."

"Tunnous, make plans to take Benjamin Kerns."

At his guarded house Kerns said to Oudi Yong, "This is my house, Father. Everyone in Israel lives in apartments, but I have a piece of the desert I fought over for forty years. I have nice high walls and iron bars on my windows," he said sarcastically. "It is more a prison. It's small and there's no grass to cut. In Israel grass is a luxury that few but the richest Arabs can afford. But I have a Jaffa orange tree that bears fruit and some miserable olives trees that would be better made into a nativity scene like they sell to tourists in Bethlehem. And I have protection." He pointed to the Mossad agents, on alert by the presence of

Samuel Scharkes who waited inside. "A prison for my retirement, yes?" Kerns managed a smile. "Best of all, I have the sea."

In the mornings, Kerns would walk on the beach with his memories. What had the Jewish people won in five bloody wars in his lifetime? A desert waste land, the great land bridge between Africa, Asia, and Europe – a narrow strip of land fought over by Assyrians, Babylonians, Egyptians, and Turks that gave access to the markets of the East and West, and useless now in the age of the airplanes and great ships. But, after all, it was the promised land – the promise, God's best-kept secret.

Here on the beach he would rest on a bench placed there by his guards and would light a doctor-forbidden cigar and think of the Countess Bonaparte, Juda's mother, and Juda, a daughter he had barely known when he brought her from Paris and trained her to serve Israel. And at times, he would think of Shamir's mother, his first woman, the beautiful and fair Druze who died by her own hand rather than live with the dishonor of being ravaged by Jewish soldiers. And he refused to remember how he killed those drunken boys, his soldiers, with his hands and gun and knife, nor would he remember his son, Raol Shamir, his bad seed, who had died against his blade.

But now, General Benjamin Kerns was happy. He was back to work and Juda was with him. He introduced Father Yong to Samuel Scharkes, the American Jew and director of Mossad.

"What does the Pope's secretary have to do in Israel, Father Yong?" Scharkes asked, taking his hand. "The Pope's trip has been canceled due to the unrest in Jerusalem." Scharkes was flawlessly dressed, his English a perfect Harvard diction, his manner, as always, repulsive to Juda and Ben.

"Religious unrest, Mr. Scharkes, has always prodded Rome. I'm here to assist in the investigation of the scroll and the murders of the religious leaders in Jerusalem."

"We've made many mistakes over these Dead Sea Scrolls, Father. Soon we may find a way to get them out of the hands of the Dominicans and into the Shrine of the Book where they belong," Scharkes remarked.

"It's true, many great Jewish scholars have been excluded from their rightful study of the Dead Sea Scrolls."

"When people are afraid they hide or fight," Juda said. "From the very beginning, Jews and Christians have been afraid of the scrolls and what they would reveal."

"And this scroll, the illegally acquired Baxter scroll, has stimulated murder, Juda. And possibly more, if the assassinations in Jerusalem are connected. That would be treason."

Kerns laughed. "Samuel, treason is a way of life in Israel. We have Arabs who are Sunni, Shiite, and Christian. Jews who are religious fanatics, moderates, even Christian and Islamic. We can't even agree on a definition of a Jew. At least the Arabs do that. The country is thick with political, religious, and racial hatred, and that's the way it'll be through all of our combined lifetimes."

As Kern's newest housekeeper served them Turkish coffee, Arabic pastries, and cubes of pistachio-dotted *hulva*, Scharkes said that skepticism and theory would not help Jerusalem. "It's about to explode into riots. I can't even quiet the Jews who are being egged on by the fanatical Hasidim. There will be blood at the Western Wall, and American, I'm afraid. And with that, half our tourism economy."

"Have you found anything in your investigations, Samuel?" Juda asked.

"I have a hundred men working on these killings and have nothing. Not a damned thing. What do you think you can do, Juda, that my entire staff has not already done?"

"Juda knows the Arabs, Samuel. More than any of us," Ben said.

"Have you any lead on the drug which was used, this haoma?"

"We can't grow milkweed in this country, Juda. That's what we think it's made of. Oh, a few plants in our horticultural centers. You already know we think it comes from Iran."

"What about the Z, the Zoroastrians?"

"Juda, we don't have any Zoroastrians in Israel now," Scharkes interrupted. He sounded annoyed. "Every other church but no Zoroastrians above ground. Secret sects, maybe, but we'd know it. And none in Lebanon, Syria, Jordan, or Turkey. One small congregation in Cairo, that's all. The main body still resides in Iran at Urmia, where Zoroaster was born. Right now, we're trying to persuade our American friends to get us satellite photographs of their site."

Before they retired, Ben told Juda that he would be working out of Mossad headquarters during this crisis and that he would provide her with a car and driver, radio, and everything she needed. "You'll find your package in your room, but you won't be needing those things." He added, "Juda, I want you to be very careful. Wars and crises are a way of life in Israel, and if we can't solve them, we go on pretending they don't exist."

"Or fence them in with barbed wire and land mines."

"West Bank. I know. A bad mistake."

"I want to visit a kibbutz, just to see how they live now. It seems like they're prisoners. Are the land mines to keep the Arabs out or the Jews in?"

"Now? I'm not sure. Ask Yitzak." Kerns put his hands on Juda's shoulders. "I'll get you a pass for anyplace in this country, but I want you to be careful. Being a pilgrim on a tour bus is one thing, a beautiful spy alone is another. We have a lot of crazies here, and, well, I want to spend time with you. If I could say the truth, I'm sick of it, and in spite of my grumbling, I liked Paris."

"Me too, Ben." She kissed her father goodnight. In her room, after some vigorous exercises and a shower, she opened the box. Her equipment, carefully packed in a leather case, was all there: gun, silencer, hand loads, hollow points, extra magazines, two knives, the shoulder holster, drugs, and syringes. Nice traveling companions, she thought, but not for me. Then she laughed at the thought that she was like a virtuous college student who carries condoms in her purse just in case she should slip. She remembered more than once putting a child's red rubber balloon on the muzzle of her gun where it acted effectively as a makeshift silencer and laughed again at the obscene imagery of the dangling balloon.

COSTA DEL SOL, SPAIN

The man in the small fishing boat cut the outboard motor and drifted. Indifferently, he baited a hook with a worm and dropped it over the side. It was warm and sunny. The skies blue. Behind him at the harbor known as Gidos, people were eating and drinking. Young, attractive people, tourists from France and Italy, and the United States, eating paella and drinking cool sangria. The dockyard was full of magnificent ships, yachts from all over Europe. Some, like the one he watched, were capable of transoceanic trips. He reached into a small bag and removed his binoculars. He scanned the shoreline then turned his attention to the ship at anchor in the Mediterranean, now less than a quarter mile from him. This was the largest of those that had docked at Gidos. A beautiful ship that required a crew of eight. Maybe a hundred-footer, he thought, and guessed how much it was worth.

On board they were having a party. After all, that was why these ships were made. He had seen their mahogany bars, their beautiful staterooms and polished brass. And now he could see the people: rich young women, girls, debutantes swimming bare-breasted in the pool, men, much older, with drinks in their hands, dressed in navy blue blazers and white slacks, one younger than the others wearing the gold-braided cap of the captain, Bill Hickman. He reeled in his line, started his motor, and went to shore. He walked to a beach bar and ordered a local beer and a hamburger. He was served a small order of deep-fried calamari, which he didn't touch; he hated those chewy sea things. What were they? He ate the hamburger with his second bottle of beer and wished they had been a Bud and a Big Mac. He sighed. That night he went fishing again.

    The large ship was still at anchor. The party had escalated. Bill Hickman, host, was enjoying himself. He had little concern for world conflicts, or B'Ann Hickman's obsessions with religion and the scroll. He indulged her whims and enjoyed doing so, as much as he enjoyed the luxury of entertaining his friends and the beautiful girls swimming in his pool, drinking his perfect martinis, eating beluga caviar by the ivory spoonful. He sipped a drink as a dripping wet eighteen-year-old pressed her body against him. The giggling girl whispered something in French. Hickman smiled and said nothing. The girl laughed again.

    The man in the boat drifted closer. A beautiful ship, he thought, as he looked through his powerful binoculars. How long had he worked for the Hickmans? Really, Mrs. Hickman. Someday he'd get her in the sack. Hardly, her being a goddess. He saw Bill Hickman gaze out into the darkness. The night sky, earlier riddled with stars, was cloud covered now. He was an invisible man, as he had always been: the silent one in Nam where he excelled at placing land mines and demolitions. Hickman seemed to stare directly at him. Gerry put down the glasses and picked up a small transmitter, extending its little antenna. Still he watched the girls and drifted closer. He pressed the button and there was light, and heat, and a terrible sound.

On the boat Bill Hickman felt the heat, heard the sound, then nothingness. The man in the boat watched as the great ship belched into a blinding white and red fireball. Flames shot up from the stern of the ship where the large fuel tanks were kept, where the night before he had carefully placed three kilograms of explosive and the receiver that detonated the plastique. The sound of the exploding fuel tanks shook his boat. Then the waves came. Big waves. Gerry Spenser dropped the small radio transmitter into the sea. He felt his heart pounding. Too close, he thought. Oh, Christ! Frantically, he tried to start the engine, but was engulfed by water as a wave from the sinking ship swamped him and his little fishing boat sank. He treaded water and looked back to the place where the large ship had been. Then he looked to shore. So far, he thought, as the last wave came.

WEST PALM BEACH

Where the old established rich of America had built their summer estates – people like the Kennedys and Colemans – and where the newcomers, young and brash, like the Trumps and the Hickmans, had come to make their statements with larger, gaudier sprawling mansions. B'Ann Hickman, seated at her desk in the blue room, her private study, received the news of a terrible boating accident that had killed her husband and twelve others. With regal equanimity she stood up, walked to the window, and stared across the Atlantic as if to see the Mediterranean where Bill had died. She would miss him, but her work would go on. That soon she would be the world's wealthiest woman barely crossed her mind. Money was only a necessary means to her end: an end that would leave her imprint on a world she genuinely believed was heading for Armageddon, the final battle between the forces of good and evil. Senator Graves had programmed her for this from childhood, when he adopted her after the death of her father.

B'Ann returned to her desk and opened a blue leather-bound phone book. She had to inform the others of the tragedy. And they would come to comfort her: her people, the leaders of the Federation of the New World Order. She would never know that their vassal, her mentor, had arranged the accident. For a moment she thought of her bodyguard, the handsome and stupidly infatuated Gerry Spenser, lost at sea. She would need another very soon.

Chapter 18

Perched three thousand feet above sea level on hills and valleys stood the ancient city of Jerusalem. Halfway between the Dead Sea and the modern city of Tel Aviv, Jerusalem was already an old city, occupied by the Canaanites, when David conquered it three thousand years ago. Surrounded by the Judaean desert, watered by the Gihon Spring in the Kidron vallaey, it had been ravaged many times over the centuries: Hebrews, Assyrians, Babylonians, Persians, Macedonians, and Romans all had had their way with the city, each leaving their carnage and destruction; and all before the birth of Christ. But with Christianity wars did not stop: Syrians, Arabs and crusaders, each had their turns at destroying the city and killing the citizens. Finally the Turks made the Middle East part of the Ottoman Empire, which lasted five hundred years – until the end of World War I, when Jerusalem was occupied by the British.

Yet, to the Jews, this city was part of their promised land, a land bequeathed to Abraham's heirs by God after the exodus from Egypt. It was the place where Abraham would have sacrificed his son as God had commanded, the land he came to after he left Mesopotamia, and the land Jacob's family and people returned to after Moses led his people out of Egypt across the Sinai.

The Jerusalem in which Juda awoke the next morning had remained throughout the centuries a sacred place for the world's three great religions – Christianity, Islam, and Judaism – and a place of eternal conflict.

In Jerusalem Jews congregated and worshipped at the only remaining part of the first temple, the Western Wall, and Christians walked the Via Dolorosa and prayed the final stations of the cross in the Church of the Holy Sepulcher. And here, more than in any other city, Palestinians carried on their war against the Jews for the conquest of their city, their land. But whose city was it? David had taken it from the Jebusites, and the Romans had taken it by rampage and had renamed it Palestine to honor the Philistines, who had battled the Canaanites for the land.

For Juda, gazing at the golden city from her suite in the King David, Jerusalem was everything promised by God and the unexpected conflict and eternal warfare born with the promulgation of every religion. That was the great paradox of religious history – God's work and perpetual bloodshed in God's name.

Even this very day, as she found her way to the house where Delbert Markham lived in the Arab district of Jerusalem, people were killing each other in other parts of the city over their religious fears. The names Abraham, Jesus, and Mohammed had been hung over the head of another crucified victim, this time a prelate of the Eastern church. The victim had been drugged, as the previous victims had been, with the strange hallucinogenic haoma. And the *Z* was carved into the forehead of the victim. True, haoma was the drug of the Persian religion that had swept through the Middle East five hundred years before Christ, but where did it come from now? The questions clouded and confused Juda's mind. On the people it was to cause anxiety, fear, and fighting. In spite of Ben's protests, Samuel Scharkes had ordered two hundred more soldiers to protect the citizens and tourists, and maintain peace. As Juda knocked on Professor Markham's door, she thought, perhaps that's what they wanted with the crucifixions and the Z – confusion and fear.

"Come, strange… Baxter's… friend here." Juda frowned, remembering her call, his one word answers. As she entered the dark apartment she understood. The professor was sitting in a chair, a light lap-scarf over his legs. Beside his chair stood an aluminum frame, a walker. His right arm was contracted against his chest. His mouth sagged. He gestured to a seat near him as he managed a one-sided smile. "Friend mine, Harold's. Understand, me well, bad talk, speak."

"You can understand me, but cannot speak well. You've had a stroke? Can you write?"

"Yes," he smiled, "and no. Left hand." He gestured with his one good hand, indicating he had been right handed.

Juda offered her hand, smiled, and said, "We'll make out, Professor. Listen to me. Harold is dead, did you know?" He nodded, dropped his eyelids, shook his head. Juda continued, "He was murdered with a drug that may have been haoma. He and his friends were working on a copper scroll." The professor became animated, tried to speak. It seemed almost painful as he tried to say what he wanted, knowing his words, not able to say them.

"You know about the scroll?" she asked.

He struggled to get up, waving Juda off when she tried to help him. Taking his walker, he went to a desk and turned on a computer. While it was booting-up, he found a chair. With his left hand on the mouse, he scrolled down and opened a file labeled 'Harold.' At the top of the document, he slowly typed with one finger:

Harold said you were his friend, and I could trust you. Over the years we wrote and talked. I helped him with the scroll, and I worked with Jean until his death. What follows is a summary of our correspondence. It is for you, Doctor Bonaparte – Juda. As he typed the last word, he turned to Juda and managed another crooked smile. Then he moved the mouse again and a noisy dot matrix printed his work. He folded it and gave it to Juda.

For the rest of the morning they talked, Juda making notes, gradually learning to understand his expressive difficulties. He told her he had been at Qumran when the others descended into the cave they had discovered. McLaughlin had fallen through an opening into a cave below after they had rolled back a large stone. It was there that they had found the scroll. On top of the cliff where they had made a camp, they had formulated their plans to hide it. Jean Legault had kept it hidden until he finally took it out of Israel. After they divided it, Professor Markham helped with historical research.

"Do you believe the scroll would reveal where the treasure of Solomon was?" The professor laughed.

"Gone, treasure gold. No! Christ… Jesus, yes." Then he struggled to get up and make tea. Juda told him she would do it. Her tone was firm but friendly.

"You think it was about Christ?" she said, waiting for the water to boil. "Harold often alluded to it being something religious."

The professor said he believed the *Testimonium Flavium* had been part of the scroll. Juda strained to remember. It was the second time in three days that the Jewish historian, Flavius Josephus, had been referred to: first by Professor d'Angello and now by Delbert Markham. Markham smiled and slowly explained that the Flavian testimony had been thought fraudulent by all scholars. It was a small paragraph that might have been inserted into his history by early Christians to add credibility to the biblical account of Christ. As late as the seventeenth century, none other than Voltaire had asserted that it was false, a Catholic fabrication and not from the hand of

Flavius. What Markham said, and only with great difficulty, and what Professor d'Angello had hinted at, was that the Baxter scroll might be a true account of Christ, one that might have been scribed when He lived and died, and one that contained the quote attributed to Flavius.

The Professor seemed tired. Preparing to leave, Juda offered him her hand and her thanks. He smiled and asked her to come back tomorrow. Before she left she asked him if he could translate the scroll if he had it. He shook his head, managing another smile, saying that Baxter had been the foremost expert and if he had not been able to do it, no one ever would.

In her car Juda told her driver, a Mossad agent, to take her to the library at École Biblique. The École was in the Arab district of Jerusalem, outside the Old City. Most of the Dead Sea scholars who had formed the strong core of the International Team under Father Roland de Vaux were Dominicans, and had come from the École, but they had soon moved to the nearby Rockefeller Museum. Juda had two hours before she was to meet Ben and Father Yong for dinner. She would then know more about this Flavius Josephus and his fraudulent quote. Two car lengths behind, driving a rented car, wearing sand colored, casual clothing and dark sunglasses, René Gervais followed her to the École Biblique.

When she left the library with a copy of the faked passage, like the scholars before her, Juda was satisfied that it had been inserted into Flavius's writings. Flavius had been a Jew, active in the revolt against Rome, who survived by joining the Roman general, Vespasian, as a historian. He wrote descriptively, and would not have written of Jesus, "He was Christ," as found in his book, for those were the words of Christians. As her driver took her back to the King David, Juda pondered the scroll. For the scroll was at the center; it moved the scholars; obsessed Harold Baxter; was coveted by René Gervais; and had driven Keeftan and Nadir to murder.

Derekh Shkhem street was filled with cars, busses, and old taxicabs, waiting to take itinerant Arab workers from Jerusalem to their towns and villages. As Juda's driver turned on Sultan Suleiman outside the Damascus Gate, the car was stopped by mobs of Arabs. A young Arab was urging the crowd of workers to enter the Old City and march to the Church of the Holy Sepulcher. The Arabs were chanting *Allah-u Akbar*, screaming curses at Jews and Christians, threatening to destroy their church and spray-paint the Western Wall for the damage done to their Dome of the Rock. They crowded around Juda's car and began rocking the Fiat dangerously. Rodriguez, the driver, withdrew his weapon from under the seat, a short barreled Uzi.

"Put that back," Juda ordered.

"Your father said I must protect you with my life. These Arabs think you're a Christian-American, and they have no doubt about me." An Arab boy jumped on the hood of the car and saw the weapon.

"He's a Jew, come to kill us," he shouted in Arabic. They continued to shake the car, which was in danger of being tipped, as Rodriguez tried to back-up. The leader continued to rouse the mob, as the now frightened youngster was shaken off the car. The mob roared and moved forward. Juda commanded Rodriguez to stop. She got out and knelt over the boy. He was conscious, but his head was bleeding profusely. She picked him up and tore a head scarf from an Arab to dress the wound and stop the bleeding. Pushing and shoving her way through the screaming crowd, pummeled and hit, clothing torn, she gained the steps outside the Damascus gate and climbed a platform with the boy in her arms.

"My father was a Jew, my mother a Christian," she shouted above the noise of the crowd. "My teacher was Sheik Ali Hashim. I am one of you." Her Arabic was perfect. The crowd listened as she chanted an Islamic prayer. "The Prophet himself granted peace and respect to Christians and Jews, and their churches. He honored Christ and Abraham. You are not Shiites. This place you would destroy is older than Islam. These killings and desecrations are not by Jews or Christians," she said, lowering her voice as they began to listen. "They are by godless men who manipulate you and frighten you with murder for the power they seek. *Allah-u Akbar, Allah-u Akbar,*" then "*Allah kebst,* God is good," and "Your god is God."

The crowd became silent. First the women began to back away, frightened by Juda's power over their men. "It's Ramadan. You're hungry and thirsty. Go home and pray with your families. Leave these murderers to the police and to their punishment by Allah." Her voice was strong, her words persuasive. A block away René Gervais watched in amazement as Juda moved the crowd. Watched as they began to disperse, listening to her words, her prayers. For Gervais, at that moment, the most important thing in his world was not the scroll. He would possess the woman.

At the hotel Juda threw herself on the bed, drained from the day. In a few hours she would meet Ben and Father Yong, who had left a message that he was bringing Father Jerome Legault with him, the brother of Baxter's friend Jean. As she fell asleep, Juda thought of Dr. LaCroix hanging in Shamir's prison like the crucified priest Father Jean Legault.

Southwest of Jerusalem in the ancient Arab city of Hebron, the city of Abraham, Abu Keeftan completed his plans for the capture of Benjamin Kerns. "He must be taken alive, Shalima, if we are to draw this woman to our camp."

"We will lose men, Rama. He travels with a Mossad guard."

"Tunnous, you will take twelve, and my woman. I will be in Jerusalem, but I will join you. There must be no mistakes. Where will you do this?"

Tunnous Mani, The Syffer, Keeftan's first officer, a handsome man of twenty-five, pointed to an area on a detailed, topographic map of Israel. "Here, Abu, where the road from Jerusalem cuts through this pass. We'll take the security guards in their cars with our rockets. Then we'll have the great general."

"Bring him to Al Khali. Have great care, he's no fool."

When Tunnous left, Shalima wrapped her arms around Keeftan. "What will you do when you have this beautiful woman who obsesses you, Rama? Will you make love to her, or kill her?"

Keeftan laughed. "Both."

"And then?"

"Nadir will taste my bullet after we have the scrolls. Then we'll buy a palace in Africa, or some small country, and you will be a princess."

"We'll leave?"

"It is over here, we've lost. The Jews will make peace with the Arabs, yet one thing preys on my mind. Jerusalem is out of control and it's not from any of us."

Chapter 19

WHEN Juda entered the dining room at the King David Hotel she was not the disheveled, bloodstained woman who had earlier that day crossed the lobby. Dressed in a simple black silk sheath, wearing gold earrings of the star of David that glistened beneath her hair, the color of desert sand, falling softly to her shoulders, she commanded a different kind of attention as she walked across the room to her table where Ben, Father Yong, and their guest were seated. She extended her hand and offered a smile to the tall, slender priest who stood up with the others. "Father Legault, I'm Juda Bonaparte." Then she embraced her father.

Ben wrapped his arms around Juda. "That was a dumb thing you did today. Are you O.K.?"

"I'm fine. You're sounding more like a father all the time and I like it. I hope you're hungry. I haven't eaten all day."

"Yes, I'm hungry, but I'm worried about you. Jerusalem is about to explode. People have been killed, and churches desecrated. Mossad believes these riots are being set-up by some Palestinian group, and Scharkes wants even more troops in here. I can't be with you, so I'm giving you another man for your car and I want you to be extra careful."

"I was in the library at the École today. I found something exciting while I was reading about Josephus, Ben." Juda reached into her purse and removed a folded paper. "It's a photocopy of a painting." She handed it to her father.

Ben whistled, holding back an expletive. It was a copy of a thirteenth century painting of a crucified man, naked, hanging from a tree, ropes strung through holes in his wrists. Strewn on the ground was a suit of armor emblazoned with a red cross. Beneath the picture were the words, Assassin Crucifixion.

"It ties these murders in Jerusalem to the Templars and the Assassins, Juda. What Professor d'Angello told us," Father Yong said, looking at the picture.

"If I go back to Scharkes with this, he'll go nuts, looking for Templar knights and Arab Assassins from the middle ages. We've got enough trouble with Palestinian terrorists." For a few moments a heavy cloud of silence settled on the small group as each tried to articulate the significance of the picture.

"They're imitating the method of the Assassins even with drugs – though from what I've read, the Assassins used hashish on themselves before their killings. Does it mean that some fanatic Arab or even Israeli group is behind these crucifixions, or is that just what they want us to believe? Like the 'Z', it may be intentionally misleading," Juda said.

"Why mislead, Juda?" Father Yong said. "It does, I see that, but I can't see why."

"I asked myself that, then I examined my feelings. Confusion, uncertainty, a sense of impending dread, that's what I found in here." Juda gestured toward her heart. "Anxiety causes mistakes, forces behaviors that we hope will reduce the anxiety. Like that near riot at the church today, it makes us want to run – escape. I've spent a lot of my life examining these things, my feelings and my unconsciously driven actions. I think these Assassins, if that's what they are, want to generate anxiety that leads to more mistakes, and ultimately to chaos and panic. The great religions have been the stabilizing force in Jerusalem, and now they're being disrupted."

"My God, Juda," Father Legault said, "You may be right. It was always political, now it's religious, and somehow it leads back to the copper scroll."

During the meal, Father Legault said that after Jean was killed, and Baxter said he was coming to Jerusalem, he had gone through his brother's office at the Rockefeller and his rooms at the monastery beside the Church of the Holy Sepulcher, looking for the copper scroll. "I knew Jean had it and worked on it regularly, but he was secretive, even with me, about the copper scroll. It's gone, or very well hidden. Maybe it should remain lost. I don't believe in curses, but many have died over it." He did not mention that he had helped Father Scantland secretly photograph it years ago because he had come to regret it.

"There are no curses, Father," Ben said, "Just some evil bas… men, after this scroll for whatever it is or what it'll reveal. Maybe the same ones that are murdering priests and rabbis, and raising hell with our citizens. Probably money. I'm skeptical about higher motives. I think this stash of Solomon is a fantasy anyway. But they have some game plan we can't see."

"Ever since the Dead Sea Scrolls were found, they've generated much of that, Ben," Oudi Yong said, his glass of wine in his hand. "Fantasy I mean. After all the years, the scholars haven't made up their minds who wrote them. Essenes, Sadducces, or Pharisees? Are they pre-Christian, Christian, late Hebrew, or pre-Rabbinic? The latest from the Jewish scholars is that they're Hebrew, and messianic, predicting a messiah who would lead them against the Romans. And this Australian woman, I forgot her name, has an entirely new theory and time frame."

"Barbara Thierer," Juda said.

"The messiah didn't come, Father, not ours," Ben said. "It was our guns and blood that got us this bedeviled promised land. And what's here? Water? Oil? We've looked. It's a desert.

The Jewish people got tired of waiting and became their own messiah." Ben turned to Juda and asked her what were her plans for tomorrow.

"I'm going back to Professor Markham's because he said he had more to tell me. After that I hope to go with Father Legault to the Rockefeller to see his brother's office."

"We may not be given full access to the scroll workroom, Juda."

"Oh, yes, we will," Father Yong said, "with the letter I have from the Holy Father. Even the Dominicans wouldn't dare."

"What then, Juda?" the General asked.

Juda smiled and said she was going to see "Bhite al-Nadir."

"What! You're going to Nadir's house? Are you crazy?" Ben said loudly. "He's been doing his best to kill you."

"Juda, I must object," Father Yong interjected. "My letter won't hold much sway with him, I'm afraid."

"Don't worry, Benjamin, Father Yong, I know what I'm doing." Earlier that day Juda had sent a note to Nadir that simply read, *I will visit your house tomorrow at four. I will be unarmed and wish to talk. Juda Bonaparte.*

That night after dinner, alone in her rooms, Juda called T.J. Troubble. "Any word from Kirnski, T.J.?"

He was very animated. "He'll be ready when you are. Was he hard to find, and excited to hear from you. Are you OK? When you coming home?"

"T.J. slow down," Juda interrupted.

"It's boring here. You got a pencil and paper? I'll give you his phone number. He's in Beirut?"

"Beirut?"

"He thought he'd have a little trouble flying into Tel Aviv, being an ex-Ruski spy and all."

"Anything with Baxter's disks yet?"

"Don't even ask, Juda. It's driving me nuts. No, nothing."

Juda then told him she had sent a letter of instruction to her bank authorizing them to release her scrolls to T.J.

"Why? What does that mean?"

"You'll take them to Father Emile Peush. It was what Harold wanted, but you do it only if… "

"You don't come back."

"Right. But I will, T.J. Take care of yourself." Juda checked the time and called her old friend, Georgi Kirnski.

"Retirement is killing me," Kirnski said from his room in Beirut. He sounded happy. "Beirut is not what it once was. Only the casino is without the scars of war, Juda. The Christians are dead or leaving. The beautiful city is in ruins. When do we go into Iran?"

"I'll need two days here, but I'll have to call you. Do you know the place?"

"Right on the sea, secluded, and heavily guarded, but I have cousins who will help us. It won't be easy. Juda, there's more going on there than God's work. KGB has a big file. I read it, but I couldn't copy it." Kirnksi laughed. "Iran is trouble, Juda. Stirring up Shiite Muslims in every country. We should have made it a satellite years ago."

"I'm going to get you a visa so we can leave from here."

"I've been in Israel before, but not with an Israeli visa." Again, Kirnski laughed. "And how will we get to the Caspian from Tel Aviv? Not with an American F16. Can you get a Harrier?"

"Leave the plane to me, Georgi," Juda said, not knowing the answer. "Will you stay in Beirut?"

"Yes, leave a message at this number. I look forward to seeing you again. This time we'll be on the same side, yes?"

After René Gervais followed Juda from the melee at the Damascus Gate to the King David he went to a building, an ancient three-story limestone structure in the Old City close to the start of the Via Dolorosa. Situated at the north east corner of the Temple Mount, the building had once been part of the Antonia Fortress. In this castle, built by Herod the Great for his friend Marc Antony, Jesus had been mocked and scourged. Restored from rubble, the fortress contained a convent of the Sisters of Zion, a Franciscan monastery, and a building once occupied by the Islamic Assassins. It was close to the Dome of the Rock and the Al-Aksa Mosque, which had been, for a short time after the crusader's conquest of Jerusalem, the home of the Templars. The Assassins and Templars, once sworn enemies, had lived side by side, much as the Arabs and Jews did today.

As René Gervais mounted the circular stone stairway, following a young man dressed in simple monk's attire to the office of the director, he was not aware of the activity below ground. In cellars and freshly dug passageways that extended beneath the Temple Mount, the inhabitants did their work. In this beehive, men had tunneled beneath Herod's platform which Solomon had built to hold the first temple.

Herod the Great's second temple, a magnificent structure, was totally destroyed by Vespasian's armies in 70 A.D., less than seventy years after Herod's death. Rome's answer to the Jewish problem was bloody carnage and annihilation. More than one million Jews died in the Roman genocide that spread from Jerusalem to end in Masada, a racial massacre that was to be repeated throughout history, culminating nineteen hundred years later when seven million of God's chosen people were incinerated by Hitler. And Jews continued to ask where was God?

With its cold stone steps and walls, the building reminded Gervais of his prison home at La Salette, France. From a tower window he could see the Dome of the Rock, the *Haram esh Sharif*, which, along with the Al-Aksa Mosque, was among the most recent major constructions on Solomon's platform. At the top of the stairs the monk silently led him into an office.

The director was an American of medium build, coarsely featured, and unshaven, dressed in tan, sweat stained, cotton clothing; he was darkly tanned and about fifty. Hanging loosely at his waist from a military webbing belt was a Beretta 9mm automatic, the standard American military issue side arm. "Come in, Gervais, I'm Charles Stourka, director of this hellhole. This is my number two man, Billy Hudson. You're late. You have something for me?" Billy Hudson said nothing as he raised his hand to his forehead, tilting his head in a half-hearted salute to acknowledge Gervais.

"Juda Bonaparte has the scrolls," Gervais lied, "and she's here in Jerusalem, protected by Mossad."

Stourka cursed. "You failed?" He addressed Billy Hudson, a younger man, lean, similarly armed, leaning back in a chair with his feet on Stourka's desk. "I told you, Billy, this is the goddamndest operation we've ever taken."

"The professors of archeology are all dead, but each had given their scroll directly or indirectly to Juda Bonaparte before my haoma," Gervais said. "What about Father Legault's scroll, the last? Do you have it?"

"No." Stourka's face screwed into a scowl. "No, goddammit, I do not have it, Gervais. The haoma didn't work with him. Why haven't you killed this woman and recovered the scrolls?"

"Why do you not have Legault's scroll?"

"Who the hell are you to question me? I have your report from France. You're a monk. You excelled in Spain, but were insolent they said. I don't give a shit about that; I want the scroll."

"Spain wasted my time. Now you tell me what I'm after, why the Arabs want this scroll, or I'm gone from here."

Stourka laughed. "The sweet life in Marseilles spoiled you, Gervais. Must have been that French pussy. How long you been in that monastery anyway?" Stourka leaned back in his chair and lit a cigar. "I'll tell you about the scroll. It's money and power, that's what it's all about. For me, a lot of money when I'm finished here. For my people in the U.S., it's power. They're after a unified world: politically and religiously."

"Communists?"

"You've been sheltered too long, Gervais. Communism is about dead as the rocks we dig. These people take up where Communism left off. No, it's global unification they want, if you can believe it. It'll never happen. They're as nuts as the commies ever were, only smoother and with a lot more money. Come on, I'll show you what I'm doing in this damned desert." Stourka stood up from behind his desk. "You want a cigar? Billy!" At Stourka's gesture Hudson reached into the desk and offered Gervais a Corona Corona.

"Your workers," Gervais said, lighting the Cuban cigar, "they're Jewish?"

Stourka laughed. "This place has been a monastery since the Middle Ages. My workers are homeless children, like you were. Jews, Arabs, who cares? They're given food, shelter, and a god to serve, although he has changed names a few times over the years. Currently it's 'God' again. When they die, there are always others to fill their rooms and new religions to fill their heads. Like you Gervais. But they're good workers. And the best thing, they're paid by the Jews. Now you tell me about this drug you used, this haoma."

"Truth, not death can be predicted from the drug as it now is." Gervais fixed his eyes on Stourka, his countenance stony cold. "All except Baxter required my final bullet. Baxter died from complications. The method of administration makes the drug unpredictable."

"You ain't telling me nothing. I about filled that priest's stomach with the stuff. He didn't say a word, just died outright."

"You gave too much and were impatient."

"Come over here, Brother Gervais," Stourka said, and walked to the room's only window. "Do you see that?" He waved his hand at the Temple Mount and the Dome of the Rock. "And that?" His voice rose with his excitement as he pointed to the Western Wall and Kotel plaza. "They're mine. Look at this!" He walked to his desk and opened a red leather-bound book that displayed a two-page photograph of St. Peter's Basilica. "This is yours." He slammed his hand down on the photograph. "They must have the scroll for this, and when the dust clears my people believe they'll have the whole world. And you, Brother Gervais, had one task and you failed. Because of a woman, I think."

René Gervais fixed Charles Stourka with an icy glare. "The woman, Juda Bonaparte, is enchanted. Arabs have tried to kill her for the scroll, and they're all dead."

"That's hard to believe, Gervais. Tell that one to the Arabs. You probably got a hard-on for this bitch and that's why you failed. But I won't, because I want to leave this place for the Jews and Arabs to fight over. And when I'm done, they will fight." Stourka laughed loudly. "I can't do anything, Gervais, until you bring me the scrolls. I've got my orders too. I don't care what it takes. I'll show you why."

Stourka led Gervais to the cellars. Billy Hudson followed. In one large room six men in dusty clothes worked with mason's tools restoring bricks. Others tediously examined, fitted, and marked them. "I've been diggin' and chippin' for five years. Look!" One wall was covered with pallets of restored bricks. "Who knows, we may find Solomon's Temple, if we keep digging. Over there we take'em out twice a week and dump them."

"You dump the restored stones?"

"I need room to work. We keep enough here to make it look good. I don't give a shit about their rubble." He pointed to a tunnel closed by a double door big enough for a truck. "Follow me." He approached a short, narrow passage blocked by a heavy wooden door. Stourka unlocked the door and said, "This is as far as we go. Tunnels, Gervais, a labyrinth of them. Built by that insane Jew, Herod, and now filled with the shit of two thousand years. The Antonio castle was connected to the first temple and later to the Al-Aksa Mosque, over there." He pointed to a partially collapsed passage branching to the right.

"It seems your Templars – that's what you're supposed to be isn't it – used to meet with their enemies the Assassins through there. Probably for a few beers and cards. Maybe dice and women. But it's not the mosque I'm interested in. Only a few feet from here and we're into the crypt under the *Even Shetiyah*, the rock. Right here the Dome of the Rock is above us and I can't do a damn thing but keep on digging until I have the scroll. We might even be standing on the Ark of the Covenant. That's what the Jews hired me to find. That tunnel took forever to clear." He pointed to a very narrow dark passage way.

Gervais frowned, "Where does that one go?"

Stourka laughed, "To the walls of Jericho."

"You believe the treasure is here?"

"As I said, Gervais, you ask too many questions. But if we find it, that's a little *vigorish* for me and you. If the Arabs knew I was digging under their temple, there would be hell to pay, and if they knew I was being paid by the Jews to do it, there would be a bloody war. You get that scroll and I'll see that you never have to go back to your monastery. You'll have enough money to keep you in the sweet life for as long as you live. Fail again, Gervais, and there'll be a French monk hanging from a church in Jerusalem with his belly full of plant juice."

Gervais had planned to return to La Salette one day just to kill that wheezing old priest, Father Lagarre, who had made him pray and force-fed him vegetables, bread, and celibacy. He had remained silent through the years, and he did so now with Stourka.

"You know who pays for this? The same people that paid for your summer camp in Spain, m'boy, and the Israelis."

"What will you do when I bring you the scroll?"

"I get my ass out of this shit-box." Stourka removed a small transmitter from his pocket. "When I'm far enough away from here, I press this little button and this whole heathen complex and the Wailing Wall gets blown all to hell." He pressed the button and laughed. "Don't worry, it's not activated yet, but the stuff is here, behind those rocks, two thousand pounds of high quality dynamite placed just right, 'cause I'm an expert."

"And every Islamic in the world will march on Israel for destroying their sacred places."

"You got it, Chester," Stourka said, "and the Christians too. Christ, what a war!"

In Nadir's guarded house fifteen minutes away, the Arab gun dealer held Juda's note in his trembling hand. His other hand was clamped around a telephone. "Keeftan, *yalan denak*, the woman you have failed to kill will be here in my house tomorrow. The *sharmuta* says she will come here to talk: talk with me in my house – the woman who killed my son."

Keeftan in his hideout in Hebron laughed and said, "The mountain comes to Mohammed. I will be there to meet this woman who kills my men so easily. I have been made a fool too long in this business of the copper scroll. Perhaps she will give it to us, *ibyn amak*, cousin."

"She will be a guest, we will do nothing when she's in my house. Do not forget you are an Arab, my terrorist friend. You arrange to take her when she leaves."

"She will not have your scroll in her arms, you can be sure of that. Are you prepared to buy it?"

"*Manuik*, she is rich. You think she wants money? I have a crazy-man for a partner." Keeftan hung up the phone.

"You heard, *khayak*, my brother?" he asked Dr. George Gamash. "You're here just in time. We'll take this French woman and, between us, my cousin, we will teach her how to be a real woman." A smile broke on Gamash's handsome face.

"Don't be deceived, my brother, she's no fool to walk into your tent without something. Don't give up your plans for her father. With him in your hands, she will dance to your music. But I'm not here to fight with you."

"Her father will be no easy matter, Gideus. He's with Mossad agents all the time. Jerusalem is on fire."

"Who's behind this?" Gamash asked.

"Some fool who has aroused Jews and Arabs, even the Christian tourists. The Palestinians have not done this thing; Jerusalem is scared." Keeftan wrapped his arms around Gamash. "Gideus, this woman is cursed. I am shamed."

"Abu Keeftan, your shame is my shame. Blood is blood."

Chapter 20

On her way to visit Professor Markham the next morning with her driver, Rodriguez, and a second Mossad man who Ben had insisted travel with her, Juda stopped to shop. She bought a selection of favorite Arabic foods: fruit, *Jibin*, fresh Arabic cheese, yogurt, black olives, halawa, and pita bread. Obviously pleased, the professor smiled and thanked her, offering freshly made coffee. After pouring the coffees, he tore off a piece of bread, wrapped it painstakingly around some cheese, salted it, and handed it to Juda. She smiled at the Arabic ways of this Englishman.

His computer was on. He had printed out a list of archeologists working at the Rockefeller. Beside one name, he had made some bracketed notes. He shook his head, pointing at the name of Father Howard Scantland. "Scantland trust, never. Friend, no," he said. He said that Scantland and Jerome Legault were close, and shook his head. Juda remembered the 'Howard' Professor Pribble had called after her visit in Manchester.

Markham said that he and Jean had worked together and that he had seen Jean's scroll many times during Father Jean's visits. Markham explained that he was a paleographer and had dated the copper scroll to 30 A.D.. He said that it was not a map to the treasure as they originally thought; like Baxter, by the time of his death Legault had believed it was a religious document.

"The Flavius Josephus insert? The 'Testimony'?"

Markham indicated he wasn't sure.

"Do you have any idea where Father Legault's scroll is?" Juda asked, pouring more coffee and offering him a cigarette.

One side of his face turned up in a smile as he produced a map of Jerusalem, the Old City highlighted in yellow. He waved away the cigarette, telling Juda she could smoke. "Here," he said, putting his finger on the Al-Aksa Mosque. "Find Buuckra Mondas," he managed, "curator, friend." He touched his chest and told Juda that Legault had been here visiting him two days before he had disappeared. He had called Baxter that night saying he was worried that others knew about the scroll, intimating Scantland at the museum.

Buuckra, Markham explained, was an Islamic Turk who had lived in Jerusalem most of his life. He had been a guide for Baxter, Legault, McLaughlin and the others many years ago. Since the scroll had been taken out of Jerusalem and the professors had left in the early seventies, he had been the curator of the Al-Aksa, but had continued his friendship with Legault and Markham. "Scroll here, with Buuckra," Markham said.

Before she left, Markham said that she must be very careful for her life. Juda embraced him, saying that Harold Baxter's friend was her friend, and that she would return for a visit before leaving Jerusalem.

After a brief shopping interlude at the *shuk*, the Jerusalem market, it was a short drive to the Rockefeller Museum where she was to meet with Fathers Yong and Legault. Opened in 1937 with a grant from John D. Rockefeller, and officially named the Palestine Archeological Museum, it had become known over the years simply as the "Rockefeller," one of three archeological centers in Jerusalem. After the discovery of the Dead Sea Scrolls in 1947, the Rockefeller had become the headquarters for the International Team and the place where scrolls were stored, indexed, and deciphered. Team members from the American School of Oriental Research and the French École Biblique worked here under the inspired direction of Father Roland de Vaux, who had led the team for over forty years until his recent death.

Oxford graduate Professor John Strugnell, de Vaux's successor and a convert to Catholicism, immediately gave Father Yong and Juda full access to the museum when he was shown Yong's letter from Pope John Paul II. He told his secretary, Margaret Bloom, to take Father Yong and Juda anywhere in the complex without restriction. Jerome Legault, a working member of the team, accompanied them.

Juda asked that they be taken to the Scrollery – the lower room under a courtyard wing where thousands of pieces of scrolls were laid out on a long table under glass plates – and the storage room, which held more scrolls.

"There were more than eight hundred scrolls found at Qumran," Legault said. "The Copper scroll, as you may know, is in Jordan. The Great Isaiah scroll is in the Shrine of the Book, here in Jerusalem." Father Legault showed them where he worked and where his late brother had worked.

"I'd like to meet Father Scantland," Juda said, examining Father Jean Legault's office, watching him closely.

"Father is in the States doing some final work on his book," Professor Strugnell's secretary said. She was tall and slender with closely cropped hair. Nun-like, Juda thought, English, guarded and stiff with every answer. Juda noticed that she did not attempt to enter Scantland's office, which was locked with a high security dead-bolt, unlike the others.

"When will all the scrolls be published?" Father Yong asked.

"By the year 2000, we project, Father Yong," Margaret Bloom answered, obviously prepared for the question that had been leveled at the International Team for more than forty years.

As they were leaving, Juda carefully noted the narrow barred windows, outside closed courts, filing room, corridors, and small locked doors marked "private." She would be back, but now someone else was on her mind: Nadir al-Nadir and her appointment at four.

Nadir had prepared well for Juda's visit. Extra guards armed with automatic weapons were posted inside the compound, near the gate, along the walls in the garden, and at each entrance. The house, a large multilevel three-story structure, was located in the rich Talbeiya district, a few blocks south of the King David Hotel. It was one of the few remaining Arab estates in this once exclusive Arab neighborhood. Most of the lands had been confiscated by Jewish authorities and sold to wealthy American Jews who had poured capital into the city since the 1967 war. The Six-Day War had won for the Israelis all of Jerusalem, a city formerly divided into political quarters much as Berlin had been after World War II.

Nadir's residence was protected by his well placed-money. He was likewise protected from prosecution for his actions against Juda in England, France, and Austria, by lack of proof and international law.

"She will not be here, Nadir," Keeftan said, smugly smoking a cigar in Nadir's palatial second floor suite of rooms. He held a small two-way radio in his hand and sat hidden from view. "She's watching us, be sure."

Nadir walked to the balcony. "This is all mine. My people, my land. It can never be taken for Jewish row housing. I pay too much for that." He looked at Keeftan. "Where is she?"

Keeftan puffed on the cigar, blowing out clouds of smoke. "If Bonaparte is here, we will soon know."

The first floor of Nadir's estate was almost windowless for security purposes. The few narrow openings for light would not permit even a child to pass through. It contained offices, guard quarters, a gaming room, a kitchen, and a large reception room. Access to the second story was by one well-guarded stairway that could be completely shut off at the top by heavy steel-reinforced doors which Nadir could close at the press of a button. Nadir turned his back to Keeftan. "It's some trick, the Bonaparte woman is too smart to walk into my nest."

"She has Arab ways and knows she would be safe as a guest in your house, but I've prepared for deception. She will not come. For twenty-four hours my men have been on the streets of Talbeiya watching for her. I agree, it's a trick, but I have tricks too."

From the darkened apartment which she had rented the day before, Juda trained her sixty power spotting scope on Nadir. She had removed the Arab disguise she had worn when she entered the building on Rodriguez's arm as a lover, her face properly covered by a head scarf. Rodriguez had temporarily balked at wearing the *kaffiyeh* Juda had purchased at the *Suk Khan* earlier that day. Held in place by a decorative black rope around his head, it draped over his shoulders and the loose-fitting suit coat he wore. "You make a handsome Arab," Juda had said, taking his arm. His lack of response troubled her.

It would be an easy shot, Juda thought as she scanned Nadir's second floor. I could end it here. She imagined Nadir's head in the cross hairs and remembered others who had died from her marksmanship. But there was no mounted Steyr rifle beside her. No Sonics silencer that would muffle the sound of the bullet that would explode Nadir's head. And now she wouldn't do it. What had changed?

Juda rested her head on the cool scope momentarily, remembering Dr. LaCroix and his last words to her. "Forgive," he had said. She shifted her view back to Nadir and the other man in the room. His face was hidden. Was it the terrorist and killer Rama Abu Keeftan? Juda waited.

Beside her, his back to the wall, Rodriguez held a two-way radio that would send two cars of Mossad agents crashing through Nadir's gate if it were Keeftan, for Keeftan was wanted for terrorism and murder. "Do you see him, Juda?" Rodriguez asked anxiously, ready to signal his men, personally wanting Keeftan more than any other terrorist.

"Why, Rodriguez? Why Keeftan more than Haddad, or Habash, or Abu Nidal?" Juda asked, straining to see the man talking to Nadir.

"For my children." The memories brought tears to Rodriguez's eyes. "One died when an Arab terrorist fell on his own hand grenade on King George Street. It happened right in front of my wife. My ten year old daughter saw it, saw her sister killed. She has been under psychiatric care since then. She no longer speaks." His head fell to his knees as he spoke.

King George and Jaffa Road intersected half a mile from the Old City in the western, Jewish part of Jerusalem, a busy shopping area. Rodriguez was referring to a vicious Arab rampage that had taken place there in 1984. One Arab, shot by a merchant, was blown apart by his own grenade. Dying on the blood-stained bricks, he had confessed that it was Keeftan who had ordered the attack, the kind so typical of the terrorist efforts in the seventies and early eighties.

Rodriguez looked at Juda. "There are Jews who would live in peace with the Arabs, Juda. I am not one. It will never happen as long as I..."

Juda, alerted by a sound, motioned Rodriguez to be quiet. He reached for his gun. She was unarmed.

The door to the room burst open and a silenced automatic ended Rodriguez's hatred as three tightly spaced bullets entered his chest. "Don't move, Juda Bonaparte, and you will live a few hours longer than this Jew," Abu Keeftan said, a smile on his face as he pointed his weapon at Juda. "Fadwi, tie her," he said to one of the men with him. The action that followed was over in less than a second. Juda threw the spotting scope like a missile, fracturing Fadwi's skull. A spinning kick connected with the Arab leader's arm, sending his gun flying across the room and a curse from his lips. Before she could recover from the kick, a third man grabbed her from behind.

"Hold her, Mheta," Keeftan said as he hit her twice with killing blows in the upper abdomen, the solar plexus. Had he used the focused energy of his straight hand and not his half fist Juda might have died instantly from the powerful blows. She collapsed unconscious.

"Carry her down the backstairs to the car," Keeftan said, stepping over the body of the unconscious man to pick up his gun. "Take her to Hebron, and do not harm her or you will join Fadwi. She's mine. And Mheta," Keeftan added disdainfully, "tie her this time." He wiped his gun and placed it in the limp hand of Fadwi.

At the rear of the hotel, Mheta, who had carried Juda slung over his shoulder, dropped her into the backseat of the Mitsubishi sedan waiting there. "You have a prize for us, Mheta," the driver said in Arabic.

"The ties; this one is a tigress, she broke Fadwi's head. Abu Keeftan says we must take her to Hebron." The driver turned into a narrow alley. In the middle, a stooped-over man walked toward them. "*Yalan denak*," Mheta screamed, opening his window. "Get out of the way or we'll run you down." The man walked slowly toward the wall on the driver's side, as the car inched by. The driver turned to him, cursing his mother and father, and was frozen by cold blue eyes that looked into his soul the second before he died. Gervais fired twice, shattering the glass. The driver and Mheta slumped forward, dead from perfect head shots. René Gervais reached through the shattered glass and turned the wheel, driving the car into the wall opposite him. He pushed the bodies out and drove away, first checking that Juda was breathing and still unconscious.

At his rented house in North Jerusalem, he placed Juda on his bed. Sitting beside her, he felt the pulse in her neck. Gervais stared at her for several moments then he touched her face, runnning the tips of his fingers down her cheeks to her mouth, tracing out her lips. He slowly unbuttoned her shirt and touched the warm skin of her breasts above the sport bra she wore. He leaned over and held his face next to hers and cried.

Chapter 21

Juda awoke looking into the handsome face of René Gervais. She remembered the fight, Rodriguez's death – Keeftan's gun. Her abdomen was painful, bruised from Keeftan's blow. Gervais smiled mischievously, boyishly. "I saved your life once more. They hit you in the upper abdomen, your solar plexus."

"I warned you I would kill you if you followed me."

"I do what I must do, what I am ordered to by my Church. You do what you have to. When I have Baxter's scroll, I'll leave you to be killed on your own." His smile was charming, but annoying. "I know you won't sell it, so I ask you, give it to me."

"You killed the others."

"No, Juda." Gervais lied easily. She watched his pupils and facial movements for signs of deception. "You saw the men I killed. They would have killed you and your father, and your friend in the wheel chair. Keeftan's men, I believe." He offered her a cigarette, one of hers. "Now I've killed again, two more of Keeftan's men who were taking you away in their car."

"You kill easily, Gervais."

"What I've been trained to do since I was a boy, as you were trained. Are you hungry? I have some Arabic food: plain cheese, flat bread, olives, a parsley salad."

"How long have I been here?" Juda asked, declining the food but lighting a cigarette.

"Two hours. I'll take you back to your hotel when you're able. Will you give me your scroll?"

"Again you ask like a child." Juda became angry; her voice rose. "Will I give you the scroll I have been entrusted with? An archeological scrap that so many have died over? Two that I dearly loved?" She thought of Harold Baxter and her servant Franke. "Give you the scroll? Hell no, Gervais!" She screamed. He looked injured from her tirade, but she continued, only with less vehemence. "A bullet would be more to my tastes. You followed me from France to Jerusalem. Why?"

"Here there are those who would kill you for your scroll. I must protect you to fulfill my sacred orders."

Juda walked over to him, her face close to his. "I could kill you right here with my bare hands – in an instant, Gervais."

Gervais smiled through pouting lips. "I think not, Juda. I'm well train…" Her hand moved with incredible speed only to be caught inches from his face before the slap could land. He was fast and his grip powerful. "I'm sorry, I might have hurt you," he said, releasing his grip. "The only woman who hit me was my mother, and… " Gervais paused, "she loved me."

His smile disarmed her and she found herself uncomfortable, embarrassed by her loss of control, but she returned the smile. "Oh, sit down and tell me about yourself, Gervais, and your society of Templar knights and why you want this scroll." And tell me about your mother, she thought. "Perhaps there will be a time when I'll give your request for the scroll some consideration."

"I'm sworn to blind obedience, Juda, but I'll tell you what I know. Come here." He walked to a window that gave a magnificent view of Jerusalem from the hill on which his house stood. "Here, in this city, three of the world's great religions converge and emanate outwards. And here our organization started… Juda, my superiors believe that the scroll was written by a historian at the actual time Christ lived and died."

"Don't tell me about Flavius Josephus, please."

"No, it was another."

"And the Templars would suppress it, bury the truth as it has been buried for two thousand years. You're afraid of what's in the scroll." Juda watched him closely, his eyes and mouth. He had a beautiful sensuous mouth, full soft lips. Gervais' face revealed only truth and trust, for he had the ability to believe his lies, and spoke the truth, as Juda wished.

"Not fear, Juda. Protection. The Christian church rests on two strong pillars: scripture and tradition."

"And a third, that which has been declared truthful by the Church fathers. Have you forgotten that, René?"

"They were inspired by God."

"Were they? René Gervais can't you see it goes round and round. To declare the truth of scriptures the Church fathers had to first state they were inspired by God, a God they got from the scriptures. The Templars would perpetrate this lie to support these pillars of clay. Were the others also influenced by God – the Prophet? Buddha? Lao-tze?"

"You're an educated woman; I don't know."

"Mohammed didn't see Islam as a new religion, only a natural extension of Judaism and Christianity, both coming from Abraham. Abraham was neither Christian nor Jew, but a *hanif*, a holy man who had surrendered to the will of God."

"*Allah u-Akbar*," Gervais said, smiling at her, remembering her words to the throng.

Juda flushed with renewed anger. "You were there, at the Damascus Gate?"

"You were marvelous, Juda. They would have destroyed the church and desecrated the Western Wall. That might mean war."

"You're hopeless, Gervais. What do you think this scroll will reveal that would be so threatening to what is found in the Gospels and declared by tradition?"

"Again," Gervais smiled, "I don't know. The scroll would have to be fully translated and it isn't, nor will it be."

"You're not after this fabled treasure as Keeftan is?"

"My order is sworn to poverty, but we don't lack wealth. There's no limit to my expenses."

"The wealth of the Templars is at your disposal? This is another fantasy." Exasperated she said, "Gervais, drive me back. And, Brother Gervais, keep away from me."

Though it was late when she arrived at the King George, Juda called Ben.

"Are you all right, Chri… I've had every Mossad agent looking for you. Rodriguez is dead. What the hell happened?"

"It was Keeftan. I'm fine, stop worrying. I'm sorry about Rod, he was very brave. René Gervais is here."

"In Jerusalem? With you?"

"He saved me from Keeftan."

"I want him, Juda. Two men were killed behind the apartment building. Shot in the head."

"A twenty-two?"

"Hell no, a forty-five, soft nose. What a mess."

"Meet me here at eight, I'll take you to him. Right now, I need a bath and some rest. And, Ben, I think Gervais is crazy."

That same night Gervais silently entered Charles Stourka's house, which was west of the Old City, not far from the Church of the Ascension and Makassed Hospital. But neither the church nor the hospital would help Stourka this night. Gervais silently cut the throat of Stourka's servant, a young Arab who slept in a ground floor room near the kitchen. Cat like he climbed the stairs and entered the bedroom. Stourka awoke with a curse, reaching for a gun on his nightstand as Gervais snapped on the light. The twenty-two hissed once, its soft nose bullet tearing into Stourka's shoulder. "I can shoot you many times before you die, so lie still and be quiet."

"Bastard, I'll kill… Oh Christ… " Stourka groaned as a second shot reinforced Gervais' message, and blood poured from a small hole in his knee. Stourka began to cry, his body trembling in pain when Gervais shot him again in the arm.

"Drink this," Gervais said, holding a small bottle to Stourka's lips as he pressed the silencer into the man's eye, "and you will live to drink again." He looked at his watch and waited for the haoma to work. Stourka slowly relaxed; the pain subsided; he drifted into a twilight sleep. Gervais smiled and began his questions.

In two hours Charles Stourka came back to a world of pain. Atheist Stourka prayed to be taken back to his haoma nirvana, but instead was jerked into hell by another hiss from Gervais' weapon. This time the small missile grazed the plexus of nerves in Stourka's neck, sending shocks of neurological pain upwards into his head and down his arm which began to shake spastically. Stourka groaned; Gervais laughed and fired another bullet, and another, and another.

While Stourka suffered his slow agonizing death from René Gervais' twenty-two, Juda dreamed. She was in Paris shopping on the Champs Élysées. The day was warm and sunny. Ahead she saw Dr. LaCroix waving to her. She dropped her packages and began running to him, her heart pounding. He turned and looked at her and she was naked.

"Were you ashamed of your nakedness?" LaCroix asked in her dream, which was now back in the analyst's office.

"You were different, Dr. LaCroix – younger. I wanted to cover myself."

"What happened?" Juda's dream doctor asked.

"You took my hand and walked with me. I was as naked as…

"As?"

"Venus," Juda said softly.

"The goddess?"

"The statue."

When she awoke, Juda took out her old notebook and recorded her dream. Then she lay back and let her thoughts flow freely as she had learned to do in analysis. She saw René Gervais, and for the fleeting moments before sleep came again, she thought of Raol Shamir, her half-brother, his decapitated skull looking at her.

Chapter 22

MOSSAD HEADQUARTERS

After they had returned from Gervais' empty house Juda was furious, enraged at the note he had left on the table.

"How long did you spend with this Frenchie, Juda?" Ben asked, amused at her annoyance. "Let me see his note."

"He's a silly child. Here, read it." Juda threw the note on the table in the small conference room next to Samuel Scharkes' office.

Ben read it aloud, " 'It was nice being with you last night, Juda. Sorry I had to leave before you came back.' He just killed two men, that silly son of a… and he writes a schoolboy letter like this," Ben said. " 'It was nice being with you last night.' Crap! This guy's been too long in the monastery, Juda. As I said before, don't trust him, whether he saved you or not, Knight Templar or holy brother. I've seen psychos like this before. Cold blooded killers with the mind of an adolescent – or less."

"Keeftan will want blood, now, Ben," Samuel Scharkes said. "The man Juda hit, Fadwi, is still in the hospital. He had a massive subdural hematoma. He's Keeftan's cousin, we think; but to the Arabs everybody is a cousin, and they're inbred for vengeance," he added scornfully.

An ignorant man, Juda thought, looking at him. As always Scharkes was fashionably dressed: an anal character no doubt, with his permanent scowl, his strong facial lines from the nose to the outer edge of his thin lips, hands scrubbed red and always fidgeting with something.

"I'm bringing more men into Jerusalem, Kerns; he'll want revenge," Scharkes said.

"On me," Juda said, "not Jerusalem. More of your young soldiers will just inflame the people." Soldiers, teenage girls and boys, armed with American M16s, their double clips taped together and loaded, were everywhere in the city. Juda had seen them at food stands, at the gates of the Old City, getting on busses, walking with the shoppers on Ben Yehuda, eating ice cream or *shawrma* sandwiches: boys and girls with guns playing at war.

That night, sitting in the subdued atmosphere of the King David's bar, Juda talked alone with her father. "And you'll go to Iran with this Russian, Kirnski? You want a visa for a Russian spy? An airplane? Juda, we can't afford another war. Two spies flying an Israeli plane over Turkey or Syria or Iraq, and into Iran? Impossible!"

"We'll land in Azerbaijan near Lenkoran. Kirnski knows the area. There's a small airstrip there. I think a private jet or helicopter will do. After that, we're into Iran."

"Is that all! We don't have a chopper with that kind of range. Do you know how far it is?"

"About fifteen hundred miles in a straight line. Add five hundred if we take the corridor along the mountains, north of Syria, past the border."

"If the Turks get you and this Kirnski, I'll never be able to get you out diplomatically. If they get you over Iraq, good-bye. I'll have to take this to the cabinet, and I already know their answer."

"Ben, this drug is our only lead. They make it in Iran and not for religious purposes. I'm going in there and that's that. I can get a plane from Isshi in Damascus." Isshi Shalhoub al

Hakum, the Fat Man, was a Damascus arms dealer who had led Juda to Shamir's stronghold in the desert.

"That fat crook almost got you killed. No! I'll get you what you need, but you may have to fly out of Beirut. And you'll have to refuel."

"I think Kirnski can arrange that. He's waiting in Beirut now. Can you get satellite pictures from the Americans?"

"I'll need a few days for this, Juda. What else do you need?"

Juda wrinkled her nose, smiled, and gave her father her list. Kerns scanned it and whistled. "Christ, I'm sorry I asked." Kerns said he would be back in Tel-Aviv the next day and asked, feigning nervousness, what else Juda planned.

"Don't worry, Ben. Tomorrow I'm having a quiet day." Juda embraced her father as they warned each other to be careful. "I'll be fine." She smiled reassuringly. "I'm going to church. I'll need a car."

"And a driver."

"No. I'm safer alone," Juda said, remembering the dead Rodriguez. "I know the city and I look like a tourist."

"I give up. Take mine." Kerns handed her the keys to his Renault. "But you'll have to drive me back to Mossad in the morning. I'll stay here tonight, if you have room."

"I have a large suite." She was obviously pleased. "Let's have another drink first. Would you like a Pernod too?"

"I'll try it."

Scharkes was right. Keeftan's rage at another failure was without limit. He cursed George Gamash who sat quietly as Keeftan wrecked his secluded house in al-Khalil, known as Hebron to the Israelis. "*Yelan denak*, bitch, woman," he screamed at Shalima, moments before he hit her, bloodying her nose, cutting her lip.

"When I stop loving you, Rama, I will kill you," Shalima said, "this I promise," as George Gamash applied pressure to her nose.

"Are you finished, Abu Keeftan? I didn't come here to doctor your mistakes. You've had fits like this since we were boys. When will you stop?"

"When he's dead," Shalima spit out.

"No! When I have that *sharmuta*, whore, dead in my hands and I have the scrolls. I curse Nadir for the scrolls, and myself for becoming his ally. No, I am his *sharmuta*, his prostitute. I'm a Judas. I bleed a thousand wounds for money. Allah strike me dead, I could have killed her. I could have easily shot her. I left her with that fool Mheta. But she was out from my blow that could have killed her, but no, I'm a fool again. Who killed them? Juda? Someone else? Why, Gideus? Why?" Keeftan's dark tormented eyes turned to his cousin. "You're a doctor, tell me. Why didn't I kill her?"

"Because she's like your sister, my cousin, and you want her. I know you. She has big *fahle* like you, and this woman you love and hurt. There, Shalima, the bleeding has stopped, and your nose is as beautiful as always."

Keeftan's sister had brought irreparable shame to her family, a "blackening of the face," by losing her *ird*, virginity, before marriage. A passionate girl of fifteen, she had sexual relations with the son of an Iraqi *shaykh*, sheik. Arab code of honor had demanded her death to restore the *wajh*, or face of the family, and the task had fallen to the young Abu Keeftan, her loving brother, the eldest son. It was an act that changed his life.

"You're right, George," Keeftan said loudly, "I want her ass."

Gamash laughed.

Keeftan laughed and poured three glasses of Arak. He dipped his finger into the drink and touched it to Shalima's lips, then he kissed her. "Let's go over our plans to take Benjamin Kerns. I'll have the blood of father and daughter to ease my pain. And after, you can tell me why you've left England, George. Why come to the desert?"

In the morning after she had let Ben off at Mossad headquarters, Juda waved at her father and turned south towards Jerusalem. A few kilometers later she knew she was being followed. Her intuition and rage told her who it was. She slammed the shifter into third and hit the pedal. No Ferrari, this little car, she thought, as she gained the distance she wanted. A few more kilometers ahead she made a fast turn against screeching tires. The Renault shuddered as she drove toward the restoration of Caesarea on the Mediterranean, a place she knew well. Now she would have this Frenchman.

Driving past the few beach houses owned by rich Jews, she entered the ruins and parked her car. The crusader castle, Roman coliseum, and parts of the palaces of Pontius Pilate and Herod the Great had all been partially restored. Juda ran through a massive limestone arch of the amphitheater and climbed the wall to the top. Lying on her stomach fourteen feet up, she saw Gervais park his car beside hers.

René Gervais looked around the complex. When he was inside the arena, Juda stood up. "I'm here, bastard," she shouted, her hands on her hips, taunting him, walking on the wall, "come and get me." Before Gervais could find a place to climb, Juda was down, facing him on the floor of the amphitheater. "I too am well trained, Gervais, and I'm unarmed. Fight!" Juda threw off the leather jacket she wore over jeans and a cotton shirt and stood waiting.

"I can't fight you, Juda."

"Then you'll die." Her spinning kick caught him in the chest – though she could have connected with his head – and sent him flying on his backside to the stone floor. Gervais, unhurt, dusted himself off and got up. He removed the sport coat and shoulder holster he wore. Juda noted the American Colt, a forty-five.

"You carry a big gun, Gervais," she sneered, "are you so unsure of yourself?"

Gervais became angry and assumed a defensive karate stance. The gladiators faced off in the empty arena. Gervais had the edge because of his greater size.

"Then we'll fight, Juda." This time her kick connected to the side of his head. Gervais went down but rolled to his feet instantly and hit her a stunning blow. Then he was on her, holding her, crushing her against his body.

"Fight, Frenchman. I'll kill you." Her leg went behind his and Gervais was down again, Juda on top. They rolled and grappled on the floor of the arena. Juda hit him again, a chop to the side of the neck, one that would have paralyzed an arm had he not been so heavily muscled. On their feet and breathing hard, Juda kicked again. This time Gervais moved fast and caught her leg, pulling her against him, smiling at her.

Then she knew. Gervais was playing with her, fighting a strange battle of sexual arousal – foreplay. She felt him hard against her, as he held her leg to his waist, pressing himself into her. Her legs weakened; her body went limp against his. He released her leg. Juda closed her eyes, submitting to the feelings. She ran her hands through his hair and pulled him to her lips. Soft warm lips sent sensations through her she had thought long dead. They danced in her pelvis, ran down her legs and up her spine. Intensely aroused, she gripped the thick muscles of his back as he still crushed her against him. Gervais moaned. Lips locked on lips, bodies melding, they swayed together. Juda touched him and stood back. Gervais' eyes rolled and closed, his neck arched.

Then it was over. A powerful and perfectly placed kick to the groin doubled Gervais over. He cried in terrible pain, vomiting as Juda's second kick landed on his chin, sending him through the air to sprawl unconscious in front of the box that had been the Roman governor's two thousand years earlier.

Juda smiled. Her chest heaving, she looked down at Gervais. "I could kill you now, you horny bastard. You won't be so frisky for a while." She put on her jacket and found a pen and card. Remembering the note he had left her, she wrote: *It was nice being with you, René Gervais, sorry I had to leave before you came to. I hope I didn't bruise your EGO too badly. You'll find your gun beside you, if it still works.* She laughed and placed it on his chest.

As she drove to Jerusalem she still felt the glow of her excitement. Somehow it pleased her. It had been a long, long time.

The Al-Aksa Mosque was built on the south end of the great platform that had once held the Jewish first and second temples, where the Dome of the Rock now stood. It was from the Al-Aksa that Nur, the son of Ibrahim Zangi, escaped the crusaders with the copper scroll in hand to hide it in a cave at Qumran. Juda removed her shoes outside the mosque, turned, and surveyed the Temple Mount.

Entering the mosque, her head covered, Juda looked for Buuckra Mondas, the caretaker and friend of the murdered Father Jean Legault. There were a few Christian tourists and Muslims in the mosque. Hebrew law forbade Jews from entering the Mount because the place of the Holy of Holies was not known. Juda looked at the *mihrab*, or portico, that faced the *qibla*, or direction of prayer. All Islamics had to face Mecca, in Saudi Arabia, when praying, for there was the place of the Masjid al Haram, the most sacred of all Islamic mosques.

A chill ran through her as she contemplated the mosque and the women praying. How many had prayed, and how many had died violently over the centuries, and how many still died because of the ideologies men had created from the simple words of the prophets? Juda felt compassion for those in prayer, mostly women, and anger at the violent games of history perpetrated by men. She gazed over the prayers looking for the man who fit the description Professor Markham had given her of Buuckra Mondas, the man who had Father Jean Legault's piece of the copper scroll.

She knew deep down where her anger came from. She knew without thinking. It was always men, like that fool René Gervais, and Abu Keeftan; men who led men with swords and guns, and bombs. Men driven by greed and passion and power. Men were born with the blood of history and their fathers on their hands, not just with the blood of their mothers on their bodies. She thought, was I? Then she saw him, an old man with a mop in his hands. She watched him bend over and squeeze the mop then wipe the marbled portico, and her own hands suddenly felt warm and sticky.

Juda bowed, touched her forehead. "Salaam, I am Juda Bonaparte, friend of Harold Baxter and Delbert Markham." She spoke in Arabic. The man returned her smile. He was old, shorter than she. His hair was white beneath the red *tarboosh*, the fez of the Ottoman Empire which bespoke his proud Turkish heritage. He wore a thick mustache.

"Father Jean said someone would come. Here," he gestured with thick and callused hands, "I have a small work room. It's humble, but I will make fresh coffee." He opened a door and offered her a chair. The room was arrayed with cleaning and maintenance supplies. On one side there was a small desk with microphone and amplifier. "Even the house of Allah must be cleaned and repaired. That's my work, but I am the muezzin too." He looked at his watch. "Soon I'll call the faithful to prayer. You want Father Jean's scroll?"

"How do you know?"

He did not answer as he measured fine coffee, sugar, and water and carefully brought the mixture to a boil, expertly raising the brass *jezves* away from the gas burner as the frothy brew rose three times to the top to create a sweet aromatic drink with a perfect crust. "Our gift to the Arabs, Juda Bonaparte," he said with a smile, "true Turkish coffee." He handed her the small cup. The coffee was excellent, sweet and strong.

"You didn't say how you knew," Juda repeated.

"Because only two people in the world knew I held his scroll, Professor Markham and Father Jean. Two days before he was murdered, Jean said I should give it to the person who came to me and asked for it. He said it would be a friend. Were you his friend, Juda Bonaparte?"

"I might have been. I loved Harold Baxter, who is also dead – murdered."

"And the others? I knew them all. Are they dead?"

"Yes. Was Father Legault afraid?"

"I think so, but he didn't say of what. Now I know he had reasons. Baxter was Father Jean's closest friend, and Professor Markham's, but not so with his brother. I'll give you the scroll, but you must come back tonight after the mosque is closed to visitors.

"Now, wait here and finish your coffee. It's time I call our people to prayer." He went to his desk and began his chant. Loudspeakers on minarets carried his message to Muslims throughout the Old City. The mosque filled, people prayed.

There was no priest, no ritual. So simple, Juda thought. She held out her hand and said she would be back at eight.

When René Gervais awoke on the arena floor in Caesarea he was in severe pain, his testicles swollen and bruised, head pounding, neck muscles aching. Juda had shamed him. Her note was a mockery. As he eased himself behind the wheel of his car, he grunted with pain at the smallness of the vehicle, then the shifter, and especially the accursed clutch. He was determined there would be no more games with Juda Bonaparte, but her kiss and touch had felt so real. Or was he a fool?

Chapter 23

When Juda returned to the Al-Aksa Mosque at eight o'clock the door was locked. She saw Buuckra Mondas sitting on a stone bench in the courtyard beside the mosque. He called her name. Juda followed him to a rear door near the edge of the mount. Far below the mosque was an area of new excavation revealing more of the City of David and what might once have been a gate into the First Temple.

"My Turkish ancestors rebuilt most of the wall, Juda," Mondas said proudly, "but the massive stones of Herod are still here." He opened the door. "Be careful, the stairs are narrow," he warned Juda as she followed him down to a room that seemed to hang on the wall below the mosque, high above excavations. He pulled a chain on the single light that hung near the center of the room. There was no furniture, just a barred window and another small door.

"Listen," Mondas said, "sometimes I hear strange noises from inside, the ghosts of the crusaders, I think." He smiled, but Juda had the impression that he believed this. She heard nothing.

"Now we'll be under the mosque. The floor is steep." A light had been installed in the narrow limestone hall that led downward. "After Jean was killed, I put the piece of scroll down here where it's like the cave that was its home for maybe two thousand years; I think." They were now deep within the Temple Mount. The passage narrowed.

"Where does this tunnel go, Buuckra?"

"To the fortress of Marc Antony, but it's blocked by rubble. The Templars lived here in the mosque, after… I forgot the time. They could visit their enemies through this tunnel."

"The Assassins?"

"That's what they were called, but there was another name – Arabic." He reached up and swept his hand along a ledge in the wall. "Here's your scroll, Juda Bonaparte. I've protected it as Father Jean wanted." The piece of copper was carefully wrapped in cardboard and secured all around with duct tape.

"Buuckra, I want to see the end of the tunnel."

He took her a dozen meters farther down the tunnel until they were stopped by rocky debris. Then Juda heard something: distant sounds transmitted through stone. "Where are we with reference to the mosque and the mount?"

"Do you know Wilson's Arch? Someplace between the mosque and there. I'll show you on a diagram I have in my work room. Will you have coffee with me?"

Back in his room Buuckra made coffee and showed Juda the diagram he had. It revealed the mosque as it was now and as it once had been – more than twice its present size until Israeli soldiers had burned it – and the relation of it to the mount and the Dome of the Rock.

"You see the Western Wall here. The tunnel descends inside the wall towards the Arch. Past that would be what remains of the fortress. Jerusalem is as complicated below the city as it is above. Have you been into the caves?"

"Tsidkiyahu's? Yes." Juda remembered the large limestone caves that descended deep beneath the Old City, reaching as far as the Temple Mount and the Western Wall. These caves were said to be the place where Solomon quarried the stones of the

First Temple. The caves were massive, steeply inclined, with convoluted passages and tunnels.

"Are there any excavations going on under the wall or the mount?"

"No, but go by during the day and watch from outside the wall on the road above the Kidron Valley. Watch the work of the excavations. There's a large cave on the left. I've seen covered trucks coming from there two, maybe three times a week, carrying stones. Why? I ask myself. They don't remove the stones of ancient ruins. I think they must stay there to be restored. But I'm not an educated man, Juda. I just watch and think a little."

"I would like to come back with some help, Buuckra, and clear that tunnel."

"It would be easy. The rocks are small and I think it's not dense. Maybe a meter or two. I've felt new air. Come back one night, we will do it. This is a mystery for you, yes?"

That night Juda met Oudi and Ben in a Middle Eastern restaurant a short walk from the King David. The food was Lebanese, Juda's favorite of Arabic cuisine. Throughout the Middle East similar foods were prepared with regional variations in spice and style. The Minaret, one of Jerusalem's best Arabic restaurants, would not disappoint Juda. Their table was immediately spread with a dozen or more classic appetizers: shiny stuffed grape leaves, dipping sauces of *hummus*, tahini, and a garlic flavored yogurt with cucumber, *kibbi* (cooked and raw), a variety of vegetables, black olives and pita bread.

"We have no true Jewish food, Father," Ben said, pouring olive oil over his *hummus*. "Jews bring their food culture from the Diaspora. So we have Hungarian, Russian, French, German, African, even American Jewish foods. Have you seen our MacDonald's?" The priest nodded and returned Ben's smile. Ben turned to Juda who was neatly rolling a bite of a tabouli salad in a piece of pita. "How was your day, daughter?"

Juda decided not to tell him about Gervais and their fight at Caesarea. "I was at the Al-Aksa Mosque today seeing Buuckra Mondas." Juda hesitated. "Ben, I have Father Jean's scroll."

"You weren't going to tell me, Juda. Why?"

"We might have a conflict of interest, and I don't want that."

Benjamin Kerns smiled and put his hand on hers. "We won't. I know your commitment to Dr. Baxter. Let's keep this private. How about you, Father?"

"I believe Harold Baxter asked Juda to give the scrolls to Father Emile Peush. So it may all get back to the Vatican anyway in the end. My lips are sealed. Now, all we need are the other two parts. Then what? If we do nothing else, I'd like to know what's in this scroll. Look how much trouble has arisen from it. And murders."

"Someone must know. It all couldn't have been started without someone knowing," Ben said. "A historical document or even another scroll must have pointed to it."

Juda listened.

"We might find the answer in the Vatican Library or in St. Peter's Vault," Father Yong said. "But that research could take several lifetimes – if the Holy Father would give scholars access." Father Yong rolled his eyes to heaven. "And that's not going to happen." He paused. "One man might know, Juda. Professor d'Angello."

"Only the Hickmans are alive who knew of Baxter's scroll," Juda said, "and Gervais."

Ben looked startled at Juda's remark. "I forgot to tell you," he said, "Bill Hickman was killed in a boating explosion off the coast of Spain two days ago. He had only recently been made a senator, filling the seat of the late Senator Johnson from Florida."

"An accident?" Juda asked.

"Who can tell? Looks like the diesel tanks exploded. Everybody was lost and the remains of the ship are all over the floor of the Mediterranean, twelve hundred feet down."

"That leaves Mrs. Hickman." Juda thought she would have to meet this last scroll survivor soon. "Now what about my plane, Ben?"

"I'm working on it. I may have you leave from Saudi, or have it look like you did. It's the flight plans over Turkey and Syria that I'm trying to avoid trouble for you. Over Iraq and Iran you'll be on your own, but you could fly north and over the Caspian to avoid them. The distance is a killer for most planes. I'll need a couple more days, but I wish you'd drop the idea."

On their way out, Juda asked Ben if there were Israeli excavations going on under the Temple Mount or behind the Western Wall. Ben looked surprised.

"How'd you know about that? It's top secret. One of the dumbest projects that ever was pushed through the Knesset. It's the Hasidim; they're powerful, our most fanatical Israelis. As crazy as hell. Sorry, Father. They don't work, only pray and cause trouble, live off the state. The answer, I'm ashamed to say, is yes, they're digging from someplace within Wilson's Arch and working out of a restoration in the Antonia Fortress. They're looking for the Ark of the Covenant."

"Under the Dome of the Rock?" Juda was stunned by the significance of it.

"A very secret, hands-off project, Juda. If the Moslems knew we were risking their sacred places there would be no holding them back. I mean we'd have a war, a big, bloody war. They even hired an American ex-Army civil engineer to run the operation. Pay him a lot of money too. He's supposed to be an expert in covert projects. How did you find out?"

Juda smiled. "I heard ghosts, Ben." Then she told him of her experiences earlier that night with Buuckra Mondas, the blocked tunnel, Buuckra's ghostly sounds, and the trucks.

In the privacy of his car as he returned to Tel Aviv, Kerns, thinking about the excavation project, uttered a stream of expletives that he had been containing all night aimed at the Hasidim. He shook his head, screwed up one side of his face, and exclaimed, "What's next!" to his startled driver.

Chapter 24

Completing her nightly calisthenics and karate workout to Arabic music on the radio, Juda thought of René Gervais and their fight that afternoon. He was undoubtedly stronger than she and fast. Juda stretched and kicked, legs straight and powerfully reaching high above her head. Her kick at Caesarea had been a perfect one, a crushing blow connecting just before the apex of her swing, a blow that had killed in the past. Juda laughed, losing her tempo. You let pleasure interfere with business, René, a *hard* lesson – she laughed again – for a horny young monk.

After her shower, Juda snuggled into a thick hotel bathrobe, poured a tall Pernod and water, lit a cigarette, and let her mind take flight as she had learned to do in analysis. Thoughts, feelings, memories, and fantasies found room to roam freely. Pleasure, that's what she had felt with René. Not victory. How long had her ability to have sexual feelings been available? Had her analysis freed them from their prison in her soul only to be choked by conscious fear? She remembered Michael George and one kiss in the line of her work. That should have told her, but there had been no time, death had surrounded them in Venice – everywhere. *Don't think it was you, René Gervais, you creepy shadow monk. I didn't spend half my life working in my analysis to attribute much to you. Where are you, Dr. LaCroix?*

Thank you. Thank you so much. Juda tilted her drink to her phantasm and smiled. The telephone broke the spell.

"Juda, you sleeping?"

"Thinking. What's up, Ben?" He sounded excited.

"That guy I told you about, the engineer we hired to excavate for the Holy of Holies under the Temple Mount, he's been murdered. About three days ago. And his servant."

"You think this connects?"

"Maybe. He was shot with a twenty-two."

"Behind the ear?"

"Every place but. Sixteen shots, probably two clips. This killer wanted him to suffer. And Juda, we found haoma in his stomach. At least, it's the same stuff we found in the others, and that's the connection. I'll pick you up in the morning. I want to meet this Buuckra Mondas and see that tunnel."

Gervais, Juda thought, as she hung up, a trained killer like she was, but was he a sadistic murderer? Another Shamir? That seemed impossible. There was nothing like that in his appearance: a passionate schoolboy, innocent, boyish, a relaxed mouth, soft lips. She shook her head as if to warn herself as she slid into bed and touched her lips. *The next time we meet, René Gervais, you'll tell me the truth about yourself.*

Benjamin Kerns had two agents with him when Juda met him the next morning. She wore blue jeans, a shirt, and jacket. Under the jacket, and for the second time in three and a half years, she carried her PPK, comfortable in its shoulder holster beneath her shirt next to her skin. "We've got some work ahead of us, Ben," she said giving her father a quick embrace.

"I brought help. I'm ready to close down that place anyway. To hell with those fanatic Hasidim in the Knesset. But we need to give them something, or my ass will be in a sling for shutting down their search for the ark, or whatever they're after."

At the Al-Aksa Mosque, Buuckra Mondas cordially greeted Juda's father, the famous general, but he wanted them to come back at night. Kerns simply shook his head and said, "Now." It took two hours for the four men and Juda to clear the rocks from the tunnel; one by one they had to be carried up the narrow incline and stacked in the room behind the mosque.

A few yards into the now opened tunnel Juda whispered to Ben, who led the procession, "Ben, look." She had her small flashlight focused on the wall just above their heads. "This has been filled in." Juda scraped the debris with her gloved hand, clearing a two-foot area which had been cut out of the wall.

"I'll be a son of a bitch," Ben said, shining his light on what they counted to be twelve sticks of dynamite. A detonating wire had been hidden along the edge of the ceiling and carefully covered beneath wet clay. Alerted now, they found three more placements in the passage ahead. Juda cut the wires as they went. "Christ," Kerns said, "what's above us? There's enough dynamite here to blow up half of the Old City."

"The mosque, and the Western Wall is to our left," Juda said, shining her light into a passage that led to the right. "And that must head in the direction of the Dome, from the map I saw."

Mondas was astonished. "The Jews would blow up my mosque? Why?"

"Not the Jews, Buuckra, others. I'm going to close down this operation and fill our jails with these bastards." He took out a mobile phone and cursed when it wouldn't work deep within the rock. He sent one of his men back to order the raid while he and the other agent took the passage that led to the Antonia Fortress.

"Buuckra and I will follow this tunnel and look for more explosives, Ben," Juda said, looking into the blackness. In the tunnel she found and cut hidden wires that connected to explosives that would have brought down the Temple Mount. When she and Buuckra returned, Ben and the second agent were huddled next to a heavy door, listening to men inside. Ben put his finger to his lips and whispered, "This door must be three inches of hardwood, reinforced with steel straps. Look at that lock. We'll have to wait until my men move in. If they hear us, they'll be gone."

Juda examined the lock. "I can open it, but they'll hear the deadbolt retract. Then we'll have to move fast," she whispered. "Ben, get Buuckra out of here."

"No! Give me a gun. They would blow up my mosque." Buuckra refused to move. Ben nodded and the agent removed a small automatic from a leg holster. Buuckra confidently eased off the safety and carefully slid back the slide enough to see that a bullet was chambered. As Juda watched, she felt better at his familiarity with the weapon. She removed two steel picks from her canvas purse and in a few minutes she was ready to turn back the heavy dead bolt.

"When I shout, go in over me. There's at least a dozen men inside," Juda said, her ear to the door.

"Who the hell's out there?" Stourka's second in command, Billy Hudson demanded, as the deadbolt retracted. He frowned and slid back the bolt of the Uzi slung from his shoulder. "And where's that bastard, Stourka, he ain't in there. Call Stourka's place again," he screamed to one of his men. The door flew open. Hudson cursed and fired. Two heavy slugs from Kern's forty-five blew him backwards. Hudson's dead finger clamped down on the Uzi's trigger letting loose a full clip that sent flying debris and deafening sound throughout the room. Juda fired from the floor, toppling a man who was taking aim at Ben. Two men screamed, dropped their weapons and raised their arms. The religious workers cowered against the rear of the workroom.

"Against the wall," Kerns ordered, motioning with his weapon. Juda shouted "Down!" as a third man, hidden behind a pallet of labeled rocks, fired. As she dropped to the floor, Juda aimed and sent a single round that grooved the top of the assailant's head. At the same time Buuckra Mondas fell to the floor, bleeding heavily from a shoulder wound. Juda held him and clamped her hand over the wound; Buuckra winced in pain. One hand covered with blood, Juda tore open Buuckra's shirt with the other. Just below his rib cage on the right a second wound oozed blood.

"Ben," Juda cried, "get an ambulance!" She folded Buuckra's shirt and pressed it over the abdominal wound, praying the bullet had missed his liver. "Hang on, you'll live," she whispered into his ear, holding him close, tears in her eyes.

The old man gasped, "My mosque is safe. *Allah-u Akbar.*"

Mossad agents sent to raid the excavation rushed in. Outside others had cleared the Kotel plaza for a small helicopter.

Two days later Buuckra Mondas was recovering from emergency surgery at the Hadassah Medical Center, the tunnels had been cleared of dynamite, and the Antonia Fortress sealed pending further investigation by the internal division of Israeli security, Beth Chen.

At Mossad headquarters Samuel Scharkes said, "I've had two men in the U.S. tracking down a company called International Contracting. They're out of Chicago. They're the people we originally contracted with for Stourka and his crew. They're gone; they were just a front. But we'll find the trail. This makes it officially ours." Mossad's mandate was national security and intelligence, comparable to the British MI 6 and the CIA. "We're searching Stourka's house and office, tracing telephone calls, military records, relatives, FBI files. Stourka and this Hudson will have a trail and we'll find it."

"And it will lead to someone who wanted to start a religious war," Juda said. "Even Palestinian terrorists wouldn't – "

" – Blow up the Dome or the Al-Aksa," Ben interrupted, "or string up holy men."

"Same with the boy who led the mob into the mosque. No connections to any Israeli terrorist groups."

"How long had Stourka been here?" Juda asked Scharkes.

"Five years. So whoever was behind him had patience and money. Arabs don't work like that."

Juda lit a cigarette. They were waiting for the scroll, she thought. It all goes back to the scroll. Waiting for Harold and the others to finish. "Ben, when will the plane be here? I think Kirnski and I'll get answers in Iran."

"Ben," Scharkes butted in, "I've said I think this is a bad idea. If she's taken in Iran, it'll be an incident we won't be able to handle. Flying over Turkey and Syria is risky enough. Where will you land? Kurdistan?"

"No. Azerbaijan, on the border. I'll have to show you on a chart," Juda said.

"Russia? That's all mountainous, the whole south shore. The Elburz Mountains, I think."

"Kirnski knows the area. But I need to know what kind of plane you're getting me, Ben."

Ben shook his head and grimaced. "I'm working on it, daughter."

Outside, alone with Ben in his car, Juda said, "I want to get into the Rockefeller first, before Iran, Ben. Show me how you and Ariel Sharon did it."

Ben remembered the black hole, the water, the rats. "Tsidkiyahu's cave, Juda. I'll show you, but we never did it." Ben's chest tightened, his skin crawled. "I panicked in there, Juda. I'll get you in, get someone to go with you, but I can't go back there. At my age I'd have a coronary."

"I didn't want you to go, Ben. Just show me." Juda touched his hand, and said something with her eyes and smile that meant I love you.

WEST PALM BEACH

The memorial service for Bill Hickman was held in West Palm Beach. Senator Hickman's body had not been found, but the search continued, with the U.S. Navy working with Spanish authorities in the recovery. After the reception, B'Ann Hickman held a private meeting with Senator Graves in her home.

"As you know, Henry," B'Ann said, "with Bill gone I'll seek his seat in the senate, as you want." She wore a black dress and a broad brimmed hat. A veil covered her eyes. Her tone was appropriately subdued.

"You've suffered a great loss, B'Ann. Be assured, when the time comes, the full influence of my office and our associates will support you. You will be senator," Senator Graves said. A tall, thick-waisted man with thinning white hair, he had been a senator for thirty years. Like many holding high political office, Graves was a Freemason. In the ranks of the society there had been thirteen American presidents, including the first, George Washington, and the current, George Bush. But Senator Henry Malcom Graves III was no ordinary Mason. He was a member of the highest and most secret level of the brotherhood, the Thirty-Third Degree. And Graves was a member of that exclusive inner sanctum, the Ring, although he had never been to their secret meetings. Senator Graves was a powerful man.

As Graves prepared to leave, B'Ann extended her hand to him, then embraced him. "I'm afraid, Henry. You ask so much of me." Graves patted her back as she cried.

Outside he told his driver to take him to the Breakers Hotel. In the morning he flew to his Washington office.

René Gervais, recovered from his encounter with Juda, boarded a TWA flight that took him to Kennedy International. The departure through security at Ben Gurion had been long and tedious, even for a French monk on a pilgrimage to the Holy Land. From New York he took an American Airlines flight to Palm Beach. Unannounced, he arrived by taxicab in the early evening at the Hickman estate. He pressed a button outside the security gates and said, "I am René Gervais from France, to see Mrs. Hickman." He was denied access until he said that he had copper scrolls for sale. In a few moments the gate opened. B'Ann Hickman met him at the door and extended her hand.

"Our renegade brother – or is it monk?" She was dressed in beige crepe slacks; a silk shirt of matching color opened to reveal the soft curves of her breasts. Her feet were bare except for simple strapped sandals that matched a thin alligator belt around her waist. Her smile was inviting, her manner gracious. Behind her a tall black man with gray-tinged hair waited silently. Fully dressed in suit and tie, he carried a gun beneath his jacket. "This is my personal attendant, Nelson Smith, Mr. Gervais." She took Gervais' arm and led him to the blue room. Her private office.

"Coffee? A drink?" She ordered both through an intercom, as she seated herself beside him on pale blue velour chairs in front of her desk. A small inlaid table separated the chairs. "You have all the scrolls, Brother Gervais?" Her voice was soft, her demeanor relaxed.

"Call me René. I've long departed from my Christian Brotherhood."

"You're the Templar knight. Do you have the scrolls?"

"Two parts, the third and the last pieces cut from the original. There are five. Two are in France, I believe. They're held by another beautiful woman." Gervais smiled and tilted his glass of cognac. "She, too, is wealthy and beautiful and will not sell them, nor would she give them to me. But she may if she believes it's right. The other part is still in Jerusalem."

"Where?" B'Ann lit a cigarette with a gold lighter and offered one to Gervais.

"I'll find it. There are Arabs after the scrolls. These are dangerous men without scruples." Gervais looked into B'Ann's eyes. "I may have to kill them." She registered nothing.

"You killed Charles Stourka?"

"He was a pig. Before he died he accommodated me with information about you and your people. He would have started a religious war in the Middle East. He crucified the religious leaders; set men out to stir the Arabs and Jews to violence, and would have destroyed the Islamic Temples and the Western Wall. You have no limits to your passion."

"No, René, none." She smiled slightly and paused. "And with the scroll, we will destroy Christianity."

"Stourka knew all this, but he didn't know why. He said you were crazy fanatics. Destroy Christianity? What do you want?"

B'Ann Hickman stood up and walked behind her desk. "They killed my husband, now I'm the wealthiest woman in America. I'm young, educated, and beautiful. My background is totally spotless. I possess several degrees from the best universities. I could have any man – anything. Soon I'll be a senator."

"And?"

"In six years, they'll make me President."

"Who are 'they,' these people with such power?"

B'Ann smiled, showing perfect teeth. "I've revealed much to you, René Gervais, and I've been truthful. Absolute truth in thoughts, feelings, and ambitions is the most necessary ingredient in a relationship. I've given you much. Now you must return that to me. Only then can our relationship continue." She looked at her watch, gold and too large for her hand. "It's late. Stay here as my guest. I'm hungry. You may dine with me."

Gervais agreed.

"Tomorrow, you'll tell me about yourself, René. Tonight, at dinner, I want to hear about this other beautiful woman, this Juda Bonaparte." She pressed an intercom button and said,

"Mr. Gervais will be my guest tonight, Nelson. Show him to his rooms. Make him comfortable. We'll eat in one hour." Alone in her room, B'Ann Hickman picked up her telephone and called Senator Graves at his Washington home. Speaking over secure telephone lines, B'Ann said that René Gervais was a guest in her home.

"Keep him with you, B'Ann. I'll have my people there in the morning, but he must not be harmed. I'll arrive later. I must be in New York tomorrow morning to report to the directors.

From its official beginning in England in 1717, Freemasonry had spread to all parts of the world. Some claimed its roots went back to the fourth dynasty in Egypt. Masons claimed responsibility for the building of the first and second temples in Israel, and the magnificent cathedrals of Europe. In the United States, one lodge was known as the Knights Templar.

Most Masons were oblivious to the organization's agenda at its highest and most secret level, the Ring. This agenda was nothing less than world unification in politics and religion. At its lowest levels it claimed no religious affinities and simply required members to believe in a higher power. However, as one moved through the higher degrees, the simplicity gave way to extremes of secrecy, blood oaths, rituals, as well as the development of international monetary, political, and cultural policies. Freemasonry was represented in every country of the world as well as the United Nations, NATO, and the Vatican.

In New York, Graves went directly to the World Trade Center as instructed. A young man approached him. "Senator Graves, please follow me." They took an express elevator to the eightieth floor and walked to a windowless office. The man bid the senator have a seat and disappeared behind a door. A minute later he returned and they took a small second elevator to another floor. There was no panel indicating what floor they were on; Graves guessed they had ascended another ten floors. The door opened into the large office of Erhardt Boeckerman, director of the Ring. The dimly lit office, paneled in book-matched cherry and furnished in leather, wood, and stainless steel, was dead silent. Two men stood to shake Graves' hand.

"Senator, I am Erhardt Boeckerman, and this is Juan Carlos Costi. Please join us." They sat in tan leather chairs around a glass coffee table on which were placed a coffee carafe and black china cups.

"Senator, we've talked many times, now I'm pleased to see you," Boeckerman said, pouring coffee. The three men sipped their coffee in silence. Finally, Boeckerman, a tall, fair Teutonic man in his early sixties, asked Senator Graves for a full update on the scroll incentive. His voice was subdued, emotionless; his gray eyes said nothing.

Though the room temperature was comfortable, small beads of sweat had formed between the few hairs on Graves' head. "I have no scrolls. The monk, Gervais, has become a loose cannon. Between him and the woman, Juda Bonaparte, they have the scrolls, or four of the five pieces. He's presently in West Palm Beach and will be held by my assistants."

"And Stourka?"

"Dead. Killed by René Gervais. Mossad discovered his operation at the temple. It's completely closed down. His men were arrested or killed in a gunfight." Graves added that Stourka had been successful in stirring unrest in Jerusalem. "The people are ready for a civil war."

"Has Mrs. Hickman fared well after the death of her husband?"

Graves smiled. "I've schooled her well. She's a queen."

"Senator, we must have the scroll, or she'll be a queen without a country. Have her offer more money to the Arab, al-Nadir."

"And Gervais." Costi added, "find out what this Gervais wants and pay him. Get the scrolls, Senator." Costi's dark eyes penetrated the senator's. "Years of planning and work depend on this one task. We're patient, and we will not fail, Senator Graves."

Boeckerman stood up. "Thank you, Senator, that will be all. Please report by the usual method."

When Graves left, Boeckerman said, "We may have to abandon our plans, Juan, if we fail again."

"I know, we've depended on the unpredictable. What about Graves?"

"A blunderer, but let's wait. He has Gervais."

"And if he fails again…?"

"I'll see to the senator," Boeckerman said.

Chapter 25

With Ben's help Juda planned to gain entrance to the tunnel beneath the Old City from a small coffee shop in the Arab Quarter. Ben insisted that they have coffee first with the owner, Samuel Shawi, a friend. He was as old as Ben, thin, dark, with a large hawk-like nose.

"It's been many years since you used my door, Benjamin Kerns. We were both young then." Shawi smiled at Juda. "I can see you in your beautiful daughter, Benjamin. She has your mischief in her eyes. But yet," he shrugged, "she's much less Jewish."

Kerns laughed. "Her mother was an Austrian woman, Samuel, a countess. Like Juda in some ways."

"You would go alone, Juda Bonaparte?"

"Have you?"

"No! No one since your father and Ariel Sharon tried. The tunnel goes to hell. No one knows it exists except me, Benjamin, Ariel Sharon, and my son. Change your mind, Juda Bonaparte." She shook her head.

Reluctantly, muttering in Arabic, Shawi led them through his small kitchen and down stone stairs to a room beneath his shop. The room was cool and damp, with rough hewn limestone walls and a worn floor. It held boxes of produce and kitchen supplies.

"My cold storage room," Shawi said, as he pushed away a heavy shelf laden with canned foods, to reveal a small wooden door. "It's been here since the time of Jesus, maybe before. The tunnel was always here. Even before you tried, Benjamin, I did, but my fear and good sense won the day. Thanks be to Allah."

"I drew a map for Juda, Samuel. Look at it." Kerns set out a rough sketch of the tunnel network as he remembered it.

"Yes, let me see." The drawing showed the tunnel snaking below the Arab section outside the walls of Solomon's caves. "Here," Shawi pointed with his finger, "is where it may have been part of the original caves. And here there's trouble." He pointed to a place where the tunnel divided into two. "You went to the right, Ben, as I did. The right goes to perdition, the bars, and the pit. That's when I came back. You remember the *wadi* that nearly drowned you, rushing through those bars and into that bottomless pit? I heard it too.

"Take the left fork, Juda. It goes down and under the right. After that you're in the hands of Allah. Before there was the Rockefeller, there was a church, very old, built by the crusaders, at that very place."

Juda opened her canvas bag and removed a cap and a flashlight. She embraced her father and thanked Samuel Shawi. "Don't wait, Ben. I'll find my way out." She descended into the black tunnel. In less than a minute she heard her father curse and call loudly, "Wait, Juda, I'm coming with you."

The night before she entered the tunnel, Juda had had dinner with Father Oudi Yong. It was to be his last night in Jerusalem. "I haven't been much help to you, Juda, but I'll continue when I'm back in Rome," Oudi had said. "The Vatican Library should yield much about the Templars' life after their near extinction. I knew you wouldn't let me go into Iran with you, so I've prepared a small document about the Zoroastrians for your library."

Juda took the file folder and opened it to see six typed pages and a map. "You've been busy, Oudi, thank you."

"Zoroaster was born there by Lake Urmia in the north mountainous region," Father Yong said, pointing to the place on the map, "about five hundred years before Jesus. Today there remain about twenty-five thousand adherents to his religion in three places in Iran: Yazid and Kernan in the south, and Urmia.

"In many ways Zoroaster was like Christ, teaching peace, goodwill, and brotherly love. His word spread throughout the Middle East and into India, and lasted for twenty-five hundred years," Oudi told her as they ended dinner with coffee.

Juda offered a cigarette and quipped, "Perhaps there would be a billion followers of Zoroaster today if Constantine had made his religion the official one for the world's greatest empire. Christianity owes much to a pagan emperor, Oudi."

"As always, Juda, you're the devil's advocate; but I know you're a closet Catholic. Remember, Zoroaster also taught that there was an eternal struggle between good and evil, and that evil coexisted with the good."

Juda smiled. "Maybe he was right. Creation has never wanted for evil."

"Juda, be careful, you may find more than you care to in Iran. It's the stronghold of Islamic Shiite fundamentalists, the *Jihad*. They support terrorism throughout the Middle East, and the Kurdish rebels in Turkey."

In the morning Oudi attended mass in the Church of the Holy Sepulcher. After the church emptied he remained, his head bowed in prayer. On his way out he felt a sharp pain in his side – the barrel of a gun pressed forcefully against his ribs. He heard the raspy whispered words, "Keep walking, Father. Say nothing and you may live to pray again."

Startled, the Korean priest looked into the face of Rama Keeftan's number one man, Tunnous Manni – the man known as the Syffer. He wore a Palestinian *kaffiyeh* of black and white squares draped over a khaki, sweat-stained shirt and pants.

Outside, on the narrow streets of the Christian Quarter, another man took up a position beside Father Yong. Manni kept the gun pressed against the priest. "Do nothing foolish, priest."

They walked through the Damascus Gate to a waiting car, an old Citröen.

At his hideout in Hebron, Keeftan was ecstatic. His mind raced with the news that Manni had the priest. "We'll use the little fish to catch the big one, and the big fish will give us the Bonaparte fish. Shalima, prepare food, drinks, and coffee for me and my men and my cousin. George, stay with me. I want you to share my successes. I'll have Benjamin Kerns and Juda, and the priest will bring me money. That pig Nadir will die from this." He removed his gun. "After that we'll go with you to Las Vegas, you and me and Shalima, where we'll make millions at the tables, and then South America." He wrapped his arms around Gamash.

"What about the scroll?" Gamash reminded him. "What will you do if you get it and Nadir is dead? Give it to Hussein for his museum?"

Keeftan's mood changed. He became morose, angry. "You make fun of me, *Gideus*."

"You're excited, Abu Keeftan. I know you. Sit and drink with me."

"Before you leave, promise me something." Keeftan's eyes, now moist with tears, took on a distant look. His voice changed into a quiet monotone. "Avenge me if I fail again. It's what I fear most. I'm cursed, yet… I know I will not fail. But… above all, swear on our fathers you'll… you'll… " He began to sob.

Shalima tried to comfort him. "Abu Keeftan, you need rest. For three nights you haven't slept. I've watched you pacing the floor. Heard you talking out loud about this woman."

"What do you want me to do, *khayak*, brother?"

"Kill this woman, Juda Bonaparte, if I fail again. I can't live with more shame."

The winter rains had started in Israel and they would pour down for five days, washing the streets, cleansing the walls of graffiti, filling the ancient Roman cisterns, leaching into the porous underground. Eventually the waters, collecting from trickles in the high country, would find their way to the deep gorges and rush four thousand feet down to the Dead Sea. There the *wadi* would sweep like a tidal wave – deadly to the unaware. In the rainy season, the Bedouin, masters of the desert, would move their camps to high ground, ever respectful of the waters. And in the water-sculpted ravines, campers and tourists had more than once been crushed against the rocks and thrown into the sea by sudden deluges.

It was still dry in the tunnel as Juda and Ben made their way under the Old City to what they hoped would be the Rockefeller Museum.

The tunnel twisted and turned, following natural cleavages in the limestone. Eventually it became too low for them to walk upright. Ben followed Juda. She could hear him breathing heavily as the path went steeply uphill.

On her hands and knees, she stopped, looked back, and said, "Let's rest, Ben. This is difficult." Her breathing was regular, but Ben was puffing hard. Her flashlight caught a smile on his face as he replied through gasping breaths:

"Yes, let's rest; this is too hard for a woman."

Facing ahead, Juda smiled. "How much farther do you think, Ben?"

"Too far!" The passage had become cool and damp as moisture, undoubtedly from rainwater, collected on the walls and floor. Wet with sweat, Ben remembered the last time he was in the tunnels – the *wadi*. A stream of mumbled expletives helped, but it was Juda's cool determination that quashed his urge to go back.

Ahead the tunnel expanded into a small cave. Now they could stand up., Juda's light picked up an iron grate overhead. "I think we're here, Ben. There seems to be a covering over it. Look! Are you OK?"

"I think I'm getting too old for this shi… stuff, daughter." Juda leaped and had her fingers into the grate.

"There's a carpet over it."

"Here, stand on my shoulders." Ben held her legs as Juda put her back to the heavy grate and moved it out of the way. She swung on the ledge and easily pulled herself into the room above, but she knew the leap and lift would be impossible for her father.

"Don't try, Ben. I'll find something." She was in a small storage room, obviously unused. "Wait there."

"I sure as hell ain't going back. If it wasn't for this damned hip, I could do it."

The room had one door secured with a heavy rusty lock that defied Juda's picks. She removed a foil package from her bag and rolled the putty-like material it contained into a three-inch piece. After carefully stuffing it into the deadbolt, she inserted a small device into the plastic and walked to the far side of the room.

"I'm going to burn the lock. Don't be startled," she warned her father. Juda shielded her eyes from the intense light while the heat from the phosphoric plastic disintegrated the lock. She pushed open the door and entered a larger room where she found an oak chair which she passed down to Ben. With that he could just reach the ledge.

Ben cursed as he failed to pull himself up. "There was a time..."

"Take my hand," Juda said. He locked his hand around her wrist. "Now the other, Ben. Hang on." She straddled the opening, closed her eyes, concentrating, and pulled him through.

"Christ," Kerns uttered, "I weigh two hundred and forty pounds. What kind of a daughter do I have?"

Juda smiled in the darkness and whispered, "I do a little weight lifting back home."

As they expected, the Rockefeller was closed and there were no guards in the lower level. They found their way to the Scrollery storage room. In neatly labeled compartments were hundreds of pieces of Dead Sea Scrolls, waiting to be translated. Through the main workroom, past the long worktable where more scrolls were laid under glass, they found Father Scantland's office off the main hallway next to Father Legault's. Juda used her picks to open the lock.

"You didn't learn that in your Mossad training, Juda."

"I took a postgraduate course from a specialist, Ben. He's in jail now." Juda opened a three-drawer file cabinet and began checking every file while Ben went through the Scantland's desk.

"What are we looking for?"

"I don't know, but something..." Juda stopped at a file folder labeled Faxes: Sen. H. M. Graves. The folder was empty. "What would a Jesuit priest be corresponding with a U.S. Senator about?" she wondered aloud. "You find anything?"

"A few notes and memos – nothing. I think he was friends with Father Legault in the next office. Look!" He showed Juda a notebook that had what appeared to be Aramaic words written in it. "I don't know what these mean..."

"They're symbols, something like Egyptian or cuneiform, I think. Baxter said the scroll had a mix of different scripts. That's what made it difficult."

"Well, he exchanged ideas with his neighbor. Maybe we better have a talk with Father Legault." Juda went over to a computer on Scantland's desk and turned it on. To her surprise, the hard drive was accessible without a code. Father Scantland, she thought, must feel very secure – or perhaps my background makes me more paranoid than those who had led quiet, normal lives. She scrolled through the various programs and opened a file which contained unfinished documents for publication. Then, in the system folder, she found a file labeled Archived Faxes.

"I've watched T.J. do this. Let's see if the professor has good computer habits." She went to a utilities folder and opened a file called UnErase. In a few seconds a screen displayed a list of deleted files. "Ben, most people forget to sweep their hard drive when they trash files." Juda clicked the file marked Archived Faxes, smiled, and printed it.

"Father Scantland has been sending and receiving correspondence from a Senator Graves and Mrs. B'Ann Hickman. I think we've struck on something Ben."

Suddenly they heard "Who's in there?" and keys in the door. A museum guard entered the darkened room with his gun drawn, shinning his flashlight on the printer. Stepping from behind the door, Ben clamped his hand over the guard's mouth.

"Don't kill him," Juda said, as she hit him on the side of his head with her gun. Ben lowered the guard to the floor, tied and gagged him.

"I wasn't going to," Ben said, taking the guard's gun.

Juda turned off the printer and computer, then fanfolded the printout and put it into her bag. "Let's get out of here, Ben."

They walked down the main lower hall looking for an exit. The windows were barred and too narrow to use. At the end of the hall, they climbed a narrow circular staircase to a small locked wooden door. Using the guard's keys, they entered the first floor library of the Rockefeller Museum. To the left they saw the main entrance and the scale model of the museum. In the distant hall, which contained Egyptian artifacts, a guard was sitting half asleep, his chair tilted back against the wall.

"Stay here, Ben. I'll get him." She approached him silently in the shadows of a ten-foot statue of Ramses and kicked the legs of his chair. The guard's arm flailed as he fell and struck his head on the marble floor. Juda checked his pulse.

"Let's go right out the front door, Ben, like we owned the place."

Thinking of the unconscious guards, the keys they had and Israel's claim to the Rockefeller, Ben said, "We do!" Juda threw the keys across the smooth floor to the unconscious guard.

Outside it was dark as they walked in the rain back through the Damascus Gate to the Old City, and returned to the coffee shop of Samuel Shawi. They were wet and dirty, but each wore a smile. "Sami," Ben said, "we're back, and we need a large cup of coffee." Shawi embraced them and thanked God for their safe return.

Chapter 26

It had been raining heavily for three days in Jerusalem when Juda Bonaparte, Benjamin Kerns, and Samuel Scharkes walked out on the runway to meet Georgi Kirnski, who had arrived by helicopter from Beirut. The former Russian agent embraced Juda with the special intimacy you feel for someone to whom you owe your life. Juda introduced him to the others.

"So the great Israeli general is your father, Juda," Kirnski said, shaking Ben's hand, smiling broadly. Kirnski was short, stocky, in his mid-fifties. Like the others, he wore a trench coat and a felt hat. "And Samuel Scharkes," he went on, "the American who became the new director of the best secret service in the world – next to the KGB, I should say."

His smile was not returned by Scharkes. The Russian's entry into Israel through customs and immigration had been reluctantly cleared by Scharkes.

They were all thoroughly soaked by the time they entered the agency car. They drove to Mossad headquarters and entered an operations room containing computers, telecommunications equipment, charts and maps, and busy technicians.

"You'll be Americans: an archeologist and an ex-Russian engineer flying out of Saudi employed by a U.S. company. You're negotiating an oil deal in Azerbaijan," Scharkes said, "civilians, in a private airplane." Scharkes scowled as if he had smelled something bad. "This is your flight plan filed in Riyadh with Turkey." He shook his head, skeptical of the whole idea. "You fly over Turkey along the southern border. The entire area is mountainous. Even if you could land the Kurds... well, they think they're a state independent of Iraq. You'd be in trouble in any case. Keep on course, I'm telling you, and at the designated altitude. Deviate to the south and Syrian MiG 21s will shoot you down. Go north and the Turks will force you down, if they don't shoot first. Take your choice; they have MiGs, Mirages, and F16s."

"Juda," Ben said, "it's dangerous just getting there. Go down and the stuff they'll find in your plane will land you in prison waiting to be shot as a spy, not to mention what may happen in Azerbaijan or Iran."

"Did you get satellite photos of Urmia?" Juda asked, unmoved.

"Over here, have a look." Ben opened a file. "Urmia is a mountainous village. Here's the church, the only Zoroastrian place of worship in northern Iran. But look at this. It's some kind of factory, a military one, close to the church. And built within the past ten years the Americans think. Something's going on there."

Juda looked at her father and said, "Ben, we've got everything except the plane."

"Tomorrow, I hope. You'll have to be briefed and take it up with the pilot. Juda, it cost six million. Do you fly, Georgi?"

WEST PALM BEACH

René Gervais awoke in the finely appointed guest room at the Hickman estate and luxuriated in the large bed. A waiter brought in a tray of coffee, cheese, and fruit and told Gervais that Mrs. Hickman wanted him to join her on the patio for breakfast in one hour. Gervais lit a cigarette, sipped his coffee, then took his time grooming himself in the extravagant bathroom.

Mrs. Hickman wore casual clothing in soft pastels that complemented the patio's decor. A vase of short-stemmed yellow roses accented with baby's breath sat on a glass-topped table. Slow moving overhead fans mixed their scent with the aroma of rich coffee, and B'Ann's perfume, heightening Gervais' excitement.

"Now tell me about yourself, Mr. Gervais," B'Ann said.

"Why?"

"So I can tell them you're to be trusted, or… " she paused, looking into René's blue eyes, "they'll kill you."

"I'm a Templar Knight, trained and educated since I was eleven for one purpose, the protection of the Catholic Church. I followed my orders and I have so far failed to acquire the scrolls. You and Stourka and a Father Scantland, who I do not know, would start a religious war in the Middle East, and you would use the scroll to destroy Christianity if you could. Why?"

"And you've gone against us by killing Charles Stourka," B'Ann said. "Now the Israelis have closed down our work in Jerusalem, sealed it. Five years of effort wasted."

"Then you deserve the same as Stourka. I can understand greed and lust, and hatred, but not madness. Stourka died because of my hatred."

"There are those above me, my young friend, who are not mad. Men of enormous power and wealth. Men I don't know. Men who have a world vision far greater than mine, or yours." B'Ann smiled. "I'm their pawn, and they'll make me the first woman president of this country. But their goal is far greater. It's the world."

"Then it's madness." Gervais pushed himself away from the table. He walked across the patio, distancing himself from the woman.

"You're angry, René." B'Ann followed, then moved close to him.

Gervais took her arms in his strong hands. "You're wealthy; they killed your husband, and yet you're their handmaiden?"

His tone and strength excited B'Ann.

"Who are these people?" He released her arms and pulled her to him. "I could kill you right here."

"I know," B'Ann said, turning her face to his, kissing him with a passion as foreign to her as this strange man with the penetrating blue eyes and soft gentle lips. His warm hands pressed on the smooth skin of her back beneath the silk blouse she wore.

She pulled herself away and said, "Walk with me on the beach, and don't touch me again until I ask.

"My father died in a federal prison where he was held for income tax evasion. I was ten and worshipped him." She kicked off her sandals and stepped off the wooden walkway into the sand. "Try it, René; it feels great. Dad," she continued, "was a midwest rancher, a self-made American to the bone, a rich and powerful man. And like you, he always carried a gun, but not beneath his shirt, here on the side," she patted her shapely hip and smiled, "out in the open."

Gervais smiled. "You do more than kiss, Mrs. Hickman. Yes, I always carry a gun."

"He despised the federal government – all governments, and believed income tax was illegal, just as he believed in his right to carry a weapon. He went to jail, and I was alone. I was adopted by his friend, a senator who surprisingly enough shared my father's beliefs. Like yours, my education was carefully orchestrated. They taught me of a higher power – not a religious one – whose goal was far more universal and would bring global peace: a world government and a simple world religion that all men could relate to."

"With you as president, doing their bidding. Virtuous goals, violent means."

"Yes. But first they would have to destabilize world governments and – where your work comes in – the world's religions."

"Do you believe all this?"

"They do. For hundreds of years their predecessors have worked in secret to realize the goals. Christianity is their enemy. With the Dead Sea Scroll, which you failed to deliver, they believed they could achieve their objectives in our times."

"And I, Mrs. Hickman, who have lived a somewhat sheltered life, have never heard such insanity. You think this miserable scroll will help them because it will destroy the fundamental tenet of Christianity that Christ died on the cross? You think that once they have proof that He lived, that there was no resurrection, and that His body is entombed somewhere in France that will be the beginning of a world order of peace? You're as crazy as my mentor who released me from my prison in the French Alps. I never believed that old fool, nor do I believe you. You're a pawn alright. A brainwashed little girl with a lot of money working for madmen."

B'Ann smiled, "Now, kiss me again, René Gervais. Of all things, I'm not a little girl."

On their way back to the house, B'Ann told René that men would come today to question him. "Dangerous men," she added.

"I'll listen to them," Gervais said.

On the patio three men waited, meeting Gervais with guns drawn. They were from Miami: a short Hispanic, a blond American, and another who looked like a Westerner. All were tough and mean.

"Sit down, Gervais," the long-haired blond said, brandishing a Smith and Wesson revolver. He was young and muscular, clean-shaven, and deeply tanned. He smelled of Brut. "Mrs.

Hickman, you can leave us." He told the smaller dark-haired man, whom he called Mic, to frisk and disarm Gervais.

"The Frenchie carries a big gun, Jasper." He handed the forty-five to the blond leader.

"Mr. Gervais is a friend, you do not need your guns," B'Ann Hickman said, seating herself.

"I said you could go, Mrs. Hickman."

"I'll stay."

Jasper shrugged and replaced his weapon in a shoulder holster beneath his blue sanded-silk jacket. He opened the slide of Gervais' automatic to see a chambered bullet.

"All ready were you, Mr. Gervais?" the third man sneered. He was the oldest of the three, lanky, unshaved, his long neck protruding forward out of a denim shirt. He laughed as he straddled a chair, holding a single-action forty-four Ruger loosely in his hand. He wore slim, flared and faded jeans that barely fit over dusty western boots that had gaudy chrome toe caps. Jasper called him Cowboy.

"Sit down, Gervais, and tell us why you're here."

"I'm visiting Mrs. Hickman," Gervais said, seating himself. He showed no anxiety, felt none. "What do you want?"

"We ask the questions, Frenchie, you answer, or we'll hurt you, real bad," the Hispanic said, withdrawing and opening in one seamless movement a Japanese clip knife and displaying its razor-sharp saw-toothed blade. "You see this little nipper? It can cut off a finger just like that or cut up a pretty face. Don't be smart."

"I said put your weapons away, this is my home."

"Mrs. Hickman, you better leave us, we got work to do," Jasper said. Unobtrusively, except to Gervais, B'Ann pressed a button on her large gold watch. In a moment Nelson Smith, her bodyguard, came to the patio, a gun in his hand. Jasper leveled his weapon at Smith's face.

"These men said you were expecting them, Mrs. Hickman." He appeared frightened of the three men holding weapons on him.

"You think you can shoot all three of us, Nelson? You just set your piece on the table and have a seat, or you're a dead man," Jasper said.

"What do you want me to do, Mrs. Hickman?" His voice trembled as much as his gun. Beads of sweat formed on his brow. "When I saw them on the monitor, I knew I shouldn't a let 'em in, but they said they worked for Senator Graves and you were expectin' them. I told them to wait out here."

"Give them your gun, Nelson. The senator will be here soon. Now, gentleman, how about some coffee."

"You make it, Mrs. Hickman, Gervais and your gunman stay here. Now, Frenchie, you got something the senator wants, some kind of scroll. Where is it?"

"In France." Gervais expressed no facial emotions. But the glare of his blue eyes on Jasper projected on a man he was beginning to hate.

"Well, ain't that cute. France! Cowboy, check his room."

"If anything happens to me, my scroll will be destroyed."

"You tell that to the senator. Mic, you go wait at the gate to let him in. And you, Gervais, you better have the right answers for the senator."

HEBRON, ISRAEL

It was the city of Abraham. He had lived here in a cave nearly four thousand years ago, and here his tomb was still venerated. Now, it was an Arab city, dangerous to the Jews. Built on hills like Jerusalem forty miles away, its cubical houses perched on the steep slopes, it proved a safe place for Rama Abu Keeftan's hideout. Behind his inauspicious plastered stone house was a well-hidden cave. Here Keeftan held Father Oudi Yong, Juda's friend.

"Are you comfortable, Father?" Keeftan asked in the small damp cell that was Oudi's prison. On the washed wood table was a half-eaten bowl of yogurt, a plate of fresh cheese, *juban*, black olives, and a basket of pita. "Do you like our food, priest? It's poor peasant food, but nutritious. Are you warm enough?"

Oudi's wide-set Korean eyes narrowed. "Why have you taken me? I'm not a Jew, and I'm not against your cause for independence, though I abhor your methods of terrorism and the killings."

"We are few, and it works. One day this will be the miserable state of Palestine, and rightfully ours, Father Yong." Keeftan offered a cigarette, which Oudi took. "You, Father, are not about politics. Soon you will be released to return to Rome unharmed. You're just bait. I want Juda Bonaparte."

"You'll force her to kill you, Mr. Keeftan."

Keeftan's eyes became distant in the dim light of the cell. "I know, Father. It's God's will."

Chapter 27

The Beechcraft stood alone on the secret Mossad runway which glistened from the continuous winter rains. A strange-looking plane, it seemed all backwards with the wings and motors in the rear, the tail up front and rudders at each end of its long wings. Juda had found it easy to fly when she went up with the young American pilot who had flown it from Saudi Arabia. Overnight its bright colors and company name had been painted a flat black, making it difficult to see, and with its seventy percent plastic construction made it almost radar undetectable. The pilot had explained that it could reach an altitude of forty thousand feet and an air speed of nearly four hundred knots, but added with a smile it wouldn't outmaneuver a Russian jet.

It was early morning when Benjamin Kerns, Samuel Scharkes, Georgi Kirnski, and Juda Bonaparte left the agency car and walked out onto the tarmac.

"Juda, you have just enough fuel for the trip. None for side trips," Scharkes warned, "and if you go down, we don't know you. There's nothing in that plane that's Israeli."

Kirnski laughed and with his Russian accent said, "We will be Americans, yes. I have finally made it!" Ben was uneasy and couldn't enjoy the humor. At the plane he took Juda aside.

"Juda, I don't like this, it gives me – "

" – You think I won't come back. Well, I will. I want to, we have a lot of ground to cover, Ben, our lifetimes."

"Take this." He gave her a tiny transmitter. "Open that door and there's a button that sends out a signal. No voice, no returns, but I'll be able to find you with our tracking equipment. And Samuel Scharkes or not, I'll come for you."

Juda hugged her father and climbed into the plane after Georgi.

"This plane almost flies itself, Georgi," Juda said, pulling back on the stick and giving the plane full throttle. At an altitude of forty thousand feet, they were over the Mediterrnean heading north to Turkey and high above the clouds that had blanketed the Middle East for the past week and filled streams and reservoirs with the nation's most precious resource – water. Juda leveled off and explained the plane to her friend. "This is a Beechcraft Starship 2000A, and it flies like a starship, First Officer Spock."

Kirnski laughed. "And we go where no man, or beautiful spy, has gone before. But our starship looks like it flies backwards."

"Those spy days are over for me, Georgi, like they are for you."

"Then what're we doing?"

"Helping my father."

Kirnski nodded, amused. "Things change, Juda. Everything changes, nothing changes."

Over Turkey they reported to the tower at Gaziantep and heard, "Where are you, Beechcraft? We cannot see you." Juda reported her altitude, course, bearings, and flight plans. She spoke in Arabic intentionally, sounding like an American troubled with a new language. She turned off her radio and said, "We're invisible on their radar, Georgi."

"Like the secret Stealth the Americans are building, and the Russians are copying as fast as their budget allows." He had opened a book of charts and was studying their land routes.

"I can get us into Iran, Juda, and to Urmia. What then?"

"We're looking for a drug-making operation. Beside the church there's a building, a large one. See there?" She pointed to a sketched-in diagram on the area map where satellite photos had shown the building site.

"What then?"

"We watch."

"What?"

"We'll see."

As they headed north over eastern Turkey, Juda commented that they were over Mount Ararat, adding that she would like to descend to see if Noah's Ark was really there. Kirnski pointed out they would have nothing to believe if everything was proved. Continuing over Russian Armenia, they turned southeast and descended through the clouds into the coastal area of Azerbaijan, Juda following Kirnski's directions. They were in the Talish Mountains, flying low in passes through the rugged terrain.

"Keep at five hundred meters, Juda. We land soon."

Ahead the mountains opened to reveal the blue Caspian Sea, the world's largest inland body of water. "We're not far from my retirement village, Juda. Follow the coast south, keep low."

Near the town of Astara, they turned into a pass and descended.

"You want me to land there?" Juda asked, looking at a road that seemed too narrow and that disappeared into the mountains.

"Yes, straight in." The area was heavily wooded with a mixed tree growth; the road offered little clearance for the long wingspan. "Good," Kirnski said as the plane bounced and landed. "Now, stay on the road and we'll disappear into the mountains."

"I can't go anywhere else, Georgi!"

Giant pines, acers, maples, beeches, and ash trees closed in forming a dense skeleton, like the arms of an umbrella, covering the road.

"Turn into the clearing, Juda, ahead on the right."

They were met by three men and a woman in her fifties who greeted Kirnski warmly. They immediately hid the plane under pine bows in a freshly made clearing.

"Kirnski, thank them," Juda said, noticing the work they had done preparing for the plane.

"They're cousins, Peter, Ivan, Jon, and Anna, and they want us to eat with them before we go. We have a long drive through the mountains. The road isn't on any map and was here, I think, when Marco Polo came through, how long ago?"

Juda looked at the old truck and tried to imagine it going along an unmarked road in the mountains.

They entered a small log cabin that smelled of fresh bread. Simply furnished, the room had an open stone hearth with firewood stacked beside it. They were seated at a long wooden table that was immediately laid out with food: coarse dark bread, yogurt, cheese, sliced cold sausage, and a diluted yogurt drink to which dried mint had been added. Anna removed a long knife and steel and deftly sharpened the blade to cut the fresh bread, although Kirnski had already broke off a piece of bread and laid the salami-like meat on it before the knife could do its work. "They make this sausage here, Juda, it is from goat with much garlic and spice."

Juda followed suit and found the food delicious. As they had coffee, one of the men showed Georgi a handmade map that would guide them into Urmia. He traced the course with his finger while speaking Azerbaijani, pointing out places of danger along the way.

He warned them that Urmia was dangerous because the new factory was run by an Iranian colonel who had a contingent of soldiers and was very bad. After eating, they returned to the airplane and loaded the old Fiat pickup truck with the items Juda had ordered from Mossad.

When the truck was loaded, Juda retrieved a small bag and returned to the cabin. Kirnski and the others had arranged the load so that a layer of slats fit across the bed, resting on supports bolted to the sides of the truck. Now they covered the load with straw followed by three layers of firewood.

Inside the cabin, Juda changed her outfit for the trip. She strapped her PPK against her chest, adjusting it so it fit snugly under her left arm. Next she applied theatrical makeup to the areas of her face and arms that would be exposed, darkening her skin. She tucked her hair into a tarboosh and wrapped it around her head. She was no longer Juda Bonaparte when she emerged from the bedroom, dressed in loose-fitting coarsely woven wool pants, old boots, and a baggy shirt and vest, held together by a wide belt. Kirnski and his cousin gave her a broad smile. Georgi changed into similar peasant apparel.

Outside he embraced his cousins; Juda thanked them again.

"It's an old truck, Juda, but strong and tuned up. We have a difficult trip ahead."

Kirnski drove the truck through rugged mountainous country before descending into lush tree covered valleys, following rivers and other natural contours for several hours. The dirt roads were narrow and tortuous. They bypassed the city of Tabriz, holding their breath when they passed two army trucks filled with soldiers. Finally, from a mountaintop they could see Lake Urmia. "For your Zoroaster, this was the Sea of Galilee, Juda. We're in Iran, and nobody knows."

They traveled around the lake, and near Urmia they hid their truck off the road in a deep thicket. Juda slung her canvas bag over her shoulder and they started an off-road uphill hike. At the crest, with Kirnski breathing hard, they hid themselves in the bushes. Juda scanned the area with binoculars. "There's the church. The town is… it's like the end of the world."

The roads were unpaved and dusty; there were few automobiles, all very old. And the people – there was something wrong. She panned to a large rectangular building and watched truckloads of vegetation being driven in past armed men. "That's it, Georgi. I bet that's where the milkweed is processed into haoma. But it's huge. Why the military?" She frowned and swung the glasses back to the town – puzzled. Then she knew. There were no children playing in the streets. She looked at her watch. Could they all be in school this late? Juda handed the glasses to Kirnski. "Have a look."

"They look like Zombies, Juda. Compare the townspeople to the soldiers."

"I'm going down there. You meet me with our truck at that shop. It looks like a bakery. Get some food; find us a place to sleep. Tonight, I'm going into that plant." Juda looked at Georgi and added, "Alone."

Late that night Juda entered the plant. Well hidden, she had watched the sentries, timed their movements, studied the building. At the rear of the structure, dressed in black and hiding in the shadows, Juda darted from one Volvo truck to another, finally gaining the roof by climbing a tile downspout. She pried open a skylight and, hanging by her fingertips, swung to the sealed top of a large stainless steel vat. Using a small lithium flashlight, its bright light shielded by her hand, she found the storage room that opened onto loading docks where the trucks picked up or discharged their loads. Nearby she found packing cases stacked high, hundreds of them, and carefully slit one open. Each contained twelve two-liter bottles filled with a clear liquid; she could not read the label. Haoma, she thought. So much of it.

Juda went to the bottling room and found one of the labels, which she placed in her bag, and plastic sealing tape, which she used to close the box she had opened after she had poured some of the contents into a small bottle. She thought of her promise to Professor Grodzinski, and was saddened because her find could never help Harold Baxter. Then she picked the lock and entered the main office.

The office was well equipped. A locked filing cabinet invited her expertise, and yielded easily to a single pick.

Slowly and methodically Juda examined files, bills of lading, shipping instructions, and correspondence. In two hours she had a stack of documents and the room was covered with opened files. She placed the papers in a copy machine and checked her watch before turning it on. On time, a guard passed the window outside. Then she turned on the copier and prayed it was a quiet one. After copying the documents, Juda carefully replaced each sheet and returned the files to their rightful places. The skylight was still open, but the leap from the vat would be too far. She left the building by the rear door that opened onto the parking lot, hoping the open skylight would go unnoticed.

That night Kirnski read the documents. "My God, Juda, they're shipping this stuff to France, by way of Marseilles. The label is in Persian. It identifies it as water for religious purposes. Juda," Kirnski smiled, "you've broken into a holy water factory."

"Would you like to try it?" Juda said, holding up her small bottle.

"No thanks, I'll leave that to the holy men in Paris who ordered it. Have some food." He tore open a bag containing black bread, cheese, olives, and meat.

"Holy men?" Juda asked as she bit into the bread and cheese.

"Yes. This stuff goes to the Brotherhood of the Rose in Paris."

"The Rosicrucians!" Juda remembered her meeting in Rome with Professor d'Angello who had said the connections between the Templars, the Rosicrucians, and the Masons were historical speculations. "What else did you learn today, Georgi?"

"You were right about the children. It's amazing. They've all been placed in schools in Tehran. And nobody cares. In Russia we would have a bloody revolt. But these people, these mothers and fathers don't care. They work in their shops, or at the bottling factory, or whatever it is, eat and sleep, go to church. And they go every day. It's the law."

"Whose law? Khomeini's?"

"No! Colonel Mudda. Omar Mudda. He controls everything – the plant, the farms, the town, the church. And you're right about the church, everybody in the town is a Zoroastrian. Mudda lives near the plant, in the only large house in the area. He must be in with Tehran. Flies his own chopper." Kirnski smiled, "Russian made." Kirnski's smile was replaced by a worried look that filled his big Russian face. "I don't like this place, Juda. When do we leave?"

"Late tomorrow night. I want to go to church before I meet Colonel Mudda." Suddenly their little room shook with a loud knock. Juda's gun appeared in her hand.

"Put that away, Juda; I'm expecting a lady." He opened the door and a short, heavy-set woman with a broad face and equally broad grin came in. "Juda, meet my cousin, Nina." Nina sat on the floor next to Georgi and Juda, the sparse room having only a bed and nightstand.

Kirnski explained that Nina was Azerbaijani and a recent widow. Her husband had been an Iranian Turk and had died a year ago.

"Nina works in the factory. She goes to their church though she's Orthodox. Tell Juda what you do, Nina." Nina pulled off a chunk of the heavy dark bread and began to tell them about her life.

"In the factory I pull the leaves off the milkweed and throw the sticks in a cart. These are loaded into the great vat with water and the lid is sealed. It's like a big Presto cooker from America. An inspector watches the valves and the temperature and the clock, always the clock. At the right time they open the valves and the holy water comes out through pipes to the filters and the bottling machines. Everything very modern, very automatic."

"Tell Juda about the church."

"It is like any church. People pray." Nina shrugged. "Only it is like school too. You must sign your name at the door before you drink the prayer water. But," she smiled, "I do not drink their water. I'm a Christian. I bow my head in front of the guard and when I walk to my seat I let it drip out into my dress or my shirt when I bow my head. See here." She showed them the stained front of her printed blouse. "They don't have the Body and Blood of Christ. So, I don't drink. I know it's the same drink that comes from the big tank in the factory." She looked at Georgi, her expressive face becoming sad. "You will help me to leave this place? I don't like it in Urmia without my husband. Everybody in Urmia is dead."

Chapter 28

JERUSALEM

As Juda prepared to pay a visit first to the Zoroastrian Church in Urmia, and then to the infamous Colonel Mudda, three cars filled with heavily armed Mossad agents left Jerusalem. The middle car held Benjamin Kerns, Samuel Scharkes, and two agents; there were four more agents in the front car and four more in the car behind. A briefcase in the trunk was supposed to contain three million dollars: the Vatican's response to the ransom demand by Keeftan for Father Oudi Yong. This ransom had divided Israel's leaders, men already tense from the fighting in Jerusalem. In principle Israel did not pay ransoms, did not yield to terrorists. It was a principle that had worked well, thanks to a highly trained counterterrorist force and Mossad intelligence.

Kerns and Scharkes had argued bitterly, with Scharkes insisting they follow the law.

"We're only middlemen, Samuel. He's the Pope's secretary, and goddammit, it's their money. Let's get him back in one piece. Keeftan's no fool," Kerns had screamed to the impassive Scharkes. In the end, it had gone to Prime Minister Yitzhak Shamir, who had circumvented his cabinet and convened with the Supreme Rabbinical Council because of the sensitive Hebrew-Vatican relations. Finally, against Kerns' warnings of a disaster, they had secured the Vatican money elsewhere and agents had stuffed the briefcase with paper. They would make the exchange and kill Keeftan.

A few miles east of Jerusalem the highway narrowed as it descended, snaking and undulating through the Judean wilderness. These were the barren rolling hills where Jesus had fasted for forty days and where the devil had tempted Him. Only now it was not the devil encamped in what appeared to be a Bedouin camp. Abu Keeftan and his men waited in ambush.

"Tell the cars to spread out, Scharkes; they're too close," Kerns said, eyeing the surroundings. The rain had stopped; the hazy morning light barely filtered through the still overcast sky, the desert hills were dark and cold. Spotting a Bedouin campsite, he said, "The Arabs are preparing for more bad weather." He looked puzzled.

"We're alright Ben," Scharkes said, reassuring the old warrior. "The exchange point is fifty kilometers from here, on the way to Masada. I've got a chopper standing by."

Ahead a large tour bus had gone off the road. Its headlights and taillights flashed a warning. Clouds of oil smoke and sand sprayed from its straining motor and screaming tires as the driver tried to free its wheels. Scharkes picked up his telephone and was about to call for help when Ben yelled, "Get the hell out of here fast, Scharkes. The Bedouins... Oh Christ!" The bus moved backwards, blocking the road as the first Mossad car exploded in a thunder of smoke and flames. One agent, his clothing on fire, dragged himself from the car. Kern's driver tried to turn around as the bus discharged its tourists – six of Keeftan's men – who immediately began a staccato of automatic fire. Behind them the third car was blown into the air by another rocket that hit the road below the car. Men screamed. Two got out, scrambled for cover, but died in a hail of bullets. Two more ran zigzag to Kerns' and Scharkes' car, joining the other two agents huddled outside their car, returning the gunfire. More of Keeftan's men, who had been hidden in the Bedouin camp, advanced along the road in the trenches.

"Use your goddamned phone, Scharkes, before we're all dead," Kerns yelled as he shot and killed an Arab firing from the ditch. "There must be twenty of them." An agent fell at his feet bleeding from a chest wound. Another died clutching his throat in the deadly exchange. Scharkes tried to call, but was hit in the shoulder. The phone went skittering across the road as Scharkes fell, while continuing to fire his weapon with his other hand; he dropped an attacker from the bus.

"Ben, I'm hit. Give up."

"No, goddammit, I'm going to kill these bastards." An Uzi in one hand, his forty-five in the other, he walked into the road firing. Men died, others came on. Then Kerns was standing there alone, waiting to die, both guns hot and empty.

There was silence as Rama Abu Keeftan climbed out of the ditch in full Bedouin dress. He walked toward Kerns in the clearing gunsmoke, mist, and dust.

"Keeftan, you bastard. Give me a gun, I'll die fighting."

Keeftan smiled as his men closed around Kerns.

"Not today, General." He walked to the car where Scharkes lay. "Are you in pain, Mr. Scharkes?" Scharkes tried to take aim, but his hand trembled. Keeftan raised his weapon, a forty-four caliber Desert Eagle, and fired, blowing away the back of Scharkes head. The other agents were dead. A small helicopter came up from behind a desert hill and landed on the road.

"Like the one you had waiting for me, General."

Kerns cursed Keeftan's mother, father, and all his family. Keeftan hit him viciously on the head with his gun. "Now I have the bait for the big fish," Keeftan said, as his men dragged the unconscious and bleeding Benjamin Kerns into the helicopter.

Two hours later Kerns was in the cell in Hebron once occupied by Father Yong. He was still unconscious. A bandage circled his head. Keeftan and two men drove Father Yong to Jerusalem and freed him two blocks from the King David. "You will be safe here, priest. The hotel is up that hill, a short walk. Tell your Pope we treated you well. The Jews have his money." Keeftan smiled arrogantly. "I knew they wouldn't pay a ransom. Go back to Rome."

He drove to Nadir's. Slowly the steel gates of Nadir's well-guarded fortress opened after Keeftan had been announced and identified. Armed men took him to the second floor suite while his men were given refreshments in the guards' quarters on the first floor. Nadir was a very cautious host.

"I have Benjamin Kerns, and Samuel Scharkes is dead. You might say he lost his head," Keeftan said, throwing his *kaffiyeh* over his shoulder and strutting to the ornate bar in Nadir's suite. He poured a shot of Arak and opened an inlaid case, helping himself to one of Nadir's cigars. "I lost eight men. Kerns is a devil like his daughter, that *shaitan*, Juda Bonaparte. But now I'll get her, and then the scrolls, and your money my fat friend."

Nadir's eyes widened in rage. "You killed Scharkes? Took Kerns as a prisoner? You've started a war, Rama. The Jews will fill the streets with soldiers, they'll seal off the cities, make house to house searches. Your actions will hurt the Arabs and you'll lose their support. They'll give up and lead the Jews to you. I have a fool for a partner. *Yelan denak*, Rama Keeftan. What have you done?"

"I'll get your scrolls as agreed. And we'll have Juda Bonaparte. This woman has shamed us." Keeftan lay back on a thick chair, easing himself into the soft cushions, crossing his long legs out in front, and lit the cigar.

Nadir paced the room. He stopped and stood in front of Keeftan, a smile on his face. He placed his chubby hands in the red silk sash that circled his waist shaping his portly figure beneath the soft white *dishdashah* he customarily wore. "You are satisfied with yourself, Rama. What will you do when this is over?"

"Retire to Mexico or Brazil. Shalima prefers Paris or Berlin, but she's a woman and will follow me."

"You would give up the cause of the Palestinians?"

"You know it's lost. But there will always be fools to follow me, like Hamas. Now I want to know what you know about this scroll. Speak the truth to me, Nadir, or I'll dissolve our partnership with a bullet."

"You demand! You threaten Nadir al-Nadir! The dog threatens the master in his house! You're the lowest of all Arabs, a peasant without class."

"And you are a pimp and a whore. I believe you would sell your mother to a Jew."

Nadir smiled knowingly. "Perhaps, Abu Keeftan, whose pregnant sister died by her brother's loving hand."

Keeftan leaped up, his gun in his hand. "You go too far, Nadir." He chambered the large caliber bullet and held the gun wavering to Nadir's head. His eyes filled with tears. "She had lost her *'ird*, purity. *Sharaf*, face, demanded her death." Keeftan's face twisted into an expression of painful anguish. He lowered his gun and began to sob. "Would you have done less?"

"Sit down, Abu Keeftan. I was wrong to offend you. Yes, I'll tell you about the scroll and Juda Bonaparte. Maybe then you'll talk before you act." As he sat down across from Keeftan, he scooped up a handful of large pistachios. "You see these? They are the pride of Iran, the best pistachios in the world. And that's where Juda Bonaparte is at this hour."

"Iran? How do you know this?"

"I have my ways, Keeftan. Juda Bonaparte has two parts of the scroll and two are held, I believe, by a renegade Catholic monk."

"What is this craziness? A monk?"

"Listen to me. In the beginning I was hired by the Hickmans, a wealthy American couple, to find the treasure in Jerusalem when the professors translated the scroll. Later this man's wife secretly agreed to pay me to obtain the scrolls even before the professors were finished. That's when I hired you to get them. By then someone had killed the professors, one by one, but two of them had entrusted Juda Bonaparte with their pieces. She has them stored in a bank in Paris. I'm not sure who has the last piece."

"This Hickman woman, what does she want with the scroll?"

"Behind her are men of enormous wealth, international bankers, financiers, I believe. Obtaining the entire copper scroll is part of their secret agenda for the world. They financed the Jerusalem riots and were set to destroy the Wall and all of the Temple Mount until Juda Bonaparte and her father discovered it and closed them down."

"They crucified the holy men?"

"Through their organization here in Jerusalem. The monk killed their director."

"Destroy the *Kubbat as-Sakhrah*? The Dome of the Rock, the Al-Aksa Mosque? Who are these madmen, I'll kill them. The monk is with Juda? I should kill you for becoming involved with such lunatics."

"This monk is Juda's enemy. Your lust for her blood has destroyed our chances for the millions they would have paid me."

"No. I'll get Juda Bonaparte and her scrolls, then I'll find this monk and get his and kill him. You can sell the scroll to your rich Americans and we'll split the money."

"Yes, we can do that, but you've killed my source of information." Nadir began to laugh loudly.

"Killed who?"

"Samuel Scharkes."

Keeftan shook his head, then buried it in his hands. "*Allah u-Akbar.*"

WEST PALM BEACH

Senator Graves arrived at the Hickman estate in the afternoon. His armed chauffeur, trailed by the Hispanic, followed him to the patio where Gervais and Mrs. Hickman waited with the other two Miami thugs. "Mr. Gervais, we finally meet," the Senator said, extending his hand, and withdrawing it coldly when Gervais did not respond. "So be it. Simply give me the scroll pieces you have and be on your way."

"Your men have searched my belongings, they're not here."

"Will you produce them? I want the pieces you have, Gervais. Do you *parlez* that?"

Gervais smiled white against his dark complexion. "Yes, I know you want these scrolls. But you must know I have only two parts. Another has three."

"Juda Bonaparte?"

"She will never sell them, or give them up unless – "

" – What?"

"Tell me why you want them. She may respond to the truth."

"From you, a murderer?"

"I did what I was ordered to do. Juda would understand that."

Graves laughed and told his men to wait outside on the verandah. He pulled a white cane chair close to René Gervais. B'Ann Hickman kept her eyes riveted on Gervais. Frightened, she said nothing, felt her heart racing, anticipating.

"What do you want, my boy?" Graves asked. "Money?"

"Yes. Five million dollars."

"That's easy. What else?"

"Some answers. Why would you and your people start a war of attrition, a *jihad* with the Muslims. And how would you use the secret of the scroll?"

"For the treasure, what else?"

Gervais laughed.

"You, you... " Senator Graves reddened. "You dare to laugh at me?"

"Senator, you're a liar. Everything is a lie."

Graves screamed for his men. Gervais slapped him hard across the face, knocking him to the floor. He took a crystal plate from the tray from which B'Ann had served him breakfast and broke it as he leaped to the door, holding the sharp fragment in his hand. Cowboy, the first to reenter the patio was the first to die as the crystal cut a deep swath through his long neck. Gervais yanked Cowboy's gun, clamped his hand on Mic's face and pulled him into the revolver, firing three times. The Hispanic flew backwards into Jasper. The bullets tore their path through Mic's body, striking Jasper in the stomach. Gervais killed Graves' driver with a single shot to the head then again turned to Jasper, who was screaming in pain, clutching his abdomen. When he had shot him again, this time through the head, he returned his attention to Graves.

"Hold it right there, Gervais," Graves ordered him. "Your gun is empty. Cowboy always carried it with the hammer down on an empty chamber for safety. And you used your five. Didn't do Cowboy any good. B'Ann are you all right?" Gervais squeezed the trigger. "You see, Frenchie, I don't lie, and nobody slaps me. B'Ann?"

"I'm here, beside you, Henry," B'Ann answered calmly. "Are you going to kill him?"

"I want him to see it coming." He aimed his snub-nosed revolver at René's face.

"You'll never see your scrolls, Senator."

"You're going to die right here, Gervais. I don't give a goddamn about the scroll. Nobody slaps me. Nobody."

"You'll never know if it's true about the body of Christ," Gervais said mockingly. Graves tightened his finger on the trigger.

"You bast…" Senator Henry Malcom Graves III died instantly and crashed to the floor, bleeding from a small hole behind the ear. B'Ann Hickman laid her stainless steel twenty-five automatic on the table and embraced René Gervais, clamping her mouth savagely on his.

"It was the right place, just behind the ear, wasn't it? Now how many millions did you want?"

Investigators attributed Senator Graves' death to a thwarted robbery at the Hickman mansion by three known criminals from Miami. Mrs. Hickman was saved by her bodyguard and the senator, who died in the shoot-out along with his driver.

Before he left, Gervais had rehearsed the story B'Ann Hickman and Nelson Smith would tell the police, and rearranged the bodies to fit the account. Shielding himself, he had fired Jasper's automatic at close range into the Senator's head, obliterating the small wound made by Mrs. Hickman's weapon. Then he had wiped the gun and pressed it back into Jasper's hand. He said he was returning to Jerusalem to find Juda Bonaparte.

Chapter 29

COLONEL Mudda's home was a few kilometers from the town and factory in a valley bounded by cliffs. The Zagros Mountains marked the border with Turkish Kurdistan; they loomed dark behind Juda and Kirnski as they waited in the shadows for the colonel to return from the haoma processing plant. Before them lay Lake Urmia.

That morning Juda had dressed as a Kurdish woman in clothing Nina had purchased for her to go to church in. She had laughed as she modeled the clothing for Kirnski and Nina and caught a glimpse of herself in an old mirror. Wearing the traditional two colorful dresses, the outer cut low over an inner dress, worn over the *sherwal,* undergarments. The *sherwal* brought the biggest laughter. These pantaloons, or underclothing, had been too big and Juda had had to stuff them with a pillow, making herself look pregnant. Trying to mimic the gait of a near-term woman, hand held against her lower back, elbow cocked, she waddled around their little room bringing tears of laughter from Kirnski and Nina.

When it was time to go to church, Juda had draped a black scarf over her head, partially covering her face. Going into the church, she had carefully kept herself from swallowing any of the sweet syrupy liquid all were obliged to drink on entering, and had spit it out as she bowed her head, imitating Nina. The church suggested a mosque, being unadorned with icons, and the sermon itself was short and simple, later to be translated by Nina.

Nina said the Zoroastrian priest had spoken of heaven and hell, angels and devils, the Truth and the Lie, the eternal conflict between the good, *Ahura Mazda*, and the evil, *Angra Mainyu*, and the necessity for obedience to the law. Those of the Truth would gain paradise, those of the Lie, damnation – words that appeared in the Dead Sea Scrolls written almost five hundred years after Zoroaster. The sermon could have been given in Christian, Jewish, or Islamic places of worship with no one the wiser.

Now, dressed in black as she scanned Mudda's house, Juda thought how Zoroaster had anticipated so much in Judaism and Christianity. How many, she wondered, would pass over their Bridge of Discrimination into paradise at the end of their lives? From what she heard, not Colonel Mudda. She was less sure of René Gervais and herself.

Mudda lived alone, Juda had learned from Nina, but he had a houseboy and three guards. Twice a week he flew to Tehran. Juda had asked Nina what languages the colonel spoke.

"Persian, Turkish, and Arabic. More, I don't know. Some English, I think. One time a large helicopter came with men in suits and a priest. They walked through the plant and talked in his office. After that we had to produce more of the milk from the plants. Trucks pick it up once a week." Nina shrugged. "I don't know what they can do with so much. Many farms in this area must grow the milkweed and nothing else. If the soldiers find potatoes or turnips, the farmers are punished…" Her voice trailed off. "Some are killed. Be careful of him, Juda Bonaparte, he's a very bad man."

"The priest, Nina, what did he look like?"

"Medium tall, about as old as Georgi, fair, a red face like a drinker." Scantland, Juda thought from descriptions given her by Professor Markham and Buuckra.

Darkness set in. Juda switched to a night vision monocular. Suddenly bright outdoor lights went on, momentarily blinding her. Now they could see the small helicopter parked on the side. Putting the monocular down, she asked Kirnski if he could fly the helicopter.

"Yes, it's a modified two-passenger HueyCobra." Kirnski smiled. "Russian – made by Bell."

A military van arrived and Colonel Mudda stepped out. Thick-set, short, wearing high military boots and in full officer's dress and carrying a holstered side arm, he reminded Juda of pictures she had seen of Benito Mussolini. He returned the driver's salute and strode into his house. Kirnski put his hand on Juda's shoulder. "I'm not staying here while you go in alone, Juda. I'll take out the guards."

"Two, don't kill them if… "

The Russian smiled. "I have tape in my pocket. No promises though. You be careful. Signal me somehow when you're inside. If you can't, I'm coming in after you. We came together, we leave the same way."

Like a panther, Juda circled the house and silently disabled her guard by clamping her hand over his mouth as she dragged him to the ground, using her knee as a fulcrum. In one swift movement, she plunged a short needle into his jugular. In a few seconds, the succinylcholine paralyzed the victim. Juda checked her watch as she taped his hands, feet, and mouth. He began shallow breathing in one minute, but was now fully immobile and unable to utter a sound. Juda dragged him to the bushes. She examined the front door and windows. No alarm system.

Inside Juda searched the first floor then went upstairs. A light was on in one room, Mudda's. In the other his houseboy slept. Fifteen or sixteen, fat, and sleeping soundly, she thought, as she quietly left him and opened Mudda's door, gun in hand, silencer attached. He flew out of bed amidst a flurry of blankets and charged Juda like a bull. Juda sidestepped, tripping him, hitting him with her gun. He crashed to the floor at her feet. She dragged him to a chair and bound his hands and feet, and gagged his mouth. As she finished, she was suddenly struck, pummeled between the shoulder blades. She fell to the floor the wind knocked out of her.

The houseboy was on her like Moby Dick on Captain Ahab, ineffectively thrashing and hitting, crushing her. The boy was not a fighter, but his great mass all but overcame her. He struck her glancing blows with his head. Juda heaved him into the air and sprung on top of him as he landed, her fingers locked stiff above his throat, ready to kill with a deadly thrust. Looking into her fierce eyes, the boy went wild with fear. "Stop, or I'll hurt you," she said. He began to cry. Juda got up and prodded him with her gun. In Arabic she said she wouldn't hurt him, but he must do what she said.

Juda tied the boy in his room, carefully checking that the filament-embedded tape was not too tight. She looked reassuringly at him and said, "Stay here and don't struggle. I'll free you when I leave." Juda returned to Mudda's room, gun in one hand, a syringe in the other, which she placed on the table beside him. "You will answer my questions and I may let you live. Refuse if you wish, but you will still answer and then you'll die."

Mudda's dark eyes widened. He shook his head affirmatively.

"Hold still," she commanded, as she twisted his nightshirt into a tourniquet around his arm and slid the needle into a vein. When she had taped the syringe to his arm, she injected three cc's of her mixture of scopolamine and lorazepam slowly into his vein.

Juda began her questioning with, "For whom do you work?" and ended two hours later with, "Are you testing your drug on the people of Urmia?" When she was finished and the syringe was empty, she wanted to kill Mudda. The truth that had come from him was horrible – and impossible; better she had allowed him to lie. She holstered her PPK, returned to the boy and partially cut the tapes holding him, "Soon you'll be able to escape. Leave this place. Leave Mudda," she cautioned. Outside she found Kirnski. "Georgi, we're almost finished, but first I'm going back to that processing plant. Let's take the chopper. Drop me off and you get Nina."

"Juda, I'll go with you."

"No, I'll meet you and Nina here in one hour. I know what I'm going to do."

As he lowered Juda into a clearing a half mile from the plant she said, "Don't wait."

Kirnski patted the single fifty-caliber machine gun mounted in front of him and smiled. "OK."

Juda gained entrance through the still-opened skylight. She closed the brass valve at the top of the huge boiler then dropped to the floor and turned up the burner. She found a large spanner in a tool room. Following a natural gas line to the gas main, she attempted to loosen the coupling that connected it to a second boiler. It wouldn't budge. Sweating from her efforts, she ran through the plant until she found a length of pipe which she slid over the handle of the wrench and was able to lever the nut free. Gas hissed. She set a strip of phosphorescent plastic from her bag on the main and inserted a detonator. Checking the time, she realized she couldn't make it back to the clearing in time. Outside she saw a truck full of soldiers following a van that was pulling into the driveway. Mudda, Juda thought, I should have killed him.

She started to run through the parking lot. Mudda screamed orders. Men fired their weapons. Juda found refuge behind one of the trucks and returned their fire. She emptied one clip: two men fell, a truck exploded. She ran and reloaded.

The hills and bushes where she might find safety were a hundred yards away. No chance. From behind his van she heard Mudda order that they take her alive. From what she had learned, being taken alive by Mudda would be an adventure in terror. She could see him, but the distance was too great for her small gun. A dozen soldiers advanced, holding automatic weapons. Juda waited, then killed two. She dropped the clip and snapped in her last. What the hell, she thought as she stepped out from behind the truck and faced the men, gun in one hand, knife in the other. Six bullets, ten men, and Mudda.

Mudda approached her from behind his van and men while screaming orders in Persian and Arabic, "Take her alive."

Suddenly, Juda heard the rotor of the helicopter behind her. Kirnski fired a burst from the machine gun that sprayed the ground in front of the men. "Drop your weapons," he bellowed over a loudspeaker, "or you will all die." Mudda ran forward, his gun drawn, pushing his houseboy ahead of him, shielding himself.

"Bastard," shouted Juda, waving the boy to fall down.

"Kill them, kill them," Mudda screamed as the boy broke away from him and ran through the line of soldiers. Kirnski's second volley, which hit the ground closer to the men, chipped clumps of dirt at them, cut down the boy. Juda gasped. Raising his weapon, a Russian Tokarev automatic, Mudda wavered a second too long between Juda and Kirnski. Juda fired twice. Mudda fell bleeding from two closely spaced wounds in his chest. Looking at his dead servant, she fired again before climbing into the helicopter. The men dropped their weapons and ran as Kirnski let loose another burst over their heads.

"Get some height, Georgi," Juda said, withdrawing a transmitter. There were two explosions: the first when the giant pressure cooker exploded, the second immediately after when

Juda sent a radio wave to the detonator at the leaking gas main. The entire building exploded into a fireball. Walls collapsed, the roof fell with a thunderous sound as flames licked the night sky. The chopper wavered and almost crashed. Nina screamed.

"Get us out of here, Georgi," Juda commanded, collapsing into her seat as fatigue swept over her. She closed her eyes against the memory of the dead boy.

As they neared Azerbaijan, Kirnski asked Juda if it had been worthwhile. She yawned and stretched, refreshed from her short nap and appreciating the crowded comfort of the Huey over the pickup truck and mountain roads they had taken getting to Urmia. "We slowed them down, Georgi. Mudda took orders from the Bashra in Tehran. They're the Shiite fundamentalists who fund terrorism and answer only to Khomeini."

"What about the haoma?"

"Mudda used the people of Urmia for his experiments. Many died. He had to determine the right doses and concentrations. Remember how passive the people were? Imagine someone taking away your children. I think the Z on the foreheads of the crucified victims in Jerusalem was to incriminate the Zoroastrians. The Muslim Shiites in Iran hate them anyway. This country is ninety-nine percent Shiite fanatics."

"Who's behind this? Don't tell me the Rosicrucians in France want to convert the world with drugs. What do they want with so much of this stuff?" Kirnski became silent, then said, "I'll go with you to Paris, Juda. We'll find out." He smiled. "You can blow up their storage places."

"Georgi look! Two MiGs. Iranian."

"Twenty-ones, we sold them to anybody, and the pilots too," Kirnski said, turning on his radio to hear a voice in Russian ordering him to return to Urmia or be shot down. He replied in Russian, "I am a KGB agent, back off." Kirnski eased his throttle to a near hover as the planes shot by swooping upwards. "We bought a few seconds, Juda, but they'll be back.

Oh hell! They needed height for their rockets. Hang on." He dove the chopper to the road and throttled back, waiting. A rocket hit the ground in front of them. "They tried to miss with that one. Do you want to go back."

"We'll be killed anyway. Do something." Nina began to pray as Kirnski flew the helicopter just above the road, which twisted and turned in the mountain pass.

"This'll be close."

"Oh Jesus!"

The road became tree covered. The rotors nipped branches as the small helicopter entered a treed tunnel barely above the ground. Rockets burst blindly around them, setting the bush on fire. "Count the rockets, Juda."

"Four."

"Four more, then machine guns." He set the aircraft down. "Everybody out fast!" More rockets blasted the ground. Then came the staccato of the strafing. The three, hiding behind rocks, were surrounded by flames and intense heat as trees burned, jets screamed, bullets hit rocks, road, and trees. Then there was silence.

"Quick! before we're roasted. They'll be back."

"Great flying, Georgi," Juda said appreciatively. "Now what were you saying about blowing up something in Paris?" Georgi steered the chopper off the road and headed into the mountains.

"We haven't enough fuel for any more games of hide and seek. More prayers, Nina."

Chapter 30

Juda had been away a week. As she approached Jerusalem she became more excited about seeing Ben and telling him what she had learned from Mudda. Clearly the Colonel was connected to Father Scantland and the American, Senator Graves. Somehow the haoma had gotten into the hands of the killer. Whoever it was that had killed Baxter and the others was after the scroll. Gervais figured in; he, too, wanted the scroll.

Was he the killer though? Juda remained troubled over this question, over Gervais. Did he have access to the haoma through the Rosicrucians in Paris? She remembered the alleged connections the Rosicrucians had with the Masons and with the Italian criminal organization once known as P2. Were they all really connected? And were these involved with the Templars through the haoma? Through the Masons? Through others such as the church? Clearly the drug was some kind of tranquilizer. Juda radioed the Mossad tower indicating that she would land in forty minutes and asked that they contact Benjamin Kerns to meet her as he had requested.

The rain had ceased, but the tarmac glistened, still wet from the last downpour. Overhead, clouds covered the area as Juda landed the aircraft. In Paris it would be snowing, she thought, wondering how T.J. was. She taxied the Beechcraft to a stop. Israel Marks and Father Yong met her as she climbed down from the plane. Marks was Samuel Scharkes second in charge. Her heart began its warning quickening. "Oudi, where's Ben?"

"Keeftan has him. He had me and released me for Ben. There was an ambush. Scharkes is – "

" – Dead," Israel Marks interrupted, "and ten agents. They ambushed us on the wilderness road outside Jerusalem. I'm acting director."

"It's me they want," Juda said, holding back tears, frozen with rage.

"And the scroll," Kirnski added. "That's what this is all about. Mudda, the murders, the haoma, all over the scroll."

"Have you heard from Keeftan, Marks?" Juda asked.

"Not a word. Our men have done a house to house search in Bethlehem and Jericho and, I'm sure, a cursory one in the City of David and Hebron. Those are dangerous places for our Jewish boy-soldiers. We've had men watching Nadir's. Nothing so far."

"Give me your file on Keeftan, Marks. Now, I want to go to my hotel. Georgi, would you mind staying with me? I have a suite."

Kirnski's Russian face broke into a big smile. "Finally you ask."

"And you Father?" Juda turned to Father Yong, her tone dead serious. "Where are you staying?"

"At the King David. That monastery was too much. With the Holy Father willing to pay so much ransom for me, and it all being saved, I thought he could bear the expense. I'm staying in Jerusalem with you. I may be able to help negotiate with Keeftan. He indicated respect for the Holy Father when I was his prisoner."

Marks, a man too young for his job, laughed. "Keeftan is the ultimate killer, Father. He respects nothing except the expedient."

"I need that file, Israel," Juda said; her expression icy cold. "I'm going to find Rama Keeftan."

At the hotel, alone in her room, Juda fell on the bed, reading the note that had been left for her at the desk. *I have your father. For the present he is unharmed. Get the scrolls. I will contact you in three days. Keeftan.*

Juda called T.J. Troubble.

"Are you all right? I haven't heard from you in weeks."

"No! They have my father, T.J. Keeftan has him and wants to exchange him for the scroll."

"I'll send the pieces."

"Address them to me, care of Benjamin Kerns. I'll see that they're cleared through customs. I'm going to fax you some material, and I want you to check out shipments to a warehouse in Paris. It's the haoma, and it's being sent from Iran as religious material to the Paris branch of the Rosicrucians. Tell everything to Inspector Gillis. He'll coordinate with the Duxieme."

"I know you're not pulling my leg 'cause I can't feel it. Rosicrucians? Jes…"

"They're in the chain, T.J. Tell Gillis to take them out."

In the morning Juda went to the coffee shop of Samuel Shawi in the Old City. "Abu Keeftan has Ben. I need to speak with someone who knows Keeftan. I'll pay them well for information."

"Ben is my friend, but I know nothing about Keeftan except that he's a terrorist, an animal of the worst kind." He half filled Juda's cup with coffee, an Arab gesture that he welcomed her and wanted her to stay for more, and asked if she would like something to eat. Juda shook her head.

"Give me someone, Samuel. I've got to find him."

"On the Via Dolorosa, there's a merchant of trinkets and souvenirs who is his cousin. His name is Amad. Don't tell him who you are, only that you must find Keeftan. Tell him some story, give him money. Be careful. Ben is a Jew and I an Arab; we're friends. There are places in Israel where there is no friendship between Arabs and Jews. Even here in the Old City, and in the City of David, Jews are not welcome. He's next to station eight."

The Via Dolorosa, the street where Jesus had walked with His cross, was crowded with Islamic shoppers, Christian pilgrims, and tourists making their way up the narrow road, praying at each station of the cross and shopping. Fresh lamb and goat hung from hooks in small shops; the scents of sumac, turmeric, zetar, and cumin mixed with fresh fruits from Jericho, roasted nuts, and breads. Two thousand years of pilgrims had worn the stone slabs smooth and concave making them slippery in damp weather. Juda watched an old supplicant ascend the stairs on her knees, her rosary in her hands. Another wept as she placed her hand at station four in the imprint said to be that of Jesus' hand, where he rested on his way to Calvary.

The shop of Amad was full of small items and clothing imported from all parts of the Middle East. These articles included inlaid gray enamel boxes of every size from Damascus; jewelry from Lebanon; curios carved in Kuwait; *kaffiyehs* from Iraq, Saudi Arabia, and Lebanon, each with their distinctive colors and bindings; and long flowing *dishdashahs* in cotton and silk. Juda walked into the shop and spoke French to a young man.

"I'm looking for Amad, the owner."

The boy, barely seventeen, taken by the beauty of the French lady, smiled and said, "I am his son, and I have full authority when I'm in the shop alone. Let me help you. What do you want? We have many things."

"Yes." Juda offered an inviting smile. "Beautiful things, young man, but it's information that I shop for today." She opened her purse furtively and withdrew a stack of American dollars held together by a gold clip.

"When my father is not here, I know everything," the Arab boy said, eyeing Juda and then the money.

"This is an *affaire de cœur*," she whispered. "Do you understand? I'm here from Paris with my husband, and I'm looking for a handsome Arab with whom I spent some pleasant hours in Monaco. He told me to find him when I came to Israel and mentioned Amad." The boy puffed up knowingly.

"Come in the back, the customers can wait." Juda followed him to the rear of the shop, which was stacked high with merchandise, and dark. "I'm young and strong – "

" – And handsome." Juda reached out and touched his smooth face. But I'm looking for Rama Keeftan." The boy trembled. "Perhaps later I will find someone younger and stronger." She touched his biceps.

"Keeftan cannot be found. Only one man may know where he is. But he lives in the City of David and you must not go there alone. Women and Jews are – "

" – Tell me who this man is, I will find him. And then I will visit you again."

"His name is Habib, but he's called Ibyn Amak by everyone. He's an old man; you won't find him young and exciting like me. Give him money. He may tell you how to find the devil Keeftan, but then, he may not. He lives on the hill beside Hezekiah's Tunnel, by the Gihon spring."

Juda took a taxicab, an old Mercedes with worn and ripped upholstery, driven by a young Jew fluent in Arabic. He told her he would not take her to the City of David until she gave him fifty dollars. With an endless chatter, he warned her of the dangers of a woman going into the city and told her he would not wait. Behind the Old City, she could see the Al-Aksa Mosque and the pinnacle of the Temple, where the devil had tempted Jesus. She wondered how Buuckra was recovering from his wound. The road, narrow and bumpy, wound round and down into the valley. Stone houses three thousand years old hung precariously on the steep sides of the hills – King David's city. The driver left hurriedly after Juda exited the cab by the Gihon spring.

Two Arab children, dirty dark-haired boys playing up and down the dusty stone stairs that led into Hezekiah's Tunnel, stared in awe at the beautiful woman who asked them where she could find Ibyn Amak. The boys held out their hands for money and asked, laughing, if she would like them to take her through the tunnel. She gave them a few shekels and the older boy ran up the road, pointing to a stone shanty on a hill. The other boy slid to a stop beside his brother, raising a cloud of dust. They watched wide-eyed as the beautiful woman with the fine high shoes strode boldly up the rocky path.

In a walled yard with a broken gate, she saw an old man smoking a *narghile*, a water pipe. His head was bare, his hair short and white. A large aquiline nose protruded proudly over a full gray mustache. His face was deeply grooved and wrinkled. He did not stand up as Juda greeted him in Arabic.

"I must find Abu Keeftan. I was told you could help. I will give you money for this information."

The old man said nothing for a few moments, just went on puffing on his pipe, gas bubbling up through the water. "Tell me why." He waved his hand, offering Juda a seat on a box beside him. The boys had followed and were pressing their faces through the lattice fence watching. Juda opened her purse and placed a hundred dollar bill on the box between them. The old man did not touch it. "Why?" he said.

Juda remained silent. The old man puffed. Four large brown eyes watched. "Go and play," the man said, waving his hand. "I'm their *gidi*, grandfather."

"If I tell you, you won't help me."

The man shrugged and yelled for his wife to bring coffee. After a few minutes of silence, a short woman wearing a black shawl over her head brought a small pot and two cups. The man poured two full cups.

"Keeftan has my father, my *bayak*, Benjamin Kerns. I must arrange his release. If he has harmed him, then I will kill Keeftan. If you cannot help me, I will still find Keeftan and kill him, but it will be too late for General Kerns."

"No. I will not help you."

Juda picked up her money and started down the hill where she ran into the youngest of the boys charging up, screaming breathlessly that his brother had gone into the tunnel and had not come out. Juda, followed by the old man, ran to the entrance. The twenty-eight hundred-year-old steps were worn and slippery, the steel gate at the entrance open. The boy screamed and pointed into the abyss; it was dark and half-filled with water. Juda dropped her coat, kicked off her shoes and pulled a small flashlight from her purse.

The water was cold and higher than she remembered from years before she had walked through Hezekiah's Tunnel. Then she had been wearing boots and slacks. Halfway in, where the tunnel bent where the excavators had met, she found the boy, his head barely above water. She dove in and felt his foot firmly lodged between two rocks. She surfaced and told him, "I'll get you out, but it will hurt."

Holding her breath under water, Juda grasped the boy's ankle tightly, supporting the small bones against fracture. Pressing down hard, she flexed his foot. The boy screamed and jerked his foot free. "You have broken my foot," he sobbed.

"Walk ahead of me. It is bruised and cut, not broken." She held him around the waist as they made their way through the tunnel.

"It's not broken, I can walk." The darkness hid his smile, but she could hear it.

They emerged from the tunnel at Shiloah's Pool, close to Ibyn Amak's house. Disheveled, drenched, and dirty, Juda examined the boy's foot. He started to laugh and said she was a mess. Juda joined him. "Your wound needs cleaning and a bandage. You'll heal up for another trip through Hezekiah's Tunnel."

From his hilltop the old man signaled Juda to come up. He said he had her coat, shoes, and purse, and had asked his wife to help her clean up and to find dry clothes for her.

When Juda came out of the small house carrying a paper bag with her wet clothes and wearing baggy cotton slacks and a loose sweater, she thanked them and headed down the hill. She faced one more impossible task, finding a taxicab in the City of David. Halfway down the path the old man called to her. His wrinkled face broke into a smile as he said, "Cabal Street, Hebron."

It was not the once international sophisticated spy who walked across the marble floors of the King David, but a ragtag urchin who had walked all the way from the City of David, breaking off one high heel along the way. In her suite she found Georgi reading. He threw down his paper. "What happened to you?"

Juda tossed her clothing and shoes into a wastebasket and fell into a chair. "I've had a day."

Kirnski poured her a half glass of Pernod and dropped in two ice cubes. "You still drink this?"

Juda sipped the drink, welcoming the licorice-flavored warmth it brought to her stomach.

"Keeftan's in Hebron, on Cabal Street. Do you know the area?"

"You going?" Kirnski asked, knowing her answer.

"As soon as I shower and change. We'll need a car."

"What about the priest? He warned me to call him as soon as you got in. Says he can talk with Keeftan."

Juda called Father Oudi Yong, and then Israel Marks. Marks said he would be on Cabal Street early in the morning with agents and the army.

"I'll be there," Juda said.

When she came out of her room, Father Yong was waiting with Georgi. Juda had changed into tight black slacks and a black turtle neck. The PPK was strapped under her left arm and two stilettos hung from a harness under the right. She handed Father Yong the small TPH loaded with twenty-two stinger ammunition and three clips. "It's small, Father, but a man of God won't need anything bigger."

Oudi Yong smiled, chambered a bullet, eased the hammer down and turned on the safety before dropping the automatic into his pocket. "Just in case, Juda."

"I have a car waiting, and we'll pick up a bag of sandwiches on the way out," Kirnski said. "You must be starved, Juda."

Juda put on her soft leather jacket, tucked her hair into a cap, and slung her canvas bag over her shoulder.

"Let's go. This may be a long night."

From his room in the YMCA across from the King David, René Gervais watched the three drive away.

Hebron, *al-Kahlil* to the Arabs, like Jerusalem was sacred to the three great religions. It had been the home of Abraham, the common patriarch. Like Abraham, who was buried in the cave of Machpelah, Keeftan's hideout was in a cave, not far from where Juda had parked her car to observe from the shadows. Kirnski scanned the street and houses with Juda's binoculars while she used her night vision scope. "He's here," Juda said, "one of these houses, I can feel it." They watched and waited.

At six in the morning, a dust-caked Toyota pickup truck began making stops at some of the houses, delivering bags of produce, meat, bread, and bottled water. At the same time large army trucks sealed off both ends of the street. Soldiers piled out and began making house to house searches. Juda watched the Toyota.

"Kirnski, Oudi, look! The truck." The house was small and cubical and, like the others, built into the mountain behind. "That's it." Instead of small bags, the driver struggled with large banana boxes filled with items from the *shuq*. When the driver went inside, Juda flashed her lights. Israel Marks drove up.

"They're in there, I'm sure of it." The truck pulled away and Marks ordered that it be detained. He called for the attack. Soldiers, heavily armed, specially equipped and trained, surrounded the house. Others went over the walls to the yard and the cliff behind. Marks and the two agents with him drew their guns and were followed by four soldiers wearing gas masks.

"We're going in," Juda said.

"The priest stays. My men first. These are crack antiterrorist troops and know what they're doing. Sorry Father."

At the door one soldier raised a heavy sledge. "Now!" The door splintered and crashed open. A woman screamed. There was one occupant and she was crying hysterically on the floor, praying between sobs for Allah to save her from the Jews. "What the hell!" Marks exclaimed. Juda opened a small refrigerator. No fresh food.

"They're here." Two men began to push on a large cabinet at the rear of the room. One was cut down by a burst from an automatic weapon inside. Juda fired into the opening. A man screamed. The soldiers rolled in tear gas and a smoke bomb and snapped on the infrared lights on their helmets. A wild staccato of gunfire, screams, and curses followed. Then there was shooting outside as Keeftan's men tried to escape through a passage from the cave. In a few seconds it was over. Silence and smoke, groans and prayers from the wounded followed as Juda stepped into the cave looking for Ben.

"The general's not here," a soldier said. He kicked a wounded terrorist who cursed in pain. "This murderer said Keeftan took him from here three days ago."

"Where, bastard?" Juda shoved her weapon into his mouth and cocked the hammer against his clattering teeth. "Where? Or die now." Father Yong who had entered house when the shooting stopped placed his hand on hers.

"Juda…" Juda looked at the priest. "No!" She squeezed the trigger.

The man fainted as the hammer fell on an empty chamber.

Chapter 31

The Israeli Negev Desert jutted like a spear separating Egypt from Jordan, pointing toward the Gulf of Aqaba. On the east, the desert was hard and barren. Here in the Paran wilderness, Ishmael, the father of the Arab peoples had lived. In the west the Negev became sandy as it merged into the mountainous Sinai Peninsula.

For three days Juda drove a Jeep south into the desert, stopping at Bedouin camps asking questions. There had not been a word from Keeftan following the attack in Hebron in which twelve of his men had died. The five survivors remained under guard in a hospital. Although repeatedly interrogated by skilled Mossad agents, they gave up nothing, and perhaps knew nothing of Keeftan's whereabouts. Benjamin Kerns was still Keeftan's prisoner – or dead.

Juda had spent the night in Beersheba at an inauspicious hotel that had a small but clean room. Wearing tan slacks and shirt under a light bush jacket, her hair covered with a *kaffiyeh*, she had had supper in a small restaurant in this Arab city at the edge of the desert. She ordered *laham mishwi*, shish kebab, a *fatoush* salad, and coffee. The owner asked if she were not afraid, being a woman alone in an Arab city. She answered in Arabic.

"I must find Sheik Ali Hashim. He's my friend. General Benjamin Kerns is my father and Hashim's close friend." Among the Arabs, Kerns was the most respected Jew.

The owner said *salaam*, bowed and tilted his right hand to his forehead. "Then you are Juda Bonaparte. I am Salim Joseph. You were a girl when your father brought you to Hashim. And now you are a beautiful woman." He signaled a waiter to bring coffee and ordered additional food. "I'll join you for a moment until your *maza* arrives. Your father was a friend to the Arabs, as much Arab himself as he was Jew. The *maza* is with my compliments."

The table was immediately spread with small dishes of hummus, *baba ghannuj*, eggplant dip, and *salatet lisaan*, lamb tongues in lemon sauce. "Our lamb is perfect tonight. The *mishwi* will melt in your mouth.

"Hashim is in the desert. I last heard he's in the *wadi* of Aqaba. But there is no road. You must find a horse or camel. I'll tell you where to find such a beast." He picked up a placemat with the Negev map imprinted on it. "At 'En Yahav you will find a thief by the name of Sharife. He will rent you a horse or camel for many dollars."

The waiter brought Juda's salad, bread, and two skewers of lamb, perfectly charred. She wrapped a pita around the hot metal and deftly slid the kebabs onto her plate. She rolled one piece in the bread with a section of blackened onion and offered it to Salim.

He waved and said, "No, I've eaten six times today. Since I have owned this restaurant I've doubled my weight." He patted his large abdomen and took the offering. Juda smiled. Salim shrugged. "Perhaps one bite to keep you company." The food was delicious.

At the door she bid Salim goodnight, but he stepped outside with her and spoke seriously. "Sharife will tell you how to find Hashim. You must be very careful. The Jews have placed land mines to keep out the Jordanians, and the Jordanians have done the same to keep out the Jews." Salim shrugged and raised his eyebrows. "On both sides the desert. Who would want to go there but the Bedouin? Sharife will tell you where it is safe to ride."

At 'En Yahav, Sharife offered her a horse for three hundred dollars and a camel for five. "If you can ride, take the camel. The way to Hashim is very difficult and dangerous, but not far. I'll show you. If you do not return, I'll keep your Jeep."

The rugged terrain, scorching heat, high cliffs, treacherous rocky passes did not hamper Juda atop the dusty camel. By the day's end she saw the large camp of Ali Hashim. She used her whip once, and the camel responded with a fast pace. The sheik was the leader of the largest Bedouin family in the Negev and was himself related to the Saudis. Old but ageless, surrounded by younger men, he roared a welcome when he recognized Juda on the camel.

"You haven't lost your way with a camel, Juda Bonaparte," Ali Hashim said, lifting Juda down, embracing her. She kissed him on both cheeks.

"Prepare a tent beside mine and a feast," he bellowed. Hashim was tall and straight with broad shoulders and a full waist bounded by a wide belt. His skin was dark like burnished leather. He took her into his large tent of coarse woven camel hair; the weave, handed down through the ages, kept the tent cool. They sat on pillows, and a woman served them coffee immediately. "Now tell me what brings you home," Sheik Hashim said.

"Rama Keeftan has my father."

"He's the lowest of all Arabs, Juda. But why would he risk the wrath of the Jews by taking their great general."

"He wants me."

Ali looked at Juda, smiled and said nothing. He placed a plug of tobacco on a water pipe and carefully lit a square of charcoal on top. "Do you remember when I taught you how to smoke the *narghile?* He handed the stem to Juda, who expertly puffed it, enjoying the heady feeling from the cool smoke. Juda told him the story of the scroll and about the assassinations in Jerusalem, the plan to blow up the Dome of the Rock, the haoma.

"Why would anyone want to provoke a war. The Jews and Arabs don't need outside help for this. And this scroll… "

"Keeftan and Nadir believe it will lead to the treasure of Solomon, and is of great value to others." Ali waved that off as if it were nonsense.

"These scrolls they found in Qumran have taught nothing. The Jews have their books, as the Christians have theirs. We have the Koran, but the Bedouin tradition is older than all the books."

"Someone murdered a man very dear to me over a scroll."

"Yes, Nadir would be moved by money, and Keeftan too, perhaps, as his ideology fails him. For both murder is of no consequence. Why does Keeftan want you?"

Juda looked into Ali's eyes. "Because I have shamed him. Killed his men, put Sabri Youssef in an Austrian prison a cripple."

"Sabri was like a father to Keeftan. Yes, he wants you above all else. And he won't release Ben. He'll kill him as you watch. Then he'll shame you. It's his way. Keeftan is quite mad, but an Arab."

"I've read his dossier. Help me, Ali."

"Stay with me. I have two hundred men, children, grandchildren, nephews and cousins, and many women too. I'll send them out to find Keeftan. Then we will go and kill him." Ali called his family for a meeting.

"Go out and find where Abu Rama Keeftan keeps my friend Benjamin Kerns," he commanded loudly from a rocky formation, standing like a proud lord. "This is my will. Isaac will stay by a telephone in 'En Yahav."

The limestone cliffs along the Dead Sea had hundreds of caves and crevasses. Many were inaccessible because of the treacherous cliffs. At Qumran two thousand years went by before the scrolls were discovered. The Hahal Dragot was one of the most forbidding gorges. Falling steeply from the Judaean mountains, its usually dry bed and walls had been eroded and gouged by millenniums of torrential flooding as mountain streams spawned from winter rains joined together in their run to the Dead Sea twelve hundred feet below sea level. The Hahal Dragot and the Dead Sea were the deepest places on the earth's surface.

In an abandoned monastery some fourteen hundred years old, Keeftan kept Benjamin Kerns prisoner. The building hung as if by a miracle to the south side of the gorge a mile from the sea. The entrance on the plateau above was well hidden by rocks and a growth of wild palms and Sodom trees and was always guarded by Keeftan's men. On this plateau, in the eleventh century, a handful of Knights Templar had fought the armies of Saladin, their mighty charge driving hundreds of the Saracens over the cliff to their death on the rocks below. But now an Arab descendent controlled the area, Rama Abu Keeftan.

Keeftan had equipped the ruins with food and water, weapons, ammunition, and radio equipment. Hidden in a large cave protected from view by an overhanging cliff was his two-passenger helicopter.

Since hearing of the attack at Hebron and the loss of twelve men, Keeftan had gone from pacing into violent rages, and finally into another stuporous withdrawal, retreating to his bed. Shalima could not comfort him. A week before, Dr. George

Gamash had left him, promising once again that he would avenge his cousin if necessary, for Keeftan had said he would take his life rather than live with another failure at the hands of Juda Bonaparte, or a Jew.

In his room, a cold stone cell, Benjamin Kerns paced the floor, cursing the leg iron and chain that limited him to a few feet. One of Keeftan's men brought him food, sliding the small tray through a cutout in the door. "Tell Keeftan I want to talk," Kerns roared at the guard.

Rama Abu Keeftan lay on his back staring at the ceiling. Juda Bonaparte and Nadir al-Nadir drummed through his head, over and over again. They had to die by his hand. Nadir, for drawing him into this debacle that had cost him his men and his dignity, and Juda Bonaparte for shaming him. He sat up, rubbed his face, and massaged his neck, rolling his head. He interlocked his hands on the top of his head and pressed his temples to ease the pain. Memories of a lifetime played a nightmarish scene in his head: the slaying of his sister, the child he had killed with his bare hands as her father, a Jewish settler watched and cried – until Keeftan's bullet had ended his agony.

"Shalima, Shalima, come to me," Abu Keeftan cried out in his anguish.

"Rama, you haven't eaten for three days. The prisoner grows fat as the captor dies of starvation. What can I do for you?"

"I'll eat, then I'll talk with Kerns."

"Will we die in this Christian place, Abu Keeftan? Inside, I'm already in hell." Rama pulled her to the bed beside him.

"A few days, my love, and it will be over."

In his cell, high above the basin, Kerns worked at the iron ring embedded into the wall whenever he could. His hands ached, but after three days it had begun to move slightly.

Abu Keeftan entered with two men. "You wanted to talk, General?"

"I want this chain removed. Only a bird could escape from here, and it makes me uncomfortable. I can't wash, or – "

" – Use the *shushma*, toilet?" Rama Keeftan laughed. "Bring him a pail, and water to wash, and remove his chains," he ordered his men. "Soon I will free you. When I have your daughter." Kerns' knuckles clenched white against his palms.

"Juda will kill you, Abu Keeftan."

Outside the cell, Keeftan asked, "The charges are all in place?"

The guard smiled and handed him a transmitter. "Push that button and the mountain and monastery will blow apart and not be rebuilt in three days."

At Ali Hashim's camp, Juda and the sheik dined alone. A small fire warmed the tent as water boiled for coffee. Between them was a large tray of boiled lamb and rice, an Arabic tradition that they ate with the fingers of their right hand, after rolling the mixture into small balls.

"It was one of the great joys of my life, Ali, living here with you."

"Yes, Juda. You learned to ride and shoot with the men, and cook with the women. But you have no husband after all these years."

"The only good men already had wives, like you – or were dead like me."

"Dead?" Ali Hashim laughed. "Every woman should be so dead! You haven't met your equal, that's why. I have many sons, perhaps… ?"

Juda laughed. "I've acquired many Arab tastes, Ali, but not that one. I'll chose my own man." She paused seriously. "Ali will your people find Keeftan?"

"Israel is a small country, but there are many places for terrorists to hide, Juda. They may not. Are you prepared – "

" – NO! I… " Juda looked at the sheik. "I must leave in the morning. Keeftan may contact me."

"Will you give him the scrolls?"

"They'll be in Jerusalem tomorrow."

René Gervais had arranged a meeting with Nadir al-Nadir. Once inside the gate of Nadir's compound, Nadir's men searched him for weapons, then escorted him to the second floor suite. He declined food or coffee.

"I have pieces of a copper scroll to sell. Two parts of five."

"And how do you know I'm interested in such a purchase?"

"Two million American dollars for two parts, three million more for the five. I do not barter, or explain." Gervais' face was expressionless. He watched Nadir's eyes.

"You can obtain the others?" His voice was over-controlled.

"I will."

Nadir fumbled for a gold-tipped cigarette and lit it nervously, holding it between his thumb and first finger. "Will you have a drink? Food? A cigarette?"

Gervais remained silent.

"You will bring the scroll pieces here to me?"

Gervais smiled. "No. I will specify an exchange place. The money must be in cash and in one hundred dollar bills."

"This is impossible. There are not that many American dollars in all of Israel. It will take me… " Nadir's dark eyes moved as if he were scanning his bank accounts, "three days. Will you have the five parts, or the two?"

"Two. If I have the other parts by then, I'll call you and give you three more days. Are we agreed?"

"Yes."

"I'll call you in three days at eleven o'clock to tell you where the exchange will take place and at what time."

That night Gervais called B'Ann Hickman. "Nadir doesn't have the missing fifth part. Juda Bonaparte must have three pieces not two." He paused, not knowing what to say. "Has anyone made contact with you?"

"No one. My only contacts were Senator Graves, Father Scantland and Nadir," she lied, "but there are others… "

"I'll call you when I'm ready to leave Jerusalem. I want you to meet me."

"Where?"

"In Boston. I must find Father Scantland."

B'Ann Hickman hung up and smiled. "You're a man of few words, René Gervais," she said to herself. But it was not Gervais' words that made her smile. She thought of Boston with its intimate bars, fine restaurants, wonderful hotel rooms, and Gervais with his innocent blue eyes, and smooth, young muscular body.

Juda called Kirnski from 'En Yahav on her way back to Jerusalem.

"Where are you?" he asked excitedly. "Father Yong and I have been worrying ourselves sick over you." He looked and nodded at the priest. They had been playing backgammon. A tray of sandwiches and a half bottle of Johnny Walker stood on a side table near Father Yong.

"I'm in the desert, and I'll be there tonight. Any word?"

"Nothing. Israel Marks called. They're going to use drugs on the survivors from Hebron. But so far they have no clue where your father is being held."

Kirnski had just hung up when the phone rang again. He listened, said nothing, and put the phone down. "That was Abu Rama Keeftan," he said to Father Yong. "He wanted Juda."

Chapter 32

The Garden of Gethsemane stood west of Mount Moriah on the lower slopes of the Mount of Olives. Surrounded by an iron fence, it contained olive trees two thousand years old. Beside the garden the Church of All Nations, which was built over the rock where Jesus is believed to have prayed after the feast of Passover, cast its moonlit shadow. This was the dark meeting place Gervais had arranged with Nadir.

Nadir's two cars slowly entered the narrow drive and parked. Usually locked after six o'clock, tonight the iron gate to the garden was ajar as Kalid, Nadir's only son, and two men entered the sacred place. All were armed and had been ordered to kill Gervais once they had the scroll pieces. Clouds moved in that forebode more rain in Jerusalem and a warm breeze caused the dense foliage of the olive trees to brush together, making an eerie sound as their shadows danced on the pavement and pathways.

Nadir waited in his car. Two armed men stood outside his Citröen sedan. Rarely away from the safety of his estate, Nadir sat alone in the backseat behind his driver, fidgeting nervously with a nickel-plated Beretta automatic. A briefcase lay on his lap. He had warned his son and prepared his men for a trap. His lust for the money the Dead Sea Scroll would eventually bring him had drawn him out, even though he knew that Gethsemane was the place of betrayal.

The garden was laced with stone paths winding among the olive trees and dotted with concrete benches for rest and meditation. The men drew their weapons and spread out. "There's no one here," one of them whispered cautiously.

"Wait."

"We've been tricked."

"No, look! Over there." Across the garden they saw the beam of a small flashlight, moving in the darkness.

"When you see him, kill him. Don't wait." Kalid and the men advanced to the light. "There! I said it was a trick." They saw a small flashlight tied to a nylon line swinging from a tree beside a bench." Enraged, one of the gunmen cursed and grabbed at the flashlight.

Kalid screamed, "No – " The explosion blew apart the concrete bench. Like shrapnel from a cannon, concrete pieces tore into the men. Kalid flew across the garden and crashed against the wall of the church, dying instantly. The other two, savagely mangled, lay moaning and bleeding on the walk.

Nadir screamed, "Drive!" as his two men ran to the garden. Gervais, from a kneeling position in the shadows, aimed and fired twice. The men tumbled and fell. Then he stood up and shot his silenced weapon through the windshield of the car. Blood and brains spattered over Nadir. The car skidded and crashed into the rear of the church. Nadir, thrown about the backseat, reached for his gun. His hand trembled helplessly as Gervais looked into his eyes and smiled.

"You would destroy Christianity?"

Nadir cringed and dropped the gun, pointing to the briefcase. Nadir al-Nadir let out a low, hopeless scream that ended with the muffled retort of Gervais' forty-five. He slumped over the brief case, blood running from the large hole in his forehead.

Juda paced her hotel room waiting for Keeftan to call. The scroll pieces had arrived by courier from Ben's house and remained unopened on a table with the third she had obtained from Buuckra Mondas. She touched the package. If they were together and translated, what would the ancient copper sheet yield? That was the ultimate puzzle. She walked to the window and looked out on the wet, empty streets. This would be the last rainfall, she thought, before the warmth of spring and the scorching dryness of summer.

From his darkened room in the YMCA across the street, René Gervais focused his binoculars on Juda and waited to fulfill his sacred mandate. Now, he had another: disconnect B'Ann Hickman from the others who would use her. Nadir had been the first, next would be Keeftan, and then the Jesuit priest, Father Scantland. Who was behind them? Gervais vowed he would find and kill them all, but first he must get the scroll.

Juda looked at her two friends, Father Yong and Georgi Kirnski, and felt comfortable. They had refreshed their drinks and were passing time rolling dice at the backgammon board.

"I'm going to bed," she said. "Keeftan is playing with me. He won't call."

The morning papers had carried the news of the deaths of Nadir al-Nadir, his son, and five men, in a gangland-style massacre at the garden of Gethsemane. Nadir had been suspected of gun dealings and criminal connections throughout the Middle East, the police spokesperson had said. There was no mention of the briefcase filled with newspapers found at the crime scene

At his hideout in the ruins of the monastery of Saint Michael, Keeftan could not contain his rage after Shalima brought him the news of Nadir's death. When the cursing subsided, he cried like a baby, his head against Shalima's breast.

"What now? Even if Juda brings me the cursed copper pieces, what do I do? Nadir has cheated me." His body trembled. "I wanted to…"

"Leave now, Rama. I will kill the general for your revenge against this woman."

"But the money. Allah curse the soul of Nadir to hell, and mine. I'm the greatest fool. No! I must kill this woman with my own hands, then we'll go." He began to laugh like a mad-man. "I'll place an ad in the newspapers in New York and sell the scroll like that crazy Metropolitan Samuel did, and the Jews and the CIA will try to take me."

Keeftan pulled himself away from Shalima. He stood up and drew his gun, crouched and turned, aiming at nothing. "I'll kill them all. This one, that one. Nothing can stop me. We'll take some Jew and hold him ransom, or a king, no, the President. And they'll give me the money, and – "

" – Rama, please." Shalima's voice was low, almost a whisper. "Sit with me, rest, and we'll think this out together." She knew his insanity would pass. It always had.

A few hours later Keeftan called Juda.

"You must come alone. Bring the scroll pieces. Your father is unharmed. Drive east. A car will follow you. No tricks, Juda Bonaparte, I will kill your General Kerns. Leave at three, exactly. My men will be watching you. No radios or telephones. I'll know."

"No!" Kirnski said, as Juda placed a call to Israel Marks.

"I'll have this with me," she said.

Kirnski examined the small transmitter. "This is a focal point transmitter, Juda. Very primitive. The range is short. In Russia we have instruments that would – "

"Juda, take a car with a two-way radio," Father Yong pleaded.

"There's one in the car, but it's easily monitored," Juda said. "This transmitter can't be detected by ordinary equipment.

When I know where he is, I'll activate it and Marks will send in a chopper. I'll use the car radio if I have no options."

"And if you're beyond the transmitter's perimeter?"

Juda smiled. "Then Marks will have to find me."

"Juda, I'm going with you," Father Yong said. "I know Keeftan. I'll negotiate on behalf of the Holy Father."

Juda tucked her gun into its holster and embraced the priest. "I know you stayed to help me, Oudi. After this, you can hear my confession. This is not the work you were trained for. Georgi will go with Marks." Juda called for her car.

"You worried, Father?" Kirnski said after Juda left. "I know her, she'll – "

"Yes, I'm worried. I know Juda too." He remembered the burning Borgese mansion where many had died. "Maybe I should be worried about Keeftan."

"Join me in a drink, Father – vodka, Russian style." Kirnski called room service to send up the bottle he had had put in their freezer.

Five minutes later the phone rang.

"There's an Arab by the name of Hashim insisting on seeing Juda," Kirnski reported to Father Yong when he had hung up. "He's on his way up."

By the time she had reached the Dead Sea, two cars full of Keeftan's men had joined her, one in front, another behind. Heavy rain and low-hanging gray clouds obscured the sea and the jagged cliffs at Qumran. Across the sea the mist-covered mountains of Jordan were barely visible. Unseen, remaining far back, René Gervais followed the procession. At Hahal Dragot gorge the lead car turned in, the driver signaling Juda to follow. They followed a narrow bumpy path on the floor of the canyon; steep walls on either side rose hundreds of feet above them. Juda lit a cigarette and rolled down her window to clear the smoke and mist on her windshield. Then she felt it. Sheik Ali Hashim had once said, "You'll feel it first. See it and you're dead, Juda. *Get to high ground.*"

Wadi!

Juda stopped her car and signaled with her headlights. She hit the transmitter button and, grabbing the scroll pieces, ran to the cliffs. An experienced climber, she had no difficulty getting to a ledge high above the canyon's base. Keeftan's men began to scream and fire at her. Behind her, Gervais, who would have been seen following in the narrow ravine, had hidden his car and had climbed the cliff, watched Juda scramble to safety on the other side. He picked up his rifle.

"*Wadi*," Keeftan screamed into his radio as forty feet of water came thundering down the canyon. Rivulets four thousand feet above them in Jerusalem, fed by the heavy rains, had joined to become a gushing, roaring avalanche of water, reaming the canyon, seeking the Dead Sea, taking everything in its path. The first car was picked up and dashed into Juda's car. Men screamed as the water sucked them in, crushing them on rocks, suffocating them, breaking them, dragging them to be pickled in the brine of the Dead Sea. The men from the rear car rushed to follow Juda's trail up the cliff. Two more were sucked in as the waters closed over them like Pharaoh's army.

Safe on the ledge, Juda watched the carnage and reached to help the first man up to where she stood. Wide-eyed with fear, cursing Allah, and then Juda, he fumbled for his gun. "I'll kill you now, you *shaitan* bitch," he screamed in Arabic.

"No, don't…" Juda said and pulled the trigger of her gun, hitting him in the throat. His head arched backwards. A last gurgling sound faded as he fell backwards over the ledge and into the fast receding water. The second survivor climbed up. Juda warned him, her weapon aimed at his head. He said nothing and withdrew his own weapon. "I'll kill you." He cocked his revolver. Juda squeezed the trigger. The Arab laughed as her PPK failed to fire.

"*Allah-u Akbar* ." He smiled and aimed his weapon just before the front of his shirt exploded in a collage of blood and tissue; the sound of a high-powered rifle followed. He lurched forward and fell at Juda's feet. Juda squinted and saw him on the far cliff, a rifle in his hands: René Gervais smiling and waving at her. Juda fell to her knees beside the dead man and vomited bile.

Hours before, Georgi Kirnski and Father Oudi Yong left Jerusalem with Mohammed Hashim, the youngest son of Sheik Ali Hashim.

"I know where Abu Keeftan is hiding. I'll take you there and we will arrive before Juda Bonaparte." He was young, had dark eyes and a flashing white smile. "Sheik Ali is my father and Benjamin Kerns my father's friend. Juda Bonaparte and you will be my friends. We'll free the general and kill Abu Keeftan. Come."

They traveled south towards Bethlehem in an old Land Rover, then they turned into the desert. Young Hashim proudly displayed his ability to navigate the treacherous path through the rolling hills and rocky crevasses.

"This is Lot's road," he said, "and only this vehicle or a camel can pass. Do you have weapons?"

Father Yong showed him the TPH Juda had given him. Hashim laughed. "You would kill the great Keeftan with that, Father?"

"And prayer, my son," Oudi Yong said nervously.

"And you, Russian, what do you carry?"

"This, and it will stop even the great Keeftan." He jacked a bullet into the chamber of his Tokarev automatic. "But I have only two extra clips."

"Behind you Father, under that canvas, there's one Uzi, two long clips, an American Colt rifle and ammunition. Load the clips. We'll be on the cliff above the monastery in one hour. If we're lucky and Allah is with us, we'll free the general."

"Allah will be on our side," Father Yong said, clutching a rosary in one pocket, the automatic in the other, each moist with his sweat, as the car leaped and bounded at the edge of a high precipice.

At Saint Michael's, Keeftan ordered his men to prepare the helicopter. "I must find out if she survived the waters, Shalima. I know my men are dead. Take this." He handed her the transmitter. "You must be on the plateau and a hundred meters back. This place and Benjamin Kerns will disappear. Do it if I am not back in one-half hour. Return to Baghdad. Something else will surely befall me before this day is over."

Down the gorge, Juda, carrying the package containing the scroll pieces, climbed the far side of the cliff to the waiting Gervais. She rested on a ledge ten feet from the top and examined the smooth wall. "I can't climb this carrying this package," she yelled to Gervais. "I'll throw it up. Don't touch it."

Gervais watched as she inched her way up, holding on by her fingertips to small ledges and cracks. At the top Gervais sat cross-legged on the ground as Juda caught her breath. "You followed me again, Gervais. What do you want from me?"

Gervais pouted and smiled, "Not what you gave me the last time."

Juda laughed.

"You climb well. You're very good with your hands, Juda Bonaparte."

She laughed again. "They serve me well. You suffered no permanent harm, I'm sure."

"I want the scroll pieces. I must have them."

Despite warnings from her head, she still felt attracted to Gervais. "Why?"

"I'm sworn to recover them."

"For your church? More treasure?"

Gervais laughed. "After all this you have no idea, do you?"

"Get down, Gervais. Look!" They peered over the ledge, lying side by side, and saw Keeftan's small helicopter flying just above the canyon floor. The copter slowed at the wreckage of the two cars then flew out over the highway towards the sea. "Keeftan, looking for survivors."

"He's looking for you, Juda."

"How do you know this?"

"Stourka told me before I killed him."

"And Nadir?"

"They would have killed me. Surely you'll understand that."

"Yes, I've killed many men, but they were evil. Only once…" Juda looked away, blinking at her tears.

"I live with sad memories too," Gervais said.

"And the others? You killed Baxter and his friends?"

Gervais looked into Juda's eyes. "I did not kill Baxter and his friends."

"Gervais, Harold Baxter was my friend. I loved him. They were not evil men, yet they were murdered over this scroll."

"Keeftan has your father prisoner. You would exchange the scroll pieces for his life. I'll help you, and if we succeed, give me your pieces."

Silent, Juda watched Keeftan circle round and round in the valley. "I will. But you must tell me what possesses you about the scroll. Why you have killed."

"You won't believe me, but – "

" – Tell me, leave the belief to me."

"The scroll, Juda, reveals where the body of Christ is buried. At some secret place in France."

"What are you talking about? The Resurrection… ? The Ascension?"

"He didn't die on the cross, Juda. That's what is written in the scroll."

Her head swam. This is madness, madness.

Chapter 33

WHILE Keeftan hunted for Juda, Mohammed Hashim, Kirnski, and Oudi Yong parked their Rover behind a rocky escarpment on the plateau overlooking the monastery. Hashim drew a map in the sand with his knife. "I've been here before, that's why my father sent me to help you. When I was a boy we camped near here. My brothers and cousins found this place and a way to get in. We're here." He stabbed his knife into the sand. "Beneath lies a large cave where Keeftan keeps a helicopter plane. And over there is the monastery and the steps, with three guards."

Kirnski climbed onto the rocks and peeked over. "We could never get to those stairs without being seen." He frowned, squinting, his jaw muscles tightened. "Maybe at night, but it could be ugly." He turned and slid down the smooth rock. "There's a chopper coming."

"Keeftan!"

"If he flies up here, we get out, and fast."

"Juda," Gervais said, "we have to walk. You can't see it from here, but my car went the way of yours. It's useless."

"We'll run, as soon as I'm finished." Juda sat on the ground cleaning her automatic, freeing up the jammed cartridge. She pried it out of the chamber with a small knife and examined the ballooned case. Then she reassembled the gun, carefully wiping each part with her shirt tail as she did. "Five bullets. What do you have?"

"Three clips for this." He showed her his forty-five. "And a dozen rounds for the rifle."

"Let me see." He gave her twelve, one hundred and fifty grain, high velocity 30.06 cartridges.

"I want you to tell me everything about the scroll and the orders they gave you. And you want them so much, you can carry them. Give me the rifle." They exchanged her package for his gun, then took off running along the plateau above the gorge. After the *wadi*, the rain had stopped. The late afternoon sun bathed the desert with long shadows and a golden-orange glow as the assassins jogged together to a common end.

"Gervais," Juda said, not losing her pace, "they've never been translated. How could anyone . . ? If . . ? About Christ, I mean, and what they told you was written on the scroll? The priest at La Salette, exactly what did he say to you? And how…?"

"He was an old fool, Juda. I wanted to be out of that prison. Did I believe him? I don't know. And I still… "

"What did he say?"

"The society, the Templars, knew of the scroll. They thought once it had been found it would reveal where Christ was buried, where His remains are entombed in a secret vault in France."

"His death on the cross was faked? He didn't die? Somehow He came to France, dead or alive, and was buried here? Gervais, this is the most bizarre story I think I've ever heard. Do you believe it?"

"After I found out about Keeftan and Nadir, and the work Stourka was up to in Jerusalem, I knew others believed it and had some grand plan that would involve the scroll. They deceived me all along. Led me to believe I was protecting the Church."

"Who else besides Stourka? Father Scantland I know about. And the American senator."

"Graves? He's dead."

"You killed him?"

"I need a rest." Gervais slowed down to a walk. "He tried to kill me, but I didn't kill him."

"Who?"

"Hickman."

"Bill?"

"He's dead. B'Ann Hickman did it, saving my life. She's a victim like – "

" – You? Are you rested? Let's go. My father's up there." They ran in silence for a hundred yards, then Juda said, "What about the haoma? Where did it come from?" Gervais had denied killing Baxter and the professors. Had he lied? Would he know about the Persian drug?

Kirnski and Yong followed Hashim through a narrow passage in the rocks. It opened into a crawl space at the back of the cave. Ahead was the helicopter, and stacked up along one wall were steel barrels of fuel, oil, and other supplies, as well as three cases of 9mm ammunition. They inched silently to the mouth of the cave and out onto a ledge high above the valley. This ledge ran to the monastery where the wall had been broken away, allowing access.

"What now?" Oudi asked nervously.

"Find the general and don't get killed. And Father, don't look down." They walked into a narrow hall with small rooms on their left. Kirnski led.

Ahead, at a stone stairway, a guard was sitting on the floor smoking a cigarette. Kirnski took off his shoes and stealthily approached the guard, hitting him hard with the butt of his gun.

"He's not on this floor," Georgi whispered after checking all the rooms. "Downstairs." Halfway down they heard Keeftan yelling at his men. Georgi signaled the others to wait and proceeded cautiously until he could see Keeftan and hear him screaming orders.

"We've got to find some other way," he said, returning to Father Yong and Hashim. "There's too many, maybe fifty, and they're all in a large common room. I bet the general's on the same floor." They turned and Father Yong walked into a Palestinian guard.

They both screamed and raised their weapons. The priest fired his first, point-blank. The guard dropped his gun and fell as the high-velocity twenty-two bullet entered his chest.

"Oh, my God," the priest said, throwing a blessing on the run. The men thundering up the stone stairs were met by the flying body of the guard Kirnski had thrown. Keeftan bellowed madly below.

"Get the hell out of here, fast!" Kirnski fired into the men climbing over the guard. One fell dead. The three intruders ran to the ledge that had been their way in.

"Run, Father," Kirnski shouted. In the cave he knelt and shot the first to follow through the narrow hole. Yong and Mohammed raced to the rear of the cave with Kirnski on their heels. "Get out fast," he said, pushing the Arab by the seat. As he entered the small space, Kirnski turned and fired twice into a barrel of gasoline. The explosion propelled him out as flame and smoke and a deafening sound filled the cave, blowing up the helicopter, sending Keeftan's men soaring into space, screaming to their deaths. A roaring fire licked the air outside the cave, followed by clouds of black smoke. The ledge collapsed, sending more men to their death.

Juda and Gervais heard the explosion, saw the smoke. They picked up their pace to a fast run. Across the gorge, the mouth of the cave spewed fire and smoke. Three men were running on the plateau. Juda squinted. "That looks like Kirnski and Father Yong. I can't believe it. There's the monastery and Ben at the window on the left." Men were running up the stone stairs to join the three guards at the top who were already shooting at the runners.

Behind their escarpment Kirnski, Yong, and Mohammed took cover as bullets hit the stones around them. At the edge of the cliff, thirty of Keeftan's men fired from behind rocks near the stairs. Two set up a heavy machine gun, an M60 Juda recognized. Kirnski yelled for Father Yong to hand him the rifle. "Save the Uzi until they rush us, and you keep your four bullets to the end, Father. We won't last long."

Three hundred yards away, on the other side of the gorge, Juda sat on the ground and aimed Gervais' rifle. Her first shot toppled a man. Two more fell moments later. Keeftan's men died in the crossfire between Kirnski and Juda. She told Gervais to start climbing down so he could get in range. "I'll be right after you." Just then a second machine gun sprayed the cliff below her, forcing her and Gervais to move back. Lying supine, Juda killed the gunner. "I have three bullets left," she said, scanning the cliff for Keeftan.

Keeftan's men regrouped and fired in both directions. Behind the rocks, Kirnski could not raise his head for another shot. A stone chip gouged into Mohammed's arm. Father Yong ripped off a strip of his shirt and bound it.

Keeftan ordered his men to flank the escarpment, while the machine gun continued a frontal barrage. Suddenly from across the canyon a McDonnell Douglas Apache rose from the desert. Then another.

"Mossad," Juda yelled and ran toward the chopper. Tracers streamed over the gorge at Keeftan's men. Keeftan kicked away the body of one gunner, took over the weapon and fired, not at the Apache, but at Juda running for it. Wildly he demanded that Allah let his bullets find their mark.

Gervais picked up his rifle and sent three rounds at Keeftan, while his men broke up and ran to the stairs for cover in the monastery.

"Gervais," Juda yelled from the chopper, "here." She threw him an AR16 from the hovering craft. "Over there," she yelled to the pilot, pointing to Benjamin Kerns in the open window of his cell. "They'll kill him. Lower a ladder." Juda climbed onto the ladder as the helicopter hovered above the monastery.

"Kill Kerns!" Keeftan screamed from inside the monastery.

"We've got to get out, Rama," Shalima said, ordering the men to fall back to an exit below them.

"Ben," Juda screamed from the swinging ladder, "get out on the ledge. Grab the ladder." Men were at the door. "Here!" She threw him a Beretta. Kerns fired six rounds through the door, then tried to reach the swinging ladder. He looked down and cursed.

"I can't do it, Juda. Get out of here."

Juda yelled to the pilot, "Get closer, he's an old man."

"I'll be a son of a bitch," Kerns said, and flew through the air, barely grabbing the bottom rung.

"Hang on." Juda yelled as she locked her knees over the second rung and hanging upside down tried to pass a webbing belt around Kerns. Unable to reach him, she let her knees slip, twisting the ropes around her ankles until she could pass the belt already secured to the third rung around her father and snap it in place. She signaled the chopper to pull them up while emptying her clip into the window as more men entered the room. From another window Keeftan, in manic frenzy, screaming and cursing, shot wildly at Juda and Ben swinging high above him. Then he fell to the floor sobbing in Shalima's arms.

Flying high over the gorge, Juda and Ben hung from the ladder like the Flying Walendas, as the chopper headed for the plateau. Suddenly the monastery and the side of the cliff convulsed and exploded into an avalanche of ancient stone, falling with an awesome roar to the canyon below.

Chapter 34

Two days later Juda, Ben, and Father Yong said good-bye to Georgi Kirnski. They sat in the lounge at the King David, the leather furniture and marble tiles taking on an orange hue from the sunset which filtered through the curtains. "The Caspian will be very quiet and very boring, Juda. I'll be waiting for you to call me out of retirement again."

"If I do, it'll be to invite you for a visit. I've already retired."

Ben laughed. "Me too."

"And I'll be back at the Vatican, pushing papers, getting the Holy Father ready for another trip." Father Yong paused and looked at Juda. "What about the scroll?"

"Gervais had the package." Her voice was soft, throaty and serious. Her eyes glistened, wet with tears. "Marks said he last saw him climbing down the cliff, carrying the scrolls, shooting at Keeftan's men. He thinks he's under the debris with Keeftan, but it'll be weeks before the area is cleared and the bodies are found and identified."

"The scrolls came from the Dead Sea, Juda, and they return to the Dead Sea," Oudi said. "Perhaps where they belong."

Juda embraced and kissed Kirnski as he stood up to leave.

"Good-bye, Juda," Kirnski said. "Good-bye, General, Father. A retired Russian couldn't have better friends." He smiled again before turning and walking to his taxicab.

That night as Juda packed for her return to Paris the phone rang.

"Where are you? Are you all right?" Juda was unable to hide the excitement she felt at hearing the voice of René Gervais.

"I'm not in Israel, Juda. Your friends at Mossad would have kept me in their prison forever."

"What will you do now? You have the scroll."

"I must find the truth, Juda. *Au revoir.*"

Gervais put down the telephone, stood up, and walked to the window. In the next room B'Ann Hickman slept. She had said that sexual relations made her hungry or sleepy. Today she had experienced both. Naked, he looked down at Faneuil Hall Market Place from their suite in the Bostonian. Somehow it reminded him of the monastery at La Salette. He had felt it at dinner watching B'Ann eat with polished gusto – the feeling of detachment, of not belonging. Uncomfortable in a new suit, he had watched B'Ann slip into a white Dior gown, silky and slithery over her bare skin. She was dressed to fit in with the very rich patrons and the elegant glass and linen table settings at the Seasons restaurant. And what was he? Mountain boy? Vegetable eater. Neither priest nor penitent. A Knight Templar living a deception for a society that had deceived him. What had they wanted with the scroll? The haoma? Whatever it was, it was not the protection of the Church, something they had drummed into his head since they took him from the bloodied farmhouse and the bodies of his parents.

"René," B'Ann called, "where are you?"

He walked into the bedroom. Naked, she had pulled the sheet over her.

"I'm leaving." His tone had a finality that brought tears to her eyes. "I don't belong. I'm going to find Scantland and make him tell me what the scrolls are really all about. I must know."

"Will you come back?"
"I think not."
"Is it me?"

"No." He sat on the bed beside her, looking at her. "I'm a monk, sworn to laws of obedience, poverty, and chastity." His eyes turned down, saddened.

B'Ann Hickman sighed. "With the scroll you will be extraordinarily wealthy. You answer to no one, kill with ease, and make love absolutely beautifully. Where is the monk, René Gervais? He died in that mountain." She embraced him, touched the smooth skin of his back, buried her face in his chest and cried. "We're alike, René. Graves raised me, trained me for one purpose, kept me a spotless virgin until I married Bill, prepared me for their one goal, to be their puppet female president."

Gervais took her head in his hands and drew her face to his, kissing her gently on the mouth.

"When you're finished," she said softly, "when your search is done, come to me. I'll wait for you."

When he left, she buried her head on the pillow and cried.

T.J. Troubble met Juda at Charles de Gaul Airport. He tilted his head as she bent to kiss him in his wheelchair.

"Am I glad to see you," he said, as they made their way to the baggage carousel. "You'll never guess: I finally cracked the code on Baxter's computer disks. It was simple after all. They contained correspondence to the others on details of his translations, what the symbols meant, how they fit with the Aramaic, and his opinions. Mostly, I couldn't understand it anyway." T.J hesitated, then said, "Juda, Harold knew the scroll held another secret; I'm pretty sure."

"It really doesn't matter anymore, T.J. The scroll is gone; Gervais had the pieces. Keeftan's dead, so is the Arab, Nadir. They're all dead."

"Gervais?"

Juda looked silently at Trouble, hesitated, and said, "He got out."

"And Ben?"

"He's helping Marks with the cleanup and interrogations going on in Jerusalem. Then he's coming here with us."

T.J. smiled. "To live?"

"I think so."

Home at last, Juda poured a drink and began reading Baxter's notes hidden for so long on his computer disks. She smiled when she read in one letter to Van Dorn something he had written about his "young assistant." She recalled their work together, her quiet interlude of happiness. "We're taking these notes to Father Peush, T.J. Harold wanted me to give him the scroll piece. This is the best we can offer. But I want to go through them first."

"He's retired, lives in Grenoble. You want to go in the van?" His voice trailed off. "I had your car brought back from Rome."

"The van."

T.J. beamed.

When Father Scantland walked out of Divinity Hall at Harvard University, René Gervais followed him. That night he answered a knock at his rented flat and looked into the youthful face of René Gervais.

"Are you going to kill me, Brother Gervais? If so, give me time to pray."

"You know me?"

"I directed you."

Gervais placed a large leather folder on the table over top of the books, the priest had been working on. "I have the scroll — all five pieces. What does it say?"

"You have all the pieces, but you're too late."

Gervais removed his twenty-two and attached the silencer.

"I may kill you, Father, if you talk in riddles. I have not failed."

"Our incentive in Jerusalem has failed. And Iran. The French have seized the haoma we stored in Paris. You've killed all our principals. Those above me have canceled their plans. I can't return to my work in Jerusalem. Kill me if you wish, Gervais."

"Can you tell me what's written in this scroll?"

The priest smiled and shook his head. "I know what's written, but I can't simply read them. For twenty years I've studied low resolution photographs and in a few weeks, I think I could accurately translate it. Baxter, more than the others, knew it was not about the treasure of Solomon, and he told me so in letters."

Gervais' mouth curled into a scowl.

"Surely you know of Manichaeism, René Gervais."

"The heresy?"

"It was started by the Persian, Mani, in the third century A.D., and was based on the dualistic concept of the universe in accordance with Zoroaster, and before him, the Egyptian monotheist Amenhotep."

"So!"

"Our new religion, Gervais, could not accept the Resurrection, which, as you know, is the cornerstone of Christianity. The belief that the death of Christ was faked, that he didn't die on the Cross, that he didn't raise himself from the dead, has permeated secret organizations, scholarly writings, and so-called heresies for two thousand years."

"You, a Catholic, a Jesuit, believe this?"

"Yes, and the scroll will be proof. Unlike the others, this scroll has been accurately dated, and it was undoubtedly written by a Greek scholar who followed Christ and witnessed everything. He went to France with Mary Magdalene."

"And the death of Our Lord?"

"Templar legend, and other heresies say He escaped to France where He joined Mary Magdalene and her sister, married, had children, and died. Have you never thought it unusual the special veneration paid to Mary Magdalene in southern France, in Marseilles? There's a strange cult to the Black Madonna and an underground worship of Mary Magdalene there to this day. They saw her as a goddess, as Ishtar. *And there are those who believe His heirs live and can be identified.*"

Gervais, flushed with anger, swept the table of Scantland's books and notes. He opened his portfolio and spread out the scroll pieces, then fitted them together. "Read them, Scantland. Show me something."

Father Scantland's eyes widened; his body trembled. He traced the embossed surfaces with his finger tips. "For twenty years I have dreamed of this moment. I can do it, I know I can. It'll take me two, maybe three weeks. You see, I've been preparing for this, Gervais."

Gervais leveled his gun at Scantland's head. "Start now, old man. In three days you'll tell me where your Christ was buried or you will die."

In a mountain chalet near the city of Grenoble, Juda and T.J. Troubble met with Father Emile Peush. Above and behind them the French Alps cast long shadows in the dense stand of pine trees around the small house. An old Renault hung precariously on the steep gravel driveway beside T.J.'s modified van. "I live here alone," Father Peush said. "I'm old, but healthy, thank God. I still drive my car to the city once a week for my needs. Someday I may need a helper." Wizened and frail, he nevertheless remained bright-eyed and alert. His place was cluttered with books.

"This is T.J. Troubble, Father Peush, my friend."

"So you do not have scroll pieces. No matter. A life is more precious." Juda had explained on the telephone how she had given up the pieces she had for her father's life.

"I've printed his notes and letters that were on computer disks. Some were to you, others to his archeologist friends, and some to a father Scantland."

"I knew them all. They were all young men in Jerusalem working at the Rockefeller when I was there." He smiled, adding that he had been an old man even then. "And now they're all dead except me."

"And Father Scantland."

"Poor Scantland." He shook his head, rubbed his grizzled chin. "A great mind, but jealous and envious because they left him out of their secret. Where is he now?"

"In the United States, working on a book."

The old man chuckled.

"They all write books about the scrolls. Will you, Juda Bonaparte?"

"No. Do you believe it, Father? That Christ survived the crucifixion? That's what the scroll is all about, I think. All the killings, everything." She had told him about Gervais, Keeftan, the haoma, the plot to destroy the Temple Mount, the Western Wall, the Al-Aksa Mosque, and the Dome of the Rock.

The priest looked at her and smiled. "Do you believe, Dr. Bonaparte?" A long silence followed as Juda scanned her memories: her childhood, the churches and nuns who had taught her, the old woman she had seen praying the rosary as she knelt on the steps of the Via Dolorosa. What Dr. LaCroix had whispered to her as he died in her arms.

"I don't know, Father."

T.J. listened intently, his gaze shifting from Juda to the old priest.

"Nor do I know, Juda. There are liberal theologians who argue that the resurrection is not necessary to the essence of Christianity. Faith is a matter of belief, not historical fact, nor the theories of scholars. Now for Baxter's notes." He picked up the file with steady hands then set it down. "Would you make tea, please, while I read."

It was late when he closed the file. "Harold was afraid of his scroll, Juda. That's why he wanted you to bring it to me. He knew I could have it archived in St. Peter's Vault forever. Or destroy it.

"He had written to Scantland, apologizing for excluding him, explaining what he feared. And from Scantland it started: the conspiracy to use the scroll. Did you see his drawing? What does it mean? A rough circle with a line over it and a wavy line below. A symbol. Baxter thought it important or he wouldn't have copied it into his notes. If we mix legend with his pictograph it may show us where he believed the scroll indicated Christ was buried. I think it means a cave in southern France. You remember, it was the unusual mixture of Aramaic and cuneiform markings that stumped Baxter."

"Yes. He said it was like no other scroll," Juda agreed.

"Do you know the order? I mean what man had which piece?"

"Baxter's was the middle piece and Father Legault's was the last, on the lower right."

Father Peush shook his head. "Do you want to find the cave, Juda?"

"René Gervais does, above all."

"Do you?"

Juda couldn't answer. She merely thanked him and bid him good night. "If the copper scroll ever comes back to me, I will bring it to you, Father Peush, as Harold wished."

As T.J. lowered the lift on his van, the priest stood in his doorway, clutching Baxter's notes. "The road ahead is dark and perilous, Juda, drive safely."

Father Scantland sat stiffly in his chair, his head at a strange angle. The room was littered with pizza boxes and empty beverage cans, half-eaten submarine sandwiches, and donuts. The priest's desk was empty, his notes and books on the floor where Gervais had thrown them. The scroll was gone. A single fly buzzed around Scantland's head, alighting on the dried blood coming from the small hole behind his right ear. Gervais had left his mark.

Juda, stretched out on the couch in her apartment, wondered where Gervais was and what he would do with the scroll. T.J. sat at his computer, a can of beer beside the keyboard. Before she could speak her thoughts, the phone rang.
"Juda, it's Ben, pick it up."
"Daughter," Ben said, "I'm coming home if you still want me."
"When?" She failed to control the excitement she felt. "We'll meet you." Something was wrong. "Why so soon? You said in a few weeks."
Silence.
"Ben?"
"Gervais got out. There was no sign of him or the scroll in the rubble. We think he's left the country."
Juda hung up and told T.J. that Ben was coming to Paris.

Chapter 35

Juda, unsatisfied after a day of shopping in Paris and a leisurely lunch with her friend Claude, a restaurant owner, threw her packages down and asked T.J. if he could get Baxter's files up on his computer. "I want to see that drawing he made, once more."

She stood behind him, watching as he found the right screen. "There's something about the curved line at the bottom. Can you change it's size? Make it smaller." Juda tilted her head, puzzled. "Make it bigger T.J."

"You have something in mind? Tell me."

"It kept coming back all day from something I saw and I can't remember. Can you superimpose it over a map of France?"

"Give me a few minutes." Juda went to her packages and began unpacking until she came to a blue and gold box from Sebastian's, a boutique. Embossed in gold on the cardboard lid were sweeping stylized lines punctuated with gold stars that located Sebastian's exclusive shops all over France. Juda traced her finger over the line of shops that extended from Paris to Nice, St. Tropez, Marseilles, Toulouse, and Bordeaux. Southern France, she thought. She called to T.J., "It's southern France, T.J., the Riviera."

"You wish. Here, have a look. It fits the Pyrenees. You can move it around a little, but the curve flows from that big bay at Marseilles into the mountains, where Baxter made his circle."

"That's where the cave is, T.J."

"And that narrows it down to about a million, I guess. They have everything there from prehistoric caves with paintings of water buffaloes or horses to – I don't know what. I think."

Late that night Gervais called Juda.

"I know where the treasure's hidden," he said without preamble.

"You mean where you believe the body is, don't you René?" She gave up fighting the feelings she had when she heard his voice, said his name.

"I must find out."

"I too know. And you'll never find it."

"Help me."

"Why? It's your obsession. I can leave it alone, René."

"Meet me in three days at noon in the town of Carcassonne."

At breakfast T.J. asked who had called so late.

"Gervais. He wants me to meet him in the Pyrenees."

"He knows?"

"I don't think so. He wouldn't have called me." Juda took a sip of coffee and lit a cigarette. "Will you come?"

T. J. smiled. "When do you want to leave?"

"As soon as we can. Order these things. We'll pick them up on the way."

T.J. examined the list and whistled. "Planning to do a little mountain climbing, Juda?"

"Maybe. We're going into mountainous country to find a cave."

"A cave in a hay – "

" – Don't say it, T.J."

On the street outside Juda's building in Paris, Keeftan's man, parked in a small sedan nearby, picked up a hand held radio. He spoke in Arabic. "They are in a black Ford van."

"Follow her and keep well back. I'll be behind you," Rama Keeftan said, starting his car. A thin smile showed on his tightly pressed lips. "I'll follow her to hell, Shalima."

It took a full day to reach the foothills of the Pyrenees. This region was a part of France steeped in bloody history. Here Hannibal, with his army and elephants, had crossed these mountains into Gaul and brought the great Roman Empire to its knees. Here the Knights Templar had built castles and churches, and acquired vast land holdings. Here, in the only crusade in history ever to be directed at Christians, crusaders responding to Pope Urban's commands had mounted a bloody campaign to quash the Cathar, or Albigensian heresy. Did Urban have other reasons for sending in his knights? For here, as in all of southern France, more than anywhere else in the world, people still held a strange and secret devotion to Mary Magdalene *who was thought by some to be the spouse of Jesus*. And here, at Lourdes, the Virgin herself had touched a girl and made miracles, announcing her preeminence over the Magdalene to the world.

Arriving in Carcassonne at dusk, Juda and T.J. took rooms in a small hotel. Keeftan, well behind them, preferred the cover of his car, and prepared to rest in it for the night. He screamed impatiently over his radio to the lead car as a sign-off, "Keep your eye on her, *yelan denak*. Lose Juda and you die."

The next morning Juda and T.J. began a systematic search of the mountains and valleys around the towns and villages. Over narrow winding roads, up great heights, and down into rocky valleys, the van bounced and rolled as Juda scanned the steep cliffs and the ancient ruins perched on top of them with binoculars. She kept referring to the copy of Baxter's sketch and a detailed regional map on her lap. After several hours she said, "This seems hopeless, T.J., we've seen hundreds of caves. Nothing fits."

"We've got two hours till sunset," he said. "Let's keep going." He turned onto a treacherously narrow road that descended into a valley below the village of Rennes-le-Chateau.

"You know, Juda, some thought this scroll had something to do with the treasure of Solomon. And you've told me about the Templars and their lost treasure. Now we got another treasure according to your friend Baxter's notes, the treasure of the Cathars. Did it occur to you they might all be the same treasure?"

"Let's go back, T.J.," Juda said, taking in his question without bothering to answer it. "It's getting dark. Maybe Gervais will know something."

"He knew it was this place, Juda, if he wasn't puttin' you on, getting us out of Paris; but he didn't have Baxter's drawing. He's using us, and I don't trust him one iota."

At noon the next day they met René Gervais and the three decided to retrace the routes Juda and T.J. had traveled. Past Rennes-le-Chateau, at the base of a steep cliff, Juda spotted a cave with castle ruins perched above. "There," Juda shouted, "the cave and the tower above, and the cross. Like Harold drew it."

She got out and examined the cliff. "Do you climb, Gervais?"

"My training didn't include that rich man's sport."

"It's about two hundred meters to the top and halfway to the cave. I'm going to place some pitons now and climb it in the morning," Juda said, smiling. "If you want to try, René, I'll make it easy for you." She belted on her equipment and started climbing.

In the back of the van, Gervais opened his large file case and carefully spread out the copper sheets, fitting them together as they once had been.

"So that's what this was all about, the scroll all back together," Troubble said, watching Gervais use a small loupe to examine the last piece of scroll in detail while holding Juda's drawing in his other hand.

"You'd like to be up there with her, T.J.," Gervais said. "I see how you watch."

"I would be if it weren't for the bullet I took a few years ago."

Juda was half way to the cave. She seemed glued to the wall as she hung precariously with by one hand, spread-legged between two pitons, hammering in another.

"What do you think she'll find in there, Gervais?"

Gervais remained silent as he too watched Juda work. Then, he offhandedly said "God." When she reached the top and disappeared into the cave, a small smile showed on his lips as he carefully repackaged the copper sheets.

Two hours passed. T.J. looked at his watch for the tenth time, and at Gervais, who was sitting against a rock, his head against his knees. "Gervais, do you think she's all right up there? What are you going to do? Goddammit, say something."

"If I tried to climb up I would slip and fall. We must wait."

T.J. beat his hands on his wheelchair and cursed – not for the first time. Gervais squinted, watching the cave.

"There she is, T.J. She survived," Gervais said. "I hope your chair does." Juda was at the edge of the cave adjusting her harness.

"She's going to rappel. God, from that height." They watched Juda pass the braided rope under one thigh, across her body and over the opposite shoulder into a cam at her waist. She descended smoothly in a few long leaps.

Juda was excited from her long climb. "It'll be easy in the morning," she said. "Are you coming, Gervais? We've found it."

"Yes. I'm sure I could follow you," Gervais answered with a new confidence. "I'll meet you here in the morning. I have my own car."

That night at dinner, T.J. said, "That Gervais is a strange one, Juda. I think he's got the hots for you. I watched him. He was studying something in the scroll, comparing it to the drawing you made from Baxter's notes, but he kept shifting those shifty blue eyes to you."

"T.J., give me the keys to the van, I have some shopping to do," Juda said.

"You want me to do it?"

"No." She took the keys. "I'll see you at breakfast. Seven o'clock?" In her room, Juda made a call to Marseilles.

"Marcel? Juda Bonaparte. I need some items." Marcel Boulanger was a gun dealer. He arranged to make the delivery by helicopter in three hours. She looked at her watch before resting. It would be a long night.

In the morning Juda and T.J. waited for two hours at the cliff. "He ain't coming, Juda. He told me he couldn't climb the cliff. I bet he didn't want you to show him up."

Juda was already out of the van strapping on equipment. "I'm going back, T.J." She hugged her friend.

The climb was easy. The night before it had been perilously difficult, when she had done it in the dark carrying the package she had received from Marseilles on her back. She had parked the van at an angle so that its headlights illuminated her way.

After entering the cave, Juda started on the difficult way down to the door with the words *Rex Mundi*, King of the World, carved in its lintel. Suddenly she slipped, tumbling and sliding to the anteroom of the great chamber. Shaken but unhurt, she dusted herself off and looked once again at the grisly guard, the skeleton of a man who had fallen on his sword centuries before. His bare-boned arm was still entwined loosely in a rope hanging through a hole carved into the ceiling.

The night before Juda had carefully examined the rope. It was frayed and weak, but she was sure that at the time it had been put there, it had been meant to tip the cradle of rocks hidden overhead. One tug would have started a landslide, which was meant to have sealed the cave.

"You figured it out, Juda. So did I."

"Gervais!"

He stood behind her, holding a gun, the scroll case strapped to his back. "I found the way in, Juda. It was on your map, the castle ruins at the top. Here." He handed her a drawing. He showed her Baxter's sketch and held it next to the one he had made from the scroll. "The scroll shows no tower, Baxter's did. No tricks, Juda. I'll kill you."

"You came down from the castle, Gervais? Now what?"

"You've been through the door. We've found it! Do you realize that? Get up."

"No. You sit down there, we need to talk about what's behind that door."

"Why? In there is the treasure: the Cathars, the Templars, or Solomon's. Who cares? Millions and millions of dollars in gold, silver, coins, and jewels. And the crypt. What everyone was after. It's mine – ours."

"Who were they, René? Who's been trying to destroy the sacred things and places? And why? I want to know."

"All I know is that they are wealthy and protected. The senator knew who."

"And he's dead. Who else?"

"Father Scantland. He's dead too."

"Did you kill Scantland?"

Gervais got up, his face contorted in anguish. "Don't you know, Juda Bonaparte. I killed them all: Baxter, his friends, Nadir, Scantland." He motioned with his gun. "Don't do it,

Juda," he ordered, anticipating Juda's impulse to draw. "I'm faster than you and I don't want to kill you. I lied to you and you believed me, because you wanted to." Tears flowed down Gervais' cheeks which he made no effort to hide. "I love you," he said.

Kill him now. She felt the cold metal of her gun against her breast, the knife on her arm. But the killer-child stood there crying.

"I did what I was ordered, but something happened to me." Gervais' gun arm dropped, he fell to his knees in front of Juda. "I began to like it – killing them. And it grew like a cancer, more with each death. And my pleasure repulsed me. I planned Nadir's death in Gethsemane. My final sacrilege." He pointed to the door. "*Rex Mundi*, Juda, King of the World. Jesus is here. Do you know what that means?"

"René, I don't know who carved that, or what they meant, but *Rex Mundi* might refer to the king of the underworld. Look what's in there – material wealth, gold, silver, jewels, and think what came from it, and what evil might have. That's not the Jesus I know."

"And if He's there…"

"I've been inside, Gervais. I've seen it. No one can know who lies buried in that stone coffin. Nothing good can come from it. So many have died already." Gervais laughed loudly, got up and opened the heavy door.

"Kill me if you want, Juda, but I'm going to find out." He walked into the cave. Juda drew her gun.

"Gervais, don't do it," Juda cried out. Turning on her flashlight she followed him into the cave, her vision blurred by tears. "Leave it alone," she shouted. She could see Gervais walking toward the back of the cave where there was a large, coffin-like stone box in a carved out niche. On the surrounding floor, chests of gold coins and jewelry filled the room. Against one wall was a large wooden box with carrying handles at each end.

"I've got to know, Juda." Gervais cried out loud.

"Leave it, René, believe what you want, but believe," Juda shouted, her voice echoing in the cave, her breathing irregular.

"I'll have the power of the world, Juda, or I'll die. If Christ is in there, then nothing matters, and I'm free," Gervais screamed back as he flashed his light around the room.

"Free? No, René. Only despair and utter hopelessness."

"If there's no good, Juda, then there's no evil. Just existence, no meaning. This is what they wanted, now I'll have it, wealth and the power to hold the world any way I choose. If not, I'm damned."

"Then you're no more than those who would control the world with their ideologies. Listen to me."

Gervais had once again fallen to his knees, flailing his fists against the tomb, sobbing, and mumbling "Jesus."

"No. Leave me now," he shouted.

"Gervais, I came back last night. I wired this evil place with explosives. I'll send it all to hell, or…"

"Do what you have to do." He was up, looking for something to lever the top off the tomb. He gave up and began tearing at the large wooden box. Juda's light reflected on something bright inside it as Gervais tore off a large plank.

"René, I'm leaving. Come with me." Juda made her way back to the opening of the cave and strapped on her rappelling harness. She removed a small wireless detonator from her bag. Now she was crying.

"Gervais, come with me; I can forgive you," she shouted. Then she heard it, a banging scraping sound, and silence. A cry welled up from deep within the void. At first it sounded like a baby, then it became louder, reaching a crescendo: a horrible, unearthly, agonizing sound that filled the cave.

"Gervais?" Juda's hand trembled; her heart pounded. "René." Her finger hesitated on the button; tears streamed down her face. "Oh Christ."

Juda was hurled into space as the mountain convulsed and collapsed into itself.

Chapter 36

"Juda, you flew out of that cave like a missile! It's a miracle you had that harness on, and got down in one piece," T.J. said as they drove out of Carcassonne, heading north to Grenoble, back to the home of Father Emile Peush.

Juda smiled at her friend. "Not a miracle, T.J., I was ready – and lucky."

"You want to tell me what happened up there?"

"Gervais is dead." Juda paused and looked away. "It had been wired with explosives. It's over T.J. The scroll and the treasure are buried forever. Only you and I know where."

"Was there anything else?" Juda didn't answer. She was looking out the window, thinking of what she had done, thinking of René Gervais.

"Are you comfortable with the mountains in this rig, T.J.? I'd like to go that way, at a slow, restful pace."

"Sit back and relax, we're on our way."

Far behind two cars followed, the last driven by Rama Keeftan accompanied by his woman, the terrorist Shalima.

"Tell Amad to take them when he can, I don't like the mountains. *Yelan denak*, that bitch will kill me yet. Where's she going now?" Shalima radioed the car ahead and relayed Abu Keeftan's orders.

"Give me the radio," he ordered. "Amad," he shouted into the radio, "I want her alive. Do you understand?"

Benjamin Kerns arrived in Paris with two agents. He had taken the first flight he could when he learned that the terrorists Abu Keeftan and Shalima had gotten out of Hahal Dragot Gorge. Keeftan would go after Juda. Kerns hadn't been able to reach her to warn her, but he would protect her now in any way he could. He and his men picked up weapons from a Mossad safe house and proceeded to Juda's building. There he spent the day trying to find out where she had gone, pacing the floor, yelling orders mixed with Jewish-American expletives. He called the Vatican and demanded to speak with Father Oudi Yong immediately.

"Father Yong is with the Holy Father," his soft spoken secretary, a nun, said.

"Sister, you interrupt and tell him General Kerns must speak to him right now; it's a matter of life and death."

In John Paul's quarters Oudi was finishing his report when the phone rang. The Pope looked weak and tired. Oudi answered, then covered the receiver and said, "I must interrupt, it's Juda Bonaparte's father with something urgent." The Pope smiled, and waved his hand.

"Like daughter, like father. Listen to him, Oudi. Help him."

When Kerns hung up, he ordered his men to get the car. "We're going to Grenoble. Where the hell's that?"

They were high in the Alps, the narrow road winding round and round through tight 'S' turns. Keeftan's hand gripped the wheel tightly. He kept rubbing one hand then the other on his pants to dry his nervous sweat.

"Call him," he ordered Shalima. "Tell him to take her now. Before we're in heaven." Over the steep edge, low-lying clouds covered the valley.

"Amad says the road is too narrow, too dangerous."

Abu Keeftan cursed madly, "Tell him to take her *now*!"

"We're near La Salette, T.J.," Juda said, half asleep, enjoying the ride. "That's where Gervais' monastery was." *I wonder if he's at peace,* she thought. "Look at the view."

"You look," T.J. said as a Renault trying to pass came up in his mirror. "Crazy bast – "

The car came on the inside, next to the mountain, spraying the van with nine millimeter bullets. Juda's gun answered, but the driver braked and fell behind. T.J. grunted. Blood sprayed from his neck as he slammed on his brakes and turned the wheel. The van skidded around to face the Renault. He clamped his hand over his wound. Juda leaped out onto the running board.

"Hang on T.J., they're coming back." She held her weapon steady, supporting it on the short hood, and took aim at the driver.

Behind, Rama Keeftan pressed the accelerator. "We've got her, Shalima," he yelled.

Juda fired. Her bullet shattered the windshield, killing the driver, as others screaming and cursing shot at her from the open windows, their car out of control. Juda emptied her clip, hitting one more man. The Renault swerved, skidded, and crashed into the front of the van before it careened off and flew over the cliff, breaking apart and bursting into flames down the mountain side. Juda barely hung on. Keeftan came up fast.

T.J. was bleeding profusely. "Good-bye, Juda," he said, pushing her off the running board and slamming the accelerator to the floor.

"Kill him, Shalima, kill him," Abu Keeftan yelled as T.J.'s powerful V8 charged at them like an avenging knight.

Shalima fired her weapon from the window. Abu Keeftan screamed *"Allah-u Akbar"* as the van and car collided and exploded in a fiery tangle of metal and bodies.

Juda, scraped and bruised, sat on the ground and cried.

Epilogue

Two months later, recovering in Paris from her injuries and the loss of her friend T.J. Troubble, Juda received a letter from Dr. Michael George and Susan Pepper, his wife. She reread it several times, remembering their friendship, forgetting the horrors of her life. Soon, she thought, as she packed for a vacation with her father and Father Oudi Yong. Las Vegas was Oudi's choice. Thankfully a destination far away from the terrors of France and the memories of the Middle East.

Together again, enjoying the spectacular glitter of the Strip, Oudi, Ben, and Juda were having dinner at Caesar's Palace after a night of gambling. "We Koreans are avid gamblers," Father Yong said, smiling. "I'm embarrassed to say, but the Holy Father ordered this. What could I do?" Oudi shrugged and smiled broadly. "He wants a report from me on this sin city. I've always wanted to come here."

Hours later, over cigarettes and coffee, Juda said, "Tell us about Professor Carlo d'Angello, Oudi."

"He'll probably die in prison before we can try him. He was the only one who had access to everything about the Dead Sea Scrolls. When I found out he was a Thirty-Third Degree Mason, I took a chance and confronted him." Looking up to heaven, he continued, "I lied a little about a confession we found at Father Scantland's and my bluff worked. He broke down and told me everything. He was the liaison between Sancta Croce, Father Scantland and Senator Graves, and the only one who could connect directly with those behind this."

"The New World Order," Juda said.

Ben said, "All the men connected with the order are clean. Mossad has people working with Langley and the French and German security services to get something on them." He added, "I'm out of it now, and for keeps. Actually, I like Paris."

"And Las Vegas, Ben. You were lucky tonight," Juda said.

Ben beamed. "How far is Monte Carlo from Paris, Juda?" They all laughed.

Before they finished, a waiter came up and gave Juda a card which read, *Please join me for some baccarat after dinner*. It was signed *Dr. George Gamash*. Juda looked around the dinning room and saw the handsome face of the London surgeon. She returned his smile.

"Somebody you know, Juda?"

"A doctor I met in London. I'm going to play a few hands of baccarat with him. Join me." She remembered their first meeting and the feeling that she had had when she saw him before.

Ben frowned. "I'm turning in, Juda. Be careful."

Gamash, impeccably dressed, stood up and took Juda's hand. He smiled, bowed slightly, touched his hand to his abdomen and forehead and said, "*Salaam*, Dr. Bonaparte. So nice to see you. It must be fate that we meet again." He had a charming smile. "So sorry to hear of old Baxter's passing away. Cards? Or would you prefer dancing?"

Juda returned his smile. "Cards, I feel lucky." She watched his eyes.

At the guarded baccarat table, Juda placed her bet with the "Players," won, and let it ride. When they quit, she was ahead seven thousand dollars, and Gamash down twice that. "That's enough for me, Juda," he said, standing up, taking her hand. "You win, I lose, but if you'll join me for a bottle of champagne in my suite, I win." Juda declined and Gamash escorted her to her suite.

When she opened the door she saw Ben tied to a chair and Oudi, his head bleeding, unconscious on the bed. Stepping into the room, Gamash leveled a small automatic at Juda. Two men held guns on Ben, who struggled against the gag and tapes that held him.

"I had to hit the Jap, boss. He tried some fancy kung fu on me."

"Now, Juda, I have a debt of blood to settle. First you will see your father die, then the priest. And after," Gamash smiled, "I have something special for you."

"Abu Keeftan?" Juda's eyes narrowed.

"My cousin. You should have accepted the champagne, Juda. You would have died happy."

Juda moved closer to Gamash.

"Then you, Doctor, will die as Abu Keeftan did, screaming all the way to hell."

Ben cursed through his gag and tried Juda's assault with the chair. He missed his mark and fell to the floor, breaking the chair. With the sudden noise Oudi awoke, groaned loudly and staggered from the bed. The distraction was all she needed. Juda moved with impossible speed. Closing in on Gamash she twisted, slammed her elbow into his stomach and kicked one man in the chin, tumbling him backwards, unconscious. Ben rolled into the second man, toppling him to the floor. Gamash recovered quickly and aimed his gun at Juda.

"Not now, bastard," Juda said, and was on him instantly. Stepping inside his gun arm, she grabbed his tuxedo lapels, yanked him backwards, falling beneath him to the floor. Her feet caught him high in the stomach. Gamash grunted as Juda's high heels tore his flesh. Then releasing his coat, she extended her powerful legs and heaved George Gamash, sending him flying across the room and through the plateglass window. They could hear him screaming all the way down the eighteen floors to the courtyard below.

Two days later the threesome said good-bye at McCarran International Airport. Oudi and Ben were flying back to Europe. Earlier when he had been alone with Juda, Father Yong had said, "Juda, I know you told me everything about Gervais and the cave, and how he was killed in the explosion, and the treasure buried. You didn't say if you had opened the crypt yourself when you were there alone."

Juda paused, remembering the tormented Gervais, the treasure and the tomb, Harold Baxter and those who had died over the secret of the scroll; and she remembered the woman crying on the Via Dolorosa, her hand pressed in Christ's hand imprint; and she heard again a million people in St. Peter's Square shouting, "Papa, Papa," as they kept their all-night vigil waiting for the Pope while she scanned the area with a high-powered rifle in her hands, ready to kill John Paul's would-be assassin.

Juda smiled at her friend and said, "I didn't say, did I."

"Well?"

Juda flipped her head back slightly, looked Oudi in the eye, and answered, "It was nothing important, Father."

The priest smiled.

Embracing Juda, Ben said, "And where are you off to now, daughter?"

Juda kissed her father and Oudi. "I'm going to spend a quiet couple of weeks in Canada, learning to fish."

"FISH!" Ben and Father Yong said together.

"And I'm going to be a godmother."

JUDA WILL RETURN IN *THE SHROUD*

Special thanks to my friends who read the early drafts and were so encouraging: Chaplain and Mrs. James Britt, Father Richard Meredith, Dr. Robert Watson, Ms. Joan Taylor, Charles Hickey, Jim Turner, Mary Marcoccia, Marlene and Benny Beach, Dr. Joe Cangemi, Dr. Tim Hulsey, my children, Dawn, Cezanne, Gregory, Richard, Jennifer, Jessica, and Kathryn. My many friends and readers of my first book all deserve special thanks.

I owe special thanks to Retired Colonel Zvi Gafni who guided me to safe, and dangerous places in Israel, and inspired me with his grasp of the history and culture of the Arab and Jew, and the Islamic, Hebrew, and Christian legacies of the promised land. The scholars who have studied the Dead Sea Scrolls are owed our honor and respect.